ASHLEY JOHN

ISBN: 1539786080
ISBN-13: 978-1539786085

ALSO BY ASHLEY JOHN

For Keri

You always go above and beyond.

CHAPTER

ONE

Ricky was looking for the perfect birdcage at the car boot sale, but the man walking in front of him was demanding most of his attention. Ricky hadn't even seen his face yet, but he knew he would be gorgeous. His massive shoulders fit his tight, white shirt and arse-fitting jeans left little to the imagination.

"Ricky, are you even looking?" asked his best friend, Tom, as he rummaged through a large box of scrap metal. "I thought we were looking for a birdcage?"

"Yeah, I'm looking," he mumbled, tearing his eyes away from the stranger and back to the stall they were standing in front of. "I'm looking."

Ricky cast his eyes over the table of junk. The old, toothless man smiled encouragingly, but Ricky doubted he had sold much all day.

"There's nothing here," said Ricky, staring longingly at the stranger with the nice shoulders and arse. "Let's keep moving."

Ricky hated car boot sales. He had terrible memories of his mother and auntie dragging him around muddy fields every Sunday afternoon in search of junk they didn't need but were convinced they did.

"It needs to be perfect," his tone was distracted as they wandered to the next stall, where the beautiful stranger was flicking through a box of dog-eared vinyl records. "Absolutely perfect."

Just as Ricky suspected, the man was gorgeous from the front too. His thick, chocolaty hair was swept casually off his face, which pushed his strong nose and jaw forward. It was the kind of beauty only years of selective breeding created. If he weren't rummaging around a car boot sale, Ricky would have sworn the man was a part of the English Aristocracy. The very idea made him delightfully unattainable, which only made Ricky want him more.

"It's got to be just the right size and the right colour. It needs to match my wig. Manchester Pride only comes around once a year, and I've been planning this outfit since before Christmas."

The man glanced at Ricky out of the corner of his eye, and they shared a small friendly smile. Dropping Manchester's Gay Pride festival loudly into the conversation wasn't subtle, but it had the desired effect.

"What can I help you with?" asked the pleasant looking woman sitting on a small camping chair behind the stall.

"Just browsing," replied Ricky, not taking his eyes away from the man. "I'm waiting for something to *jump* out at me."

Tom loudly huffed his disapproval. If Tom had his way, Ricky would settle down and marry, just like he had, but that wasn't on the menu for Ricky. Ricky preferred gorging on the appetisers, before moving swiftly onto the next restaurant.

"Such a great album," said the beautiful stranger, in a thick Yorkshire country accent, holding up a faded copy of David Bowie's *Aladdin Sane*. "I've always felt drawn to Bowie."

Ricky's bedroom had been filled with posters of Bowie and his pink lightning bolt, but he had left that obsession in his teenaged years. He faked a sound of interest and moved closer to the stranger.

"One of the best," echoed Ricky. "One of a kind."

"Quite." The man smiled, before dropping the album back into the box and crossing over to the next row.

Ricky almost chased straight after him, but he decided to play it cool. On the next cluttered table, he spotted a birdcage. It was too big for what he needed, but he feigned interest to show Tom that he was committed to their search, even if he was only interested in finding a way to bed the man.

"I never did ask why you wanted a birdcage?" mumbled Tom as he followed behind. "I should probably get back to the farmhouse. I told Cole I'd watch Eva so he could run into town."

"You can't leave me now." Ricky closed the small door on the birdcage and crossed to the next row. "This is crucial. Pride is in August, and if I don't find one, the entire performance will be ruined."

"Because of a birdcage?"

"It's the centrepiece of my entire outfit, sweetheart. I plan my calendar around Pride, and this year, I'm performing on the main stage, so I need to step up my game."

"You swallowed fire last year. How can you step it up

3

more than that?"

"Fire was easy. I've swallowed worse things," Ricky said playfully, poking his un-amused best friend in the ribs with his elbow. "This is *drag*! It's all about constantly evolving and taking risks. I want to mount a birdcage on my wig, with a live bird inside."

"You're crazy," sighed Tom with a soft chuckle.

"I know."

They stood next to the David Bowie enthusiast again. This time, he was examining a set of crystal champagne flutes. He held them up to the light, as though he had found what he was looking for.

"Look how they sparkle," he said in Ricky's direction, seeming to know he was there without even looking. "Beautiful."

"Aren't they just?"

Ricky didn't need to look at Tom to know he was rolling his eyes again. He could practically hear them falling into the back of his head.

"What about this?" Tom tapped Ricky on the shoulder, holding up a square birdcage with an electronic rocking bird perched inside. "A bit of spray paint and you'd never know it was plastic."

"Too tacky, sweetheart."

"I thought you said there was no such thing as too tacky?" Tom mumbled under his breath, ditching the plastic birdcage.

"Sometimes you need a bit of quality." He joined the stranger in examining the crystal wine glasses. "*Exquisite*."

"Quite," agreed the stranger.

Once again, he replaced the item and moved onto the next stall. Ricky lived for the chase. He didn't like fucking people he could easily get. He wanted to stalk his prey and toy with him before devouring him whole.

"I don't even think he's gay," Tom whispered into his ear as they followed the man to the next stall.

"When has that ever stopped me?"

"Maybe it should. You chase these guys, and you can never keep hold of them. One of these days you'll have to take another chance on love."

Ricky's stomach knotted as his mind cast darkly to Bret. He saw him on his deathbed, making Ricky promise he would find somebody who made him happy. He shook those thoughts to the back of his mind and focussed on the man in front of him. He wasn't going to let himself get trapped in that painful memory.

"You know my rules," he reminded Tom.

"You and your stupid rules!"

"No names, no second dates and –"

"And *no* breakfast," mocked Tom. "Your rules keep you single."

He hadn't told Tom his fourth, secret rule: no love.

"*Exactly*, sweetheart. Isn't it great?"

They repeated the dance around the car boot sale for the next twenty minutes. They followed the stranger to every stall, shared a comment about an item Ricky had little interest in, and then moved on. When they were coming to the end of the market, Ricky knew he had to strike before the stranger got away.

"Sweetheart, will you grab us some coffees?" he said as he thrust a five-pound note into Tom's hand. "There's a good boy."

Tom didn't argue. He pointed his eyes angrily at Ricky, scrunched up the money and walked off, muttering something about Ricky not acting like the thirty-eight-year-old man he was. Ricky had no interest in acting his age, especially when the mirror still generously told him thirty-three.

"Did I hear you were looking for a birdcage?" said the stranger, picking up a perfect, metal birdcage from the table in front of them. "The craftsmanship of this piece is rather charming."

"Very charming." Ricky accepted the birdcage and turned it over in his hands, feeling its strength and weight. "This will do perfectly."

"What kind of bird do you own?"

"A cock, or two," he said with a straight face. "Needs a new cage."

"A cockatoo?"

"Something like that, sweetheart."

The man tightened his eyes, but he smirked wickedly. Ricky handed over a twenty-pound note for the cage, and they wandered past the final table toward the food truck.

"Do you come here often?" he asked.

"Why don't we drop the niceties?" whispered Ricky slowly. "Do you want to come back to my place for a fuck, or not?"

"*Excuse* me?" he choked on his own words.

"You heard me. Do you want to come back to my house, so I can fuck your brains out? It's a simple question."

The man stared wide-eyed at Ricky in disbelief, but he didn't reject the invitation. Ricky knew he had caught his prey, and now it was time to play with him.

"I'll take your silence as a yes," he said airily. "Follow me."

Ricky started walking, ignoring Tom's eye line as he cut across the field, clutching two coffees. Tom didn't understand the thrill of picking up a guy in the most unlikely place, but it was a feeling that kept Ricky getting out of bed in the morning.

He didn't need to turn around to know the man was following him, keeping just enough distance between them.

He reached the top of the winding lane back to the village and paused. Footsteps crunched on the gravel, and the man appeared next to him, glancing nervously over his shoulder back at the busy market.

"We don't even know each other's names," said the man.

"Let's not ruin it, sweetheart. This way."

***

Chase turned up the speed on the treadmill as his trainers pounded into the rubber. He grabbed his towel and wiped the sweat from his tattoo-covered neck. Every muscle in his body burned, reminding him that he was alive.

He turned up the speed once more, pushing his body to the brink of destruction. His lungs cried out for air and his brain for water, but he didn't dare stop to provide either. He ran and ran until the very last second that he felt he could run no more. He hit the big, red, emergency stop button and his legs slowed to a halt, threatening to give way under him.

Chase unscrewed his bottle and poured water into his mouth and down his exposed, inked, chest. A salty mixture of water and sweat dripped from his short, dark hair and down to his lips. He caught it with his tongue, finding the taste strangely comforting.

The gym had always been his safe place, so co-owning his own with his brother meant that he could work out when he wanted, for as long as he wanted. He particularly liked Sundays in his own gym, because Hebden Bridge was such a small village, there was always something else happening on a Sunday afternoon, keeping the gym relatively quiet.

"You know it's against the rules to work out with your

shirt off," said his older brother, Danny, as he tapped his finger on the sign sitting on the counter. "You love the look of yourself too much, little bro."

Chase caught sight of himself in the mirror. He had dark tattoos running from his jawline, across his heavy-set chest, down his toned thighs, only stopping once they reached his ankles. He rubbed his hand down his flat, sculpted stomach, each muscle extra defined from his workout. He loved the way he looked because he felt a sense of achievement, not vanity. He would never forget the chubby loner he was before he discovered kickboxing as a teenager, no matter how low his body fat percentage got.

"I'll hit the showers and then I'm going to head off. I thought I'd take Dylan to the park or something."

"You're scheduled all day," mumbled Danny, barely looking up from the advanced copy of next month's *Men's Fitness* that had hit their doormat yesterday. "Natalie has him."

"Your wife has enough to worry about without throwing my son into the mix. I promised I'd do something with him today."

"You promise that boy too much," said Danny. "Kids don't need constant attention. They thrive when they're left to find their own way. That's what Natalie says."

Danny's wife, Natalie, was a bestselling author of parenting guidebooks. Chase couldn't do anything without her giving her own over-stuffed opinion. She thought she was the knowledgeable parent, which Chase found ironic because she didn't have any of her own children.

"We just make it up as we go along," said Chase as he crammed a protein bar in between his teeth. "I've raised that boy from birth, and I'd like to think he's doing fine."

"By choice. There are plenty of women out there, bro."

"I know," he mumbled through the artificial chocolate

flavour. "But I'm not going to introduce any woman into Dylan's life for the sake of it."

"Nobody is asking you to." Danny slapped his *Men's Fitness* shut and folded his arms across his chest. "You don't even give birds a chance! When did you last go on a date?"

Chase had to really think hard about that. He could only remember a handful of dates since Dylan's birth, and none of them had led to a second one.

"I'm not ready to date."

"You're never ready to date." Danny rolled his eyes. "You know Beth is mad about you, right?"

"Beth, the yoga instructor who works here on Saturdays?"

"*Yes!*" Danny slapped his hands on the glass countertop. "Please tell me you've noticed? She always mad flirts with you."

Chase tried to remember how Beth had been yesterday. She was a sweet girl in her mid-twenties. Chase just assumed she was nice to everyone because of the inner peace that yoga brought her. Was he really that rusty?

"She's too young for me."

"You're thirty-two. You've got life in you yet, Granddad," said Danny, reaching across the counter to tightly pinch his cheek. "Let me hook you two up, and –"

"No, don't," Chase interrupted. "She works here. If it doesn't work out, we'll have to let her go, and her yoga class is one of the few full classes we have."

"If I didn't know better, I'd think you had something to tell me," joked Danny, with an air of sarcasm. "Are you batting for the other team and not telling me, bro?"

Chase laughed off the suggestion, but he didn't reply. He didn't feel like he could lie to his brother's face, especially when the question had been made in good humour. He still hadn't figured out a way to tell his brother that he spent most Friday nights on Canal Street in Manchester's gay village, picking up guys.

"You're funny," said Chase, trying not to sound awkward. "I'm hitting the showers. I can smell myself."

"I didn't want to mention it." Danny held up his hands and winked. "You stink, mate. Before you go, the tickets for the Annual Trainer's Weekend showed up this morning. I'm gonna have to back out, bro."

"Oh, why?" Chase took the envelope out of his brother's hands and peeked inside at the two tickets. "We had such a good time last year."

"I know, but Natalie has this TV thing in Germany, and I promised I'd go with her. You can still go. The cover staff for that weekend is still booked."

Chase considered it for a moment before folding the envelope and stuffing it in his pocket. They had bought the tickets at last year's event because it had been so much fun. It was supposed to be a convention for personal trainers and fitness professionals to see new products and learn new programs, but it ended up being a weekend in a large country house with a free bar and more alcohol than Chase could remember. It wouldn't be as fun alone.

Chase left his brother at the counter and stripped off in the small changing room. He usually went into a cubicle, but he was the only man in the gym, so he enjoyed being able to let everything hang free. He yanked off his socks, tossed his clean towel over his shoulder and walked into the cold, communal shower block.

The chill in the air made his nipples stand to attention. He brushed his fingers over them, remembering the young guy he had fucked on Friday night. He twisted the bulky tap, and hot water spat out of the showerhead, relaxing his tense muscles.

He knew he wasn't technically lying to his brother. He

did still see himself settling down with a woman one day; he just enjoyed fucking men too. He didn't know if that made him bisexual, or just curious, but the two things felt very separate. When he imagined his future, he knew his brother was right. Dylan was only six-years-old, and he was starting to notice that he didn't have a mummy like the rest of the kids in his class at school. Chase didn't know how long he could put off telling his son that his mother had been more interested in party drugs than her own newborn baby.

Running the bar of soap over his solid abs, he let his hand wander to his manhood. When the hard, foamy bar hit his shaft, it reacted instantly. Glancing over his shoulder, he made sure that the changing room was still empty before he started to work his shaft.

The hot water ran down his body as he panted through his rhythms, giving himself his second workout of the day. When he could feel the blissful release edging closer, he thought back to the lay from two days ago. He came in seconds, and before it had even been washed away by the water, he was back to cleaning his body, as though nothing had happened.

CHAPTER

TWO

"**D**o you want to grab some lunch together?"

Ricky rolled off the bed and tore off the condom. He tossed it into the bin and pulled on his tight, black briefs. In the mirror, he watched the man from the car boot sale light a cigarette in bed, his cock still hard under the sheets.

"*I said*, do you want to grab some lunch?" he repeated. "There's a great little pub up in the countryside. I know the owners. I'll run home and jump in my Range Rover, and we can drive out there."

Ricky didn't know how to break it to the man that they wouldn't be grabbing lunch. The sex had been great, but Ricky had long since learned not to muddy the waters. Sex was sex, and dating was off limits.

"I'm not hungry," he said, as he fought with the window's tricky brass lock. "You got more of those cigarettes?"

The man held out the pack and Ricky pulled out two. He pushed one between his lips and slotted one behind his ear. It had been four days since a cigarette had passed his lips. It had also been four days since he had last fucked a guy. It didn't matter that he was trying his best to kick the filthy habit; it was almost impossible not to want a cigarette after sex.

"This cottage is beautiful," said the stranger, wafting his cigarette up to the ceiling. "Just from the beams, you can see how old it is. Is it listed?"

"I don't know. It's rented." Ricky leaned in and let the stranger light the end of his cigarette with the end of his own. "Listen, I have somewhere I need to be later, so you should probably get dressed and make your way out."

"If you're not hungry, we can just go for a drive," the man said, squinting through the thick cloud of smoke growing between them. "Or a drink?"

"Sweetheart, *listen*, I think you've got this twisted. It was fun, but that's all it was. *Fun.*"

"It was fun." The stranger smiled, rolling onto his side so that the sheet fell off his toned, hairy body to expose his still solid cock. "I like you."

"You don't know me," said Ricky, holding back the laughter. "Get dressed and go. You've outstayed your welcome."

"Don't be like that," the man said with a soft smile, clearly not taking Ricky seriously. "I'm Malcolm, by the way. What's your name?"

"I said I didn't want to do names." Ricky pulled on his black jeans, the cigarette still balancing from his lips. "Don't make this more complicated than it needs to be."

"At least tell me your name. Look, I get it. You don't want anything serious. That's cool. I'm not exactly looking for a relationship myself. I think Mum would have a heart attack if she found out about this. Just tell me we can do this again?"

"I'm not going to lie to you, Martin."

"*Malcolm.*"

"Whatever." He stubbed out the cigarette on the edge of the window before letting it drop to his garden below. "Like I said, I have somewhere I need to be."

Ricky pulled on his white t-shirt and tossed Malcolm his clothes. Post-orgasm, he was still the same good looking man Ricky had followed at the car boot sale, but he had lost his sheen. In the glow of the afternoon sun, his skin was slightly weathered, telling of a life spent outdoors.

"*Richard Thompson,*" said Malcolm. "So your name is Richard. I didn't have you down as a Richard."

Malcolm flicked through the stack of letters on Ricky's nightstand.

"What do you think you're doing?"

Malcolm turned around, clutching the framed photograph that had been hiding under the pile of letters and said, "Is this why you want me gone? Because you have a boyfriend?"

Ricky snatched the frame out of Malcolm's hands and tossed it onto the bed. He scooped up Malcolm's clothes, thrust them into his arms and pushed him towards the bedroom door. He hit his forehead on the low doorframe as he went through.

"Get out," seethed Ricky through gritted teeth. "You have no right looking through my stuff."

He pushed Malcolm across his living room, towards the exit. When Ricky tossed open the door, Malcolm jumped back and dragged the clothes down to hide his softening cock.

"You can't kick me out like this," he laughed awkwardly, his tone apologetic and desperate. "At least let me get dressed first."

"No."

With one firm shove, he pushed Malcolm over the threshold, slammed the small door shut and slid the old, brass lock into place. He heard some grumbling, but he didn't stick around to listen to what the man had to say.

Ruffling through his hair, he wandered into his small kitchen and tore open the fridge. It was pathetically bare. He poked the old block of cheese and opened the empty egg box. The milk was days out of date, and the half an iceberg lettuce had started to turn purple. He gave last night's Chinese takeout a quick sniff and he assessed that it was still okay to eat. With a fork in hand, he took his leftovers into the living room.

His garishly bright and modern furniture stuck out like a sore thumb in the four-hundred-year-old cottage, but that's exactly the way he liked it. It was an almost perfect representation of who he was as a person.

Sitting on the yellow, leather couch, he started to pick at the cold food. It only took a couple of mouthfuls for the slight guilt in his stomach to dull. He hated it when the guys he brought back to his house tried to force the length of their welcome. He preferred picking up guys in the bars because most of them knew to call a taxi the second they had their underwear pulled up.

He stared at the birdcage sitting on the neat stack of magazines on his coffee table. It was the product of an afternoon well spent. He pulled his phone out of his jeans and sent Tom a quick apologetic text message. They both knew Ricky's cock had a mind of its own.

He dumped the Chinese next to the birdcage and

walked back into his bedroom. He straightened out the ivory silk sheets and arranged the pillows and the bright yellow throw cushions against the ornate, gold headboard.

Perching on the edge of his bed, he picked up the photograph and looked down at the snapshot of Bret and him from a happier time. It felt like a lifetime ago, and yesterday at the same time. He kissed the glass and said a silent apology for hiding the frame under the letters.

Placing the frame upright on the mirrored surface of his nightstand, he knew if Tom had been a fly on the wall, he would have pushed him to accept the offer of a date.

Ricky looked down at the photograph, sadness filling his heart. He had already lived that life, and he knew how painful it was to lose.

Casting those thoughts to the back of his mind, he walked over to the built-in wardrobes covering half of his bedroom. He pulled on the mirrored doors, revealing rows and rows of glittering gowns in every imaginable colour. On the shelves above the gowns, his different wigs sat neatly on pink floating heads. He plucked out his curly blonde Marilyn wig and a floor-length red gown.

After tossing them on the bed, he sat at his dressing table and turned on the vanity lights around the mirror. He stared at his reflection, wondering when he had gotten so old.

"Right, Miss Kitty Litter," he said, pushing his eyebrows up with his fingers. "You ready to come out and play, sweetheart?"

***

Danny and Natalie's kitchen looked as it always did. It was perfect down to the last detail. White gleaming cabinets lined the walls. All of the appliances were stainless steel and gleaming under the soft spotlights. In Chase's flat, they wouldn't last two seconds before being covered with Dylan's fingerprints.

A bulging glass vase of short-stemmed white lilies adorned the giant marble island in the centre of the kitchen. A stack of Natalie's own parenting books had been neatly displayed. They were taunting guests to pick them up so Natalie could talk about her favourite topic: herself. Chase had all of the same books, but they were currently holding up his coffee table after he accidentally kicked off one of the legs.

He leaned against the island and waited for Natalie to return with Dylan. She had offered him every drink in her glass-fronted refrigerator, but he didn't want to stay any longer than he needed to. Whenever they were left alone without the buffer of Danny, Natalie used it as an excuse to lecture Chase. She always made him feel like he was doing every single thing wrong, and he probably was, but he didn't want to hear it from his sister-in-law. As far as he was concerned, her books weren't worth the paper they were printed on.

"Daddy!" Dylan ran into the room and jumped straight into Chase's arms. "Are we going home?"

It had only been a couple of hours since Chase had seen his son, but he hugged him as though it had been weeks. Chase worked around Dylan's school hours but Natalie always watched him on the weekends, and he knew Dylan hated every second of it as much as Chase hated leaving him there.

"Have you been a good boy for Auntie Natalie?" he asked as he put Dylan back on the ground.

Dylan nodded, but Natalie pursed her lips and crossed her arms under her bust. Her blonde hair was scraped off her face into a tight roll at the back. She had a pretty, open face, which seemed to translate well on TV and in photographs, but in person, her expression was as blank as the white marble tiles she was standing on.

"I'll be going then." Chase grabbed Dylan's hand and walked around Natalie, already pulling his keys from his pocket. "See you next weekend, Natalie."

"Can I have a quick word, Chase?" she said with a tight smile. "Alone."

Chase passed Dylan the car keys and told him to go and wait in the car. Natalie kept her tight smile until the front door slammed and they were alone. Chase wondered if Natalie thought she looked friendly.

"How are things?" she asked casually.

"Things are great, Natalie. I really do need to get going, so if –"

"There is something I want to tell you."

Natalie walked into her kitchen and put a white china cup under a white coffee machine. She pressed a button, and it started to grind beans. She didn't bother asking Chase if he wanted one. When her coffee was finished, she added a dash of Soy milk and mounted one of the high chairs under the island. She sipped her coffee and ran her finger along her books, before reapplying her smile and sending her piercing blue eyes back in Chase's direction.

"I can't watch Dylan over the summer," she said softly, as though she were talking about something as casual as the weather.

Her words were a blow to Chase. He had been counting on Natalie babysitting Dylan over the summer, so he could take longer shifts at the gym and build up his savings before Christmas hit. He had put every penny of his funds into opening the gym, and he had nothing left to put into childcare. The gym had been open for nearly a year, but he had made sure to ask Natalie if she could look after Dylan for the six weeks he had off school. For Chase, it had been one of the conditions of how much money he could invest. He hadn't wanted to dump Dylan with his auntie every day of the summer, but Natalie had seemed more than happy to help out.

"But you agreed."

"I have a North American book tour planned from the fifth of July until the end of the month." Her tight smile turned genuine, as though she was really pleased with herself. "I really am sorry, Chase."

She didn't sound the slightest bit sorry, but Chase couldn't argue with her. He wondered if he could take Dylan to work with him. Danny wouldn't mind, but a gym was no place for a child.

"I have nobody else," he said, almost to himself. "I was counting on you helping. You promised you would."

"I'm sure you have somebody you can ask." She reached out and adjusted one of the lilies so that it was aligned perfectly with the ones surrounding it. "There's always childcare."

"I can't afford childcare. You know that."

"Well, maybe if you worked harder, you'd be able to provide more for your child," she said in a sweet, but cutting tone. "Like Danny and I."

Chase bit his tongue. Natalie had been argumentative since the first moment he had met her. One of the first things she had said to him was that his tattoos were a bad influence on Dylan and they were corrupting his moral compass. He didn't want to mention that he worked just as hard as her husband, doing the exact same thing and they earned the same amount of money from the gym.

"I work hard, Natalie," he said firmly.

"That sounds like you've not read my new book, Chase," she said, narrowing her eyes, without faltering her cold smile.

"I skimmed it," he lied.

"Well, if you had read chapter six, you would have known how important I think it is to save for expected events in life, such as childcare."

Chase clenched his fists by his side and inhaled deeply. Her eyes glanced down to his hands, and she seemed pleased with her words.

"I need to go," said Chase, before he said something he couldn't take back. "See you around, Natalie."

Chase didn't wait for her to say anything else. He opened and slammed her front door so hard, the heavy knocker rattled against the wood. Dylan was sitting in the passenger seat, with the keys in his hands and the doors locked, just as Chase had taught him. When he noticed his father, he clicked the keys and the doors opened.

"Let's go to the drive-thru," said Chase. "How does a cheeseburger sound?"

"Auntie Natalie said wheat is poison and cheese will stunt my growth," Dylan said in a serious tone, which didn't suit his six-year-old face. "What's wheat?"

"Ignore anything Auntie Natalie says from now on, okay? The woman probably doesn't even know how to tie her own shoelaces."

Dylan laughed. Chase slotted his keys into the ignition and pulled the car out of Natalie's paved drive. The electronic gates opened up as he approached and he drove away quickly.

"Can I have a meal with a toy?" asked Dylan as they drove across town.

"You can have anything you want."

Chase knew there was probably something in one of Natalie's books about giving children toys, but he didn't care. He lived his life for his son and he wanted to make him happy. It was hard enough doing everything on his own, without the added pressure of having a so-called expert in the family.

They pulled into the drive-thru and as Dylan stared up at the backlit menus, Chase watched his son. He knew it was only a matter of time before Dylan started asking serious questions about his mother, and that thought broke his heart. It had been six years, and Chase still couldn't fully understand what happened, so he had no idea how he was going to explain that to a little boy.

CHAPTER

THREE

Ricky loved Friday nights. The week had been long, and he had been looking forward to his DJ session at London Bridge all week. He sipped the cocktail a hot twenty-something had bought him and admired his full dance floor.

Ricky loved drag. He didn't care if people didn't understand it because he understood it perfectly. It was a way of applying a mask, becoming a new person and expressing different sides of his personality, which only seemed socially acceptable when he was wearing a wig and a dress. Of course, nothing about drag was socially acceptable, but part of him enjoyed that. The people who got it understood it was an art form; no different to painting on a canvas, but the people who didn't get it thought it was a perversion. Ricky didn't know how many times a week he had to explain he never had sex in drag.

Being sworn off relationships made being a part-time drag queen easier. Bret had loved Miss Kitty Litter, but Ricky didn't know many men who could live with a drag queen full time. Most of the guys he pulled in drag knew the man he was underneath, but he doubted they would like to share Ricky with another woman.

Sipping his cocktail, he laughed to himself at the thought of any man ever getting that close to care. It wasn't that men didn't try, because they did, but Ricky was hardly going to let any of them get close enough. Even if a man who accepted the feminine side of his personality materialised in front of his eyes, it would take a lot for him to even consider giving love a second chance.

"Don't forget, sweethearts, Miss Kitty Litter is here all night, every Friday and Saturday, playing you the best chart and cheese music right through till the early hours. Now, which one of you am I taking home with me tonight, you beautiful bunch?"

A couple of guys cheered, but Ricky recognised them as regulars he had already fucked. Most of them didn't get a second invite back to his cottage.

He eased Madonna into Britney and watched the crowd go wild. He drained the last of his cocktail, and he caught sight of his best friend, Tom, wading through the crowd with his husband, Cole. They both looked nervous of the full club. Tom had never been one for clubbing and even though Cole had worked at the bar before marrying Tom, he had gone the same way as his husband. Ever since adopting their daughter, Eva, Ricky had been trying to get them to go on a night out with him, and now that Cole's auntie was back from her second cruise of the year, they had no excuse to stay at home.

"Hello, boys," he said over the microphone. "*Everybody*

say hello to Tom and Cole. They're a beautiful married couple, and they're boring as fuck. They also happen to be my best friends."

Ricky turned down the music and the people who were paying attention chanted '*Hello Tom and Cole*' in perfect unison.

"They've also got a little girl, Eva. She's only five!"

The crowd said '*Awww*' and Tom and Cole hid their faces as they waited at the bar to be served. Embarrassing his friends was a simple pleasure, but being the drag queen DJ gave Ricky every right to do so.

"I thought being gay meant we didn't have to change shitty nappies and be kept awake from teething," he said over the microphone. "Well, that doesn't sound too long ago for some of you in here. You're all getting younger with each passing weekend. I miss the days of hiding in the closet until your late twenties! There's nothing wrong with a little self-loathing every now and then, sweethearts. Frankly, I think it's *quite* rude that you come in here with your smooth skin. You're making this thirty-three-*plus*-five-year-old drag queen look old. *Old*, I tell you! *Tina! Bring me the axe*! I'm about to chop through the prettiest to make me feel better."

The crowd all chuckled as Ricky lined up the next couple of songs. When the club was back to dancing, he grabbed his cigarette packet from his bra and dismounted the stage, steadying himself by putting his large hand on a young man's head. Ricky was usually the tallest man in the room, and that was without the six-inch heels and the tall wig. Miss Kitty Litter loomed above everybody, and that was exactly how Ricky liked things. She had the confidence Ricky had to fake.

"I thought you quit smoking," said Tom as he handed Ricky a pink cocktail.

"I have," he said as he placed a cigarette in between his lips. "I'm just having a little relapse."

After taking two of Malcolm's cigarettes last weekend, he had gone straight to the corner shop and picked up a packet. All week, he had been telling himself that he was going to quit again, but the thought of doing drag and not having hourly cigarette breaks sounded like too much of a chore.

With the cigarette pressed between his lips and a drink in hand, he took Tom and Cole out to the front of the club. Young boys and girls all lined up neatly behind the barriers, waiting for the bouncers to pat them down, take their money and let them in. Ricky's face was proudly plastered on the posters in the window, calling the children in. He felt a small twinge of pride.

"I hear you're performing on the main stage at Pride this year," beamed Cole, slamming Ricky on the shoulder. "Congrats, man."

"Thanks, sweetheart." Ricky leaned in and kissed Cole on the cheek, leaving behind a red imprint. "I thought it was about time they asked me. I am, after all, a *local* legend."

"For all of the wrong reasons," mumbled Tom under his breath as he wafted the cigarette smoke away from his face. "I thought you were doing so well quitting smoking!"

"I was, sweetheart. But you know how it is. *Stress.*"

"What do you have to be stressed about?"

"Life, sweetheart. *Life!*"

He finished his cigarette while Tom and Cole sipped their drinks, looking awkwardly around the busy streets. It was obvious they hadn't taken Ricky's advice to pre-drink at the farm before coming out. He had always said the gay village was a better experience blind drunk.

"We can't stay out too late," said Tom.

"In case Eva wakes up in the middle of the night," added Cole.

"You're not going home until I say so." Ricky pulled a pair of handcuffs from his bra. "I brought these, just in case."

Tom and Cole both took a cautionary step back. Ricky had brought them as a joke, but he was seriously considering handcuffing one of them to him, even if he had no idea where the key was.

Part of him admired their relationship. When he had first met Cole, Ricky had been enamoured by his good looks. His hair was dirty blonde, his skin was sun-kissed, and his body was muscular to the point of model perfection. He had been raised on a farm, so he was too down to earth and wise to go anywhere near somebody like Ricky. Tom, on the other hand, fit him like a glove. Tom had been working as a journalist when he had met Cole. Tom had always sworn off casual sex and spent his weekends on his own with his cat. Ricky had practically forced them together, but even he was surprised when Tom traded in journalism for working on Cole's farm. Five years later, they were married, had a daughter, a farming empire, and everything seemed perfect.

Despite being a cynical old queen, Ricky knew their love was pure. He didn't know if it warmed his heart or turned his stomach. He was happy that his friend had found somebody, but he knew better than anyone that the most perfect things could come crashing down.

He finished his cigarette and tossed it into the road. They bypassed the long line and pushed their way back into the full club, just as the final song he had lined up neared its end.

"Stay where I can see you. I need to get back to work, but this place closes at two, so we'll go out then."

Tom yawned, but they both nodded their agreement to the plan. Ricky doubted they would both last the three hours until closing.

He resumed his place behind the DJ box and played Beyoncé's *Single Ladies*. The crowd roared, and the hands and bad dancing started.

An hour later, he was surprised to see that Tom and Cole were not only still there, but they were on their third drinks. Tom seemed to be easing into the night, and his hips were even starting to sway a little. Cole seemed like less of a lightweight, but even he had an easy smile on his face.

"I love this song!" wailed Tom from next to the DJ booth as Ricky played Kylie Minogue's *Locomotion*.

Ricky laughed. He had known all it would take for his friends to relax was some cheesy music and some sugary, strong cocktails. When Ricky took Tom and Cole outside for his next cigarette break, the fresh air showed how quickly the couple were getting drunk.

"I don't feel too good," said Tom as he clutched his stomach. "How did I used to do this?"

"You didn't," said Ricky. "You went home before midnight, sweetheart!"

"It's past midnight?"

"A little past."

"I'm having fun," said Cole. "Let's stay out a little longer."

Ricky pressed the cigarette between his lips and lit the end. He inhaled the smoke and relaxed. If his friends continued drinking the way they were, they would be on their arses within the hour. Ricky wasn't in the mood to babysit drunks.

Cole went back into the club to find the toilet, leaving Tom and Ricky leaning against the club window.

"So," slurred Tom, "you and the car boot sale guy?"

"We fucked and I kicked him out butt naked," Ricky mumbled through the cigarette, ash tumbling to the floor. "He found the picture of Bret and started asking questions."

"What did you tell him?"

"I told him it was none of his business and he should leave."

"Oh, Ricky." Tom clumsily dropped his hand on Ricky's shoulder and leaned his body weight against him. "He seemed nice. You should have gone on a date with him."

"I have my rules –"

"Fuck your rules, '*sweetheart*'," mocked Tom. "Your rules are stupid. *You're* stupid."

"Well, thanks." Ricky tossed his cigarette onto the road. "Maybe it's time for you to go home."

"No! I'm having fun!" Tom stood up and steadied himself. "I'm fine. *See*! I'm fine."

"You're slurring, sweetheart. I doubt many bars are going to let you in like that."

"I'll drink water. I promise," said Tom with a nod, tapping the side of his nose. "Water."

They went back into the club, and Tom went straight to the bar. He ordered a bottle of water, but he also ordered two straight shots of vodka. He gulped down some of the water and dropped the shots into the bottle. He fastened the lid and shook it up, looking guiltily over his shoulder; unaware Ricky was watching him from behind his DJ booth.

"I think I've found you a man," Tom shouted over the music, sipping his water cocktail as though it was really water. "He's so lovely."

"I don't need you to find me a man, sweetheart."

"No, he's *super* lovely!"

"You just said that."

"But he is! He's called Jerad. He buys milk from us. You'll love him."

Ricky didn't respond. Cole reappeared from the toilets, complaining about the long line and seeming a lot more sober.

"What are we talking about?"

"Jerad!" cried Tom.

"Oh, he's lovely."

"So I've heard," sighed Ricky. "I'm trying to work up here, guys."

"You should go on a date with him," said Tom.

"He's so lovely," repeated Cole. "You'll love him."

"You're giving me tinnitus," quipped Ricky. "I don't want to go on a date with '*lovely*' milk-buying Jerad."

"He owns his own business! And he's *so* handsome. He's thirty-nine, and he's divorced, but he doesn't have any kids. He came out two years ago, and he's looking to settle down."

"Good for Jerad!" snapped Ricky, frowning as he focussed on his laptop screen as he lined up the next track. "And you think '*lovely*' Jerad wants to settle down with a drag queen?"

"We've told him about the drag, and he's cool with it!" said Tom, standing on his tiptoes and peering over the edge of the booth, his curly hair hanging low over his eyes. "Just say you'll go on a date with him."

"If I say yes, will you two shut up?"

Tom and Cole both looked at each other, clearly surprised. Ricky had no intention of going on a date with anyone, but he doubted his drunken friends would remember.

"Seriously?" asked Tom.

"You'll love him. He's so –"

"*Lovely?*" snapped Ricky. "I'll think about it."

"No! You said yes."

"Give me his number and I'll text him tomorrow."

Ricky handed over a pen and ripped off a corner of the poster of his face on the wall behind him. Tom read out the number from his phone and Cole scribbled it down. He handed it to Ricky. It said '*Lovely Jerad*' with a huge smiley face and his eleven digits below it. Ricky folded it up and stuffed it in his bra, and he wondered how quickly he could lose the number.

"I'm gonna be sick," mumbled Tom, his lips suddenly looking wet. "I don't feel -"

A pink stream of liquid spurted from his mouth onto the floor before he finished his sentence. The bouncers didn't see, but the people around Tom jumped back as the vomit splashed against their feet. Before word travelled across the club, Ricky quickly lined up a song, jumped down from his podium, and escorted his friends out of the emergency side entrance and into the dark alley.

"Home time."

"But we were having so much fun," mumbled Tom, still drooling.

He leaned over and vomited again, this time splashing the edges of Ricky's toes. He jumped back as Cole rubbed his husband's back. Ricky was glad Tom had Cole because he wasn't the type of friend who would nurse him all night.

After the second round of vomiting, Tom didn't object to being pushed in the direction of the row of cabs waiting outside the takeaway across the road.

"Promise you'll call him?" asked Tom woozily.

"I promise." Ricky crossed his fingers behind his back and slapped Cole on the shoulder as Tom stumbled into the taxi. "Look after him."

Cole promised that he would, kissed Ricky on the cheek and ducked into the taxi. They sped off down the street, turned the corner and vanished from sight.

"Jesus Christ, love. You're a beast," a man's voice called from the shadows. "Look at this one, lads. Is that a bloke in a wig?"

Ricky turned around to see a group of four overweight, middle-aged, bald men in polo shirts, baggy jeans and the type of shoes usually worn at funerals. They were painfully heterosexual, and desperately out of place amongst the rainbow flags and same-sex handholding.

"Don't come into my house and shit on my doorstep, sweetheart." Ricky gave them his middle finger and walked back towards the club.

"Don't let them blokes in," Ricky said to Gary, the straight doorman who had a similar appearance to that of the group, but without any of the ignorance. "Troublemakers with a capital *T*."

"You got it, boss."

Ricky went back into the club. The music had stopped playing, and people were looking awkwardly around at each other.

"Alright, *alright*! Mother is back! I'm just defending your gayness, but God help me if the music stops playing. Also, Jackson, can we get a clean up in front of this DJ booth? There's a pile of pink slime, and it's only a matter of time before somebody twerks into it."

The rest of Ricky's set went by quickly. He was surprised that he wasn't annoyed at Tom for getting too drunk and going home early. He had half expected it, but as he had been getting into drag earlier that night, he had sworn that he wouldn't let Tom and Cole leave no matter how drunk they got. A small part of Ricky was looking forward to getting a taxi home when the club closed, something he rarely did. He was usually the last queen on the scene, stumbling out of AXM at six in the morning and straight into the kebab shop, with whatever lucky guy he had granted the special privilege of going home with him. Tonight, going home alone seemed more tempting. Whether that was because of the fix the day before with the mailman, or because he was getting old, he didn't actually care.

People moved on from the club earlier than usual and at half-past one in the morning, Jackson pushed the leftovers out onto the street and closed early. The music stopped, the lasers stopped flashing, and the harsh, fluorescent lights were turned on. Ricky stared at the mess on the dance floor, happy it was written into his contract that he didn't have to do any of the manual labour at the end of the night.

He went into the tiny changing room, which also doubled up as a cleaning supplies storeroom. He unlocked one of the few working lockers and pulled out his boy clothes. To his own amazement, he wriggled out of his skin fitting, black, latex dress in the cramped space and snatched off his wig. Using a makeup wipe, he wiped off as much of his makeup as he could. He looked in the smudged mirror on the back of the door. He still had eyeliner around his eyes, but it suited him. It only emphasised the dark, Italian features he had inherited from his grandmother's side.

"Not going out tonight?" asked Jackson when Ricky emerged from the changing room, his drag stuffed in his backpack. "You feeling alright?"

"Early night for this queen tonight."

"Early night for Ricky?" Jackson laughed and leaned against the mop. "You sure about that one? I've got some weed back at mine if you want to come back."

Jackson smiled playfully and winked. He was young and good looking, but also naïve. He had been the manager at London Bridge for three months, and he was the third manager they had gone through since Rox, the longest and best running manager the bar had ever seen, had jumped ship to work at Tom and Cole's farm café. Rox had had a strict '*no fucking the staff, Ricky*' policy, which he usually ignored, but he had heard whispers that Jackson had already fucked his way around the rest of the male staff and he wanted the complete set. Ricky didn't mind making men just another notch on his bedpost, but he wasn't about to be a notch on somebody else's.

"I'll pass, kid," he said as he walked past Jackson, slapping him on the backside. "You've missed a spot. See you tomorrow night, sweetheart."

Instead of taking the shortcut through Canal Street, he opted for the longer route of going down the dark alley. The destination was the same, but he was likely to know most of the people on the main street, and he didn't want to turn them away.

A drop of rain hit him on the end of the nose. He looked up at the dark sky, and even darker clouds had drifted over the city. He was glad he was going home. Rain was a drag queen's natural enemy. Smiling to himself, Ricky tossed his backpack over his shoulder and set off into the dark.

Walking behind the clubs, he could hear the pumping pop music as he passed. When he got to the back of The New Union, he heard one of his favourite songs: Gloria Gaynor's '*I Will Survive*'. Lip-syncing along to the words, he made a mental note to consider it for one of his Pride performance songs.

Before he reached the end of the alley, a beer can rolled out of the shadows, followed by a deep laugh, interrupted his bliss. He stopped dead in his tracks and looked in the shadows, instantly recognising them as the guys who had hollered at him in the street over an hour ago. They hadn't seemed to spot him, so he didn't move, wondering if he should turn around and cut through the well-lit street after all.

"These fucking faggots," said one of the men as he sipped from a can of lager, leaning against a yellow skip. "Who wants to go in their puff pubs anyway? Full of a bunch of shirt lifters, ain't it, lads?"

There was a mumble of agreement as they all gulped down their store bought cans. Ricky squinted into the dark at the men, but he didn't recognise the one who had called to him before. For a mad moment, Ricky decided he was going to carry on walking. He only had twenty or so steps until he reached the yellow glow of the streetlamps.

He doubted they would recognise him out of drag, but that didn't concern him. He wasn't scared of a bunch of homophobic men. He had dealt with men like that his entire life, including his own father. He had grown up being called a 'sissy' and a 'queer' in his own house. It had only made him tougher and more resilient.

What made him change his mind was the thought of his bed and how nice it would be to go home and crawl into bed without any drama. Resigning himself to the fact he was getting old, he turned on his heels to head back the way he came.

He only took one step before the main guy from earlier emerged from the shadows. Zipping up his jeans, he looked as surprised to see Ricky, as Ricky was to see him.

"What do we have here?" he smirked at Ricky. "Got lost, little boy?"

"I'm not so little," Ricky inflated his chest and deepened his voice. "Piss off and get out of my way."

"Who do you think you are?" growled the man, his eyes filling with a drunken rage. "The last idiot that spoke to me like that ended up in a box."

Ricky wasn't sure that was true, but he wasn't about to

take his chance. He stepped to the side and walked past the man, and for a moment, he thought he was on his way back to safety. He was yanked back when the man pulled on Ricky's bag, dragging it off Ricky's shoulder.

"Give that back," demanded Ricky, holding out his hand.

The man did what Ricky hoped he wouldn't. He stepped back, holding the bag above his head, a devious, sloppy smirk on his wide face. A single, silver earring hung from his left ear, glittering in the glow of the distant streetlamp.

Popping the zip, he ripped open the bag, and Miss Kitty Litter's blonde wig fell to the ground. Rain started to pour from the sky, and Ricky had to stop himself from dropping to his knees to rescue the three-hundred-pound lace front wig from the dirty cobbles.

"Well, well, well," slurred the guy. "It's that queer in the frock from before, lads."

The other three men had stood up to see what was going on, but they stayed back. Ricky knew he had seconds to act before things turned messy. He almost turned and left behind his wig and dress, knowing he could outrun the drunken slobs. What stopped him was his Pride performance. He had planned his entire main stage outfit around the birdcage he had found at the car boot sale and the wig on the ground was the wig he had chosen. Without it, he would look a mess, and that thought terrified him more than anything.

Against his better judgement, Ricky swooped in for the wig and clasped the bag in the man's hands. Unluckily for Ricky, the man's inebriation didn't seem to affect his strength. He yanked on the bag, pulling Ricky closer than he would have liked to be.

Without thinking, Ricky clenched his fist around the

blonde wig and sent his knuckles square into the middle of the man's face. It worked. He let go of the bag, and without sticking around to see the consequences, Ricky set off at a sprint.

His assumption about outrunning the men had been correct. Before he knew it, he was way ahead of their heavy footsteps, and the glow of the streetlamps was within touching distance.

But something heavy struck him in the back of the head. At first, he thought it was a can of beer, so he decided to keep running, but when he heard the sound of the brick bouncing against the cobbles, he realised it wouldn't be that simple. He fought the pain, but it was all-consuming.

His vision blurring, he dropped to his knees, his fingers still clutching the wig. His last moment before he blacked out was that he had been right about somebody going home in an ambulance. As darkness clouded his mind, he took a second to appreciate the irony that the siren would probably be turned off and he would likely be in a body bag, not strapped to a stretcher.

CHAPTER

FOUR

C hase loved Friday nights. Once a week he would put aside one night to indulge. It had been a tradition since opening the gym to leave Dylan with a babysitter and head into the city centre for a couple of drinks on his own.

It was time he treasured, and this week was no exception. When it almost didn't happen because of his regular babysitter, Helena, cancelling because she had taken a more profitable late-night shift at the call centre she worked at, he had almost reluctantly given up on the idea. He was glad his kind neighbour, Annie, had stepped in.

Annie lived in the flat next to him on the fifth floor of their concrete high-rise building on the outskirts of the city. She was always on hand to offer cups of tea whenever Chase was smoking a cigarette over the edge of their walkway. It had been one of those cigarette breaks at the very moment Annie was walking back from the shop with a pint of milk that had saved him. When she offered him a cup of tea and asked why he was walking around under a grey cloud, it had been her idea to watch Dylan for the night.

Normally, he wouldn't have left Dylan with somebody who didn't regularly watch him, but he trusted Annie. She was a sweet lady in her early eighties, and she seemed to crave the company, even if it was from a six-year-old boy. Her own children were grown up and rarely visited, and her husband had died before Chase moved in.

Flicking the last of his cigarette over the glass railing and into the canal, he turned to VIA and went inside just as it started to rain. The pink-bearded doorman greeted him and opened the door. Chase nodded his appreciation and hurried inside.

When he had first started showing up in the bars around Canal Street, it had been hard to gain entry. From his tattoo-covered body, exaggerated muscles and masculine vibe, he wasn't surprised it had taken repeat appearances for trust to be gained. He didn't mind. He knew they were just trying to keep the gay bars safe from the troublemakers who looked like Chase.

Sometimes he wondered if covering every inch of his body in tattoos had been the wisest decision, but he couldn't imagine his life any other way. The only blank areas of skin were on his face, his palms, his arse cheeks, and his manhood. He rubbed his most recent tattoo on his forearm, his fingertips gliding over the healing ink. It was a patch he had been saving for years, so he could fill it with a portrait of Dylan. He had wanted to wait until Dylan was older, and now that he was starting to grow into his face, he thought it was the best time. It wasn't until his son's face was immortalised on his skin that he really noticed how much he looked like his mother.

"Pint of lager, please," he said to the good looking man behind the bar, "and whatever you want to drink, if you're allowed."

The bartender smiled, naughtiness filling his eyes. He looked like he was in his mid-twenties, and he wasn't Chase's type, but there was a certain mystique in his beauty. His face was almost elf-like in shape, with tilted brows, sleek eyes and pointed ears. A subtle, silver nose ring hung between his nostrils and his soft smile and gleaming teeth were framed with dark stubble.

"I won't tell if you don't," he said with a wink as he poured himself a shot of white Sambuca, along with one for Chase. "This one's on me."

Chase gladly accepted the shot, despite barely being able to tolerate Sambuca. They both tossed back the shots, and the barman looked over his shoulder as the other men dressed in black hurried around him to service the rammed bar.

He poured the lager and pushed it across the bar. He charged Chase for the pint and one of the white Sambuca shots. '*Bailey*' flashed up in blue on the tiny LED screen.

"Nice drinking with you, Bailey," said Chase. "Cheers for the shot."

"Anytime," twinkled Bailey, his teeth biting the inside edge of his rose petal lips. "I'll see you around."

"I hope so."

Taking his pint, Chase walked through the busy dance floor, past the elevated DJ booth, and onto a raised platform. He loved drinking in VIA. From the outside, it looked like a tiny, narrow bar, but there was an entire secret section hidden in the back, which spanned three levels. The entire building was made up of reclaimed church wood, which Chase had always felt was an ironic theme for a gay bar.

He walked along the wooden bridge to the other side of the bar, looking down at the level below. He spotted two men kissing in the mock confessional booth, and he instantly felt horny. He tugged at the soft bulge in his jeans. Last week he had gone home alone, so he felt extra pressure to pull.

Sitting in a seat on the balcony, he scanned the faces of the people below. None of them caught his eye like Bailey had. Just as he was hoping to see Bailey's striking features again, the bartender ran down the stairs on a glass collection run. As he stacked the pint glasses, he seemed to be looking around for someone. When he looked up, he caught Chase's eye and smirked. Bailey had been looking for Chase.

Bailey ditched the glasses on the second bar and lingered by a set of stairs leading to the toilets and the lounge under the club. The lounge bar was themed like a church crypt, and Chase usually found himself in there in the early hours of the morning, watching the drag shows.

Ditching his pint, Chase met Bailey at the stairwell. Neither of them spoke, but Bailey's smile told Chase to follow him. Two men passed them on the stairs, nodding to Chase as they went. He recognised them as other regular Canal Street visitors, but he didn't know their names.

He assumed Bailey was leading him to the unisex toilet cubicles. It wasn't the classiest location, but the doors locked. Instead, he turned left to the crypt. A red rope was tethered across the door, signalling that the basement level of the bar was closed tonight.

Throwing caution to the wind, Bailey pulled back the rope and opened the door. Chase waited for a group of women to come out of the bathroom and to pass him on the stairs before he walked into the dark room. The only light came from the illuminated drinks display behind the bar. It cast an eerie glow across the chiselled stone ceiling.

Bailey skipped the vocal explanation and chose to grab Chase's hand. He pulled him up onto the small stage in the corner, which usually housed a drag queen performing covers of Adele and Susan Boyle. Chase thought it was an odd choice of location, until he realised it was the only part of the underground bar that couldn't be seen when peering through the door.

"You're so hot," Bailey mumbled through shaky breath as he danced his fingers over the exposed parts of Chase's tattooed chest.

Bailey was considerably shorter, but that didn't stop him from locking lips with Chase. Most men were shorter than him. Just like his brother, he stood six-feet-four-inches proud. He had learned as a young boy that it was impossible to fade into the background, which retrospectively, he knew was the reason he had chosen the tattooed life.

Bailey didn't waste any time in unbuttoning Chase's shirt. His kisses trickled down his torso, stopping above Chase's waist. He tugged at his belt buckle and frantically unbuttoned his jeans, all the while glancing over to the door.

He pushed Chase against the sequin backdrop attached to the wall and peeled back his white Calvin Klein briefs. His solid cock sprung out, and Bailey's eyes looked up to his with a mixture of shock and wonder.

"Bloody hell, man," he mumbled. "You're gonna poke somebody's eye out with that thing."

Bailey's hand wrapped around Chase's shaft, his fingers barely touching. He knew most guys were average sized, and the ones who weren't were usually thicker or longer, but rarely the two combined. Chase's almost ten-inch penis hung thick and strong.

Clutching the back of Bailey's hair, he closed his eyes and pushed as much of his cock into his mouth as the bartender could take. He gagged as the tip hit the back of his throat, but it was barely past halfway. Chase had yet to meet a man who could take his full length into his mouth, and he would be surprised if he ever did.

Resisting the urge to force himself deeper, he handed the control back over to Bailey. He gently massaged his hair as the young bartender worked his shaft with his tongue and hand. Chase watched in wonder as he expertly worked him. It was clear he had done it enough times to perfect his technique, but Chase didn't care.

Bailey uncovered Chase's secret weakness when he looked up and locked his eyes with Chase's. He didn't know why, but making eye contact with a man as he was having his cock sucked was his biggest turn-on. Just staring into Bailey's hazel eyes, he felt his orgasm already brewing.

He wanted to slow things down so they could savour the moment, but Bailey seemed to be in a rush. In between looking up into Chase's eyes, he kept looking at the door. Chase gave in and stopped holding back.

"I'm close," he warned Bailey.

Instead of pulling away or slowing down, Bailey sped up even faster, tightening his grip and twisting his shaft in a way that nobody had ever done before.

Every muscle in his body clenched as his forced orgasm shot out of his body. Straining his eyes to keep them open, he looked down into Bailey's eyes, as he looked up hungrily, with a waiting tongue. Chase released, and Bailey gladly accepted his load, seeming to savour every last drop. A guy swallowing was second on Chase's list of biggest turn-ons.

When it was over, Bailey stood up, a teasing smile on his lips. He winked at Chase and took a step back so Chase could pull up his underwear and jeans. He looked down at Bailey's cock, where a strained erection pushed through his trousers. Chase reached out to unleash it, but Bailey took another step back.

"We close at two. Wait around for me," Bailey said softly. "I live around the corner."

Chase nodded as he buttoned up his shirt, his cock still jutting out through his jeans. Bailey looked down at it, tugged on his own and reluctantly doubled back to the door.

When he was redressed and starting to soften, he made his way back up to the bar and ordered another pint, this time with another barman. He watched Bailey work, wondering what it would be like to fuck someone so slender. He hoped he would be able to take his cock.

Two o'clock rolled around before Chase had even had a chance to finish his pint. He lingered outside of the bar, leaning against the glass railing shielding the canal. Ten minutes past two, Bailey emerged from the bar, in a leather jacket with a canvas bag over his shoulder. He seemed shyer out of the comfort of his workplace. He winked at Chase and nodded down Canal Street for him to follow him, just as he had done at the top of the stairs.

"We'll take the shortcut," he said. "This way."

Chase followed him around the corner of G-A-Y, past a mural of Batman kissing Superman painted on the wall, and into the dark alley behind The New Union. He only took two steps before he noticed a man slumped up against the wall. Bailey walked past him, like most people in Manchester did when they saw a homeless person on the side of the street. It was hard not to overlook them, because they were perched on every street corner, begging for money.

Something was different about this man. He wasn't

ASHLEY JOHN

begging, and he didn't look homeless. His clothes looked expensive, and his nose definitely looked bent out of shape. Chase squinted into the dark, approaching the man carefully, as not to alarm him.

"Are you coming?" Bailey called from further down the alley.

"There's a man. I think he's hurt."

"He's probably a sleeping tramp. Leave him be."

Chase took another step forward, and he pulled his phone out of his pocket and shone the screen on his face. The man groaned, but he looked barely conscious. It was then he noticed the fresh blood trickling from the man's nose and mouth and two fresh black eyes.

"I'm calling an ambulance. He's been beaten up bad."

"How do you know?"

"Because I've had my nose broken enough times to know what it looks like."

Bailey approached him, and his hand drifted up to cover his mouth when he saw the man close up.

"I know him. He works at London Bridge around the corner. I can't remember his name. Ronnie, or Kyle, or something like that."

Chase pushed the phone deeper into his ear and called for the ambulance. He told them exactly where he was, how badly hurt the stranger was, and they said they would be thirty minutes and couldn't promise they could be any quicker on a Friday night.

"Come on, let's go," said Bailey, tugging on Chase's shirtsleeve. "You've called the ambulance. There's not much else you can do."

"We can't leave him like this!"

"Do you want to stay here and wait for half an hour for an ambulance, which is just going to cart him to the hospital? Or do you want to come back to my flat, which is a three-minute walk away, where you can fuck me?"

Bailey's offer was tempting, but not when Chase looked at what it was stacked up against. He crouched next to the man and picked up his wrist. His pulse was there, but barely.

"I'm staying here," he said adamantly.

"Time waster," Bailey mumbled under his breath as he pushed his hands deep into his jacket pockets and set off into the dark.

Chase watched his shag turn the corner and disappear from view. He knew he would have to give his favourite bar a wide berth for a couple of weeks, but he didn't care.

Sitting on the ground next to the man, he did the only thing he could think to help. He picked up his hand and held it. With his thumb, he caressed the back of his hand, and the stranger reacted by clenching as much as he could, which was limp by anyone's standards.

Chase noticed the bag on the ground at his feet. A wallet poked out of the pocket, and it looked like it had been stripped of its cards and cash, but whoever had done it had been kind enough to leave behind an out of date provisional driving licence.

"Richard, it's going to be okay," he said louder as he clutched his hand tightly. "I've called an ambulance and they're going to help you."

Chase wasn't sure if he was trying to convince the stranger or himself that everything was going to be okay. As he listened out for the sound of sirens, he closed his eyes and leaned his head against the back of The New Union, the music pounding into his skull.

He hoped and prayed Richard would survive the next thirty minutes.

CHAPTER

FIVE

Ricky's first thought as he started to wake was how harsh he was going to look under the fluorescent lighting. It pierced through his fluttering eyelids, but he couldn't seem to open them. His second thought was that every part of his body ached.

He opened his eyes as wide as he could, but he felt like he was looking through narrow slits. He stared ahead, taking in his surroundings. How much had he drunk last night?

Knowing he should probably get home, he attempted to stand up, but he only managed to roll onto his side. A sharp pain shot through his ribs, and he immediately knew some of them were broken. It was only when he lifted his hands in front of his face that he realised he was in the hospital. An IV drip jutted out of the back of his hand, and a heart rate monitor was attached to his finger.

He waited to fully wake, but his mind was cloudy. Had somebody drugged him? He tried to think back to last night, but it was a blur. He remembered putting Tom into a taxi and leaving the bar, but whatever happened next was foggy.

Twisting his head to the window next to his bed, he almost had a heart attack when he saw a man slumped down in a chair, fast asleep. If it weren't for the tattoos covering every inch of the man's body, Ricky would have assumed he was a doctor. Squinting into the light, he stared at the sleeping stranger, trying to place his face, but he was sure he had never seen him before. Even through his medicated haze, he would have recognised such a beautiful face.

Ricky observed the man as he slept. The top three buttons of his white shirt were open, exposing his rising and falling chest. He looked like he was dressed for a night on the town, but it seemed too early for that.

The door to his room open and Ricky twisted his neck as quickly as he could. The man slept soundly in his chair, undisturbed by the appearance of a young, smiling nurse.

"How are you feeling, Richard?" she asked softly as she walked across the room.

"Sore," he said, attempting to laugh, but only coughing. "Where am I?"

"You're at Manchester Royal Infirmary, love," she said with a friendly smile as she checked the notes at the end of the bed. "Do you remember anything that happened last night?"

Ricky raked through his cluttered memories, but nothing was surfacing. The pain was too intense to focus on anything else.

"I was working," he mumbled. "I was going home, I

think. Who's this man?"

They both looked at the stranger sleeping in the chair. Despite his rugged exterior, there was something childlike and soft about the way he slept.

"He was your knight in shining armour. He brought you in at the beginning of my shift. He's not left your side all night."

"What time is it?"

"Just gone eight. I thought I'd come and check on you before I clocked off. You've had quite a night."

"I – I can't remember anything," he said, frustrated with his own mind.

"That's perfectly normal. It will all start coming back to you eventually. The police will want to ask you a couple of questions when you're feeling better, but you don't have to talk to them until you're ready."

"Police?"

The nurse looked up uneasily from Ricky's notes, a worried smile on her face. He tried so hard to remember, but he was still pulling a blank.

"This man found you slumped in an alley. It looks like you were attacked and mugged."

Ricky felt a sharp jab in his stomach, and he felt water on his face. Had it been raining?

"Can I get you anything before I go?"

"Water," he croaked. "My throat is dryer than Gandhi's flip flops, sweetheart."

The nurse chuckled and picked up a jug of water off the stand next to his bed. She poured a little into a plastic cup, added a straw and held it at his chin. He sucked on the water, but it hurt to swallow. He felt ridiculous having someone hold the cup for him, but he wasn't sure if he could keep his arm lifted for long enough.

He drank the tiny amount and he felt nowhere near

hydrated, but it hurt too much to swallow, so he told the nurse he didn't want anymore, and she headed for the door. It snapped shut behind her and the man jumped out of his sleep, looking as surprised and startled as Ricky had when he woke up.

"You're awake," he muttered faintly as he rubbed his red eyes, squinting at Ricky. "I must have nodded off."

They both sat in silence for a moment. Ricky felt uncomfortable knowing that he probably looked like shit and the man had been there all night looking at his face.

"How are you feeling?" he asked as he leaned forward against his knees eagerly.

"Sore," he repeated. "What happened?"

"I found you behind The New Union. It looked like somebody turned you over pretty bad. I called an ambulance."

"The nurse said you've been here all night."

"I couldn't just leave you," he said anxiously. "I'm Chase, by the way."

"Ricky."

"Ah," he said with a more natural smile. "I checked your wallet, and it said Richard. You've been fleeced of your cards and money."

"Only my mum calls me Richard," he said, attempting to laugh again, but it turned into another painful cough.

Ricky didn't care about his money. He suddenly remembered the wig and dress he had been holding in his bag. Why did that wig feel so important? He closed his eyes, and he saw its blonde hair flying past his face in slow motion. Had he thrown it at someone? Nothing made sense.

"I can't remember. Was it raining last night?"

"Yes. It's normal to forget things after you've taken a blow to the head. It'll come back."

"That's what the nurse said," he croaked, fidgeting uncomfortably under the itchy, cotton sheets. "How do you know that?"

"Fifteen years of kickboxing," he said proudly. "I run a gym. *Fitness World Pro.*"

"I know that name," he furrowed his brow, hating how his memories felt like a jigsaw puzzle with all of the pieces crammed in the wrong slots. "I think."

"It's on the high street in Hebden Bridge. It's a little village just outside of —"

"I live there." He was sure of that, at least. "You opened last year."

"That's right," he said, seeming pleased Ricky was remembering something. "I run it with my brother. Is there somebody from the village you want me to call? They tried to get in touch with your next of kin on file, but the number has been disconnected."

For a moment, Ricky couldn't think of who they had been trying to call, but he remembered the last time he had been in the hospital. Twelve years ago when his appendix nearly burst.

"Good luck with that, sweetheart," he said with a wince as he tried to sit up. "Unless you've got a phone that can contact the afterlife. Believe me, I've tried."

"Oh, I'm sorry," Chase jumped up and picked up the remote from the side of the bed. "Let me."

Chase pressed a button, and the top half of Ricky's bed elevated so that he was forced into a sitting position. When his head adjusted to the new angle, he felt less like a corpse lying on a slab.

"You've probably got somewhere to be," said Ricky. "Thanks for — *y'know* — thanks for not just leaving me, sweetheart."

"I couldn't have," he said, as though it was obvious. "It's

still early. Annie always wakes up at nine every day."

"Who's that? Your wife?"

"My eighty-two-year-old next door neighbour," Chase said with a smirk. "She picks up the milk bottle from her doorstep every Saturday at nine."

"People still have milk delivered?" Ricky attempted to laugh again, but he felt like he was about to cough up a lung. "You don't have to stay on my account. You're probably as knackered as me."

"I'm fine, honestly," said Chase as he stood up and walked over to the window. "Although I'm dying for a cigarette."

"Me too."

"Probably not the best idea in your situation," said Chase apprehensively.

Just the mention of a cigarette made every fibre of Ricky's body crave nicotine. He looked up at the ceiling, but there were two smoke detectors ready to beep at the first sign of smoke.

"Grab me a wheelchair, sweetheart," he said, nodding to the door. "They'll be dotted all over the place."

"I don't think that's a –"

"Just do it. I'll be fine. This machine thing is on wheels."

Chase reluctantly walked over to the door, not without giving Ricky one last hesitant look. He popped his head out into the corridor before slipping out of the door. Less than a minute later, he returned with a bulky push-along chair with huge, cream coloured wheels.

"Help me get in there." Ricky tossed a finger at the chair. "I just need to roll into it somehow."

Chase lined the chair up with the side of the bed. He put his arm around Ricky's shoulders, and Ricky thought he was just helping, but his second arm slid under the sheets and cupped under his buttocks. The back of Ricky's gown was missing, and Chase's knuckles grazed the bottom of his arse cheeks.

"Wrap your arms around my neck," he instructed.

"I don't think you'll be able to lift me, sweetheart," he said as he slowly lifted his arms around the man's thick, tattooed neck. "You're gonna need a lie down in my bed if you throw your back out."

In one swift movement, Chase lifted Ricky effortlessly, as though he was no heavier than a small child. Every inch of his body cried out in pain, but he felt oddly safe in Chase's arms. He clutched tightly to Chase's neck as he lowered him carefully into the huge chair, making sure not to catch the wires on the arms. Remnants of a clean aftershave on his skin tickled Ricky's senses. Why did it smell familiar?

When he was in the chair, he felt exhausted and ready to crawl back into bed, but the promise of a cigarette gave him a new lease of life. He grabbed the heart rate monitor, Chase grabbed the handles, and they started to move.

They snuck past reception easily and quickly to the lifts at the bottom of the long, white corridor. They floated down to the ground floor in the lift, smirking at each other in the mirror. There was something quite exciting about breaking out, even if it was only temporarily.

They glided through the rotating entrance doors and out into the early morning cool air. Ricky inhaled deeply, appreciating the crisp British air.

Chase placed a cigarette in between Ricky's lips and cupped his hands around the end as he lit it for him. Ricky could have probably attempted to light it himself, but there was something comforting about the muscular man being so helpful.

"Oh, fuck," mumbled Ricky through the first drag of

the cigarette. "That's just what I needed. I'll be right as rain in no time."

Chase chuckled as he lit his own cigarette. He leaned against the wall under the hospital's sign, next to Ricky. People worse looking than Ricky were slumped around him in wheelchairs, puffing hard on cigarettes. It almost seemed ridiculous, but he felt like he was growing stronger with each hit.

"I remember somebody holding my hand," he said out of the blue as the memory floated to the top. "I think. *No, I know* there was. Somebody clutched my hand tightly. Maybe it was a dream."

Chase didn't say anything as he puffed hard on his cigarette, his brow furrowing. Ricky wondered if it had been Chase holding his hand, or if he had really imagined that.

"I think that was the nurse," said Chase. "It was touch and go for a while."

They quickly finished their cigarettes and made their way back to Ricky's room. On the way, he caught sight of himself in the lift mirror and gasped. He didn't recognise his own face. When they returned to his room, nobody had even noticed they had gone anywhere.

"I should probably get going," said Chase after chatting to Ricky for another half an hour. "Is there anyone you want me to call?"

Ricky almost felt sad that Chase was leaving, but he couldn't expect the tattooed hunk to hang around forever. He couldn't quite place his finger on why, but Chase had a soothing presence. This was one of the few times Ricky didn't mind admitting he probably couldn't get through life on his own.

"My best friend, Tom," Ricky said, knowing that he was going to lose his mind when the call went through. "His number is in my phone."

"That was taken too."

"Oh. Do an internet search for Barton Farm. He lives there."

Chase checked his phone signal, but he was out of bars, so he ran back down to the reception area without saying goodbye. Ricky sat for nearly fifteen minutes, wondering if Chase was going to come back. He didn't owe Ricky anything, but it felt like they had been through something together.

Just when Ricky had given up hope, the door to his room opened, and Chase slipped back inside.

"He's on his way," he said, with soft, friendly smile. "He was in bits when I told him."

"And I thought I was the drama queen."

Chase walked across the room to the side of Ricky's bed and clutched his hands around the plastic railing.

"Is there anything else you need before I go?" he asked.

Ricky shook his head. Chase had already done more than enough, and he couldn't ask any more of the man who had literally saved him.

"Thank you," he said, dropping his hand on top of Chase's. "For everything."

"You really don't have to thank me," he said, looking down at Ricky's hand on top of his. "Anytime."

Ricky pulled his hand away and dropped it down to his side, feeling foolish for reaching out in the first place. He realised that the man had seen him as vulnerable as a person could get, but it was probably a step too far. Chase didn't seem as affected as Ricky.

"See you around," said Ricky, trying his best to smile through the thick dressing shielding his nose.

Chase nodded and backed away to the door. He turned and grabbed the handle, but he didn't open it straight away. Instead, he turned back and pulled his wallet from his tight jeans. For a moment, Ricky thought the man was going to give him money, but instead, he pulled out a small card.

"Come by the gym when you're back on your feet," said Chase. "I can show you some self-defence stuff in case any arseholes try to do this again."

He put the card on the edge of the table next to Ricky's bed and tapped it hard with his finger. Ricky smiled and nodded gratefully. As he watched Chase leave, he knew it was probably the last time he was going to see him, but he appreciated the offer.

Wincing in pain, he reached out and picked up the business card, turning it over in his fingers. Before he had even decided what he was going to do with it, Tom burst through the door in his farm clothes, smelling like horse manure, with clear traces of a raging hangover in his eyes.

"Oh my God! Ricky! What happened to you?"

***

"I was beginning to worry!" said Annie as she wrapped her robe across her floral nightdress. "Dylan is still asleep in the box bedroom. I was restless all night listening for you to come home."

Chase almost told her about everything that had happened but it was a long story, and he was exhausted. He thanked Annie, slotted a twenty-pound note under the ceramic statue of a bulldog on the edge of her kitchen counter and took his sleepy son back to his own flat.

Yawning, he poured Dylan a bowl of cereal and drowned it in milk. He wasn't sure how much sleep he had actually gotten in the hospital, but it didn't feel like much. Tiredness tugged at his eyelids, but he was more than sure he wasn't going to be able to sleep. Ricky was on his mind, and he couldn't shake him away.

Accepting that he was awake for the day, he made himself a bacon sandwich, a strong coffee and cuddled up to Dylan on the sofa to watch the early Saturday morning cartoons.

Dylan seemed engrossed by the bright colours, but Chase just looked straight through the television. If he hadn't needed to get home, he would have hung around at the hospital for longer.

He couldn't believe a man could inflict so much pain on another man, just for a couple of quid and a phone. Chase could more than handle himself, but it still made him nervous. He had always thought the gay village was a place exempt from that kind of hate.

A knock on the door brought him from his thoughts. He looked down at Dylan, whose cereal bowl was empty. How long had he been staring into space thinking about Ricky?

Through the frosted glass, he saw the police uniform, opened the door and said, "Dad, what are you doing here?"

"Nice to see you too, son." His father, Patrick, stepped into the flat and slid off his hat. "I was doing some follow up on the first floor, and I thought I'd come up and see my favourite grandson."

"Granddad!" Dylan jumped up and flew into his Granddad's arms.

Chase knew Dylan valued that they had a close bond. He had grown up without grandparents, so he was glad Dylan had at least one. Patrick was a better grandparent than he had been a father. It had crossed Chase's mind more than once that he was trying to make up for lost time, but Dylan wasn't Chase.

"Did you hear about Natalie not watching Dylan for the summer?" he asked as he set to making them both cups of coffee. "I have no idea what I'm going to do with him."

"Don't look at me!" he held his hands up. "I can't take any more time off work after that cruise with Barbara."

Just hearing Barbara's name sent a shiver down his spine. For all of his childhood, his mother had only ever uttered Barbara's name with pure venom. She was the woman who had stolen Chase's father and forced him into having another family. Chase didn't speak to his father for most of his childhood and teenage years, and they only reconnected when Chase and Danny's mother succumbed to cancer when he was eighteen.

"No milk for me," he said. "Barbara's got me on no dairy. She's trying to make me slim down before my retirement next year. I told her that I had the body of a God."

He patted his protruding belly, which Chase knew was made up of beer and pies. He had offered him a free gym membership more than once, but he had never accepted.

Chase stirred in the sugar and handed his father the black coffee. He gladly accepted and leaned against the kitchen counter, casting his eyes over to the garish colours on the TV, frowning as he blew on his hot coffee.

"TV will rot his brain," said Patrick. "It's no good for kids."

Chase bit his tongue. He wanted to ask his father how he knew that, but he remembered his two stepbrothers, who Patrick had raised as his own. A couple of years ago, he would have taken any excuse to throw that fact in his father's face, but he had since learned it was better to live in harmony, especially for Dylan's sake.

"I don't need more parenting lectures," he said as he sipped his own coffee on the other side of the counter. "Natalie attempted to rip me another one the other day."

"What did The Wasp have to say this time?" he snarled, rolling his eyes heavily.

There was nothing like a common enemy to unite a strained father and son relationship. Patrick hated Natalie as much as Chase did. Chase had kept most of his thoughts about his brother's wife to himself, but Patrick had told Danny on more than one occasion what he really thought of her.

"The usual. I'm doing everything wrong, I should read her new book, and I need to find Dylan a replacement mother."

Patrick sipped his coffee uneasily, wincing as the hot liquid hit the end of his tongue.

"I hate to say it, son, but she's not wrong. That boy needs a woman's touch."

"That can't be helped."

"I know," he backtracked. "I didn't mean it like that. What happened with Tracey was just awful, but it's been six years now. You could have found yourself another woman in that time."

Chase bit his tongue again. Patrick had found another woman while he still had a perfectly fine one at home with two of his biological children. He sipped his coffee to shut himself up.

"It's not that easy."

"Of course it is," his father said. "By the looks and smell of it, you were out on the town last night. Did you pull?"

Chase looked over at the TV uneasily. A lack of a relationship growing up had led to the usual parent and child boundaries being blurred. Patrick tried to act like a buddy and less like a parent. Chase wasn't sure if he wanted him to act like a parent. After so many years, he was sure it would feel forced.

"No," he said. "I was home early."

"Liar." Patrick sipped his coffee and winked. "You're still wearing last night's clothes. Crawl in this morning, did you? Don't worry, son, we've all done it."

Chase almost denied it, but he decided it was better to let his father think that than try to explain the truth. To explain where he had really been would mean he would have to explain everything leading up to it and Chase didn't feel comfortable lying. He could tell the story, leaving out crucial information like the blowjob and which part of town he was in, but his brain didn't have the energy to stitch together a convincing story that didn't indict him. His father had made his feelings on that *funny lot* clear, on more than one occasion.

"I'll ask around about the summer," said Patrick as he drained the last of his coffee. "Barbara might be able to have him."

"No, it's alright. I'll find somebody," Chase cut him off. "I'll sort it out."

"Well, I better be off, I'm still on the clock," said Patrick, slapping Chase heartily on the shoulder, awkwardly avoiding eye contact. "See you around."

"Yeah, see you around."

His father showed himself out, slamming the door as he went, sending a shudder through the flat, just like he did every time he visited. Chase gathered up the morning's cups and dishes and dumped them in the sink. As he covered the mugs in soapsuds and scrubbed away the coffee rings, he wondered if he could squeeze in a visit to the hospital before his afternoon shift at the gym.

Dismissing the idea almost immediately, he dumped the cups on the draining board. He headed to the bathroom, stripped down and turned on the shower. As the hot water trickled down his body, his mind involuntarily wandered back to seeing Ricky's naked body as the nurses had stripped him out of his clothes.

CHAPTER

SIX

T wo weeks after being discharged from the hospital, Ricky returned to have his stitches and bandages removed. He was now sporting a new bump on his nose, but he didn't mind it so much. He thought it gave him an edge.

He stepped off the train and walked through the village, making sure to walk the long way around so that he passed Fitness World Pro. He looked through the window, hovering by the door to see if he could see Chase. He wasn't going to go inside, he just wanted to know if he could spot the beauty again. He would be lying if he said Chase hadn't come into his mind more than once over the last couple of weeks.

Abandoning the shop window, he set off up the winding country lane to Barton Farm. Tom and Cole had insisted he stay with them while he healed. At first, he had wanted nothing more than to go home and be on his own, but when he found it difficult to so much as wipe his own arse, he gave into his friends' offer.

"Look at you!" Auntie Belinda planted a heavy kiss on Ricky's cheek. "Good as new! What did I tell you? You've healed up nicely. Let me cook you some breakfast! Sit! *Sit*!"

Ricky hadn't wanted to stay longer than the time it took him to pack his bags, but the offer of breakfast was too good to pass up.

After wolfing down Belinda's famous full English breakfast and two mugs of coffee, he went in search of Tom and Cole. He found Tom first, in the newly built row of stables. He was shovelling manure out of the sawdust and dumping it into an overflowing wheelbarrow. He tossed a nugget, and it missed its mark, rolling towards Ricky and tapping the edge of his shoe.

"I'd like to say that was the first time somebody had flung their shit at me, but I'd be lying."

"Jesus, Ricky!" Tom jumped, his dark curls bouncing and his eyes clenching. "You scared the shit out of me!"

"I can see that," said Ricky, nodding at the full barrow. "Let me empty that for you."

He picked up the barrow and wheeled it behind the stables to the huge, elevated trailer. Ricky had been doing what he could around the farm as a subtle thank you for their help, and it had worked as cheaper physical therapy. His ribs still ached a little, and he still had half a dozen yellow bruises that were refusing to leave, but it was nothing time, and a handful of the good prescription painkillers wouldn't fix.

"You're going to injure yourself again," said Tom disapprovingly. "Go and put your feet up."

"I'm fine, sweetheart. I'm going stir-crazy. I'm feeling so

much better. I was thinking about sleeping back at the cottage tonight."

"*What*? You can't!"

Cole rode towards them on the back of his horse, completely shirtless and wearing nothing more than jeans and a riding hat. Ricky tried not to check out his friend's body, but it was a marvel that had to be admired.

"Can't what?" he asked, jumping down from the horse and patting her mane.

"Ricky wants to go home!"

"Aw, why?" he frowned. "Eva's loving having Uncle Ricky here."

"I've loved it, and I'm grateful. I really am, but it's time for me to spread my wings! I was thinking of going back to the bar this weekend."

"No!" Tom planted his hands on his hips. "I won't allow it."

"I'm not a kid, sweetheart."

"Tom's right," said Cole. "It's too soon. What if whoever beat you up comes back?"

"Well, if they do, I won't recognise them, will I?"

Ricky had hoped his memories would have returned, but with every passing day, they seemed to drift further away. He could remember short bursts of scents and colours, but nothing his fingers could grip onto. The entire event was a dream, which had unfolded and already slithered away.

"You're not thinking straight," said Tom, shaking his head and pinching in between his nose. "How long does a concussion last? Web-search it, Cole."

"I'm not concussed. I just want to get back to normal, sweetheart."

"You almost died!"

Tom's face turned bright red, and he was breathing out of control. Ricky looked at Cole, and even he looked surprised by his husband's reaction. Ricky knew Tom was sensitive and he knew the mugging had scared Tom as much, if not more than Ricky, but he hadn't expected Tom to hold him hostage at the farm.

"I'm a big boy," he said. "And besides, I've been offered self-defence classes, so I'm good."

"You have? Are you going to take them?"

"Sure," he lied. "Jackie Chan will be shitting himself when I'm finished."

Ricky's lie seemed to ease Tom, but only a little. It had slipped out of his mouth, and it had seemed to work. He still had Chase's business card in his wallet, along with his new bankcards, but he hadn't dared call the number on it. Every so often, he would find himself taking it out and spinning it between his fingers without even realising it.

"Just put off the bar until next weekend," said Tom. "It's too soon."

"Fine," he relented. "But I'm going home tonight. I want to be in my own bed and around my own things. I'm forgetting who I am up here. I get why you two never want to go down into the real world. It's like being on that island from *Lost*, isn't it, sweethearts? Time just passes us by."

"Isn't it great?" sighed Cole, smiling effortlessly as he inhaled the country air.

"It's bloody awful."

Before he had the chance to offend either of them anymore, he went into the farmhouse and gathered his things, stuffing them into the overnight bag Tom had packed for him after taking him home from the hospital.

"There was a call for you, love," said Belinda, tearing the top piece of paper from the pad next to the phone. "Some copper. Wanted to know if you're ready to make your statement."

Ricky looked down at the hastily written telephone

number, along with the name, Chief Inspector Patrick Brody. He screwed up the paper and sighed, tossing it straight into the bin. He didn't know how much longer he could evade police questioning, but he was going to try for as long as possible. He didn't know how many times he could tell them he still didn't remember anything.

"Is that wise?" said Cole, opening the bin and pulling out the piece of paper, which was now covered in fresh, damp, coffee grounds. "They might have some information."

"I just want to forget the whole sorry affair!" he said, more hysterically than he had expected. "Have you seen my cigarettes?"

Clutching his heavy bag in his hand and a cigarette between his lips, he started to walk down the country lane back to the village. Tom had offered to drive him, but he needed the walk to think. He was tired of everybody fussing around him.

When he reached the bottom of the lane, he tossed his cigarette into the road and clutched his ribs. The morning's painkillers started to wear off, and he remembered how much pain he was still in. He tried to suppress it, but it was sharp and chronic.

Inhaling deeply, he shook his head back and set off walking through the village. Tightening his hand around his bag, he walked slowly past the gym. He glanced inside again, but he couldn't see Chase. He could see his cottage up ahead, but he didn't move.

Learning self-defence wouldn't be the worst thing to do. His promise to Tom had been flippant, but standing outside of the gym made him think more seriously about it. What if they came back to finish what they started? Without really thinking about it, Ricky opened the door and walked into the air-conditioned gym.

He approached the counter, dropped his bag and pulled Chase's business card nervously from his wallet. He turned it over in his fingers while he waited for the muscular man behind the counter to approach him.

"I'd like to sign up for a trainer. Is Chase available?"

***

Chase yawned wildly as he worked through the dull stock check. The large vats of protein powder all blended into one, and he lost count for the fourth time.

He couldn't remember the last night he had slept right through. It was no coincidence that his sketchy sleeping pattern started when he lost his childcare for summer. The days were ticking down to Dylan finishing school, and he still hadn't found a replacement.

He counted the whey protein tubs again and scribbled down the number, sure it was wrong. Flipping over the sheet, he looked at the items Danny had told him to grab for behind the counter display.

His stomach deflated when he checked his watch. He had been at the gym since opening at six in the morning, and he was already more than ready to go home and crawl into bed. The idea of a mid-afternoon nap before picking Dylan up from school excited him more than the thought of lunch.

He rummaged through a box, wondering if Danny would mind him clocking off early. He counted out twelve chocolate protein bars and dropped them into the box, along with the other stock he was taking.

People had told him that setting up his own business would be the best thing he would ever do, and they weren't wrong, but most of those people also failed to tell him how much hard work it would be.

Chase wasn't work shy. He had kickboxed as a teenager, so he was more than used to early starts and sacrificing his time for a cause. His first professional job had been working as a cleaner in a gym, and he had naturally drifted his way up through the ranks. When his brother had come to him with the idea of starting up their own gym in a small unit in Hebden Bridge, he had jumped at the chance. He was already the manager at a gym in the city, so he hadn't expected it to be much of a jump in duties.

He couldn't have been wrong. His workdays were longer, his schedule was fuller, and he had less time to spend with Dylan. Everything he did, he did for his son, which was a strange thought, because the harder he tried to provide for him, the less time he seemed to have.

"Chase, are you nearly done in there?" Danny called through, breaking Chase's daydream. "There's some sap wanting to sign up with you for a training session. I told him you were fully booked up until Christmas, but he isn't taking no for an answer. Will you come and deal with him?"

Chase scooped up the box and heaved it through the door, re-emerging from the darkness into the brightly lit gym. The sound of feet hammering the treadmills and weights hitting the floor told him he wasn't likely to be clocking off anytime soon.

He dropped the box on the counter and slid it to the side, ready to tell the man requesting him that he had already filled all of his training slots, and then some. He was already staying later and later on Fridays to fit in all of the extra work he had taken on.

The man smiled at him, in a way that no other man in his gym had smiled at him before. He squinted at the face under the harsh lighting. It took him a moment to recognise him without the bruises.

"Ricky?" Chase grinned. "You came."

"*Ta-da*, sweetheart." Ricky shook his hands, as though he had just been unveiled as a low-level prize on an eighties game show. "Your brother tells me you can't fit me in."

Chase looked at his brother, who was hiding out of Ricky's view around the side of the drinks machine. He smirked smugly and waited for Chase to back him up.

"Danny, why don't you go and finish up this stock check? I didn't finish counting the boxes of water."

"What? That's your –"

"Danny," he cut him off with a stern look only a brother would understand. "Please."

Danny surrendered and disappeared to the stock room, not without giving Ricky one last look up and down. Chase stared at Ricky's face, amazed at how different he looked from the man he had been remembering. He hadn't even realised every time he was subconsciously thinking about Ricky, he was seeing him with a packed up broken nose and two black eyes. He looked like an older version of the fresh, sullen face he had seen on his driver's licence, just much more handsome.

"I was beginning to think you weren't going to turn up," he said, noticing the nerves in his own voice.

"I like to be fashionably late, sweetheart." He shrugged, stuffing his hands in his pockets. "To tell you the truth, I had no intention of coming, but I had the stitches taken out today, and I feel like a new man."

"You look like one." His words sounded much more complimentary than he had intended. "Have you –"

"Remembered anything? Nothing concrete. Little flashes here and there, but nothing enough for the police. They're hounding me to say something just so they can close the case. I'm thinking about dropping it entirely, to tell you the truth."

"You shouldn't. Whoever did this to you should be brought to justice."

Ricky smiled uncomfortably. They didn't know the first thing about each other, but Chase could feel a bond from what they had been through. It was impossible for Chase not to feel drawn to Ricky. He felt protective over him; even though he knew it wasn't his place to. It was a completely different protective feeling than the one he had for Dylan, but no less intense.

"I hear you're fully booked?" said Ricky, sucking the air through his teeth. "I can go somewhere else, if you want. I don't want to cause trouble."

"No trouble." Chase opened up the schedule on the laptop under the counter, trying to hide his horror at how full every slot was. "I'm sure I can squeeze you in somewhere."

"Little old me won't take up much room."

Chase couldn't help but laugh. He even felt his cheeks blush, which was a strange experience. He usually fucked guys; he didn't exchange enough words with them that they could make him laugh. He thought back to Bailey, and how he had just left Chase with Ricky in the street. If he had gone home and fucked Bailey, he wouldn't have cared about the lad's morals, but seeing them exposed so coldly had left him troubled. He hadn't been back to Canal Street since.

"We close on Mondays at six, but I can stay on and do you then," he stumbled over his words, his cheeks burning brighter. "I meant – I can *train* you then."

"You sure you don't mind staying on?" he asked cautiously. "I honestly don't want to inconvenience you. Like I said, I wasn't even going to turn up."

Chase thought about Dylan and his stomach writhed with guilt. His dad looked after Dylan every Monday until Chase picked him up at six. He almost backtracked and changed it to another day, but he remembered how happy Dylan was every Monday night after having dinner at Granddad's. His dad wouldn't say no to an extra hour.

"If you can do Monday at six, I can do Monday at six," Chase said certainly. "A session usually lasts an hour, if that's okay with you?"

"An hour for one session?" Ricky smirked, winking again. "Impressive. I'll see you Monday then, sweetheart."

"Yes," he said, nodding a little harder than he'd intended. "Monday it is."

Chase added Ricky onto the end of the day. The system flashed red, telling him it was an invalid action. He overrode it and added him onto the end of the schedule.

Ricky turned and headed for the door. Chase almost expected Ricky to look back as he left, but he didn't. He watched Ricky walk down the street, and he didn't allow himself to breathe until he was out of view.

"*I can do you then,*" he whispered sarcastically under his breath. "Smooth, Chase. *Smooth.*"

Danny resurfaced and slapped the clipboard on the desk. He checked in Jack, one of their regulars and then turned to his brother and waited for him to speak.

"He's just a friend of a friend," said Chase. "He's cool. I've fit him in out of hours."

"What friend?"

"You don't know him."

"I know *all* of your friends, mainly because you don't have any."

"Just somebody from school," he snapped defensively. "It's fine. It's sorted."

Danny grumbled under his breath before starting to input the figures from the stock check into the system. He raised an eyebrow when he saw the out of hours booking.

"He seems a little gay to me," Danny mumbled under

his breath. "Just saying."

"Well don't."

"Why so protective? He's just a mate of a mate."

Chase didn't bother responding. He jumped onto a treadmill, and as his feet hit the rubber, he realised how much he was looking forward to Monday.

CHAPTER

SEVEN

Ricky took Tom's advice and avoided the bar. He was still marked down as '*sick*', so they hadn't been expecting him, but he had planned to surprise everybody by turning up in his most fabulous drag. He knew word of his attack would have spread quicker than an Australian summer fire, and he wanted to show everybody he was alive and well and he wasn't going to let those bastards get him down.

When it came time to get ready on Friday night, he didn't get past gluing down his brows. He had sat at his dressing table, staring at his reflection for nearly an hour, unable to bring himself to go any further. It was a feeling he had never experienced before, and it scared him more than the threat of being attacked again. Drag had always been his escape. Whenever life got him down, drag lifted him back up, but it had been tainted.

His weekend was spent ignoring his phone and only answering the door for the take-out delivery driver. When Monday came, he was almost glad of his gym session, because a weekend of binge eating and binge watching television had developed a small gut on his otherwise normally flat stomach.

Glancing at the clock, his gut flipped when he saw that it was half-past five. He still hadn't decided if he was going to show up early or late. He appreciated Chase fitting him in, but he didn't want to seem too eager. He wasn't sure if that was for his benefit or for Chase's. He couldn't ignore the rumbling fire of excitement that had been growing in his stomach all week.

He wandered through to his bedroom to get changed. The stunning pink and black silk gown he had picked out for Friday night was still slumped over the edge of his bed. He had hoped it would inspire him to want to be Miss Kitty Litter again, but it only seemed to have the opposite effect.

He tossed the dress into the wardrobe and slid the door shut. Ignoring his wardrobes filled with drag, he crossed his bedroom to the relatively smaller collection of male clothes he owned. It was true of all drag queens that they spent so much time and money on their drag, their male counterpart's fashion suffered as a result.

Playing it safe was something Miss Kitty Litter would never dream of doing, but Ricky rarely ventured out of black, white and grey form hugging t-shirts and black or blue skinny jeans. It was safe, simple and it meant he didn't have to spend his time trying to keep up with the ever-changing trends.

He opened his bottom drawer and dug right into the back for his old gym shorts. It had been nearly a year since he had stepped foot in a gym. In the months after Bret's death, going to the gym had been a way for him to cope and distract himself. Bret would have laughed at Ricky going to the gym, but he actually grew to enjoy it. Since moving into his new cottage, he had neglected working out, and his gym clothes had found their way further and further to the back of his drawers. Ricky thanked his high metabolism daily, because even though his muscles weren't as firm and pronounced as they had been, his body fat was still low enough for him to slide effortlessly into his tightest dresses.

Ricky stripped out of his clothes and examined his reflection in the mirror. His ribs were still slightly bruised, but he was looking more like himself than he had in weeks. On his last visit to the hospital, they had told him to avoid exercise for at least another month, but he had never been one to follow the rules.

He pulled on electric blue compression shorts, which left little to the imagination in the cock department. He used to go to a gay-friendly gym, so he hadn't minded everybody being able to see the definite outline of his manhood, but he didn't want to scare Chase away. He hadn't spotted a wedding ring, but he was sure a man that masculine and gorgeous would have an equally gorgeous tattoo-covered girlfriend waiting for him at home.

He pulled on a pair of baggier black shorts over the tight blue ones, satisfied that it was more appropriate. After pairing them with a white tank top, he admired his reflection. He looked like a real man. He knew he was a real man, but he was so used to seeing Miss Kitty Litter looking back at him in the mirror, he was almost surprised. Weeks of no drag had allowed his skin a break from the constant shaving and he had developed a dark shadow of stubble. He had never been able to imagine himself with more than a light dusting of facial hair, so he liked the change.

When quarter to six rolled around, he filled up a water bottle and decided he was going to turn up early for once. Chase was staying late for him, so the least he could do was to show his willingness.

Clutching his water bottle in one hand and his phone, wallet and keys in the other, he headed for the door. Before he reached it, heavy knuckles pounded on the other side of the wood.

Ricky took a step back. For a moment, he forgot who he was and where he was, and the thought of a stranger on the other side of the door made him want to run and hide where nobody could find him. It was a feeling he had felt before, but not since Bret's death.

"Mr. Thompson? It's Chief Inspector Patrick Brody," the familiar voice boomed through the wood. "I can see your shadow through the frosted glass, Mr. Thompson."

Resigning himself to the fact the police officer wasn't going away, he reluctantly unlocked the door and plastered on his friendliest and widest smile.

"How can I help you, Chief Inspector? I was just about to go out."

Patrick looked Ricky up and down, almost confused by his appearance. Had he been expecting Ricky to be draped in a blanket with a tub of Ben and Jerry's in one hand and a bottle of wine in the other? If that's what he had wanted to see, he should have come around on Saturday night instead.

"It won't take long," he said. "We've had a breakthrough with your case."

"A breakthrough?" he said, the shock loud and clear in his voice. "What kind of breakthrough?"

"If I can come in, I'll be able to show you better," Patrick looked around Ricky. "Unless this is a bad time."

Ricky looked back to the giant clock on his mantelpiece.

The dial was edging closer to ten to six.

"Make it quick." He stepped to one side and let the Inspector in. "Shouldn't they have sent somebody else for this?"

"I was passing by and I wanted to ask you some questions myself."

Patrick strode into Ricky's cottage and sat on the yellow leather couch uninvited. His eyes wandered around the room, pausing on the obnoxiously large black and white canvas of two hugging naked men hanging proudly over the fireplace. His jaw tightened, and he looked down at his shoes and pulled a phone from his inside pocket.

"What kind of developments?" asked Ricky, hovering behind the sofa.

"We found some CCTV footage that we want you to review. We think it might be helpful in finding the perpetrators of this crime."

"I thought that alley didn't have CCTV cameras?"

"It didn't," he said carefully, nodding as he scrolled through files on his phone. "And the surrounding bars didn't pick anything up, but a café down the road came forward and handed over this footage after we did a door to door appeal for information. They were closed at the time, so they never thought to immediately check."

Ricky's stomach churned when Chief Inspector Brody selected a file. His finger hovered over the play button, but he didn't immediately press it.

"Before I play this, I just want you to keep an open mind. You're claiming not to remember anything, and this might be distressing for you if you do recognise something. On the other hand, I don't want you to try too hard, just in case this isn't connected. Do you understand?"

Ricky looked up at the clock as its hands ticked closer to six. He nodded and attempted to gulp the lump in his throat, but it felt like swallowing sand.

Chief Inspector Brody pressed play and the silent CCTV footage started. It was black and white, grainy and dark, and at first, Ricky wasn't sure what he was supposed to be looking for. All of a sudden, a man ran across the screen, and then he was gone in a flash.

"Play that again," said Ricky, leaning in closer.

Patrick slid his finger back along the footage and the video played again, but it was so fast, Ricky couldn't make heads or tails of it.

"Can you slow it down?"

"Erm," Patrick mumbled. "Let me try."

He pulled up a menu and tapped a couple of buttons, and the footage slowed down. He replayed the man running down the street, and Ricky saw a flash of something familiar. He snatched the phone out of the Inspector's hand and pulled it up to his face. With shaking fingers, he slid the footage back and his heart sunk when he realised what he was holding and why he recognised it.

"That's him," his voice shook out of control. "That's definitely him."

"How can you be sure?"

Ricky tossed the phone down onto the couch and took a step back.

"Because they're brandishing *my* fucking wig like a prize," he said. "I'm going to be late for the gym, Chief Inspector Brody. If you don't mind –"

Ricky held open the door, his shaking fingers clinging onto the wood for support. He heard Patrick tell him that he would need to go to the station to make another formal statement, but the words floated over Ricky's head.

Something broke through the haze, like a ray of sunlight through storm clouds. He remembered punching somebody. He remembered the wig in his hands. He had spent weeks wondering if the attack had been a random mugging for his phone and money. If it had, he would have been able to deal with that.

It was more than clear to him it wasn't the case. He had been attacked for who he was and in a place he had always felt safe. The only thing stopping him from crawling back under his covers was the promise of seeing Chase again.

***

Chase had never been happier to announce the gym was closing. He watched Paul finish his last set of weights, tapping his foot every time the bulky man lifted the bar over his head. When he dropped the bar to the ground, Chase allowed himself a small smile.

"See you tomorrow, Paul," he said as the sweaty bodybuilder walked past him to the door.

"Fancy a quick one at the pub?" asked Danny as he changed out of his shorts and into his jeans behind the counter. "I'm gasping for a pint."

"Not tonight," he said, almost glad of the excuse. "I've got that extra training session tonight, haven't I?"

"Oh yeah," he mumbled, a pinch forming between his brows. "With *that* guy."

Chase knew exactly what Danny was getting at. He didn't need to say it for Chase to know his brother thought Ricky had no place in their gym. Chase wasn't sure if it was because Ricky was obviously gay, or because he wasn't their usual type of client. Either way, he wasn't going to push it.

"You get off, I'll finish wiping down here," he said as he glanced at the clock, noticing that it was almost six.

"You sure?" Danny arched a brow. "You hate wiping down the machines."

"I'm feeling extra generous tonight, bro," he said, with

an involuntary nervous laugh. "Go home and see your wife."

Danny tightened his eyes for a flash, but he didn't question Chase. He shrugged, grabbed his bag and headed for the door without another word. When Chase was finally alone, he leaned against the counter as the nerves bubbled away.

Chase still hadn't figured out why he was nervous, but he had felt the same feeling every time he looked at the invalid booking on the schedule. Folding his arms across his chest, he watched as the small clock above the changing room door ticked right past six.

All week, he had wondered if Ricky was going to show up. He didn't strike Chase as the time-wasting kind, but he also didn't strike Chase as the kind to agree to a personal training session. The man wasn't out of shape, but Danny's unspoken reservations were right; Ricky didn't fit in.

But Chase liked that. Ricky's oddness drew him in. It wasn't until Ricky had left the gym after turning up out of the blue that Chase had realised how much he liked being in the man's company. He couldn't explain why, but he made him feel at ease. He was almost jealous of how Ricky seemed to walk through life letting nothing faze him. If he festered the same insecurities and worries as the rest of the world, he hid them well.

When the clock struck five past the hour, he started to pace the gym. Ricky lived somewhere in the village, so even if he were running late, it wouldn't take more than five minutes to walk to the gym.

Promising that he would leave at quarter past, he was more than a little relieved when Ricky burst through the door at twelve minutes past, with sweat dripping down his red face and a half filled water bottle clutched in his hand.

"Sorry I'm late, sweetheart," he said through the

panting. "I just went for a little jog around the block to warm up."

Ricky doubled over and clutched his knees as he filled his lungs with air. Chase rubbed his back, unsure of why Ricky would go for a jog before their session.

"You ready to get started?" he asked, stepping back and slapping his hands together. "Lots to get through."

"Would it be rude to have a cheeky ciggie before?"

If anyone else had asked to smoke before a training session, Chase would have laughed them out of his gym, but coming from Ricky, it sounded like the best thing he had heard all day. A little nicotine in his system would rid him of the nerves that were still bubbling away. He had hoped they would vanish when he saw Ricky again, but they only seemed to grow.

Ricky offered Chase one of his Marlboro Lights when they were standing on the street outside of the gym. Cars and busses hurried up and down the small high street as the shops closed and people commuted home. He had found Hebden Bridge a fascinating place ever since Danny had suggested they make it the location for their first gym. It was unlike any other Yorkshire village he had ever seen. It had a strange, quirky, cosmopolitan vibe that almost felt like a slice of a big city, crammed into a small, rural dwelling.

Chase wasn't sure he would fit living in such a place, but Ricky fit Hebden Bridge perfectly.

"I hope you don't mind staying back for me," said Ricky again. "I almost feel bad that I'm making you work later. I know you said you'd give me a free session, but I insist on paying."

"You really don't have to," he said, not knowing how to tell Ricky he wasn't doing it for the money.

Ricky wasn't going to take no for an answer. He pulled

thirty pounds out of his pocket and stuffed them into Chase's shorts, tapping the side of his nose.

"It's only twenty for an hour's training."

"Call it a tip," he said. "For, y'know, saving my life, and all that."

Chase laughed. He dragged hard on the cigarette, finishing it right down to the filter.

"I'm no hero," he said. "I just did what everyone else would have done."

"Well," said Ricky as he blew the last of his smoke from his lungs, "we shall agree to disagree, sweetheart. Now that my nicotine levels are back to an acceptable level, shall we start?"

They went back into the gym, and Chase locked the door behind them. The last thing he wanted was for somebody to wander in, thinking they were open. He watched Ricky clumsily limber up in the mirror as he printed off the training sheet he had devised especially for Ricky.

"We're going to start with some circuit training, so I can assess your fitness levels and what we need to work on," he said, scanning over the sheets. "And then I thought I'd show you some self-defence techniques."

Ricky snatched the piece of paper out of Chase's hands and skim read it at arm's length through squinted eyes.

"Burpees? Jumping jacks? Squats?" he scoffed. "This is child's play. I was hoping you were going to show me how to kill a man with one finger."

"All in good time, my friend," he pulled back the paper and slapped Ricky on the shoulders. "Let's just see how we get on with this, shall we?"

Ricky rolled his eyes as he pulled loosely on his hamstrings. Chase was almost amused by how little Ricky seemed scared of the circuit Chase had designed. He had seen men built like brick houses throw up during his training sessions.

"Alright, let's start with some warm-ups," said Chase as they walked over to the open mat area where Beth held her yoga sessions. "Nothing too strenuous or stiff. Let's keep it fluid and moving. One hundred jumping jacks, on the spot. *Go!*"

Ricky started jumping, his fingers barely touching and his legs hardly spreading. Chase usually did his training sessions alongside his clients. It was a good excuse to keep in shape, and he found that it spurred them on to push even harder. He started doing his jumping jacks correctly, and Ricky adjusted his technique as he observed Chase in the mirror.

When they passed fifty, Chase noticed the sweat breaking out on Ricky's forehead. He contained his laughter, not wanting to put his new student off.

"Almost there!" he cried. "Just a couple more."

"I'm fine, sweetheart," Ricky said firmly through the panting. "Child's play, remember?"

Chase laughed and looked down at the mat as they headed into the last ten. As he looked back up, he caught the sight of Ricky's manhood bouncing up and down in his shorts. He seemed to be wearing compression shorts under his actual shorts, but that didn't make it any less impressive. He adjusted his gaze quickly.

"How are you feeling?" he asked as they both took a water break.

"Peachy." Ricky nodded. "I just need *five* minutes."

"Nope. Thirty squats. Go!"

Ricky laughed awkwardly, as though not believing Chase, but Chase dropped into a squat, letting him know he was more than serious. Ricky's technique was a little sloppy, but it was nothing he couldn't refine in time.

After their squats, Chase allowed another quick water break, but it was straight into the burpees, which he knew would finish Ricky off. After the last set, he collapsed on the floor with his eyes closed and his hands clutching his ribs.

"Still child's play?" he said as he offered Ricky a hand up.

"Easy peasy." Ricky accepted his hand and Chase pulled him up with ease. "How far are we through this?"

"About a quarter?"

"A *quarter*?" he cried. "Are you sure?"

"We can stop if you want?"

"No, *no*," he said, shaking his head and waving his arms. "What next, Rambo?"

They worked through the rest of the circuit and to Chase's surprise, Ricky matched him step for step. His complaining trailed off, and his breaks for water became shorter and shorter. As they started the circuit from the beginning for the second half, he noticed a switch in Ricky's attitude. He looked like he had something to prove.

"Five more bicycle sit-ups and we're done," he said. "You can do this."

"I can do this," Ricky panted through the pain, sounding like he was trying to convince himself. "One, two – *Jesus take the wheel* – four and five -"

They both collapsed on the mats and stared up at the ceiling, panting for breath. Chase was feeling the workout, and he was a trainer, so he could only imagine how Ricky was feeling.

"The police turned up as I was setting off," said Ricky when he had caught his breath. "I was going to be early."

"I hadn't noticed you were late," he lied. "I thought you went for a jog?"

"I did. I started running, and I wasn't sure why. It wasn't until I had passed my cottage again that I realised I was supposed to be coming here. Something took over me."

"What happened?" Chase rolled onto his side and leaned his head against his hand. "Bad news, I take it?"

"I don't know if it was bad or good." Ricky copied Chase up onto his own side. "They found some video footage of this guy running through the streets. I didn't think anything of it, but he had something of mine in his hand."

"Did it trigger your memory?"

"Not really," he sighed, screwing up his face and clenching his eyes. "I can see parts if I really think about it, but the second I pin it down, it slides away before I even have a chance to say it out loud. It's infuriating."

Chase watched as Ricky wandered through his memories, his eyes twitching aggressively behind his lids. It was then he realised Ricky was more affected by what had happened than he was letting the world see.

"We've done enough for the day," said Chase as he got up to his feet. "We'll carry on next Monday."

"No, I want to finish this. I want to know how to defend myself."

"Ricky, you don't have to push yourself for my benefit."

"I'm not!" he snapped, a bite in his voice. "I'm doing this for me. Whoever those arseholes were, they attacked me because I was gay. It wasn't random. Do you know what that means?"

"No."

"It means it can happen again. Tomorrow, next week, next month, next year," Ricky said with steely determination in his eyes. "And when it does, I want to be ready. There is no shortage of arseholes out there at the moment, and I need to know how to defend myself."

"Okay. I believe you. Let's do this."

Chase screwed up the training sheet and tossed it to the

side. He ran over to the counter and hooked the laptop up to the speaker system. He selected his favourite workout playlist and cranked up the volume. He flipped a panel on the wall and turned off all of the lights, except for the ones over the mats.

"Are you turning this place into a fight club, sweetheart?" Ricky cried over the drum and bass music.

"It helps get the adrenaline going," he said with a smirk. "Are you ready?"

"Ready for what? Are we about to wrestle?"

"Wrestle?" chuckled Chase. "How about we start simpler than that? I'll throw some punches and you have to the defend yourself."

"Alright," said Ricky, a little apprehensive, but he raised his fists to his face anyway. "Just stay away from the face, yeah, sweetheart? One broken nose is *enough* for me, thank you."

"Don't worry, I'll go gentle on you."

They circled each other like stray alley cats as the music throbbed through their veins. Chase lifted his fists, but he didn't strike straight away. The anticipation of a blow was scarier than knuckles hitting the skin. He wanted all of Ricky's senses sharp as a knife before he struck, even if he knew a real opponent wouldn't be so kind to allow him the courtesy.

Chase's first punch was a gentle one. Ricky blocked it easily with his forearm, jumping back as an extra precaution. He seemed pleased with himself, if not a little wary. Chase struck again almost immediately, but this time, Ricky's instincts weren't as sharp and he missed entirely. Chase stopped before his knuckles struck skin.

"It's alright," Chase cried over the music when he noticed the irritation in Ricky's eyes. "We're just warming up. You try to hit me, and I'll show you some stuff."

Ricky arched a brow, but he shrugged and sent a punch in Chase's direction. He grabbed Ricky's fist with one hand, bent his wrist and twisted his arm into a gooseneck hold. Ricky yelped and pulled his arm away from Chase.

"Bloody hell, sweetheart!" he cried, rubbing his wrist. "That hurt!"

"It was meant to. You try it."

Ricky pursed his lips. He stopped rubbing his wrists, shook out his hands and clenched his fists once more. Chase attacked and Ricky performed the move, pulling Chase into a sloppy, but adequate gooseneck hold.

"From here, you can do many things," said Chase, not moving out of the hold. "Kick me in the back of the leg to ground me, keep twisting to snap my wrist, or just hope you've done it fast enough to scare them away."

Ricky's toes collided with the back of Chase's knees, and he crumbled to the ground, staggered by the abrupt movement. Ricky distorted his arm even further, and it sent a sharp pain running down to his shoulder. He looked up into Ricky's face to see him smirking down at him.

"Like that, sweetheart?"

"Something like that." He nodded through the pain, not wanting to show Ricky how much he was really hurting him. "Pretty good. I'm surprised they got so many punches in with you. You know what you're doing."

Ricky suddenly let go of Chase, and he stumbled backwards. Chase thought he had offended Ricky, but his eyes were glazed over, as though he was seeing something before him that wasn't really in the room.

"I think I just remembered something," he mumbled, his hand dancing up to the back of his head. "These stitches on the back of my head. I think I remember how I got them."

Chase got up off the floor, rounded the corner and hit

the space bar on his laptop to stop the music. When he returned, Ricky was perched on the edge of a stack of aerobic steps with his head in his hands.

"What do you remember, Ricky?" Chase sat alongside him on the step, their bodies touching. He resisted the urge to put his arm around Ricky. "Tell me."

Ricky continued to cover his eyes with his palms for what felt like a lifetime. When he finally looked up, his eyes were filled with tears.

"It was my fault," he said, clearly holding back the cries. "I threw the first punch. They took something off me, so I punched them and ran. They threw something at my head - a brick or a rock - I think. I didn't stand a chance, but I started it."

Chase gave into the urge and wrapped his arm tightly around Ricky's shoulder, his skin clammy to the touch. He pulled him in and Ricky let his weight push up against the inside of Chase's chest.

"If they took something from you, it was still self-defence," said Chase. "And even if you did punch first, they were the ones who hit you with a brick and left you for dead. You did nothing wrong."

Ricky looked up with a small, gloomy smile prickling his lips. A tear trickled down his cheek and into his thick, dark stubble. Why did seeing him cry upset Chase so much?

"Didn't I?" he said in a small voice.

Chase leaned in and wiped away the tear. He hooked his finger under Ricky's chin and tilted his face so that they were looking eye to eye. Ricky's eyes darted down to his lips and Chase mirrored the move. He could feel his heart pounding in his throat.

"You did nothing wrong," he repeated again. "Nothing."

Ricky nodded as another tear escaped the inside of his eyes. He closed them, and more tears tumbled down his face, but he didn't open them. He leaned in and his trembling lips touched Chase's.

It was so tender and quick, but it felt like it lasted a lifetime. Chase's stomach knotted as Ricky pulled away from the kiss. It was over too quickly. Before Ricky could speak again, Chase hooked his hand behind Ricky's ear, and he pulled him in.

This time, Chase opened his mouth to Ricky. Their tongues brushed up against each other nervously. Chase had no idea what was happening, he just knew he wanted it. He had wanted it since first meeting Ricky, but it had taken Ricky making the move for him to realise it.

Chase wasn't sure where the kiss was going, he just knew he didn't want it to stop. When he heard the gym door open and the sound of the street drifted in, they both immediately pulled away from each other.

"I forget my bloody house keys," called Danny from around the corner. "I got all the way home and – *oh*, you're not alone."

Danny's narrowed eyes darted between the two of them. Had he noticed how close they were sitting? Could he see the bulge in Chase's shorts? Chase wanted to move, but he was frozen to the step.

"I was just going," said Ricky with an awkward cough as he stood up, evading Chase's gaze. "Thanks for the session."

"Sure," he mumbled. "See you next week?"

Ricky glanced over his shoulder, but he didn't say anything. He smiled stiffly and walked past Danny, avoiding his eye contact too. The gym door slammed, and it sent a shockwave through the building and through Chase's body.

"He's a bit weird, isn't he?" Danny's expression relaxed as he folded his arms across his thick chest.

Chase waited for his brother to turn around before he

stood up. He tucked his penis into the elastic of his shorts, and he checked out his reflection in the mirror. His lips were still red and damp from the kiss. He ran his tongue along his bottom lip, Ricky's cigarette and sweat was still fresh to taste.

Chase didn't know what had just happened, but he knew it was going to complicate things. He couldn't ignore the intense burning he felt deep in his core. If his brother hadn't turned up, he wasn't sure how far they would have gone.

CHAPTER

EIGHT

"**H**e said he's told you everything he knows." Tom's words fired across the table at Chief Inspector Patrick Brody. "You're treating Ricky like he's the one who has done something wrong!"

Ricky was surprised it had taken Tom so long to snap. He had been drumming his foot throughout Ricky's statement, which had somehow descended into an interrogation.

"I just want to make sure we cover all angles," said Patrick calmly, holding his hands up as he leaned back in his chair. "I just want to go over this one last time, Ricky, okay?"

Ricky nodded, wishing he didn't have to. It was as though Patrick was expecting Ricky to go out and arrest the men for him. If only Ricky understood how his own memories worked.

"You were hit with a brick, and then beat up? The next thing you remember is waking up in the hospital the next morning?"

"That's right," he said sternly. "That's everything I know."

He gulped hard, knowing that he had purposefully forgotten to mention the part about him throwing the first punch. He repeated over and over in his mind what Chase had said about it being self-defence.

"What about the man?" Tom mumbled under his breath. "The trainer guy?"

"What man?" Patrick snatched up his pen and leaned across the table. "There's been no mention of anybody else in your statement."

Ricky shot hot daggers across the table at his best friend. Ricky hadn't mentioned Chase because he hadn't wanted the trouble being dragged to his doorstep. He had done nothing but try to help him.

"It's not important," he said dismissively, shrugging it off. "It was just some guy. He was the one who called the ambulance. He was there when I woke up. He doesn't know anything."

"I'd like to be the judge of that." Patrick pulled a small pad out of his top pocket and flicked through several pages to a blank sheet. "Do you have a name? A number? An address?"

"It has nothing to do with him."

"He's called Chase," said Tom, instantly apologising to Ricky with his eyes. "Don't look at me like that! The Inspector is right. He might know something and not realise it."

"Chase?" Patrick wrinkled his forehead. "That's an

unusual name. Do you have an address?"

"He works at the gym on the high street in Hebden Bridge," said Tom. "Covered in tattoos. You can't miss him."

"Jesus, sweetheart. Do you want to wipe my arse for me too?" cried Ricky. "I knew I shouldn't have told you about any of this. You *can't* keep your nose out, can you?"

"Bit rich, coming from you," Tom mumbled under his breath.

Ricky looked away from his friend and to the officer. Patrick's eyes had glazed over a little, and he was gritting his teeth so hard, his jaw was protruding through the haze of silver stubble.

"Problem?" asked Ricky.

"No," he answered immediately, snapping the pad shut. "Thanks for coming down. I'll be in touch."

Patrick showed them out of the station, and the moment they were outside, Ricky produced a fresh packet of cigarettes from his leather jacket pocket, unpeeled the plastic seal and pressed one of the rolled up sticks between his lips.

"Is that really the best idea right now?"

"What are you? My mother?" Ricky lit the cigarette and blew the smoke into Tom's face. "You don't have to bother about dropping me off. I'm going to walk into town and stop by the shop. I haven't been in for weeks, and I want to make sure Brendon hasn't burned the place to the ground."

"You wouldn't be going to the bar, would you?" Tom arched a brow and folded his arms suspiciously.

"If I was, sweetheart," he paused and blew another cloud of smoke into Tom's face. "It has *nothing* to do with you. Ta-ta!"

Ricky left Tom standing outside of the station and headed in the direction of the city centre. He knew he had been harsh with Tom, but he was tired of having to constantly explain every decision since the attack. When he was standing at the top of Canal Street and looking down at the bars, he finally felt like he had come home.

"Afternoon, Ricky." Suzie, one of the promoters for one of the clubs, tipped her ringleader's hat to him. "Haven't seen you around here in a while."

"Taken some time off, sweetheart, but I'm back now."

He lit up another cigarette and walked past the open bars, avoiding the eye contact of the day drinkers. It seemed news of his attack hadn't spread all over the village after all, which would explain the lack of sympathy cards and flowers on his doorstep. He had started to think they didn't care about Miss Kitty Litter after all.

He reached G-A-Y on the corner and paused before turning towards London Bridge. He looked down the dark alley behind The New Union. He stared at the cobbled road, hoping he would suddenly be able to remember the face of his attacker. He couldn't.

"Ricky." Jackson dropped his cloth and ran across the empty bar, wrapping his arms around his neck. "Jesus Christ, it's good to see you. I heard about the attack. I was going to come and visit, but I haven't had a moment to myself."

"Don't worry about it, sweetheart. I'm back now."

Ricky looked around the bar and smiled. It felt good to be back. It may have been empty, but just being in his fortress, he felt more at ease than he had for weeks. He walked over to the DJ booth and ran his finger along its edge. He looked up at the poster of his face behind the DJ booth, but the ease didn't last for long. He climbed up onto the small stage and walked behind the booth, ripping down the altered poster.

"*Toxic Tonya?*" Ricky pointed at the sticker that had

been plastered over his name. "You've had Toxic *fucking* Tonya in here?"

"We needed a DJ," Jackson said defensively. "What did you want me to do? I didn't know when you would be back!"

"Why her? If I were Superman, she would be Lex Luthor. She's been pissing on my patches for years. You know she stole my first drag job in VIA right from under me? She's a sneaky little witch troll from hell. She's so devious, the Blair Witch is jealous of her tricks!"

"Well I've paid that witch up until the end of the month, and she's been keeping the place ticking over, so you might want to thank her."

Ricky screwed up the poster and tossed it across the bar towards Jackson, who ducked out of its way. Ricky gripped the edge of the booth and stared down at the club. Tom might not have thought he was ready, but if he spent another two weeks at home eating his feelings, he was never going to fit into any of his drag ever again.

"Call Toxic Tonya and tell her Mother is back," he said confidently. "I'll see you on Friday, sweetheart."

"Are you sure that's a good idea, Ricky?" Jackson frowned disapprovingly. "After what you've been through?"

"I'm fine. I had a self-defence class."

"Just the one?" Jackson scoffed.

"One is all I need," said Ricky. "I don't need another."

It had been six days since the kiss, and he had been able to think of little else. For that reason, he had to stay as far away from the gym and Chase as he could. He had avoided walking down the high street in his own village all week. Just the thought of feeling what he had felt during the kiss made him anxious. It had been intense and raw, and it made him feel more alive than he had in years, and that was why it scared him half to death.

"I'll see you Friday," Ricky pulled a pair of sunglasses from his top pocket and opened the bar door. "I better go home and see if I can still remember how to beat this mug."

Ricky set off to the train station. At the mouth of the alley, he paused and almost walked through the street, but he decided he couldn't avoid it forever. As he walked quickly along the cobbles, staring into the dark corners from behind his shades, he realised that he probably wasn't fully ready to return, but he needed to get back to his land of fantasy before the real world threatened to claim him forever.

***

"Can you remember the last time we were summoned to Dad's house for Sunday lunch?" whispered Danny as they took their jackets off in the hallway.

"I think it was three years ago when Barbara wanted to show off her new conservatory," said Chase.

"Ugh, that dreadful thing," said Natalie through a wrinkled nose. "*Don't* remind me. It's the mark of a commoner."

Patrick's call late last night had come as a shock to Chase. His father never called him, especially not to invite him around for Sunday lunch. If he hadn't been put on the spot, he would have backed out. He almost cancelled first thing in the morning, but his brother texted asking if he wanted a lift, so he knew he couldn't be the son not to show up or he would never hear the last of it.

"Boys," Barbara chimed in her soft singsong voice when they walked into the kitchen. "So good to see you. We're eating in the conservatory. Your father is already in there, so why don't you go ahead and I'll bring through some drinks. Beer for you two, and Natalie?"

"A glass of chilled white zinfandel would be lovely, Barbara."

"The wine is red or white. White's in the fridge, red's under the sink. Help yourself." She smiled faultlessly through her bright red lipstick. "Oh, that is a lovely blouse you're wearing."

"Vivian Westwood," said Natalie airily. "Next season's collection but I have a man on the inside. I can try and pull some strings and get you one? What size are you again? Sixteen?"

Barbara looked down at her own floral blouse and patted her stomach, a chink appearing in her usually perfectly plastered on smile. Chase had always thought Natalie and Barbara were cut from two ends of the same cloth, which was probably why they despised each other.

"Boys, good to see you," Patrick jumped up from the wicker chair at the end of the conservatory and muted the TV. "Just in time. The game's about to start."

Danny clapped his hands together but football had never interested Chase. When his brother was getting up for early morning football matches as a kid, Chase was already training at the kickboxing club.

Patrick and Danny sat watching the football game while Chase and Natalie sat at opposite ends of the table ignoring each other, which he didn't mind. Ever since she had landed him with a childcare problem, he had even less desire to talk to her. Dylan stayed in the kitchen with Barbara, no doubt picking at the food before it was ready. She was tapping away on her phone with a playful smirk, no doubt texting her friends to tell them that she was sitting in a conservatory that looked like it had been pulled out of a 1989 catalogue. The house was dated and clearly reflected Barbara's set ways, but Chase would kill to be able to raise Dylan somewhere like it. He looked out into the never-ending garden, knowing how much Dylan would thrive if they lived somewhere like it. His tiny flat was nowhere to raise a cat, let alone a child.

"Lunch!" Barbara explained as she carried in a large roasted leg of beef on a platter. "It's not up to my usual standards, but I wasn't given much notice, *was I*, Patrick?"

She fired daggers at Patrick across the table, but he was oblivious to them because he couldn't seem to take his eyes away from the football.

All of Barbara's food filled the table. It was clear she had been at the supermarket the second it opened and cleared them out of ingredients because she hadn't missed a trick. Crispy roast potatoes surrounded the perfectly cooked beef, along with honey roasted parsnips, tender Yorkshire puddings, sliced baby carrots, creamy mash, pigs in blankets and an overflowing gravy boat, which looked homemade and thick. Natalie pursed her lips as she glanced over the food suspiciously. Chase, on the other hand, was ready to eat.

"This looks amazing, Barbara," he said.

"Oh, thank you, Chase."

"Yeah, Nana, it looks well good," said Dylan as he scrambled up to his chair. "Can I have two pigs in blankets?"

"You can have whatever you want!" she beamed.

"You should watch his saturated fat intake," quipped Natalie. "It's not good for children to eat refined fats. It messes with their hormones and it makes them gain weight."

"Gain weight?" Patrick sighed. "There's nothing on the lad! Look at him! He's skin and bones. Pile his plate up, Barb, it doesn't look like that son of mine is feeding him."

Patrick laughed, but Chase took his dig personally. When he left, Chase's mum had tried to make up for it by overfeeding him, which was why he discovered his love for fitness in the first place. Chase had always been careful not to substitute his love for food because he never wanted Dylan to know what it was like to be that overweight kid.

"Just one slice of beef for me," said Natalie as she held out her plate. "I'm trying to stay away from red meat."

"It's brown," Barbara said through gritted teeth. "I'm not into that raw stuff, Natalie."

"No, I *mean* –" Natalie's complaint was cut off by Danny and Patrick's cheering when their team scored. Dylan joined in, but he didn't seem to know what he was cheering for.

When their plates were cleared and half time was called, Patrick turned his attention to the table for the first time since his guests' arrival. Chase hadn't wanted to be cynical, but he knew there must have been a reason behind his father's invitation. Just from the way his eyes kept scurrying over to him, Chase knew it was something to do with him. Danny and Natalie had been invited as a cover.

When they were all scooping up Barbara's overly sweet, lumpy, homemade trifle, Patrick finally got to the point of their visit.

"So, Chase," he said carefully as he licked the back of his spoon. "Your name was brought up in one of my cases."

"At the station?" asked Danny. "What've you been up to, little bro?"

"Nothing that I know of."

He was genuinely confused. He looked around the table at the suspicious eyes, wondering if they were all in on something he didn't know about.

"Does the name *Ricky Thompson* ring a bell with you?" he asked, his tone calm and casual. "Because he seems to know you."

"Ricky?" mumbled Danny through a mouthful of trifle.

"Isn't that the name of the new guy you're training? The weird one?"

Chase's heart sunk. He looked around the conservatory for the nearest door. If his sudden exit wasn't likely to create even more questions, he would have grabbed Dylan and headed straight for it. Instead, he decided to play it cool, and he put a spoonful of trifle in his mouth. He chewed it awkwardly and slowly as everybody stared expectantly.

"He's just some guy I helped out. I found him all beat up, so I called him an ambulance."

"And stayed with him all night," said Patrick. "Or so *he* says. I don't trust him, if I'm honest with you."

Chase squinted at his father, hoping he wasn't going down the road he thought he was about to. He bit his tongue and thought of the best way to keep things calm and rational, without giving away too much.

"I wanted to make sure he was okay. He was seriously hurt, and they couldn't contact anyone for him. I fell asleep at the hospital, and when I woke up, it was morning and he was up."

"And now he's at your gym?" Patrick's jaw clenched, and his eyes darkened.

"I offered him some self-defence classes."

"You know he's *queer*, don't you?" Patrick said sternly.

"Patrick!" Barbara cried. "Not at the dinner table. There are children present."

"What? You can't say that anymore? I've given up knowing what I can and can't say. It's political correctness gone mad! I can call him queer because *that's* what he is."

The slur went through Chase like a knife through butter, and not for himself, but for Ricky. It hadn't even crossed his mind that his father might be the one working his case at the station. Now he wasn't surprised as to why Ricky was keen on pulling his statement.

"I think the *correct* term is *gay*," said Natalie.

"Same difference," he spread out at the head of the table, as though he was holding court. "Gay, Queer, Faggot – all means the same *bloody* thing, doesn't it? None of it is normal."

"*Patrick!*"

"Oh, come on Barb," he snapped. "It's a bloody agenda. They're trying to *force* it on us decent folk, trying to make us think it's what the future is. Well, it bloody isn't. Some of us like the things the way they are, *thank you* very much."

Chase looked awkwardly around the table, but everybody was silent. None of them even seemed that offended by what he was saying, not even Natalie, and he knew she had a huge group of gay friends.

"And don't even get me started on gay adoption," he scoffed, spooning in another mouthful of trifle. "It's bloody *barbaric*! You wouldn't just hand over kids to a paedophile, would you?"

"That's enough," said Chase, in his calmest voice.

"Well, it's true!" Patrick laughed bitterly. "The world has gone bloody mad. Between the gays and the immigrants, I don't know who is bloody worse!"

"I said *that's enough!*" Chase's fist struck the table, causing the plates to jump. The movement of spoons lifting trifle to mouths stopped for a moment as all eyes were on him again. "Ricky is a good guy, regardless of what you think, and he's been through the wars."

"Maybe if he didn't flaunt it around so much, he wouldn't have been mugged," said Danny, throwing his two cents into the ring. "He forces it down your throat."

"That's just how he is!" Chase could feel his blood boiling in his veins as he tried to defend a man who wasn't there to defend himself.

"Well, maybe if he toned it down, people wouldn't take

such exception to it," said Patrick, even louder this time. "It's bloody sickening! You should see his house. *Tacky* isn't even the word. He's got some naked men above his fireplace. You think that's a place to raise kids? It's disgusting!"

"So you're saying you'd rather a child was raised by a single straight parent rather than two loving gay parents?" asked Chase, unable to contain the shaking in his hands. "That's mad."

"No, a child needs a mother and a father!" cried Patrick, slamming his own fist down on the table. "God made Adam and Eve, not Adam and *bloody* Steve."

"You're not even religious!"

"I was christened!"

"When did you last go to the church, Patrick?" Barbara sighed. "Let's drop this. I didn't slave away over a hot stove for you to ruin everything *again*."

Barbara's words fell on deaf ears because it was clear to Chase that his father wasn't going to drop it anytime soon. He glanced back to the muted TV as the second half of the match started up. It didn't grab his attention, thanks to the dining table talk.

"A child needs a mother *and* father," he said again. "Look at you, it's about time you found yourself another bloody woman. That boy needs a mother!"

"I'd have to agree," said Natalie. "Dylan needs a female influence in his life."

"He has one!" said Barbara. "I love that child like my own grandchild."

"It's not the same, is it?" added Danny. "I keep telling you that you need a woman, little bro. You can't escape the truth."

Chase felt like his head was going to explode. He closed his eyes and tried to centre himself as the chatter engulfed him. It wasn't enough. Both of his fists collided with the table, and silence fell.

"How I raise my son is *my* business and nobody else's," he said sternly, making sure to look each of them in the eye one at a time, landing on his father last. "If you think having two parents is so *fucking* important, why did you jump ship and leave me with one? Get your coat, Dylan, we're going home."

Dylan slid off his chair and shuffled silently into the hallway. Chase looked around the table one more time, but nobody dared challenge him. Danny and Barbara both looked scared, and Natalie looked amused, but it was Patrick's expression that shocked Chase the most. He looked angry that Chase would even dare bring that up.

Chase pushed his chair out, the wooden legs screeching on the tiles, he walked slowly around the table, but nobody said a word. He grabbed his jacket, grabbed Dylan's hand and headed outside.

"What's a queer?" asked Dylan as they walked down the street to the bus stop.

"Don't listen to your granddad," he said, squeezing Dylan's hand firmly. "He's a silly old man."

As they waited for the bus, Chase wondered if he would have reacted the same way if he hadn't met Ricky. He had heard similar conversations around the same table before, but he had always managed to check out of them, wanting to keep his curiosity to himself. Had he given away enough pieces of the jigsaw that they would all be able to figure it out after a couple of glasses of wine? For once, he didn't care.

He hadn't been able to stop thinking about the kiss all week, and he was just hoping and praying that Ricky would turn up for their second training session.

CHAPTER

NINE

At six o'clock on Monday, Ricky was sitting staring at the clock, drumming his fingers on the couch arm. He had been sitting in the same spot for nearly an hour, staring at the workout clothes from the week before, which were still slung over the back of his armchair.

It was only in the last ten minutes that he decided he wasn't going to the gym. He just hoped Chase wasn't going to sit around expecting him for too long, if he was waiting at all. After their awkward kiss, he doubted Chase was anticipating him again.

Breaking his eyes away from the clock, he heaved up and drifted into the kitchen. He dumped some dry, wholemeal pasta into a pan and filled up the kettle. He wasn't really in the mood to cook, but he knew if he left it any longer, he would order another pizza, and he was scared he and the pizza delivery guy were going to be on first name terms soon.

When the kettle finished boiling, he poured it over the pasta and lit the back ring on the stove. As the pasta bubbled away, he looked in the cupboard for something to put with it. His cupboards were pretty bare, but a jar of red sauce caught his eye. Ricky ate out most nights, but because he hadn't been working, he had been forced to use his kitchen. Bret was always the one who had been great at cooking; Ricky was great at eating.

He unscrewed the lid with a satisfying pop and added it to a second pan. When both were bubbling away, he pulled out his phone and his finger went instinctively to his hook-up app. He had been avoiding it since the attack, mainly because he didn't want anybody to see him looking like Quasimodo. Now that he was looking more like himself, he was ready.

Stirring the sauce with one hand, he scrolled through the endless pictures of overly edited selfies and vapid torso shots. The nearest guy, BiBoiXO, was only thirty metres away. Ricky clicked on his profile and read his bio. He was cute, and looking for '*discreet fun now*', which suited Ricky perfectly.

He hovered over the chat button. Chase sprung into his mind, and he felt guilty. Looking at the time on his phone, he imagined Chase waiting at the gym right now. Ricky could do quick and meaningless sex; he couldn't do surprising and intimate kisses. He clicked on the button and sent the guy a message.

"Shit!" he cursed as his sauce bubbled over.

He quickly drained the pasta and poured it into a bowl with the sauce. He carried it through to the living room, taking a bite and almost burning his tongue off.

BiBoiXO replied. Ricky slid down his notification bar

and tapped on the message.

'Hey, where r u hot stuff? Can be there in fifteen xo.'

Ricky hesitated before typing in his address. He hovered over send as he shuffled another hot mouthful of pasta into his mouth. Looking around his living room, he knew fifteen minutes was enough time to quickly clean up the mess that had built up over the last couple of days.

'See you soon ;) xo.'

Ricky ditched his pasta and sauce and hurried into his bedroom. He picked up the scattered heels, wigs and dresses from the floor and flung them into the wardrobe, making sure to close it tightly. After quickly making the bed, he pulled out two condoms and a sachet of lube, and he placed them on the nightstand.

He picked up the picture of Bret, kissed the glass, silently apologised and set him carefully in the drawer. He quickly changed out of the sweatpants and tank top he had been wearing all day and wriggled into a pair of well-fitting, pale blue jeans, and pulled on a simple black t-shirt. After a quick squirt of his spicy aftershave, he was ready.

Five minutes earlier than expected, there was a knock on the door. Ricky was so used to strangers waiting on his doorstep for sex, but it had been a long time since he had felt nervous.

Ricky hurried through his living room, checking his breath as he went. He paused behind the door, inhaled deeply and wrapped his hand around the brass doorknob. He opened the door, but it wasn't the cute face from the picture.

"Chase?" Ricky smiled awkwardly. "What are you doing here?"

"Is this a bad time?" Chase peered around Ricky's shoulder into his house. "I was worried about you. I wanted to make sure you were okay. I still had Tom's number from calling him at the hospital, so I asked him where you lived."

"And he just gave it to you?" Ricky grimaced through the smile. "*Of course* he did."

"I was worried when you didn't turn up. I just wanted to make sure everything was okay, but you look fine."

"*Ta-da*, sweetheart!" Ricky held his hands out and shook them. "Still in one piece."

"I can see that." Chase nodded awkwardly. "Well, I'll leave you to it."

Ricky couldn't ignore the disappointment on Chase's face. He had hoped he wouldn't have even cared if Ricky hadn't turned up, but it was clear he did. He looked as though he was waiting for Ricky to say something, but when he didn't, he nodded and turned on his heels.

"Wait," Ricky called out. "I should probably apologise."

"No need," Chase said without turning around as he unhooked Ricky's gate. "I get it."

Ricky wasn't sure he did. He ran barefoot across his small garden and spun Chase around by his shoulder.

"I really am sorry," he said. "I didn't want to make things awkward between us."

"Why would things be awkward?" Chase looked genuinely confused. "I thought you wanted to train."

"I did, but *y'know*, what happened. I thought you were straight. I assumed you were straight."

"I am," Chase said, shrugging uncomfortably. "Straight-*ish*."

"You don't kiss like a straight guy, sweetheart," Ricky said with an arched brow. "Do you want to come inside for a minute so I can explain?"

Chase looked at Ricky, before looking back down the street. Ricky wouldn't blame Chase for leaving without hearing him out. Why did Ricky care so much? He had never had trouble throwing guys out of his house, and now he was trying to invite one in, minutes before his shag was about to turn up.

"I left the gym unlocked," he said, hooking his thumb over his shoulder. "I should probably get back. I only ran up to see if you were – *never mind*." His voice trailed off, and he stuffed his hands into his short pockets. "It doesn't matter. I'll see you around, yeah?"

Chase turned around and unlatched the gate. Ricky watched him walk quickly down the street and out of sight. An impulse deep in Ricky didn't want to see Chase leave so suddenly. He ran back into his house and grabbed his gym clothes off the back of his armchair, along with his keys.

"Chase, *wait!*" He hurried down the street and caught up with him. "Is it too late for that training session?"

Chase stopped in his tracks and turned around with a small smile. He shook his head and jerked it towards the gym. Ricky exhaled and followed Chase down the high street, unsure of what he was doing.

On the opposite side of the street, he spotted BiBoiXO looking at his phone and heading in the direction of Ricky's cottage.

***

At the end of the hour, they both collapsed onto the mats and leaned against the mirror. Panting silently, they caught their breath as sweat dripped down their equally red faces.

"That was great," said Ricky, wiping the sweat from his cheeks. "I'm going to feel that tomorrow."

"That's how you know you've had a good training session."

"Well, you're a good trainer."

"And you're a good student."

"You think?" laughed Ricky. "You can tell that to my

boss, Jackson. The little shit is half my age and thinks I take direction badly."

It suddenly dawned on Chase that he hadn't asked Ricky what he did for a living. He remembered Bailey mentioning something about Ricky being a DJ, but he had taken that with a pinch of salt. He looked at Ricky and tried to assign a career to him. He couldn't imagine it being something dull like working in a gym or answering phones in a call centre.

"What do you do for a living?" he asked as his breathing finally levelled out.

"By day, I run a bookshop in the village," he said. "And by night, I'm a DJ."

"In a club?" asked Chase. "In the village? I might have seen you. What club is it?"

"It's just some tiny bar. You probably haven't heard of it," Ricky said, clearly not wanting to talk about it. "I'd just finished work before the attack. I was walking home. I went to the police, and I told them what I remembered, but I don't think it made much difference."

Chase shifted uncomfortably on the spot before standing up. He still hadn't told Ricky it was his father who was handling his case. After his outburst at the dinner table, he wasn't sure he wanted to tell Ricky. He didn't want to be associated with such an awful man.

"An officer came and asked me a couple of questions," he said tactfully. "They said you gave them my name, but I told them everything I told them at the hospital."

Ricky held out his hand, and Chase pulled him up to his feet. They stood face to face for a moment, and Chase almost thought they were going to kiss again. Ricky pulled away and turned to fiddle with his hair in the mirror before that happened.

"Tom gave them your name. I didn't want to lump this

on you. You've already done enough. He can't help but stick his nose into my business."

"He seems pretty concerned about you. He was telling me on the phone that you were planning to go back to work."

"I bet he loved that," laughed Ricky, rolling his eyes. "I love him to pieces, but he seems to forget I've been on this planet longer than him. I've done enough living for the both of us to know what's best for me."

A glint of sadness took over Ricky's eyes for a moment, but like a skilled actor, it vanished as quickly as it had arrived. Chase could feel that Ricky was hinting at something traumatic from deep within his past, but he didn't elaborate, so he didn't ask. Chase had his own secrets, and he appreciated the need for them.

"He seems nice enough," said Chase. "From what I could tell."

"Oh, he is lovely, sweetheart. Sweet to a fault. He's married to a farmer called Cole, and they have a little girl, Eva. It's all very Disney, but it's not for me. If you typed up 'perfect gay family' on your laptop, a picture of them would pop up first. He seems to think that's the only life for people like us, but can you imagine me living like that? What else did he have to say about me?"

Chase wondered if he should tell Ricky everything Tom had said. They had only talked for a couple of minutes, but Tom had crammed as much information into that conversation as he could. Chase decided it was best not to tell Ricky that Tom had called him a self-destructing, self-sabotaging, responsibility dodging man-child.

"Not much," he lied. "I'm about to hit the showers. I can smell myself."

Their eyes caught in the mirror for a split second and Chase's stomach squirmed. Ricky wasn't the type of guy he would ever go for in the club, but there was something irresistible about him. If he wanted their training sessions to continue, he would have to be an adult and resist.

"I might join you," said Ricky as he sniffed his own pits. "We cooked up quite a stink in there."

"It's a communal shower block," Chase warned.

"Oh, sweetheart. We're all adults here. It's not like I've not seen a naked man before. I'm quite intrigued to know where those tattoos end."

They walked into the changing rooms and sat on the benches and unlaced their shoes.

"Thanks for giving me another shot," said Ricky out of the blue. "I think I needed to get that out."

"Don't mention it," he said. "I expect to see you here next week at six, no excuses."

"I'll think about it, sweetheart," he said with a wink. "No promises."

Chase was the first to strip down to his underwear. He caught Ricky looking out of the corner of his eye, but he pretended not to notice. He left his clothes on the bench and wriggled out of his briefs, cupping his junk with one hand. Not wanting things to turn awkward, he quickly rounded the corner and hurried onto the cold tiles, twisting the tap so that the showers started up. He opted for a shower in the middle.

The water was ice cold when it hit his skin. It soothed his muscles and helped keep his urges at bay. It didn't stay cold for long, and steam soon filled the row of showers.

It felt like an age before he heard Ricky's heavy footsteps behind him. As he soaped his armpits, he instinctively turned around. He hadn't meant to, but his eyes landed straight on Ricky's soft cock. It was big enough to give Chase's a run for its money.

To Chase's surprise, Ricky chose the shower directly by

his side. Standing under the water, he cleaned his eyes as it drenched his body. Chase followed the water down to the ground as it ran along Ricky's defined form. Through the steam, he could barely see the bruises.

"I wish my shower was this powerful at home," said Ricky, breaking the silence. "Mine's like being pissed on by a tramp."

"Mine too. I love showering here."

"Must be alright having your own gym. You can come here whenever you want."

"I spend most of my working day here. I actually like going home at the end of the night. Not that I don't want to stay back for these sessions. I enjoyed them."

Ricky ran his hands through his hair, and he let the water run down his chest. He smiled and said, "Me too."

Chase ran the bar of soap along his defined, tattooed abs. He thought he caught Ricky watching out of the corner of his eye, but he couldn't be sure.

"Did those hurt?" asked Ricky. "The tattoos, I mean."

"Some of them," he answered as he ran the soap under his balls, avoiding touching his shaft, which felt like it was going to stand to attention with the smallest brush of contact. "It's a pain you learn to crave."

"I understand that."

Chase looked up and down Ricky's body, but he didn't seem to have any tattoos. He wondered what pain Ricky was addicted to. For a second, he thought it was connected to the attack, but everything Tom had said hinted to something else. Chase almost asked Ricky to elaborate, but he stopped himself. If there was something, he knew it would be better to let him open up about it on his own.

"Can I borrow the soap?" he asked. "I wouldn't ask, but I didn't bring any."

"Sure," said Chase. "Here."

He held out the soap, but it slipped out of his hands and disappeared into the steam.

"You've dropped the soap, sweetheart," Ricky smirked. "Let me."

They both bent down to grab the soap at the same time. In a flash of stupidity, their foreheads collided, sending them both tumbling backwards. Chase clutched his forehead, the sharp pain spreading quickly. Through the steam, he heard Ricky laugh.

"Sorry," said Chase.

"My fault," he laughed. "Really, let me this time."

Chase straightened up and he let Ricky bend down to grab the soap. On his way back up, Ricky paused, staring directly at Chase's crotch. Looking down, he hadn't noticed that his cock was hard.

"Jesus *fucking* Christ," he mumbled.

"Shit, I'm sorry," Chase apologised again. "*I – I – I* don't know how that happened."

"Don't apologise, sweetheart," Ricky said, straightening up and running the soap over his body. "You're a man. It's natural."

Chase wondered if Ricky thought it really was random, and not because of how attracted he was to Ricky. He was such an enigma and unlike any man he had ever met and that only turned Chase on even more.

Chase hid his embarrassment by plunging his head under the heavy flow. He let the water pound against his skull, and he tried to think of anything apart from Ricky's body. The more he tried to rid himself of his unwanted erection, the more it seemed to harden.

Stepping back from the water, he was about to leave Ricky to finish up when he noticed Ricky's cock had also stood to attention. He paused as Ricky ran the soap over his neck. Ricky was unaware that Chase had spotted it, so he took the moment to admire its impressive length curving up to Ricky's stomach.

Chase walked towards the changing room, his feet splashing in the puddles. He couldn't believe he was walking away from a guy he was so attracted to, especially when Ricky seemed to share that attraction, unless his erection was really random.

He almost did leave Ricky alone, until he remembered the kiss. Ricky had kissed him. Chase had wanted to, but it had been Ricky who had closed the gap.

Turning on his heels, Chase marched through the steam. He spun Ricky around and the soap fell to the ground once more. Against the backdrop of the splashing water, he pushed Ricky up against the tiles, clutched Ricky's stubbly cheeks and joined their lips. The passion between them erupted like a volcano, ready to destroy anything that dared stop them. Their tongues lashed against one another urgently as their throbbing cocks touched.

Chase pulled away from the kiss to stare at Ricky. He wanted to tell him how beautiful he was, but he didn't want words to ruin the moment. He didn't know where things were going, he just knew he needed to get there, or he would go home with an ache in his pants and regret in his mind.

It was Ricky who broke the silence with a lead balloon statement. "We shouldn't," he mumbled through the steam.

Chase wasn't about to give up so easily. He could feel the heat between them, and it wasn't coming from the water. Being daring, he let go of Ricky's face and ran his fingers down his wet torso, not stopping until his fingers were clenched around his thick, pulsing, curved shaft.

"Why not?" he whispered, his voice trembling deep within his throat.

Ricky's eyes darted from Chase's eyes to his lips. Had

Chase overstepped the mark? Ricky didn't strike him as the prude type, but had he read Ricky completely wrong?

"Fuck it," said Ricky, his words biting through the steam like a bullet.

It was Ricky's turn to grab Chase's face. He pulled him back towards him and their lips joined once more, and this time, they were both giving as good as they were getting.

Gripping hard, he pumped up and down on Ricky's impressive shaft, enjoying the feeling of its hardness between his fingers. Ricky let out a tiny moan, and their tongues deepened. His fingers slipped from his cheek and to the back of Chase's head, his nails digging into his short hair.

As though he could hear its cries for attention through the water, Ricky's hand disappeared below, and he grabbed Chase's cock with an expert touch. Ricky groaned through the kiss, letting Chase know how much he wanted it. Chase wanted nothing more than to spin Ricky around and fuck him right there, but he couldn't seem to stop his fingers working Ricky's shaft.

The water reached its time limit and ground to a halt, but that didn't stop them. The air suddenly grew cold, and Chase could feel it licking his bare arse cheeks, but the burning passion between them was creating a sweat as the water started to dry.

He felt that he was reaching his limit quicker than he wanted to, but Ricky only sped up as his cock twitched. He tried to pull away to tell him to slow down, but Ricky held his head firmly in place as his fingers quickly massaged his shaft.

Chase understood what Ricky was saying. He matched his speed. His climax was growing closer and closer, but he was powerless to prevent it. Just as every muscle in his body started to tense, he felt Ricky's do the same.

In the final sprint to the finish line, their hands became clumsy, but that didn't stop them sending each other over the edge at the same moment. Their lips and tongues stopped moving, but neither of them pulled away from the kiss.

A deep and primal groan escaped Chase's throat as the darkness behind his closed lids was banished by a blinding light. For a moment, his body didn't belong to him, and he was sure he was about to crumble to the ground.

He released, over and over against Ricky and Ricky did the same. For a moment, they gripped each other's faces, their hands still holding their cocks as their kissing slowly ground to a halt. With an exhausted smile, Chase leaned his forehead against Ricky's. He could have stayed like that forever if his body hadn't suddenly noticed how cold the tiled room had become.

He reluctantly broke away from Ricky and twisted the shower tap again. Once more, they shared the soap and cleaned themselves down in silence.

Back in the changing room, Chase pulled his towel and change of clothes from his personal locker. An envelope fell from the pocket of the shorts and two, blue tickets poked out of the edge. He picked them up, remembering they were for the Annual Fitness Event Weekend. He scanned over the tickets, sure that he had missed the event. When he noticed it was that weekend, he had a crazy thought.

He watched Ricky dry himself down with one of the communal towels. He didn't expect Ricky to agree, but it was worth a short.

"Are you doing much this weekend?" he asked as he hooked the towel around his hips, still holding the tickets.

"I'm back at work," he said, turning as he dried his balls, not caring that everything was out on show. "Why?"

"Oh, it's nothing." He sat on the edge of the bench and

looked down at the tickets again, remembering how much fun it was last year. "I just have these tickets for this thing. It's a weekend in a country manor for this fitness thing. It sounds really boring, but it was tons of fun last year. I was supposed to be going with my brother, but it doesn't matter. Forget I mentioned it."

Ricky sat next to Chase and pulled the tickets from his hands. He looked over them and turned them over in his hands.

"This weekend?"

"There's a free bar."

"A free bar?" Ricky slapped the tickets against the palm of his hand. "*Fuck it.* I'm in. Toxic Tonya can hold down the fort for another week."

"Who?"

"Doesn't matter," he said as he stood up. "I'll come."

Chase tried to hide his excitement. He had no idea if they were going anywhere serious, but he was enjoying the ride.

They both dried and dressed and headed back through to the gym. Chase powered everything down, flicked off the lights, and they headed out into the dark of the night.

"I guess I'll see you this weekend, sweetheart."

"I'll pick you up at lunchtime. It's an hour drive to the place."

"You know where I live," Ricky smiled as he backed away down the street. "See ya."

Chase watched Ricky until he disappeared into his cottage. Clutching the tickets in his hands, he bit into his lip and grinned. He jumped into his car, wondering how Annie would feel about taking Dylan for the weekend.

CHAPTER

TEN

I t was a beautiful early summer's day as they drove to Coltrane House out in the Yorkshire countryside. With their bags for the weekend on the backseat, they drove with the windows down and the radio blasting. When they drove up the long and winding private driveway of Coltrane House, Ricky almost felt like he was on holiday.

"Jesus *bloody* Christ, sweetheart," exclaimed Ricky when the manor house came into view. "Looks like something out of *Downton Abbey*! This must have cost a fortune."

"It's a spa and hotel. The event booked out the whole building for the weekend, so we got a good deal," he said as they pulled into the already packed car park by the side of the house.

They grabbed their bags and walked across the gravel towards the grand entrance. Roller banners stood either side of the door letting them know they were at the Annual Fitness Event Weekend. Ricky heaved his bag over his shoulder, wondering how much fitness they were going to be getting up to with a free bar.

"Chase!" a tall, handsome man crossed the entrance hall and slapped his hand in Chase's. "Good to see you again! Where's that brother of yours?"

"He couldn't make it, Mack. This is my friend, Ricky. He's one of my training clients at the gym, so I thought I'd drag him along to show him how it's really done."

Mack's smile faltered when he spotted Ricky. Everybody already seemed to be in their shorts and Lycra t-shirts, even Chase. Ricky had opted for his comfy jeans, t-shirt and leather jacket.

"Ricky, nice to meet you." Mack leaned around Chase to shake his hand. "I'll let you two check-in. Make sure you're in the main hall at two for the orientation."

Mack walked away to greet more guests, leaving them to head to the reception desk.

"Maybe this wasn't such a good idea," he said. "This isn't my crowd."

"Don't be stupid," Chase laughed off the suggestion. "This is going to be a great weekend, you watch."

Ricky dropped his bag on the floor and drummed his fingers on the desk as they waited to be checked in. He had been wondering all week why he had agreed to go. He had almost cancelled more than once, but he had stopped himself every time. When he told Tom how he was spending his weekend, he had almost had a heart attack.

"Good morning," said a well-dressed woman with an Eastern European accent as she approached them from behind the desk. "Can I take your name?"

"Should be under Brody." Chase leaned across the desk. "Chase or Danny."

"I've got you right here," she said through a smile. "A double room for the whole weekend, prepaid. Would you like to put a card on file for extra room charges?"

"Did you say double room?" Chase frowned. "My brother would have booked a twin."

"It's definitely a double. It was booked last year and hasn't been amended since."

Chase looked uncomfortably at Ricky. Ricky hadn't even thought about the sleeping arrangements until now.

"Is there any way to change it to a twin?"

"All of the twins are booked up," she said as she typed away on the keyboard. "I do have two single rooms, but they're on separate floors. There would be an extra charge, but I can change that for you?"

"We'll take the double," Ricky jumped in. "We're both big boys."

The woman smiled and continued to tap away at her keyboard. She produced two key cards, slid them across the desk and told them they were on the second floor in room forty-two.

"Are you sure you don't mind?" asked Chase as they walked up the grand, oak staircase to the second floor. "I can still go back and change it."

"Would you have changed it if your brother was here?"

"Probably not. We just would have topped and tailed or something."

"Then we'll do that," said Ricky with a wink. "I hope your feet don't smell."

"I just don't want you thinking that I've brought you here with an ulterior motive."

"You mean a weekend of fucking?"

"Something like that. I just want to get to know you better, that's all."

Ricky's hands tightened around his bag as they walked

along the ornate second floor corridor. A weekend of fucking made him feel a lot more comfortable than a weekend of Chase trying to unlock his boxes. Tom had told him to not be afraid of getting close to Chase, but it was easier said than done.

Chase slotted the keycard into the electronic lock, and the door opened with a satisfying click. They both looked into the room and then to each other.

Ricky didn't know what he had been expecting, but it wasn't what they got. They walked into the grand bedroom and dumped their bags by the door.

"I think Danny was still drunk when he booked this. He must have paid for the upgrade," said Chase as he walked over to the floor-to-ceiling windows with views for miles of the gardens and the countryside. "We didn't get any of this last year."

Ricky bounced up and down on the edge of the giant four-poster bed. He looked around the impressive room, thinking it wouldn't look out of place as a honeymoon suite for newlyweds. The gold flowers on the deep red wallpaper glittered in the bright sunlight, reflecting the pattern on the luxuriously embossed sheets.

"Have you seen this bathroom?" Chase's voice echoed from the adjoining room. "It's got one of those free-standing baths with gold feet. This room alone is bigger than my entire flat!"

Ricky stopped peering in the fully stocked minibar under the mahogany writing desk and walked through to the bathroom. Chase lay fully clothed in the bathtub, grinning like the king of the castle as he stared around at the dark emerald tiles. Another window looked out onto the grounds.

"This is mad," he laughed. "Can you believe this?"

Ricky sat on the edge of the bathtub and hummed his

agreement. He was as impressed as Chase, but he was also nervous. It was a much more romantic setting than he had imagined his weekend being set against. When Chase had offered him a weekend in the countryside at a fitness event, he had imagined muddy fields, portable toilets, and itchy sheets.

After unpacking their weekend bags, they headed back down to the reception area and Chase led the way to the main hall. It was no less impressive than the rest of the manor house. Fine art paintings lined the wood walls and the same windows from their bedroom lined the back wall, letting in so much natural light it made Ricky suddenly hate the small windows in his little cottage.

Any other time, he could imagine it filled with decorated tables for an extravagant wedding, or rows of tables for a banquet. Today, small booths cluttered the floor and hundreds of people in every shade of Lycra imaginable wandered around. They couldn't have looked more out of place in the beautiful setting if they tried.

Chase explained that they could sign up for as little or as much as they wanted to over the weekend. Each class they signed up for was a chance for them to learn new techniques and for the teachers to sell whatever new product they were pushing.

"The trick is to sign up for the things you know you're going to learn something new from," he whispered to Ricky as he put their names down for a '*Beginners Introduction to Aikido*' class. "The classes start in about an hour and most people jump straight in, but I've always found today is the best day to take advantage of that free bar, so we can focus on the real fitness tomorrow and Sunday. Sound good?"

"You're the boss," said Ricky, feeling more out of his comfort zone than he had ever felt before.

They walked over to the '*HIIT Techniques 2.0*' booth

ran by two men who seemed to know Chase as they approached. It took Ricky a moment to notice they were twins. From their name badges, he learned they were called Paul and Justin. It wouldn't be hard to tell them apart because Paul had a large scar down the left side of his cheek.

"Chase, my good man!" beamed Paul, shaking his hand. "Good to see you. Your brother said over email you weren't making it this year."

"Last minute change of plans. This is my friend, Ricky."

"Welcome to the mad house, mate," Justin reached across and shook Ricky's hand heartily. "First time?"

Ricky looked down at his outfit. Did he really stick out as obviously as he thought, or was it in his mind? He could smell the testosterone in the air, and he was sure they could smell his homosexuality.

"Is it that obvious?" he asked.

"Not at all," said Paul. "You look in good shape. We've been coming here for the last six years, so we learn the faces. Can I put you both down for our Sunday morning class?"

"It's a tough one," said Chase, sucking the air in through his teeth. "You sure you're up for it?"

"What are you insinuating, sweetheart?" Ricky snatched the pen from Paul and scribbled their names down on the end of the growing list. "I can keep up with the best of them."

"That's what I like to hear!" Paul said with a grin. "A man who isn't afraid to sweat is a friend of mine. How's Dylan doing, Chase?"

Ricky didn't know who Dylan was and he wouldn't have thought much of it if he hadn't noticed Chase's cagey expression.

"Yeah, he's doing good. C'mon, Ricky. Let's see what's outside."

"See you tonight in the bar?" asked Paul. "Both of you?"

"I could never turn down a free drink," laughed Ricky. "See you both."

"That's my man! I like this one, Chase."

They wandered past the booths and towards a set of double doors, which led out onto a stone patio. There were more booths, but most of them were for Yoga and Chase didn't seem very interested in them.

"Who's Dylan?" asked Ricky.

"Oh, just an old friend."

Ricky couldn't put his finger on why, but he didn't believe him. He hadn't heard a mention of Dylan before, and he hadn't seen Chase look so uncomfortable at a question.

Ricky was about to ask more questions when he spotted Mack wandering around the gardens, puffing on a cigarette and talking on his phone. Mack's eyes caught his, and he looked at him the same way he had done in the reception area. Ricky had thought it was the same way Chase's brother looked at him, but it was different. He almost looked scared, even disgusted.

"Who's that Mack guy?" he whispered to Chase as they leaned against a low stone wall and pulled out their own cigarettes. "He's giving me weird vibes."

"Really? Mack? He's a good guy. He's the bookings coordinator, so he's already hovering around trying to get people to book for next year. He's good for a laugh. He's usually one of the last in the bar because he doesn't really get involved in the fitness side of things."

"So he'll be there tonight?"

"Is that a problem?" Chase arched a brow as he lit Ricky's cigarette for him.

"I don't know," he glanced over his shoulder in Mack's direction. He wasn't talking on the phone, but he was finishing his cigarette leaning against a tree and staring in

Ricky's direction. "It's probably nothing."

"You're safe here. You don't have to worry about anything happening."

"I'm not, sweetheart. I don't think every straight guy is going to jump on me. I'm not that cynical, yet."

"Oh, Mack isn't straight," he said. "He got married to a guy last year, I think. I was invited, but I couldn't make it."

Ricky glanced back over his shoulder, but Mack had vanished. Was Mack just trying to suss him out? It felt like more than that, but Ricky couldn't place his finger on what. No matter how much he tried to convince people that the attack hadn't changed him, he couldn't deny that it had made him more paranoid.

***

Chase jumped out of the bath and wrapped a thick towel around his waist. He pulled the plug and watched the bubbles disappear down the drain. He made a mental note to take pictures of the bathroom before going home. Dylan would never believe he had stayed in such a palace.

He wiped down the mirror and examined his face through the condensation. He rubbed shaving foam over the lower half of his face and quickly dragged his razor over the tattoos on his neck, up to his cheekbones. He splashed his face with cold water and patted it down with a hand towel.

He examined the bottles Ricky had neatly displayed on the counter next to the sink. He picked up a tall bottle of aftershave in the shape of a man's torso. After giving the cap a sniff, he squirted it on his neck. He immediately smelled like Ricky.

With the towel around his waist, he walked back into the bedroom. Ricky looked up from behind his book as he read on his stomach on the bed.

"How was the bath?" he asked as he slowly turned the page.

"Big. How's the book?"

"Boring." He tossed it to the side and rolled onto his back to look at Chase upside down. "Agatha Christie is hit and miss."

"I didn't have you down as the reading type."

"Why not?" Ricky rolled back over and sat cross-legged on the edge of the bed. "I was an A* student in high school, I'll have you know. It was probably the only thing in high school that was straight about me."

"I didn't mean that," he said as he flicked through the few shirts he had hung up in the closet. "I just couldn't imagine you sitting down and reading a book until now."

"I'm a mystery wrapped in a riddle, sweetheart. There is a lot you don't know about me."

"Oh, I don't doubt it." Chase looked over his shoulder and smiled at Ricky, who he was sure had been staring at his bare, tattooed back. "Black or white shirt?"

"The white brings out your tattoos."

Chase plucked the white shirt from the hanger and pulled it over his solid arms. He buttoned it up from the bottom, leaving it open halfway up. He liked how it emphasised his well worked out chest muscles. He wriggled into a pair of tight white briefs and let the towel fall to the ground. He caught his reflection in the mirror hidden on the other side of the closet door. The shirt hugged his muscles, and the tiny briefs hugged his manhood. He considered changing into some boxers, but he hated the way the loose fabric felt against the denim. There was something about feeling the rough denim on his smooth thighs that he liked.

"Is that my aftershave?" Ricky appeared in the reflection

and sniffed at his neck.

"Hope you don't mind."

"No, it suits you," he said, catching Chase's eye in the mirror. "It smells sexier on you than me."

Chase didn't agree. Every time he smelled the same dark, spicy scent on Ricky, it did something to his insides he couldn't explain. Was it doing the same to Ricky?

He crossed over to the bed and sat on the edge, leaning back on his elbows. He picked up the book and turned it over in his hands. Ricky pulled his white t-shirt off and quickly pulled on a similar white shirt. Chase noticed the bruising had faded completely.

Tossing the book back onto the bed, he thought more about what Ricky had said about high school. He hadn't even begun to imagine Ricky's life that far back yet. He barely knew anything about the man standing before him.

"Did you have a tough time in high school?" he asked.

"What makes you think that?" he asked, turning around as he buttoned up the shirt. "Because I'm a big, raving queer?"

"That's not what I meant."

"I know," said Ricky. "I'm being sarcastic, sweetheart. You can add that to the file, seeing as you wanted to get to know me."

"Noted."

"High school was high school. It's never easy. You're too gay, too geeky, too fat, too thin, too ugly, too spotty. I didn't have it any harder than anyone else."

Chase thought back to his high school days. When he first made the leap from primary school to high school, Danny had been in his last year at high school, but they had been total opposites. Chase had been a chubby little thing who wasn't good in lessons, and his brother was the school's football star, and he was a Senior Prefect. The gap between them didn't close until Chase discovered his love of kickboxing in the second year when the local instructor came in to an assembly to talk to the kids about self-defence.

"Did you not get bullied for being gay?" Chase asked, remembering his own experience being called '*Chubby Chase*'. "Kids are tough."

"I didn't say that. I got called every name under the sun, every day of my life. It was murder, but I got through it."

"How? Did you always have that wall?"

"Wall?" Ricky frowned. "What wall?"

Chase felt like he had crossed a line, but he couldn't believe Ricky was even questioning his statement. He had only known Ricky for less than a month, but even he had noticed there were two definite versions of Ricky. He had even noticed before Tom mentioned it during their brief conversation on the phone.

"You know what I'm talking about. There's the real Ricky, and then there's the sarcastic, biting Ricky."

"We're one in the same, sweetheart."

"Were you like that in school?"

"No," he said bluntly.

"Well, who were you?"

"Does it matter?" he snapped and turned back to the mirror as he rolled his sleeves up. "What's with the questions?"

Chase paused and picked up the book again. He flicked to the page Ricky was reading, noticing a business card for a bar called London Bridge saving his place. It was a bar in the village he rarely went into. Was that where Ricky DJ'd?

"I'm sorry. Ignore me," said Chase, tossing the book on the bed and standing up again. "I'm just trying to make conversation."

Ricky crossed over to the window and stared out into

the grounds as the sun started to fade from the sky. Chase went back to the closet and pulled out a pair of tight, faded jeans. He wriggled into them and turned on the small, ornate lamp sitting on the writing desk. Opening the mini bar underneath, he pulled out two tiny cans of beer and tossed one to Ricky, who caught it firmly.

"You really want to know what high school was like for me?" he said, turning around the occasional chair under the window. He straddled it and cracked open the beer can, sipping away the froth. "It was hell. I had this friend, Morgan. I told him I was gay when we were twelve, and he kept it secret until we were sixteen and in our last year. I'm not saying it was a walk in the park until then, because it wasn't. People seemed to know I was gay before I even opened my mouth. When he told everyone after we fell out, it was tough. I didn't have any other friends, so I had to toughen up. Word somehow made its way home, and my dad beat me up pretty bad. We never really spoke much after that. He died when I was away at university. Is that what you wanted to hear?"

"I'm sorry. I didn't mean to pry."

"It's okay, sweetheart. I knew I was gay before I knew what gay meant. I realised at an early age that life was going to be against me. It was harder back then. When I left home at eighteen, I stopped caring about what people thought. I never did, until –"

Ricky's voice trailed off, but he didn't need to say it for Chase to know what he was about to say. Chase checked his watch, and they were five minutes late for dinner.

"My family doesn't know anything about me," said Chase. "About me liking guys too."

"Are you going to tell them?"

Chase sipped his beer and imagined telling his father he had kissed the guy he had ripped into over Sunday lunch.

In any other world, he would tell him and not care about the repercussions, but he had Dylan to think about. He wasn't about to deprive him of any more family members.

"I think my brother would be okay, eventually," he said. "But my dad is like yours. He doesn't understand any of that stuff."

Ricky finished his can of beer and crushed it between his hands. He tossed it into the bin, stood up and straightened up his shirt.

"Well, sweetheart, you either make him understand, or not care that he doesn't. Living with secrets that big will only rot inside of you."

"But you got your secret out young."

Ricky smiled, but it was a sad smile. Chase had always thought there was something more to Ricky's life that he was keeping tight to his chest, and the look in his eyes only confirmed it. Chase almost pushed it, but he felt like a hypocrite. He still hadn't told Ricky about Dylan, even though the perfect opportunity had presented itself earlier in the day. He didn't even know why he was keeping it so secret, but part of him enjoyed just being Chase without having to explain his past, even if it was a fantasy. Perhaps he and Ricky weren't so different.

"Let's go down for dinner," said Ricky. "I still haven't seen this free bar you promised me."

Chase nodded and stood up. He quickly finished his beer and tossed the can in the bin with Ricky's. He suddenly wanted to tell Ricky about his son, but he decided it could wait until the morning. For a crazy moment, he imagined Ricky being more than a fling, even if he knew that was impossible.

He didn't know what their weekend away would hold, but he knew when he returned to the city, Dylan still needed a mother.

CHAPTER

ELEVEN

After a bland dinner of unseasoned chicken and steamed vegetables, Ricky was more than ready for a stiff drink. He followed Chase through the busy manor house. At the end of a long, dark corridor, they walked into the bar. Ricky hadn't expected such a building to have its own dedicated bar room, so he was pleasantly surprised to see it busy. It was nothing like London Bridge, but it served alcohol, and that was all he cared about.

The mahogany bar ran along the back wall, with regency style lights hanging from the ceiling along its length. All of the barstools were occupied, along with the booths. It was standing room only, but Ricky hadn't expected anything less from a free bar.

"Beer?"

"Make mine a vodka. I feel like getting drunk."

"Two vodkas it is," said Chase with a subtle smile. "Go and see if there's anywhere to sit and I'll get the drinks in."

Ricky wandered around the small bar, but the only spare seats were on the edges of bursting booths. He almost gave up, but one of the twins from earlier in the day caught his eye and waved him over.

"Ricky, how's it going man?" said Paul as he hugged his pint. "Where's Chase? We've saved you some room."

Paul and Justin scooted over in the booth, along with some other guys Ricky didn't recognise and one he did. He caught Mack's eyes again, and he immediately felt uncomfortable.

"Actually, we were just going to sit over -"

"Oh, hey lads." Chase appeared behind him holding two vodkas on the rocks. "Mind if we join you?"

Before Ricky could object any further, Chase squeezed into the full booth, leaving just enough space for Ricky to perch on the edge. He let the ice hit his lip as he tossed back the drink in one go.

"That's my man." Justin reached behind Chase and massaged Ricky's shoulder. "Let's kick off this weekend in style."

He held up his drink, and they all followed. Ricky waved his empty glass into the middle of the table as he wiped the vodka from his lips. Mack didn't take his eyes away from him the whole time.

Chase introduced Ricky to the two other guys sitting at their table, Bobby and Simon, two gym owners from Essex who had travelled up. They were real masculine blokes, usually the type Ricky stayed far away from, but they seemed nice enough.

After half an hour of drinking, the inevitable questions Ricky had dreaded started coming his way.

"So, Ricky. What do you do for a living if you're not in

fitness?" asked Justin when the waitress brought over another tray of free drinks.

"I own a bookshop," Ricky said tactfully. "And I DJ some weekends at a bar."

"DJ? Anywhere we might have heard you play?" asked Paul.

"It's just some little backstreet bar," he said, not wanting to go into too much detail. "It's nothing special."

"And how do you two know each other?" This question came from Mack, he narrowed his eyes on Ricky as he stared across the table. "Where did you meet?"

"It's a long story," said Ricky.

"The night isn't going anywhere," he said, darting his brows up and down. "Tell us."

Ricky looked at Chase, who looked as uncomfortable as Ricky felt. If Chase hadn't told his parents about his curiosity, the group of casual friends he saw once a year wasn't going to know.

"He's a client at my gym. I'm his trainer," said Chase. "We just became friends through that."

"That's not a very long story," said Simon as he sipped his pint. "Pretty boring, actually."

"I was attacked," said Ricky bluntly. "Chase found me and called the ambulance. He recommended that I take some self-defence classes."

"Shit, man," said Paul. "Good shout, Chase. You can never know too much self-defence these days."

"Who attacked you?" asked Mack.

Ricky tossed back his fourth vodka, his eyes trained on Mack. He didn't know what Mack's deal was, but he was starting to tire of his questioning. It was obvious to Ricky that Mack had an agenda. Was he trying to out Ricky to the group of masculine men? Hadn't they already figured it out?

"I don't know. I haven't remembered yet."

"Yet? So it's quite recent."

"About a month ago," said Chase. "It was pretty bad."

"So you've only known each other for a month, and here you are," said Mack. "You must have a lot in common."

It wasn't just Ricky who was looking strangely at Mack. The rest of the boys all turned to Mack with confusion loud in their eyes. He seemed to notice because he leaned back in his chair and the questioning suddenly ceased.

"Fancy a game of pool?" asked Paul, standing up. "The table's free."

"Now that's a good shout," said Justin, joining him in standing up.

Bobby and Simon shuffled out of the booth, and Paul and Justin followed. Chase waited for Ricky to move, but he wasn't in the mood for a game of pool.

"Mind if I just stay here?" he said. "Pool isn't my sport."

"You sure?"

"Yeah, go ahead. I'll be fine."

Ricky let Chase out, and he followed the rest of the lads over to the pool table. Just as Ricky had suspected, Mack didn't join them. They both sat on either side of the booth, staring at each other in silence for what felt like the longest time.

"You don't remember me, do you?" said Mack angrily. "You don't *fucking* remember me?"

"Should I?"

Ricky stared at Mack's face. He had thought there was something familiar about him, but he couldn't place it. The thought that he might have been one of Ricky's attackers had crossed his mind, but he was sure he would have recognised him sooner if that were the case.

"Last January," he said. "January twenty-fifth, to be precise?"

"Is that your birthday?"

"Cut the crap, Ricky," he said. "Or should I call you Kitty Litter?"

"That's *Miss* Kitty Litter to you," he snapped, leaning across the table. "What's your game?"

"I don't believe you actually don't remember me. Jesus Christ, man. You almost ruined my life."

"I did? Couldn't have been much of a life to ruin if I don't remember what I did."

Mack laughed sarcastically as he hit his head against the chair. He tossed back the dregs of his pint and sucked the air through his teeth as he looked angrily around the bar.

"You fucked my fiancé," he said in a low voice. "The day before my wedding."

"I fuck a lot of people. I don't keep tabs."

"You're *unbelievable*. You took my fiancé, Johnny, back to your place and you fucked him. Don't you remember me finding your cottage in the morning and dragging him out of there?"

Ricky's memory suddenly triggered. He had been so hung over and confused by the banging on his door, he hadn't taken much interest in memorising faces. It had happened so fast.

"Vaguely," he said. "From what I remember, your fiancé loved it."

"You almost ruined our wedding."

"That wasn't me, sweetheart. That was your fiancé. I wasn't the one who put a ring on your finger. I didn't force anybody to do anything."

"You knew he was my fiancé before you took him home! You congratulated us over the microphone! I almost didn't recognise you when you first turned up, but I knew I'd seen your face somewhere."

Ricky finished his drink and sighed heavily. It wasn't the first time he had met the scorned other-half. Perhaps he should make it one of his rules to only fuck single guys in the future. It would make things a lot easier.

"Listen, Mack, I'm sorry that I didn't do a background check on your fiancé before I had sex with him, and I'm sorry that I failed to remember your rather generic face. Now, if you'll excuse me, I'm going to get another drink because that barmaid doesn't look like she's coming back over here anytime soon. I'd offer you one, but quite frankly, I don't want to."

Ricky was about to stand up, but Mack wrapped his fingers around Ricky's wrist, forcing him back to the table. For a moment, Ricky felt pure terror rush through his body at the man putting his hands on him. He looked over to the pool table, but Chase was deep in conversation as he leaned over the table.

"I don't know what you're doing with Chase, but he's a good guy. Too good for you."

"We're just friends."

"Yeah, sure," said Mack with a laugh. "I've seen him around Canal Street before, even if he thinks he's hidden from me. He's a nice lad. Too nice for you."

"I don't know what you think me and Chase are to each other, but you've got it all wrong. We barely know each other."

"You know each other well enough for him to bring you here. I know all about you, Ricky Thompson. You're poison, pure poison. Everything you touch turns to shit. I know you were engaged once, but the poor idiot had a lucky escape getting away from you."

Ricky tore his wrist away from Mack and walked quickly across the bar, anger flowing through his blood and tears welling in the corner of his eyes.

He wasn't angry because of what Mack had said, he was angry because he knew he was right. He had only agreed to the weekend away with Chase because a small part of his brain had lied to him, telling him he deserved a slice of happiness.

Wiping away the tears, he walked out of the bar and along the dark corridor back towards the staircase.

***

It was Chase's turn, but he dropped the pool cue and ran across the bar after Ricky. He caught the door before it closed and hurried along the corridor after him.

"Ricky? Where are you going?"

"I have a headache," said Ricky, without turning around. "I need an early night."

"Headache? You were fine earlier."

"Just get back in there and enjoy your game of pool."

Chase jogged to catch up with Ricky at the bottom of the stairs. Before his foot hit the bottom step, Chase grabbed Ricky's arm and spun him around. Tears were rolling down his face. Chase did the only thing he knew to do, and he reached out and wiped away the tears, the same way he would if Dylan fell over and scraped his knee.

"What's happened?" he asked carefully, staring around the dark, empty reception. "Is that about Mack? What's he done to you?"

"Nothing. It's what I've done to him. It doesn't matter," he tried to pull away from Chase. "I just want to be on my own."

"You know him?"

"Not really," he said. "I had sex with his fiancé the day before their wedding. I don't know if he was more pissed off that it was me or that I didn't remember him."

Chase let go of Ricky. He had heard all about that. Mack had almost called off the wedding, but he decided to go through with it last minute. Over his emails, Mack had made the man who had slept with Johnny sound like the devil incarnate.

"Do you feel guilty? Is that why you're crying? I hear they're fine now and they've worked it out."

"Guilty?" Ricky laughed, wiping away the tears with his own arm. "That's not in my range of emotions, sweetheart. I don't even *remember* the sex. It's just –,"

He stopped himself and inhaled deeply, his face turning a deep shade of maroon. Chase let go of his shirt and stroked his arm gently.

"What?" he urged.

"He said I was poison, and he's right."

"Poison?" Chase screwed up his face. "Why would he say that? So what if you fucked his fiancé. *Who cares?* You're not poison."

"I am, sweetheart. He hit the nail on the head there."

Chase let go of Ricky's arm and glanced over his shoulder at the long corridor to the door. A group of women walked down the stairs and walked around them. Ricky hid his face from them as they walked past. They headed towards the bar, giving Chase an idea.

"Just wait here, okay? Don't move."

Ricky nodded and wiped away the final tears before sitting on the edge of the bottom step. He dug his fingers deep into his hair and stared deep into the grooves of the wooden floor.

Chase ran back to the bar and pushed his way through the crowd trying to get served by the two bartenders. He waited until neither of them was looking in his direction and he reached across the bar and plucked out a bottle of vodka. Before anybody questioned what he was doing, he headed back to the entrance area, where Ricky was still sitting on the bottom step.

"Follow me," he said, shaking the almost full bottle of vodka with the metal pourer still attached. "Unless you don't want a drink?"

Ricky laughed and stood up. He snatched the vodka from Chase's hands and poured a generous amount into his mouth. He swallowed it as though it was nothing more than tap water. Chase snatched it back and searched back into his memory for the direction of the pool.

CHAPTER

TWELVE

icky followed Chase down the never-ending dark corridors. He had no idea where he was being taken, but he didn't care. Chase was holding the vodka and vodka was the only thing to stop him from thinking about Bret.

Eventually, they reached a set of double glass doors. Ricky noticed the illuminated blue pool through the windows. Chase rattled the door handles, but they were both locked.

"Shit," he mumbled. "This way."

He led Ricky further down the corridor to the changing rooms. He pushed the door, and it opened. He turned back to Ricky with a devious smile, and he headed into the dark room.

Ricky followed Chase into the pitch black, and he waited for his eyes to adjust to the lack of a window. When they did, he noticed just how creepy the tiled room was at night.

"Where are you taking me?" whispered Ricky into the dark. "I can't bloody see a thing."

Chase reached back, and his fingers looped around Ricky's. His instincts told him to pull away, but he liked how it felt to have a strong hand in his, guiding him.

A shivering, blue light broke through the darkness as they walked past a block of showers. They turned the corner and walked out into the poolroom. A full-length pool ran down the middle of the room. Small lights dotted the blue tiles under the water, making the calm surface glow sapphire. Windows filled the walls and ceiling of the room, giving them the perfect view of the empty gardens. The almost full moon hung in the black velvet sky above.

"Better than going back to the room?" asked Chase as he dragged two huge, wicker loungers from the edge of the room.

"Perhaps."

Chase positioned the loungers by the edge of the pool, and he pushed them together to resemble something like a bed. He lay on his front and patted the one next to him, shaking the bottle like a toy for a dog.

Ricky sat on the edge of the second lounger and snatched the bottle from Chase. He drank some more vodka, and he felt his mind start to swim like the radiant water in front of him. Copying Chase, he lay on his front on the comfortably cushioned lounger and nursed the vodka like a child's bottle.

"Fuck Mack," said Chase, his voice echoing around the empty pool. "He's a dick."

"You said he was nice before."

"That's before he upset you. I might say something to him tomorrow. If he had a problem, he should have just kept it to himself."

"You really don't have to," said Ricky. "I don't need you to fight my battles."

"I know," said Chase, taking back the vodka, "but I want to."

After swigging the vodka, he leaned on his arm and stared into the water. Ricky copied him, and he felt more at peace as he watched the water ripple under the luminosity of the moon.

"Why did you invite me here?" Ricky asked after a moment of silence.

"Because I wanted to."

"But why?"

"I wanted to get to know you better."

"Why though?" he asked sternly. "Why do you care about me? Is it pity?"

"Pity?" Chase scrunched up his brow. "I don't pity you, Ricky. Why would you think that?"

"I can't think of another reason you would want me here with you. I'm not into fitness like you are. You're just my trainer."

"I'm just your trainer?" Chase sat up. "I'm *not* just your trainer. I can assure you, I've never done those things with my clients in the shower before."

Ricky had wondered that. It wasn't the first time Ricky had done something sexual in a gym shower, but he doubted Chase made a habit of it.

"Why do you want to give me the time of day?" he asked. "I'm not your type."

"How do you know what my type is?" he laughed. "I don't have a type."

"But if you did, it wouldn't be a man like me."

"A man like you? Who do you think you are, Ricky? I think I'm seeing something else."

Ricky thought about drag and who he really was when Chase wasn't around. It wasn't that he had intentionally kept those things from Chase because he didn't care who knew he was a drag queen. He hadn't felt the need to be a character around Chase. He put it down to how vulnerable he had been when they had first met, but it felt like more than that.

"What do you see?" he asked quietly, taking back the vodka and taking another long sip. "I want to know who you think I am."

Chase smiled through the dark. He relaxed his body and started pulling on a loose thread on the edge of the cushion as he stared around the room.

"I see someone strong and resilient," he said softly. "I see pain and confusion. I see someone funny and caring. I see you, Ricky."

"That doesn't sound like me, sweetheart," said Ricky, almost uncomfortably. "I think you've got me mixed up with someone else."

"Nope," said Chase, pretending to think for a moment. "I'm *definitely* thinking about you."

"There's so much you don't know."

"I know." Chase nodded. "But that doesn't mean my perception of you changes."

"It might."

"I doubt it," he said seriously. "You're a good man, Ricky."

Ricky almost brought up Miss Kitty Litter, but he decided not to. He thought he was ready to bring her back to life, but he had been glad of an extra week of just being Ricky. The longer he stayed away from the bar, the more distant he felt from his alter ego.

"What do you see when you look at me?" asked Chase, flipping the question back on Ricky. "Aside from tattoos and muscles."

"I see a lot of tattoos and a lot of muscles." Ricky nodded. "But I see kindness. More kindness than I would have expected from a man like you."

"A man like me?"

"Y'know." Ricky danced his finger up and down Chase. "*Macho*. I don't have a type either, but I usually stay away from men like you."

"Why?"

"Because the thought of the rejection scares me," he blurted out without even thinking about it. "My dad was a sailor in the navy. Tattoos and muscles were his thing. It's probably not even connected. I just always assumed men who are outwardly masculine are all the same."

"We're not."

"I know that. I'm not dense, sweetheart. I told you, I'm complicated."

"I like it," said Chase with a wink. "You keep surprising me."

"You still haven't answered my original question," sighed Ricky. "Why do you like me?"

Chase stared deep into the water, the ripples reflecting against his rugged features. He looked so beautiful and soft in the glow. Even without the tattoos and muscles, Ricky wouldn't have been able to deny the beauty in his face. He looked so much like his older brother, but there was a softness to his eyes that radiated from within.

"Because you're Ricky," he finally said. "I can't explain it. I don't want to. I don't make a habit of talking to men about the way I feel. It's never gotten this deep before. It never gets past sex."

"You sound like a man after my own heart. You've already made me break one of my rules."

"You have rules?"

"Of course!" he laughed. "No names, no second dates and no breakfast."

"We'll be eating breakfast tomorrow," he winked. "Those rules sound like you're cutting yourself off from anything serious."

"Isn't it wonderful?"

Chase pursed his lips. It was obvious he didn't agree. Without telling Chase about Bret, how could Ricky explain why he had an iron cage around his heart?

"I was surprised you said yes to this weekend, Ricky. Why did you?"

"Why did you ask me?"

"Because I wanted to."

"Then there's your answer, sweetheart."

They shared a small smile for a moment before they both looked into the pool. Chase pulled the vodka from Ricky's fingers, took a deep swig and jumped up off the lounger, startling Ricky. He quickly unbuttoned his shirt and tossed it over a giant potted plant along the wall.

"What are you doing?"

"What? You didn't think we'd come to the pool and not take a dip?" Chase bit into his lip as he worked the belt of his jeans. "Don't argue with me."

"Arguing is my favourite hobby, sweetheart. I'm not going in there. It's probably full of chemicals this time of night."

"Says the man who drinks vodka like mountain spring water." Chase kicked off his shoes and peeled off his jeans so that he was standing on the edge of the water in nothing more than his tiny, white briefs, which Ricky could right through to spot the outline of his thick, meaty cock. He dipped his toe in the water and jumped up and down like an excited child. "That is *freezing*. You might want another shot of vodka before joining me."

Chase dove perfectly into the pool, barely making a ripple. Ricky watched as he glided under the water like a snake through sand. He broke the surface with a playful smile on his wet lips. He brushed his short hair back and his tattooed biceps dripped water back into the pool.

"Come in!" he urged as he swam back. "It feels so good."

"I'm alright, sweetheart." Ricky took another sip of the vodka, which was nearly half empty. "I'm happy watching."

Chase swam up to the edge of the water and rattled the lounger. It shook, but Ricky's weight kept it on the ground. He scrambled back to the end, clutching the vodka.

"Baby!"

"And proudly so! Ricky doesn't swim."

"Ricky can't swim?"

"That's not that I said. I just don't swim. It's a choice. Some people choose to wear Crocs, I choose not to set fire to those people. We all have choices."

Chase kicked back off the side of the pool like a mermaid and circled around. His soaked briefs peeked through the water momentarily, and Ricky could see everything on display. He gulped and took another sip of vodka. His mind was more than loosened and he had long since lost count of how many shots he had slurped from the metal teat.

Chase surfaced again, an even bigger smile on his face. He seemed content lazily paddling on his back. Ricky hoped he was off the hook. After a couple of minutes of drifting around the pool, Chase swam to the ladder and pulled himself out of the water, taking no notice of how dangerously low the weight of the water was dragging down his briefs. Ricky took another shot.

"You know I can pick you up," threatened Chase with an extended finger. "Don't make me force you!"

"Sweetheart, *nobody* has ever been able to force me to do

something I didn't want to. Good luck."

"Don't make me."

"I said, *good luck*," he said through gritted teeth as he clung onto the edge of the lounger. "I'm not going in!"

"Yes, you are."

Chase ran over to Ricky, a devilish smirk consuming his face. In the low light, he looked somewhere between beautiful and terrifying. Ricky's stomach did that twisting thing he hated. Was it because of Chase or the vodka? He took another swig, just to be sure.

Chase loomed over Ricky, his brows raised high up his forehead and his eyes expectant.

"Chase, I've told you –," Ricky was cut off when Chase scooped his arms under Ricky, as though he was nothing more than a baby. "What are you doing?"

"Exactly what I said," he said as he carried Ricky to the edge of the pool.

Still clutching the vodka, Ricky flew towards the water's surface. The last thing he saw was Chase's face, illuminated with childlike joy. The water collided with his backside like a sharp whip and the blue light consumed him. He thrashed and kicked, his mind and body tumbling in circles as he clung helplessly to the vodka bottle.

He broke the surface, gasping for air at the same moment Chase took a running jump and cannonballed into the water. Ricky relinquished the vodka bottle and splashed the surface to keep his head above water. His clothes felt like lead weights pulling him down, or was it the vodka again? He wiped his eyes and pushed his dark hair out of his face.

"See, I told you this was fun!" cried Chase, his voice echoing in the dark shadows.

"They treat prisoners of war better than this, sweetheart," shivered Ricky, paddling towards Chase to splash him hard with water. "*That's* for manhandling me."

"How else was I supposed to get you in?" Chase splashed him right back. "You're stubborn, you know that?"

"Stubborn is my middle name." He splashed Chase again, his toes finally finding the bottom of the pool. "Well, it's Jeremiah, but I don't shout that one from the rooftops."

"Jeremiah?" he laughed. "You don't look like a Jeremiah. My middle name is Christopher."

"It's an old family name. Richard Jeremiah Thompson. It's a mouthful, isn't it, sweetheart?"

"Think of the Scrabble points!" Chase started to swim to the far edge of the pool. "Let's have a race."

"What are you? Twelve? My limbs don't work that way."

"You came here to workout, didn't you?"

"I came here because you asked me, and I'm starting to wonder why."

"Admit it, you're having fun."

Ricky swam to where Chase was waiting for him. If he really thought about it, it was good to be away from home. His cottage had become a prison, and he was enjoying Chase's company. The vodka was making his mind and heart looser than they usually would be, but he suppressed those particular thoughts, knowing it was the vodka's fault.

"You can't swim in clothes." Chase tugged at Ricky's shirt. "Take them off."

Ricky unbuttoned his shirt and dragged it off his shoulders. It was heavy and awkward, and he had no idea how he was going to get out of his jeans. Before he had to figure it out, Chase swam in front of him, his tiptoes balancing him in the pool. Looking Ricky deep in the eyes, their noses only an inch apart, he unbuckled his belt.

Chase submerged into the water and dragged the jeans down Ricky's legs. He yanked off Ricky's shoes, and they floated to the surface, quickly followed by the blob of denim. Chase popped up between them and wiped his eyes.

Ricky looked down into the water. His Calvin Klein boxers were floating in the water, and his socks felt like weights. He jumped up on the edge of the pool and yanked off his socks. When he started to pull his underwear off, he knew he was drunk.

His underwear landed with a thud on the tiles, and he dropped back down into the water completely naked. It felt so freeing to be one with the water. He bobbed up and down on the surface, with a satisfied smile on his face.

"Well, if you insist." Chase jumped up onto the edge of the pool, and he pulled his briefs down his buttery, inked thighs. Ricky didn't even try to hide that he was staring at Chase's impressively huge flaccid penis. "Ready?"

Ricky tore his eyes away as Chase dropped down into the water and he nodded. He hadn't swum for years, but he knew it was like riding a bike. He grabbed the edge of the pool and got into the starting position. Chase followed and he counted down.

On three, they both kicked off. Ricky clenched his eyes and tore through the water, scooping his cupped palms and kicking his feet like he was a resident of the ocean.

When he reached the other side of the pool, he gripped the edge as Chase came in behind him.

"You let me win," said Ricky as they both caught their breath. "There's *no way* I won that."

"I didn't!" he said. "I'm more of a doggy paddle kind of guy."

"Liar!" Ricky hit the water hard, splashing Chase once again.

Instead of splashing back, Chase jumped on Ricky and pushed him under the water with both hands. Water filled Ricky's mouth as he struggled and kicked with his eyes clenched. He opened them and caught sight of Chase's cock floating in front of him.

Chase let go, and he floated to the surface inches away from Chase's face. He gasped for air as Chase laughed. Ricky couldn't help but join in. Wiping the water away from his face, his laughter slowed, and he detected how noiseless the pool was.

To his surprise, Chase's hand cupped his cheek and caressed his stubble softly. He bit into his lip as water trickled down his skin.

"You're not poison," he whispered quietly. "Don't ever think you are."

Ricky's heart clenched tightly in his chest. This time, he knew it wasn't the vodka. He swallowed hard, but his throat was dry, as though the chlorine water had claimed all of the moisture from his body.

Chase pulled Ricky's face towards his own, and he didn't fight it. Their lips joined and Ricky suddenly didn't feel so intoxicated. His senses became so sharp; he could still smell his own scent on Chase's skin.

Ricky pulled away from the kiss, not because he wanted it to stop, but because he had a better idea.

"Let's go up to the room," Ricky whispered, his breath shaking as he started to shiver in the water. "Now."

Chase nodded, and he didn't say a word. He scooped up Ricky's hand, just as he had in the dark changing room, and they swam to the water's edge. Chase climbed out and then helped Ricky up onto the cold tiles.

"What about our clothes?" asked Ricky. "We can't put them back on."

"I can't see any towels." Chase scooped up his clothes and tossed Ricky his. "It's late. Let's make a run for it."

"Are you crazy?"

"As a box of frogs," Chase said with a playful wink.

"Who cares if somebody sees?"

As they crept through the dark changing room, hand in hand and clutching their damp clothes to their chest, Ricky couldn't believe what they were about to do. When they reached the changing room door, Chase paused and turned to Ricky.

"Ready?" he smirked, darting his brows.

With their hands still joined, they ran down the deserted corridor completely nude. The air licked Ricky's skin, and the vodka washed around in his mind.

They burst into reception, but they didn't slow down. It was dark and empty, so they sprinted for the staircase. Taking them two at a time, they reached the top in no time.

As they ran down the corridor in their birthday suits, a man in a tuxedo pushed along a room service trolley. He stopped in his tracks, his eyes darting from each of their faces, to each of their penises and to their joined hands. He looked like he was about to speak, but no words came out.

"Lovely night for a stroll, isn't it?" said Chase as they passed the man.

They walked carefully until he resumed walking and hurried to the end of the corridor and out of sight. They ran to their room, and Ricky scrambled for the wet keycard out of his pocket. He slotted it into the electronic lock four times, and when it eventually clicked, they fell into the bedroom.

"*Lovely night for a stroll*, sweetheart?" Ricky laughed as he slammed the door. "The poor guy is going to need counselling."

Still holding Ricky's hand, Chase pulled him away from the door and into his arms. They stared into each other's eyes, both of them on the brink of laughter.

"You're beautiful," whispered Chase. "I hope you know that."

"You're not too shabby yourself, sweetheart."

Ricky felt Chase's cock twinge against his own. A fire ignited deep in his core, and their lips joined once again in a heated flurry of passion. Falling backwards together, they landed on the soft mattress in a pale strip of moonlight piercing through the darkness.

Ricky edged up the soft sheets and rolled over to his nightstand. He tore open his wallet and pulled out a small silver square.

Without saying a word, he dropped it onto the bed next to them. Chase crawled up Ricky's body, his kisses easy against his skin. Their lips joined again, and Chase's weight pushed Ricky into the soft mattress. He needed to feel Chase inside of him. It was hunger that had long since deserted him, and he wasn't going to ignore it.

"Fuck me," whispered Ricky, pulling away from the kiss to bite Chase's earlobe. "Fuck me, Chase."

Ricky squirmed under Chase's weight to turn over, but Chase's arms fired up and clutched Ricky's wrists, pinning him to the bed. Ricky stared up into the dark, the cool moonlight barely lighting up the burning expression taking over Chase's features.

"No," he said. "I want to look you in the eyes."

Ricky could do nothing but nod. He shrunk into the sheets, feeling so unlike the man he thought he was. Chase leaned in and planted a soft kiss on his lips. He pulled away to look deep into Ricky's eyes. He repeated the move, kissing him even deeper. Each time he pulled away to look at him, the fire burned more ferociously.

Chase dove in once more. His tongue probed Ricky's mouth, delicately flicking and dancing against his own. Ricky's hands found their way into the back of Chase's short hair. With a gentle nudge, he guided Chase back down his body. His tongue ran softly in a perfect line down

Ricky's form, his eyes not breaking contact.

When he felt his tongue hit the solid head of his cock, Ricky tossed his head back into the bed and moaned. He moaned louder than he knew he should have, but any concern about anyone hearing them had vanished when they ran naked through the country house.

Chase took Ricky's length in his mouth, his eyes looking deeply into Ricky's the whole time. Ricky had never liked it when his fucks looked up into his eyes, but there was something different about the look in Chase's. He wasn't looking for approval or praise; he was looking deep into Ricky. He was looking deeper than a person had dared to look in so long.

Chase's tongue travelled from Ricky's shaft to in between his thighs. He spread them slowly and dragged Ricky's hips upwards. His playful tongue hit Ricky in the sweet spot, and he moaned once more. Chase had discovered Ricky's biggest weakness, and encouraged by his moans, Chase lost all shyness.

Chase pulled away and reached out for the silver packet. He tore down its side with his teeth, and he slid the condom down his thick shaft. It snapped around his base with a satisfying pop.

Everything suddenly felt real for Ricky. He suddenly remembered who he was and how he was breaking all of his own rules, the spoken and the unspoken ones. It went against every fibre of his being, but he couldn't summon the energy to stop Chase. He wanted it too badly; he craved it.

The tip of Chase's shaft brushed against Ricky, teasing him. Ricky knew if he waited any longer, his true self might break through and stop everything. For once, he wanted to feel all that life had to offer. He reached down and guided Chase to where he needed to be.

As he slowly slid into Ricky, Chase shot down and

enveloped Ricky's mouth in passion. His hands wrapped around Ricky's head, fixing him in place. Ricky felt Chase's entire length fill him and he moaned out, begging for more. Chase heard his cries, and he pushed himself as deep as he could go. Ricky breathed in deep, his stomach vanishing into the sheets. His cock rubbed against Chase's skin, sandwiched between their bodies.

Ricky wrapped his arms and legs around Chase so that every part of their bodies were intertwined. Chase rocked his hips with the rhythm of a graceful dancer, gliding in and out of Ricky. The vodka lubricated his mind, drowning Ricky in a sea of heightened desire.

Chase pulled away from Ricky's lips, and he stared down into Ricky's eyes, his lips parted. His tattoos blended into the dark causing his face to glow like a lighthouse on the horizon. Chase bucked his hips, his gaze unwavering and unblinking.

Ricky felt something he had forgotten he could feel during sex. He felt a connection. He ignored the urge to close his eyes, or to roll over and bury his face in the sheets. He looked back at Chase and he saw deep into the man, just as Chase had done with him. It didn't matter that Ricky didn't know everything about Chase, or his life. Their connection was so much deeper than the confines of their physical existence.

Chase's rhythm sped up, but he didn't look away. Beads of sweat fell from his face onto Ricky. One hit his lip, and his tongue caught it. In the sweat, he could still smell his own fragrance, clinging mercilessly to Chase's skin.

Ricky was so used to being fucked, he had forgotten what it felt like to have real sex. He had forgotten that it wasn't about what was happening on the outside, but what was happening within. He had missed the swirling cocktail of emotions that pumped through his body. The true feelings of intimacy had evaded him for far too long.

Chase dove in to kiss Ricky once more, but he didn't close his eyes, so neither did Ricky. They pressed their lips hard together as they breathed through their noses and looked into each other's souls. Ricky's fingers dug into the back of Chase's scalp, and his gentle thrusting increased. The harder he breathed, the harder he fucked Ricky. No matter how hard and fast he went their connection never broke.

Chase's fingers wrapped around Ricky's hair, and he pulled his head to the side. He nuzzled Ricky's neck, discovering another one of his sweet spots. Ricky moaned loudly, but he couldn't hear it over the pounding of his heart.

He let go of Chase's head and slapped down on the bed, his fingers gripping handfuls of the expensive sheets. He had handed all control over to Chase, and it felt amazing.

Chase's mouth found its way up Ricky's jaw and back to his mouth. Ricky closed his eyes, but when he opened them, Chase was looking deep into him once again. He pounded harder and faster, more and more sweat gathering on his brow. Ricky knew what was coming. He wanted to prolong it, but he also wanted to feel everything he could, right at that moment. Just like Chase, he wasn't sure he could wait any longer.

As though he could hear these thoughts, Chase's fingers disappeared between their bodies and he massaged Ricky's shaft. He knew it wasn't going to take long.

"I'm close," Chase grunted, breaking the silence. "I'm so close."

Ricky leaned up and joined their lips once again. Chase didn't look away, his eyes wanting and begging. Ricky nodded, knowing he was also on the edge. He felt Chase tighten up on top of him. Ricky stopped trying to hold back, and he released. His cock jerked between them as Chase's fingers gripped it tightly. The thrusting stopped and so did their kissing. Every cell in Ricky's being exploded and vibrated as a mist devoured his eyesight. He blinked and panted into the dark, searching for Chase.

Chase's green eyes claimed him once more in the blackness, and for that moment, they were the only two people in existence.

And then it all stopped. The silence was broken with a ringing in Ricky's ear and Chase pulled out and rolled onto his side next to him.

Ricky knew there was plenty to regret, but he would leave that for the morning. He closed his eyes as he caught his breath. Chase toyed with his hair, looping his dark strands around his fingers. Ricky fell asleep thinking dangerous and enlightening thoughts about the man lying next to him.

CHAPTER

THIRTEEN

The light pierced through Chase's heavy sleep like a sword through flesh. He darted upright and grabbed his head, the promise of a hangover already on the horizon. Looking around the room, it took him a moment to realise he wasn't at home. Ricky slept softly by his side, clutching a pillow to his chest on top of the sheets.

Chase leaned in and kissed him softly on the forehead, remembering what they had done the night before. Ricky didn't wake, but Chase didn't mind. Ricky looked peaceful in his sleep, something he rarely did when he was awake.

Chase walked naked across the room to the menu next to the phone. He flicked to the breakfast section and spotted two overpriced, full English breakfasts. Speaking quietly into the handset, he ordered the breakfast, suddenly remembering what Ricky had said about his rules, and wondering if they were beyond that.

Sitting in the occasional chair by the window, he watched Ricky roll over across the bed. He opened and closed his mouth and licked his lips, but he didn't wake. Chase wondered how they had gotten to the point they had last night.

It wasn't until he had been on top of Ricky, looking into his eyes, he realised he had been nervous to have sex with him. There was no going back from sex. During the act, he hadn't worried about the repercussions, but in the cold light of day, he wondered how things were going to change.

Ricky had freaked out about their kiss in the gym. Was that going to happen again when he opened his eyes? Chase hoped not. He turned and looked out over the gardens as a man mowed the neat lawn far in the distance. He realised he had never had sex like it before, and that scared him.

Ricky didn't slot easily into his life, and outside the confines of the gym or Coltrane House, he knew they didn't work. How could they? Chase had to think about his son, and he couldn't see where Ricky fit into his life.

He turned back to Ricky and his heart burned. It had only been a month, but it burned so brightly. Could he ignore those feelings?

There was a soft knock at the door. Chase grabbed one of the hotel robes from the closet. Ricky stirred from his sleep and rubbed his eyes, yawning and groaning. Chase crossed the bedroom and opened the door to a man with a silver trolley.

"Good morning, sir," he said, avoiding Chase's eye contact. "Shall I come in and serve?"

"Sure," he croaked, his voice raw and tired.

Chase stepped to the side and let the man push his trolley into the room. It wasn't until he passed within an inch of Chase's eyes that he recognised the man as the same man from the corridor the night before.

He pushed the trolley across the bedroom, avoiding looking in the direction of the bed where Ricky was sitting up, hugging the large pillow to his naked body. He looked dazed and confused as he stared ahead into space, his brows heavy and his jaw tight.

The man set out the two plates of breakfast along with a brimming French press filled with coffee, two cups, a selection of sugar, milk, and two full glasses of orange juice. When he was done, Chase grabbed his wallet from his still wet jeans and pulled out a soggy ten-pound note and handed it over. The man accepted it gladly and hurried out of the room, casting an apologetic glance in Ricky's direction. In the light of the morning, he didn't look any older than twenty.

"What's all this?" mumbled Ricky through the sleep haze. "What time is it?"

"Breakfast and I don't know. Early. Not too early to order room service, though. Come and eat."

Ricky stared silently at the food on the table, as though he had never seen a full English breakfast before. Chase sat at the table and poured them both coffees. Ricky stumbled naked across the room and sat in the chair opposite him. They ate in silence for a while, until Ricky finally spoke.

"What time do we have to be at these classes?"

"We don't have to be at any of them," said Chase. "Not if you don't want to."

"Isn't that the whole point of coming here?"

"Maybe." He bit hard into a sausage. "It's up to you. I'm happy to stay in this room all day."

Ricky scooped a spoonful of beans and chewed silently. Chase picked up on the awkwardness between them and wondered if Ricky was like this every morning. If he was a DJ, he probably wasn't a morning person.

After they finished eating, they sat drinking their coffee in silence. With every sip, Ricky seemed to become more alive. When they were finished, he walked over to the closet and put on a grey t-shirt and a pair of black boxers.

Chase followed his lead and climbed into a pair of sweatpants. He grabbed his cigarettes off the writing desk and heaved open the giant window. Leaning out into the fresh air, he placed a cigarette between his lips, wondering how he had fallen asleep last night without his usual after-sex smoke. Ricky appeared by his side and plucked one from the box.

Chase lit both of their cigarettes, and they blew their smoke into the air. It felt like an unspoken acceptance of what had happened. Part of Chase wanted to talk about it, but an even bigger part didn't want to ruin what had happened with words. Their bodies had said more than their words could, even if it took vodka to get them there.

It turned out Ricky did want to check out the 'Introduction to Aikido' class Chase had signed them up for in the afternoon. At noon, they sauntered downstairs to the front of the manor house, where the class was being held on the front lawn.

They breezed through the class, learning the different techniques of the martial art. No matter how hard Chase tried to memorise the techniques, so he had something to show his brother, he couldn't seem to take his eyes away from Ricky.

After Aikido, they headed into the main hall for lunch. They grabbed some food from the self-service buffet and joined Paul and Justin on a table in the middle of the buzz.

"Where did you two sulk off to last night?" asked Paul as he bit into a raw carrot. "We were the last ones in the bar. They had to brush us out in the early hours."

"Ricky had a headache, and I wasn't really feeling it

either," the lie rolled easily off Chase's tongue. "I'm getting old."

"If your brother was here, he would never have let you go to bed early. What's happened to you, Chase?" said Justin.

Before Chase could say anything, Mack joined their table, sitting directly next to Ricky. He had almost forgotten what Mack had said to Ricky the night before, but Ricky's body language quickly reminded him.

"Where did you two get off to last night?" Mack asked the same question. "Up to no good?"

"Headache," said Paul. "I told them they missed a good night."

"Yeah, it was great," said Mack. "Although there were two people having a better time than us. Two idiots broke into the pool last night."

"Broke in?" laughed Justin as he stirred a pot of yoghurt into muesli. "How do you break into water?"

"It was closed," Mack said through gritted teeth. "They snuck in through the changing room."

"Hardly a break in then?" added Paul.

"Same difference. Pool's shut this morning for extra cleaning. We wouldn't have even known, but there was a pair of wet underwear hanging over a plant, so we looked back through the security footage."

"Sounds like somebody got lucky last night!" hooted Paul. "Good on him."

"It was two guys," said Mack suspiciously, looking directly into Chase's eyes.

"Well, good for them."

"Streaked through the halls naked," he said. "Almost gave one of the servers a heart attack."

"Jesus," laughed Justin. "Seems like we missed out on the real fun. I wonder who it was."

"I don't know," said Mack. "CCTV was fuzzy, but I'm sure we'll find them."

Mack's eyes spoke a thousand words. Chase knew there wouldn't be many men covered from neck to ankles in tattoos. He hadn't even considered the security cameras. Was Mack trying to embarrass Ricky for what he had done, and dragging Chase through the mud as collateral?

The rest of the lunch went by quickly, and Paul and Justin excused themselves to set up for their HIIT class. Before Mack could say another word, Ricky stood up with his plate and Chase followed.

"He knows," said Ricky. "What's he trying to do? Out you?"

"I don't care," said Chase. "He's just bitter."

"Can you blame him?"

They headed back to their room and Chase headed into the bathroom for another bath, leaving Ricky to his book. Lowering himself into the hot water, he considered outing himself to Paul and Justin before Mack had a chance to. He knew Paul and Justin wouldn't care because they were nice guys, but how long until that news spread back to his brother? An hour? A day? A week? A month?

Rubbing the bar of soap over his chest as he relaxed in the bathtub, he wondered if that was such a bad thing. He tried to imagine Ricky somewhere in his future, but he still didn't know where he fit in, if he did at all. Ever since he had found Ricky in the alley, he had been hoping they could spend more time with each other, and that feeling had only intensified.

Pushing those thoughts to the back of his mind, he decided they were a problem for another day. Right now, he had another full day in the Yorkshire countryside with Ricky, and he didn't want anything to spoil that. If they only had the weekend, it would be a perfect weekend.

Deciding he was going to confront Mack the first chance he got, he sunk deeper into the bath and he closed his eyes.

When he opened them again, the bright afternoon sun had faded from the bathroom. He jumped out of the cold water and rubbed his eyes. He checked his phone and it was nearly four. How long had he been asleep?

He scrolled through his contacts and stopped at '*Annie – Next Door*' and hit the green button. It rang three times before she answered in her best telephone voice.

"Annie, it's Chase. How's Dylan?"

"Chase!" she cooed down the handset. "How's the fitness camp going? Dylan is fine. He's just here doing some colouring. I'll put him on."

"Daddy!" Dylan cried down the phone. "I'm having the best time. Annie lets me have ice cream and trifle! She's ace."

"Are you being good?"

"Yeah. Annie has these weird things she calls videos with old cartoons on them. They're so weird. When are you coming home?"

"I'll be home on Monday. Two more days."

"I miss you," he said. "Be quick."

Chase's heart clenched in his chest, and he felt guilty for leaving Dylan to be with Ricky. Remembering he would have done the same to spend the weekend with his brother, he pushed that guilt away.

When Dylan bored of him, he passed the phone back to Annie. She assured him everything was perfect and she would call if there were any troubles. He tossed his phone on the side and started to dry himself with the towel.

It struck Chase that he still hadn't told Ricky about Dylan. He felt guilty, but for a completely different reason. He hadn't intentionally hidden his son from Ricky. How could he? Dylan was his whole world, but the longer he didn't mention him, the more he had found himself biting his tongue whenever he almost came up in conversation.

Chase looked at the door and wondered if he should tell Ricky now. He climbed back into his clothes, remembering how he wanted the perfect weekend. He made a silent promise that he was going to explain everything to Ricky when they were back home.

He spritzed Ricky's aftershave on his neck and basked in the spicy cloud. Feeling calm and refreshed, he unlocked the door. Walking into the bedroom, he expected to see Ricky having a nap on the bed.

Ricky wasn't on the bed. He wasn't even in the room. Chase flicked on the lamp on the nightstand and looked around for a note. He couldn't see anything. He opened the closet, but all of Ricky's stuff was still there.

Turning on the spot, he wondered where in the hotel Ricky could have gone. He was about to walk back into the bathroom to grab his phone to ring Tom for Ricky's number, but something sitting on the edge of the bed caught his eye.

It was Chase's wallet. Its brown leather skin almost blended into the deep, red sheets, but some colour jumped out, catching his attention. It was open. He spotted the picture of him and Dylan at Dylan's Christmas carol concert from two years ago. Dylan was on his shoulders dressed like a little elf, and Chase was wearing a knitted jumper that Barbara had helped Dylan buy him. In bright green letters, the words 'World's Best Dad' beamed up at him, burning him like a brand.

Telling Ricky when they got back home wasn't going to work, because Ricky already knew. Grabbing his phone and keycard from the bathroom counter, he headed out of the room, with no idea where to start looking.

***

Ricky leaned against the tree and smoked his cigarette. He looked up at the manor house, trying to spot their bedroom in the dim light. Grey clouds had moved over the countryside and they had been teasing rain in the hours Ricky had been standing smoking in the garden.

He didn't know how many cigarettes he had smoked. Each one had been more bitterly disappointing than the last, not providing the clarity he had hoped for.

Chase had a son. Ricky didn't know how much clearer things could get. He had allowed the possibility of happiness to cloud his judgement, and he had done the one thing he had avoided doing for a decade. Letting Chase in had been a mistake; he knew that now.

Tossing the cigarette into the grass, he blew out the smoke and walked towards the manor house as the sun drifted out of the sky. He checked his phone and it was nearly seven. The only reason he hadn't gone straight to the bar was because it hadn't been open when he had left Chase in the bath.

Ricky had stumbled upon Chase's wallet by accident. The European lady, who he learned was named Helen, called up to the room and asked for a card to charge the morning's room service too. Ricky was going to use his card but he hadn't been able to find his wallet. Chase's had been sitting on the side, so he grabbed it and hung up immediately when he saw the photo.

It had only taken him seconds to figure out the situation. He didn't blame Chase for keeping it a secret. Ricky had his own secrets and more than one of them. He didn't feel angry towards Chase, he felt angry with himself. How could he let his barriers down like that?

Swearing he wouldn't do it again, he walked into the

empty bar and sat on one of the stools. He ordered vodka on the rocks and knocked it back, which was quickly replaced and also knocked back. It didn't even touch the sides.

The bartender gave him a look he had seen many times before. It was disgust, followed by pity. Ricky ordered another drink and took it to a booth, out of view of the prying eyes behind the bar.

He laughed bitterly and shook his head. He had let everything happen the way it had and he only had himself to blame. He checked his phone and there were multiple missed calls from an unknown number and even more calls from Tom. He pressed the button on the side and watched the screen fade from life.

Tom would love to see him now. He would lecture him and tell him to believe in the dream again. Ricky knew he had to wake up from dreams and they had a habit of slipping away.

Sipping the vodka, he wished the sex hadn't been so great. The connection had lulled him into a false sense of security, but his body still ached for it. It was a craving he knew he couldn't satisfy.

Why had he ignored his own rules? He should never have eaten the breakfast. It would have been easier if he had thanked Chase for the gesture, dressed and caught a taxi home.

His rules were his armour. After Bret, he didn't know how he could live his life without the man he loved. The armour was put in place for a reason, to protect him from this feeling.

He twirled his phone around in his fingers, wondering why he hadn't called a taxi yet. His wallet was in the leather jacket he was wearing, where it had been since setting off from Hebden Bridge. Sticking around was only making things more complicated, but Ricky always had been a glutton for punishment.

The door opened and in walked Mack, and he immediately noticed Ricky. He had half expected to see Chase. Mack crossed the bar and joined him in the booth without an invitation.

"What do you want?" Ricky sneered. "Come to cry about your marriage again?"

"Chase is looking for you," he said dryly.

"So?"

"I know it was you two in the pool."

"Good for you. Do you want a cookie?"

"What?"

"Piss off, Mack. I'm not in the mood."

"Trouble in paradise already?" he laughed, shaking his head. "From what I've heard about you, that's to be expected."

"You don't know what you're talking about, so shut your mouth."

"No." Mack clicked to the barman and ordered a beer. "Drinking alone is pathetic."

"I am pathetic."

"At least you know it. I don't know if that's brave or even more pathetic."

The bartender put a beer in front of Mack and a fresh vodka in front of Ricky, and this time, it was a double. He tipped his head to the barman and tossed it back.

"I guess I'm more pathetic than I thought then," he said. "If you don't mind, I'm going to go somewhere else. Anywhere else in fact, as long as you're not there."

"But I just ordered a drink."

"So drink it alone, and you can be the pathetic one," he snapped, already irritated by Mack. "What do you want from me? To berate me for fucking your man? To embarrass me for streaking through the halls? To out me to these ball-scratching straight men? *I don't care*, Mack. When are people like you going to realise? I don't care about any of that anymore. I'm Ricky. I'm a mess and I don't care."

"I pity you."

"Join the club."

"I pity you because you actually believe you don't deserve to be happy." He crammed the neck of the bottle in his mouth and downed a good mouthful before wiping it away with the back of his hand. "I built you up to be the devil in my mind, but it's actually quite sad to look at you."

"It's nothing I don't see in the mirror."

"What happened to you, Ricky?" he asked, sighing heavily as he clung to his bottle of beer. "What made you so bitter?"

"Life."

"We all have it tough. We're not all like you."

"One of me is enough."

"That's true. You're a handful."

"Are you trying to be a mate here, or are you trying to make me feel worse? Because I don't need either, not from you."

"Leave then," he said with a casual shrug. "See if I care. You can be pathetic here, or you can be pathetic somewhere else. Here, there's free alcohol."

Ricky looked at the bar, admitting that Mack had a point. He sat back in the booth and signalled to the bartender for another top up. The drink was swiftly replaced, and it was the first one to finally take the edge off.

"Why did you marry him if he cheated on you?"

"I loved him," Mack replied. "I *still* love him. It's not been the same since. You ruined my life."

"That wasn't me, sweetheart. If Johnny hadn't fucked me, it would have been someone else."

Mack stared into the opening of the beer bottle, his jaw tight and his eyes focussed. It was obvious he knew Ricky had a point, even if he didn't want to admit it.

"It was still *you*. You charmed him."

"I have a habit of doing that."

"You have this aura. You suck people in. You're doing it to me right now."

"Believe me, I'm *not* trying."

"It's just you, Ricky. It's sad you don't see it."

"Are you my shrink now?" Ricky rolled his eyes, looking at the door and wondering if being on his own was better than a free bar with a psychopath. "If you are, good luck with what you find."

"You're such a cliché," he said in a low voice, leaning across the table. "You know that, yeah?"

Mack's words struck Ricky. He tried to figure out what he meant, but he couldn't put his finger on it.

"Something clearly happened to you, and you're lashing out at the world," Mack explained. "You're transparent. It's not original, it's not unique, and it's not doing you any favours."

"Maybe this is my lot in life."

"It's self-inflicted."

"Maybe this is what I want."

"Nobody wants to be miserable," said Mack, clearly irritated. "You're an idiot if you think you really want to be miserable. Are you going to tell me what happened to you?"

"Tell you?" Ricky laughed. "Have I just woken up in *The Matrix*?"

"So something did happen?" Mack asked, rather pleased with himself.

The worst year of Ricky's life flashed through his mind. He thought about Bret's grave, sitting under the dark clouds, only a couple of miles away. How long had it been since he had visited?

"I was engaged."

"I don't see a ring."

"He died."

"Oh. I'm sorry."

"No, you're not. I ruined your life, remember."

"At least I got to marry my fiancé, flaws and all. You never got the chance to mess your own marriage up."

Mack's words once again struck Ricky the wrong way. At first, he felt seething anger and he had to stop his hand from smashing his glass into the side of Mack's head. It took a minute for his words to sink in, but he knew he was right. The worst thing in the world had happened to Ricky, and he was somehow still standing.

"The only way for you to fix your marriage is to get even," said Ricky. "You'll resent him forever if you don't."

"Sleep with somebody else?"

"You're gay, sweetheart. It's in your DNA."

Ricky didn't really believe that. He had never cheated on Bret, and he never would have. He didn't doubt for a second if they had gotten married that they would still be together and happy. Sometimes he lay awake at night thinking about that version of Ricky and how much better he would probably have been. Instead, Ricky had spent his life living up to the stereotype that gay men were promiscuous, just to further his own self-inflicted prison. He reminded himself that it was armour, but he knew he could have that armour without the constant stream of men in his bed.

They carried on talking and drinking. Ricky didn't know how long they sat there for, but he drank himself sober. Eventually, it felt like they were almost friends, in a twisted way.

"Let's just say I did sleep with someone else?" Mack

pointed his bottle at Ricky. "Do I tell Johnny?"

"No, you just need to know you did it."

"But what's the point in that?"

"Johnny isn't the one who is beating himself up. He knows I was just a mistake. I was nothing to him, and he was nothing to me. You just need to have easy, quick, casual sex with someone to get it out of your system. You're probably jealous that he got to fuck somebody, one last time. You still put a ring on it."

"Because I love him."

"Exactly."

"So what you're saying is, I should fuck someone else because I love him?"

"To *save* your marriage." Ricky tapped his finger hard on the wood. "It's the *only* way. I'd say the same to anyone else."

"So let's do it," said Mack. "Let's fuck."

"*What?*"

"You and me. Who else? You fucked Johnny, so I fuck you and the loop closes."

"That makes no sense at all."

"It makes perfect sense."

"No, it really doesn't."

"Ricky, it does. Come up to my room and I'll show you."

Mack stood up and swayed on the spot, clearly not able to handle his drink as well as Ricky. Ricky thought about Chase and he instantly felt guilty for even considering it. He knew that was the reason he had to do it. If he didn't fuck somebody else and purge his system of the feelings he was starting to develop for Chase, he wouldn't be able to move on.

Maybe he was drunk after all, but he didn't care. It was what Ricky did. It was his own loop, but he was just rebooting the cycle. He needed to, for the sake of protecting his heart.

He followed Mack up to his room on the third floor. His room was smaller than the one he had shared with Chase.

"You got a condom?" asked Mack, bumping into the post of the bed. "I can't call them jonnies. Johnny doesn't like it."

"Yeah, in my wallet," said Ricky, looking around the room as he produced the small, silver packet. "Here."

He tossed it onto the bed and Mack picked it up. He unbuckled his belt and let his jeans fall to the ground. It was nothing like the sex from the night before, but it was everything like the sex Ricky was used to. There would be no kissing, no tenderness, and no build up. He didn't have to worry about feelings and breakfast in the morning. He knew Mack's name, but could easily forget it again.

He watched Mack cram the condom down his semi-erect shaft, and he knew the vodka hadn't numbed his attraction to Chase. He tried to ignore that attraction, to push it to the back of his mind. He was Ricky; this was what he did.

CHAPTER

FOURTEEN

"Tom, I'm getting really worried now. His phone is switched off, and it's dark out. I've asked everyone and checked everywhere, twice! *Yes*, I've checked the bar. He wasn't in there. I think he's left. Can you check his cottage again? Oh, you're still there. Just let me know if he comes home. What caused it? I caused it. I lied to him. Well, it wasn't a lie. I just didn't tell him something."

Chase collapsed onto the bed, explaining everything to Tom. He poured his heart out and Tom listened to every word. At the end of his confession, Tom wasn't so surprised at Ricky's sudden disappearance.

After hanging up, Chase picked up his wallet and stared at the picture. It always brought a smile to his face every time he opened his wallet. How could he even try to keep his happiness a secret?

A soft knocking at the door made him snap his wallet shut. He jumped up from the bed and hurried across the room. Chase tore open the door expecting to see Ricky. It wasn't Ricky.

"Excuse me, Mr. Brody. We still need a card for your account and your line has been engaged for most of the day."

"Of course," he said, pulling his card from his wallet and handing it to the woman. "Take it for as long as you need it."

"I'll be right back up with it, Mr. Brody."

Chase closed the door and collapsed back onto the bed. He knew he should eat, but he felt sick from worrying. He no longer cared what Ricky thought about him. Ricky could hate him all he wanted, he just wanted to know he was okay.

There was another knock at the door, and he walked back across the room, already knowing what to expect. He opened the door and held out his hand for his card.

"Do you want me to shake it, sweetheart?"

Chase looked up and his heart stopped pounding in his chest. Sweet relief spread through his body and he couldn't stop himself from wrapping his arms around Ricky and squeezing him tight. The protectiveness he had felt for Ricky since their first meeting was just as alive as ever.

"I was so worried about you!" Chase pulled away and grabbed his Ricky's face. "I was thinking the worst."

"I'm fine."

Chase stepped to one side and let Ricky into the room. He didn't have to inhale too deeply to smell the strength of the vodka on Ricky's breath. Ricky crossed the room and stood next to the window, staring out into the darkness.

"Where have you been? I've looked everywhere for you!"

"Around. I'm sorry."

"You don't have to apologise. I should be the one apologising. Let me explain everything."

"You don't have to explain. I need to explain," Ricky mumbled, still staring into the dark. "I've done something terrible."

"So have I."

"Not as terrible as me, sweetheart," Ricky tried to inject lightness into his voice, but it sounded sad. "Me and Mack, we – *I* –,"

Chase's stomach knotted, and he sat on the edge of the bed and dropped his face into his hands, readying himself for the worst. He didn't own Ricky. After what had come to light, he doubted anything else was going to happen. Tom had told him Ricky's biggest fear was commitment. He wouldn't say why, but a child was the biggest sign of commitment Ricky could see. He shied away from anything conventional, and the perfect family was as taboo as it got for Ricky. Chase had heard those words from Ricky's own mouth, but he hadn't put the pieces together.

Despite their sudden lack of any future, Chase still didn't want to hear that Ricky had slept with Mack, especially after what they had shared last night. He didn't want to muddy the waters of the memory.

"I don't want to hear it," said Chase. "Just forget it."

"No, I can't," said Ricky. "I need to explain."

"I said I *don't* want to hear it."

Ricky didn't seem to be listening. He picked up the occasional chair from under the window and turned it around to straddle it, just as he had done when they had first arrived at the hotel the day before. Chase almost couldn't believe that had only been just over twenty-four hours ago. So little had happened, but so much had changed, and then changed again.

Ricky lit up a cigarette without opening the window. It became apparent to Chase he was going to tell him every gory detail if he liked it or not.

"I was looking for a card to give to reception when I saw that picture of your kid. Your son, I mean. I don't even know his name. He looks like you. I grabbed my jacket and I left. I didn't know what else to do. It all got too serious. It was all too much. Too much for me to deal with."

Ricky paused and inhaled deeply on the cigarette letting the ash tumble from the end onto the expensive carpet. Chase knew Ricky would probably be the same without the aid of vodka.

"I stood outside for a while. I was trying to figure out which windows were ours. I didn't get them right. I waited for the bar to open and I went there to drink myself stupid. All of this is too much for me to deal with. I know I've said that, but it is. Stuff happened to me. I don't want to go into it, not tonight. It reminded me of a dark time. Reminded me why I don't do things like this."

He stood up from the chair and walked slowly over to the minibar. Despite clearly having already drunk a lot, he seemed scarily sober. He plucked out the two remaining beer cans and tossed one to Chase. He caught it, but he didn't open it. Ricky on the other hand, opened the can and sipped at the froth. He sat back on the chair and stubbed his cigarette out on the windowsill.

"Mack came into the bar. I think he was looking to gloat. I wound him up. We wound each other up. We kept drinking and I convinced him he should cheat on his husband to get even. It was stupid. I was just toying with him, but then he convinced me it should be me. I couldn't give a fuck about their marriage, but it made sense to me, *y'know*, sweetheart? If I fucked Mack, I wouldn't care about you. I'd ruin it. Spoil whatever happened last night and I'd be able to move on."

"Ricky, you can stop there. I get it."

"No, I don't think you do, sweetheart. We went up to his room. He asked for a condom, so I gave him one. It was so sterile, so cold. He couldn't even get it up properly. I nearly started laughing."

"I said I don't want to hear it!" cried Chase, tossing the beer can onto the bed and standing up. "If you came to get your stuff, take it and go. Don't torture me. It's not fair, after everything I did for you, don't fuck with me!"

"I'm not." Ricky stood up and put the beer can on the table, next to the plates that were still there from breakfast. "Just let me finish."

There was a knock on the door. Chase knew it had to be the woman from reception again. He almost ignored it, wanting to be left alone with Ricky, but she had his card.

"Yes?" He tore open the door.

It wasn't the woman from reception. It was Mack. A rage grew over Chase's vision; a red haze filled with every angry thought that had crossed his mind that night. All of them erupted out, and Mack was in the firing line. He clutched Mack's jacket and fired him into the opposite wall.

Chase had been invited to his wedding. He thought Mack was a friend. Why would he do this to him? Staring deep into Mack's striking, fear-filled, blue eyes, he tensed his fists around his collar, wanting to squeeze the life out of his body.

"Chase, stop!" Ricky tore him away from Mack. "We didn't do anything. We almost did. I wanted to, but I couldn't."

Mack clutched his throat and coughed looking as confused as anybody could look.

"What?" Chase asked, turning back to Ricky. "You said

you went up to his room."

"I did, but I couldn't go through with it. Mack was getting on top of me and the minute his hands touched my skin, I got out of there. All I could think about was you, Chase. About what we did last night."

"I only came to give you this." Mack thrust Ricky's wallet in front of him. "You must have dropped it. You two are both insane. You're welcome to each other."

Mack left and the receptionist appeared and handed Chase his card back. She must have been able to sense the tension in the air because she scurried off as quickly as she had arrived.

Chase walked back into the bedroom and Ricky followed him. Chase paced on the spot for a moment, trying to absorb what he had just heard.

"I don't care if you had sex with him."

"I didn't. I promise you."

Chase believed him, but he still didn't understand what it meant. He couldn't clear his mind quickly enough to think clearly. Even if Ricky hadn't had sex with Mack, it didn't change things. Chase still had a son and Ricky was still Ricky.

"What now?" asked Chase.

"I don't know." Ricky perched on the edge of the bed, clearly exhausted from the day. "I came straight here. I needed to tell you. I don't know why, I just did. My mind hasn't stopped whirring all day and I couldn't shut it up with vodka, or casual sex. I thought telling you what happened would help, but it's buzzing as loud as ever."

"What's it saying?"

Ricky paused and he looked up to Chase, his eyes filled with sadness but his lips quivered into an empty smile.

"It's telling me to jump," he said coldly. "To take a leap of faith. A big bloody leap if you ask me, sweetheart."

"And because of this thing that happened in your past, you're scared to do that?"

"Bingo. I guess you've been talking to Tom again."

Chase felt guilty for even discussing Ricky with his best friend. It felt like a betrayal.

"You don't have to do anything you don't want to do."

"That's the problem, sweetheart. I don't know what I want."

"If it helps, neither do I." said Chase, sitting next to Ricky on the bed. "This isn't how I planned things to happen either. Last night caught me off guard, just like you. I never saw me feeling that way about a guy."

"Straight-ish, you said," laughed Ricky. "I guess we're not so different."

"We seem to keep discovering that."

"It doesn't change things," said Ricky dismissively, suddenly standing up and walking over to the closet. "I'm going to go home. You stay here. Enjoy the fitness and the booze, and I might see you around."

Chase watched Ricky pack for a few moments, but then he realised he didn't want to see Ricky go. If thinking the worst about Ricky's fate had taught him anything, it was that he genuinely cared about what happened to Ricky. He couldn't bear the thought of Ricky going home and beating himself up.

"What happened last night?"

"Let's just forget it. Draw a line under it. You said it yourself, we can't work. You're straight-ish, and I'm Ricky."

Chase's head whirred. He knew what Ricky meant about the buzzing not stopping. He could hear his father and his brother telling him his son needed a mother. That thought was holding him back. Ricky just didn't fit into the life he had with Dylan. How much would they have to bend to make it work?

He was almost on the same wavelength as Ricky, until he remembered how he had felt during the sex. He had felt like a half of a whole. He had felt similar things with people when he was nearly ten inches inside of them, but never as strongly and never as brightly. He had expected the feeling to fade after his orgasm, but it still ached the morning after. It still ached now.

"What about last night?" he repeated, pulling Ricky away from packing his bag. "I know you felt it too."

"So?" Ricky laughed, yanking his arm away. "That doesn't mean shit, sweetheart. It's just hormones. You can ignore them, I should know better than anyone."

"I don't want to ignore them," he said. "I want to see where they go."

"And what if they go nowhere? What if they go haywire and blow up in our faces?"

"Then we at least enjoyed the ride and learned a lesson along the way," said Chase, trying to calm his shaking voice. "This isn't easy for me either. You're not who I expected to end up with."

"Oh, well thank you very much, sweetheart." Ricky got back to packing his bag, even more furiously than before. "I'll call a cab from reception."

"Ricky, just wait. I didn't expect to end up with a man, full stop. I still don't know if I do, but fuck, I'm not just going to ignore how I feel about you. I know you feel it too."

"You can't prove that."

"I don't need to," he said calmly. "I felt it as real as you felt it last night."

Ricky paused his packing and looked down at the floor. It was clear Chase hadn't imagined that intense connection. Something that real couldn't be faked for all of the awards under the sun.

"Just let me go, Chase."

"I can't," he said. "Not yet. Not until we know for certain there's no way we didn't at least give it a chance. There are one hundred different ways this can end, and ninety-nine of them are bad, and you're probably right, it will go tits up in five minutes, and we'll both look like idiots."

"I'm glad you're seeing my way."

"But despite all of that, Ricky, I like you. I really like you. All of those things you hate about yourself, I like them."

"Well, you're crazy."

"I know I am." Chase shrugged, slapping his hands by his side. "But so are you. You're the craziest person I've ever met. I suggested we streak through a hotel naked and you didn't even blink."

They both laughed for a second and Chase could see that he was getting through to Ricky.

"I've done crazier things."

"And I believe it," he said, grabbing Ricky's hands, "but I want you to do something even crazier than that. Crazier than streaking naked through a hotel."

"If you're about to say swallow fire, I've already done that too, sweetheart."

Chase laughed. It didn't surprise him that Ricky had. He knew there were thousands of things he still hadn't learned about Ricky. If he had fifty years to learn all of those things, there were sure to be more stories for another day.

"Just go on a date with me," he said. "That's all I'm asking."

"I think we're past the first date."

"So let's call it a second date," he said, clutching Ricky's hands tightly. "Break your third rule. You've already broken the first two. Be reckless."

Chase knew he was going out on a limb. Staring into Ricky's eyes, he knew there was a one in a million chance he would agree to it. He had thought the same about Ricky turning up for the self-defence class, but he had, even if he had taken him some time. The Ricky he saw was never far from the surface, if still hiding under a layer of stone.

"Fine."

"Fine?"

"I'll go on a second date with you." He said, tensing his jaw. "But that's not a promise of anything more. Everything I said about all of this being too much, it still is."

"I don't doubt it," said Chase, concealing his smile, surprised that his plan had worked. "Since you're packed, shall we head back? I'm not sure this place is as fun as I remembered."

"Oh, I don't know." Ricky shrugged. "The streaking through the corridors was pretty fun, sweetheart."

They packed up the rest of their things and headed down to the reception. It was closed for the night, so they slotted their key cards into the express checkout box and headed for the front door. The night air was crisp, and Chase could smell rain was on its way.

With their bags on the backseat, they drove slowly down the dark, winding driveway. Chase had never been happier to go home in his life.

Neither of them spoke until they finally hit the motorway.

"What's your son's name?" asked Ricky as he stared out of the window into the darkness.

"Dylan."

"I thought so," he said. "Just wanted to check."

CHAPTER

FIFTEEN

On Sunday morning, Ricky was glad to be standing behind the counter in his shop, *Books and Bondage*, for the first time since the attack. He knew he wouldn't get many customers through the door, but it was nice to feel normal.

Waking up that morning, it almost felt like the weekend at Coltrane House had been nothing more than a bizarre dream, but unlike a dream, it didn't slip away from him when he woke up.

When they got back to the village, Chase dropped Ricky off at his cottage. They exchanged numbers for the first time, and Chase went home with a promise to call Ricky. After what they had done, it felt like a step backwards, but it felt like the right step.

Ricky had been surprised to see Tom sleeping in his

armchair when he walked in, and Tom had been just as surprised when he jumped out of his sleep. He attempted to give Ricky another lecture, but he pushed him out the door before he had a chance. He fell asleep the moment his head hit his familiar silk pillow.

After Ricky realised everything wasn't a strange dream, he had to accept what he had agreed to. It felt peculiar having a second date on the horizon. It was a feeling he wasn't sure he liked, but he couldn't back out, he wasn't sure he wanted to.

He flicked through the mail that had been left for him on his cluttered desk in the office. Brendon had sorted the important from the junk, but in the middle, a heavy white envelope with familiar messy handwriting caught his attention. He ripped it open, but he already knew what it was. He glanced over the note attached to the front of the Canary Islands holiday brochure and smiled as he read Brian's note.

'Just in case you change your mind one day, pumpkin. There are plenty of jobs here. Miss you. At least consider a holiday to come and see me! It's been too fucking long Miss Kitty Litter! Call me xxx.'

Ricky tossed the brochure onto the desk without needing to open it. Brian had been sending them annually for the best part of a decade. They had started drag together, but Brian had fled the doom and gloom of Manchester for the never-ending sunshine of Gran Canaria. Brian had been trying to get Ricky to follow ever since.

Ricky thought about life under the sun for a fleeting moment, but his daydreaming was broken when his phone started violently vibrating on the counter in front of him. His first thought was that it might be Chase's newly added number, but it was probably Tom. It was neither. It was Chief Inspector Patrick Brody, who had been added to his phone under '*The Pig*'. He didn't want to answer it. After everything that had happened, he had almost forgotten about the case and the attack. Much like a rash Ricky had once had in his intimate area, the more he ignored it, the worse it got.

He answered the phone, and twenty minutes later he was walking into the police station, blowing fresh smoke out of his lungs. He told the receptionist who he was, and five minutes later, Patrick walked through a door to lead Ricky deep into the station, and into a dark room with a single window, looking out into another, much brighter room.

"Like I said on the phone, we've been following some lines of inquiry, and we've brought some guys in. All I need you to do is tell me if you recognise any of them. Got it?"

"I'm not dense, sweetheart."

A couple of minutes later, a row of men stood before him. All similarly dressed, all similar ages and all similar heights. Ricky wasn't sure he could tell one from the other, never mind pluck one from memories he couldn't trigger.

Ricky stared at the line-up of men. He could feel Chief Inspector Patrick Brody breathing down his neck, but Ricky didn't recognise any of the men. He narrowed his eyes and studied each face, but nothing jumped out at him.

"Nothing." Ricky sighed with exasperation. "I don't recognise any of them. It's been weeks, and I barely remember a bloody thing."

"Just take your time. Have another look."

Ricky walked up and down, assessing each man. They were all forty-something, slightly overweight men with little or no hair. They looked no different than the men who gathered in any pub, on any corner, in any city, on any given day of the week. How was Ricky supposed to pick any of them out as one of his attackers?

"Still nothing."

"They can't see you. This glass is one way. Just take your time."

"I've taken my time, and I still don't remember a thing. This is useless. What's the point in all of this?"

Ricky leaned his hands against the glass and stared into one of the man's eyes. He knew he couldn't be seen, but it didn't stop his stomach from wobbling. He was very aware that one of the men who attacked him could be in front of him right now and he had no way of knowing for sure.

"I remember the brick, I remember him taking my wig. Their faces all look the same." He paused to close his eyes but the harder he tried, the foggier his memory grew. "That's it. I need a cigarette."

"You can have a cigarette soon, Mr. Thompson. Please, just take another look at these men."

"I don't want to. I'm tired of all of this."

Ricky turned away from the window, his hands shaking by his side. He stuffed them in his pockets and fiddled with the packet of cigarettes.

"The longer this goes on, the less likely we're going to find the perpetrator of this crime."

"What are you saying?" Ricky frowned, staring dead into the Inspector's eyes. "That I should drop the case?"

Chief Inspector Patrick Brody's cold expression didn't flinch, but Ricky knew that's what he was hinting at. Ricky had considered withdrawing his statement from the start, but it didn't feel fair.

"I didn't say that," said Patrick. "But it is a possibility you might want to consider."

"But that scumbag who attacked me could do this to somebody else if you don't find him. How am I supposed to live with myself if they get their hands on someone else and do even worse?"

Patrick's eyebrows dropped ever so slightly, casting dark shadows over his eyes. He couldn't have cared less about it happening to somebody else, because he hadn't really cared about what happened to Ricky.

"You dress like a woman in your spare time, Mr. Thompson," Patrick said coldly. "If I were to guess, I'd say these men, whoever they were, took exception to that and that's why you were attacked."

"Are you trying to blame me?" Ricky whispered darkly, suddenly feeling sick. "It's an art form, not a perversion. I didn't ask for this. I was just walking home. I wasn't even in drag when it happened."

"I'm not trying to blame anyone, I can assure you."

"I think you are." Ricky looked the Chief Inspector up and down and stepped around him. "I'm going for a cigarette. You have my number if you find anything else."

Ricky marched through the police station, anger building with each step. He knew the twisting corridors from his all too frequent visits over the last month. He burst out into the reception and headed straight for the door, a cigarette already between his lips.

When he reached the door, something shiny burned brightly in his mind. Was it the fluorescent lights? He clenched his eyes and pulled the cigarette from his lips.

The memory burned brightly for a moment, and he turned back on his heels and hurried back through the station, back to the room he had just stormed out of. The men had already gone, but Patrick was still there, shuffling through paperwork.

"Let me see those pictures," Ricky said, holding out his hand.

Patrick sighed and pulled the mug shots from the file. He dropped them on the desk and sat back in the chair, pinching between his brows as he checked the time on his watch.

Ricky shuffled through the pictures, and when he saw the same shiny thing he had seen in his mind, he felt like he had just kicked the door open. How could he have forgotten that face?

"This one," he said. "This was him. He was the main guy."

"How can you be sure? You didn't remember a thing two minutes ago."

Ricky stared down at the face and he couldn't believe he had forgotten it so easily. He ran his thumb along the name underneath it. His name was Terrance Hoole.

"The earring." Ricky tapped hard on the photograph and pushed it across the table to the lacklustre Inspector. "I remembered his bloody earring, sweetheart."

***

Chase pushed the swing hard and Dylan cried out with joy. It had been so long since he had spent a Sunday at the park with his son. He was taking full advantage of the gym having cover for the rest of the weekend.

"Higher!" Dylan cried. "Higher Daddy!"

"That's as high as you can go," Chase said as he pushed his son. "Otherwise, you'll spin around the bar and then you'll fly off and shoot off into space."

Dylan giggled wildly. The sound of his son's laughter warmed Chase's heart.

When Dylan tired of the swings, they walked to the grass in front of the bandstand. Chase laid out the red blanket, and they sat and ate the picnic he had prepared. When they finished eating, they both leaned back in the grass and looked up at the blue sky, watching the white clouds drift by.

"That one looks like a dragon." Dylan pointed out.

"What about that one? That one looks like a monkey."

"No, it doesn't," he giggled. "You're so silly, Daddy."

Chase inhaled the warm air, completely content for the first time in weeks. He pulled out his phone, resisting the urge to call Ricky. He knew if anything was going to work, he needed to give Ricky space and move at a pace that wouldn't terrify him. Chase looked at Dylan, knowing taking things slowly was the only option. He tried to envision a day when he would introduce Dylan to Ricky, but that day felt so far off, it wasn't even in Chase's reach.

"Daddy, what's a fag?"

Chase sat up and stared down at his son, wondering where that question had come from. Did he mean a cigarette? Chase had always made a conscious effort not to smoke in front of his son.

"Where did you hear that?"

"Granddad said you were a fag. He said that's why I don't have a mummy."

"You ignore your granddad," said Chase, trying his best to contain his anger.

He lay back again and stared up at the sky, trying not to worry Dylan. The clouds drifted by, but he didn't pay them any more attention. Dylan chattered away to himself, but Chase's mind was only focussed on one thing.

Knowing he needed to confront his father, he packed up their picnic, and they jumped on the bus home. He hurried along his walkway, but instead of going to his flat, he stopped a door early.

"Oh, Chase. I was just baking a cake. It will be ready in ten minutes so get yourself in here."

"I can't, Annie," he said. "Can you watch Dylan for half an hour?"

"Of course! Is everything okay? You've got a face like thunder."

Chase hadn't realised he was scowling until he saw his reflection in Annie's glasses. He plastered a fake smile on his face and told her he was fine.

After calling Barbara, he found out where his father was, jumped in his car and drove to the suburbs. When he pulled up into the driveway of his brother's house, he noticed his father's car and his blood boiled.

"Chase," Natalie opened the door, a glass of champagne in her hands and a look of surprise in her eyes. "I didn't know you were coming. Come in."

Chase walked into her house and quickly realised he was gate-crashing a party he hadn't been invited to. Natalie's middleclass friends cluttered her kitchen, a couple of them flicking through the books on the kitchen counter.

"Is Patrick here?"

"Somewhere around. Can I get you a glass of champagne?"

"What's all this for?" he asked. "Is it your birthday or something?"

"That's in November," she said coldly, her lips pursed. "I found out something amazing in Germany. I'll let your brother tell you. Ah, here they are."

Danny and their father walked in from the living room, each of them clutching a bottle of beer. They both looked as surprised to see Chase as Natalie had.

"Bro." Danny slapped him on the shoulder. "I thought you were at Coltrane until tomorrow?"

"I came home early," he said, stuffing his hands in his pockets as he looked around the party uneasily. "What's all this for?"

Danny smiled over his shoulder at Natalie. When her hand wandered down and patted her stomach, the jigsaw piece slotted into place.

"I thought it was my gluten intolerance playing up, but I did the test just before my TV spot in Germany, and it said I was eight weeks pregnant."

"Isn't it awesome?" Danny grinned from ear to ear. "I'm going to be a dad, and Dylan will have a little cousin."

Natalie pursed her lips and sipped her champagne, which Chase guessed was alcohol-free and likely just as expensive as the stuff everybody else was drinking. She gave Chase a sour look, as though his mere presence had ruined her party, and she left them to join her friends in the kitchen.

"I would have invited you," said Danny in a low voice. "I honestly thought you were still away. It was all so last minute."

"It's fine. I didn't come for the party. Congratulations by the way."

"Cheers bro. It's pretty major. I was as surprised as you look when I found out."

Chase didn't have the heart to tell his brother that his perplexed expression wasn't about the baby, or the party.

"I called Barbara and she told me you were here," he said to his father, who had been silently sipping his beer and keeping his distance the whole time. "We need to talk."

"What's happened?" asked Danny, looking between them. "Is this about that Sunday Lunch again? Chase, you need to let that go, man."

Chase hadn't brought up the Sunday Lunch since it had happened, nor had he spoken to his father. He guessed that was why he was being so silent. Chase knew he was waiting for an apology, which he was never going to willingly give.

"I need a word," Chase said sternly. "In private."

"Let me grab you a beer."

"I'm not staying."

"What's this about?" Patrick narrowed his eyes as he hovered the beer bottle over his lips. "What have I done now, son?"

Chase looked over to the kitchen, and he caught Natalie looking suspiciously over her shoulder at him. It was obvious she was gossiping about him to her friends. His ink exterior had never fit in with her strictly beige and white style.

"We can do this here, or we can do this somewhere quieter," he said.

"Let's go upstairs," said Danny as he walked over to the spiralling white staircase. "I don't want you to cause a scene on Natalie's big day."

Chase stepped back, and he let Patrick go first. He followed them both upstairs, wondering how he was even going to broach the subject without incriminating himself. They walked along the soft-carpeted hall into Natalie's home office where she wrote her books.

"We're turning this room into the nursery," said Danny proudly. "Natalie doesn't know that yet, but I'm not giving up my gaming room."

Patrick crossed the room, and he sat in Natalie's writing chair. It was the biggest chair in the room and clearly a move to outline his power. Danny sat on the small sofa and spread out his arms, ready to spectate. After softly closing the door, Chase crossed his arms across his chest and stared at his father.

"Why did you tell my son I was a fag?"

"What?" laughed Patrick, shaking his head. "I didn't."

"My son doesn't lie."

Chase clenched his fists under his arms in an effort to stay calm. It was taking all of his strength not to raise his voice.

"He must have overheard me and Barb talking," Patrick

said casually as he sipped his beer. "You know what kids are like, son."

"Is that all this is about?" Danny rolled his eyes, almost looking disappointed that it wasn't something more serious.

"Why did you say I was a fag and that's why Dylan didn't have a mother?"

"Can you blame me? You haven't been with a woman in over six years, and you've been hanging around with *that* idiot."

"So I can't be friends with someone who is gay?"

"It's not normal."

"I'll tell you what's not normal. The amount of shit you keep saying in front of my impressionable six-year-old son. He already doesn't understand why he doesn't have a mum, without you saying stuff like that to confuse him."

"He's got a point, bro," said Danny. "You have been hanging around Ricky a lot recently."

"So?"

"Well, it's a bit weird."

"Would me being gay be the worst thing in the world?" Chase said, before even thinking about it.

Danny and Patrick both looked at each other, their eyes narrowing, as though not sure if they should take him seriously. Chase inhaled deeply, trying to keep his cool, but he could feel a sweat breaking out on his forehead.

"Are you?" asked Patrick, his voice dark and serious.

Chase knew he wasn't gay. If he had to pick a label, he would opt for bisexual, but he knew it was just as bad in his father's eyes.

"No," he said. "I'm not gay."

Even though it wasn't technically a lie, it felt bitter on his tongue. It felt like a denial of what he and Ricky had shared over the weekend.

"So why won't you start dating?" asked Danny. "It's

about time you moved on from Tracey."

"I have."

"Really?" Patrick laughed, spinning to the side in his chair to put his beer bottle on Natalie's writing desk. "From where I'm sitting, I'd say you were still pining after that addict. Let it go."

"You didn't even love her, bro."

"I'm not pining after anybody," Chase snapped, hating how casually they were talking about the death of Dylan's mother. "I've met someone."

Patrick and Danny looked at each other again, even more surprised than his possible admission of being gay. A bead of sweat trickled down the side of his head, anticipating that he was about to wrap himself up in a lie.

"Who?"

"How long has this been going on?"

"It's early days. You don't know them."

"What's her name?"

"Rachel," he said, wondering why that was the first name that came to mind. "I met her on a night out."

"Why didn't you say anything?" said Danny, his eyes narrowed questionably. "Is she a fat bird?"

"Jesus, Danny. I didn't say anything because of questions like that!"

Danny shrugged and sipped his beer. Danny had always been closer to their father. Chase had always wondered if that was because Danny was older and he remembered him more from when they were kids, or because they were naturally more alike. The older Danny got, the more he spoke like their father and the more disappointed Chase felt every time something ignorant left his lips.

"When can we meet her?" asked Patrick.

"When I'm ready. I have Dylan to think about, so I'm taking things slowly."

The door rattled against Chase's back. He jumped away, and Natalie stuck her head through the small gap.

"What are you doing up here? Matt and Rebecca are here. They're asking about you."

"Chase has a girlfriend."

"What?" She slipped into the room and closed the door. "When did this happen?"

"Quite recently, apparently," said Danny. "She's called Rachel."

"Rachel what? I might know her."

Chase looked around the room as he scrambled for a name to give his fictional girlfriend.

"Rachel White," he said. "She's not from around here."

"Does she have a brother called Simon? Simon White?"

"I don't know," he sighed heavily. "Listen, I need to go."

"When can we meet her?" Natalie asked.

"Not yet," said Danny. "When *he's* ready."

"You kept that quiet." Natalie pursed her lips and arched one of her artfully shaped brows. "Don't plan any weddings in the next seven months. I don't want it clashing with my baby."

When the questioning finally stopped, they all made their way downstairs. Danny tried to offer Chase a beer again, but he didn't want to stick around. He hated lying, and he wasn't sure how many fake details he could invent about Rachel White before people became suspicious.

"Bro, you know you can tell me anything," said Danny when they were both at the front door. "I'm a little hurt that you didn't tell me."

"Like I said, it's early days."

"When you're ready, I do want to meet her," he slapped Chase on the shoulders. "I need to make sure she's not imaginary."

Danny closed the door, leaving Chase standing on the

doorstep feeling guilty. If he was ever going to introduce Ricky to his family, he needed to make sure he was really sure it was the right thing to do.

He jumped into his car but before he drove anywhere, he pulled his phone out of his pocket and he scrolled to his newly created contact.

"Ricky, it's Chase. About that second date? Are you free on Thursday night?"

CHAPTER

SIXTEEN

"Wherever you're taking me must be pretty special if you've asked me to wear a suit, sweetheart."

"I wanted to make a good impression," said Chase as they drove into the city. "Have I told you that you look handsome?"

"Twice. If I didn't know better, I'd think you were nervous."

"Nervous?" Chase laughed awkwardly as he pulled off an exit on the roundabout. "A little. You're a hard man to impress, Ricky."

"Me, sweetheart? I think you've got me mixed up with someone else."

They crawled through the city behind a double-decker bus. Ricky looked at every restaurant they passed, wondering when they were going to stop. He watched as Chase drummed his fingers on the wheel. Ricky had never seen him so nervous.

Getting into his suit, Ricky had felt like the most nervous man on the planet. He had been close to cancelling the date at every stage of getting ready, but he resisted. He looked at the suit Chase has crammed himself into, his tattoos poking out of the collar and cuffs and he was glad he hadn't cancelled.

"We'll have to park here," he pulled them into a small multi-level car park tucked down a dark alley.

They left Chase's car in one of the few available spaces on the open top of the building, and they headed back down. Ricky's cigarette was already lit before they reached the street.

"It's not far," said Chase, rubbing his hands together. "I hope you like it."

They walked past the Manchester art gallery with its tall, illuminated, Romanesque columns casting a shadow across the street. Ricky almost hoped they were going to take a left and head into the gay village. That would be comfortable, but they were both wildly overdressed.

Dodging the trams, they crossed the road and walked past Manchester's library. He looked up at the white stone round building, blowing his cigarette smoke into the air. Ricky never found a reason to head into this part of the city.

"It's just up ahead," said Chase as he stuffed his hands awkwardly into his pockets. "I hope we're not too late."

Ricky tossed his cigarette into the road and waited for the tram to pass. When it did, it revealed a grand, red brick building.

"The Midland Hotel?" Ricky mumbled as he read the gold lettering. "Why have you brought me here, sweetheart?"

"The restaurant," he said. "The French. Have you heard about it?"

"Have I heard about it?" he laughed. "I don't live under a rock. Now the suits make sense. It's bloody fine dining, sweetheart."

Chase looked from Ricky to the building. He looked like a scorned child, and Ricky suddenly felt guilty for his tone.

"Is it too much?"

"I've always said there's never such a thing as too much. Lead the way."

They crossed the road and walked up towards the towering Victorian hotel. It had a charm and beauty that Ricky could appreciate, even though he had never stayed there. The rooms were notoriously lavish and expensive, with the restaurant usually booked to capacity most nights. When it had first opened, the press had called it Manchester's first fine dining experience, so naturally, Ricky had stayed far away from it. As they headed up the steps to the manned door, he couldn't understand why Chase would bring him to such a place. It didn't seem to fit either of them.

"Reservation?" The man standing behind the reservations book smiled coldly, his eyes honing in on Chase's tattoos.

"I don't have one, but we only need a table for two."

"Oh, sir," the man laughed, seemingly amused by Chase's greenness. "We're booked up for the next three months. If you don't have a reservation, you can't come in."

Chase looked from Ricky to the man, whose name badge read '*Bruce*'. A bead of sweat trickled down the side of Chase's face and down into his collar. He tugged awkwardly at his tie, looking a little desperate.

"Look, man, it's just a small table for two. Stick us in the back. Help me out here."

"I've got Tuesday on the 28th," he flicked through a book in front of him, "of November."

"Seriously?"

"Chase, let's just go somewhere else," said Ricky, tugging at Chase's sleeve. "It doesn't matter."

"No, it *does* matter." Chase pulled away from Ricky. "You must have something. A cancellation?"

Bruce looked behind him into the full restaurant and turned back, his smile even colder than before. Ricky had known men like Bruce. He didn't doubt for a moment that Bruce had a tiny penis.

"If you're not going to make a reservation, I'm afraid I'm going to ask you to leave."

Chase looked like he was going to launch on Bruce, but another little tug of his suit jacket edged him towards the door. As quickly as they had entered, they left The Midland, and they were back on the street. Ricky pulled his cigarettes from his inside pocket and offered one to Chase. He gladly accepted.

They sat on the bottom step and stared across the street at the giant library. Ricky decided not to speak until they were half way through their cigarettes.

"It was a sweet idea, but I don't need fancy restaurants." He nudged Chase with his shoulder. "Stuff like this doesn't impress me."

"I just wanted us to have a nice night."

"And I'm flattered." Ricky nodded. "That idiot isn't going to ruin it. You've got me all dressed up in a suit and we're in the city. That's an achievement in itself, sweetheart."

Chase finished his cigarette and tossed it into the street. He ran his hands through his short hair and stared up at the ink black sky.

"I'm such an idiot," he said quietly. "As if I thought I could just walk up to the best place in the city and get us a table."

"That *was* pretty stupid," he winked.

"I thought if I bamboozled you with something amazing, you wouldn't even notice you were on a date."

"Bamboozle?" he laughed. "It will take more than a blob and a drizzle of snooty food to bamboozle me, sweetheart."

Ricky finished his cigarette, and he stood up and stretched out. He hated wearing suits. It reminded him too much of funerals.

"Are you sure you don't mind?" said Chase as he stood up. "I feel like I've got you all dressed up for nothing."

"I've always been more of a bag of chips on a street corner kind of guy."

"Honestly?" said Chase, his brow furrowing. "I have an idea. Follow me."

Chase waited for a tram to turn the corner and he ran across the road, signalling for Ricky to follow him.

Ricky was surprised that he hadn't used it as an excuse to go home. Despite the uncomfortable suit, he was happy to be spending the evening with Chase, even if he had no idea where they were going.

***

"This is more like it! A box of wine, and fish and chips."

Chase tossed a vinegar soaked chip into his mouth. He felt like a fool for trying to impress Ricky. He should have known he hadn't needed to try so hard.

Ricky licked his fingers, tossed the empty paper onto the bench and guzzled wine from the spout. Chase wondered if Ricky knew how funny he looked in his suit, drinking cheap box wine. Chase took the wine and had a mouthful.

He had never been a wine person, but it wasn't as bad as he had expected.

Chase set the box on the ground and dragged off his tie. He unbuttoned his top buttons, finally feeling free. After stuffing the tie in his inside packet, he stretched his arms over the back of the bench and looked up at the concrete blocks of flats surrounding them on either side.

"That's mine there," he pointed to his dark window on the fifth floor. "It's not much, but it's mine."

"Where's your kid?"

"Dylan? He's with my neighbour, Annie. She's lovely."

Ricky nodded. Chase couldn't tell if Ricky wasn't interested, or if he still hadn't come to terms with the shock of finding out Chase was a parent.

"As second dates go, this isn't all too bad," said Ricky after guzzling more wine.

"So this is still a date?"

"I don't drink box wine on benches with everybody, sweetheart. Only on special occasions."

Chase believed him. He didn't know how long it had been since Ricky had agreed to a date, but he knew it was probably a long time. He was itching to know what had happened in Ricky's past, but before he could ask, Ricky jumped in first with the questions.

"How does a thirty-two-year-old man like you end up a single parent?" Ricky asked as he stared up at the starry night sky. "Not that I'm judging."

"Dylan's mum died when he was a baby."

"Oh." Ricky sat up straight. "Right."

"It's complicated."

"Sweetheart, I invented complicated."

Ricky produced his cigarettes and placed one between Chase's lips. He lit it for him and did the same for himself, as though an invitation to start talking.

"It was a one-night stand. I met her in a club. Her name was Tracey. She was pretty, but she was a complete party girl. I knew her through a friend of a friend, and I was itching to get laid. I'd had a huge argument with my dad that day and I just wanted to blow off steam. She was the first girl who showed an interest. She turned up on my doorstep nine months later with a baby in her arms. He still had the hospital tag on his wrist."

"Jesus Christ, sweetheart," Ricky mumbled through his cigarette. "The worst thing us gays have to worry about is somebody turning up with STI results."

"I didn't believe he was mine at first. I took Dylan to Tracey's mum's house, but she didn't want to know. She said it was Tracey's mess and she should sort it. I tried to find Tracey but she vanished. I heard through people that she was going off the rails taking drugs. I knew she had always been into that, but I didn't know her enough to stop her. She came around to see him a couple of times, but she was off her face. By that point, I'd bonded with him and given him a name. It wasn't instant, but I couldn't just abandon him."

"And you knew he was yours for sure?"

"That went through my mind. My dad got a DNA test through forensics. It wasn't above board, but it worked. He was only two months old when she died. The toxicology report said her body just gave up. They said after giving birth, she was already weak, and she was taking enough pills for ten men. I didn't know her, not really, but I knew she picked partying over her son, and I can never forgive that. I don't know how things would have turned out if she hadn't have left him on my doorstep. I probably would never have known."

Ricky exhaled the smoke from his lungs, and he tossed the cigarette stub into the grass. He looked as though he was taking everything in slowly.

"And you've been on your own ever since?"

"Between working and Dylan, I never really had time to think about it." Chase paused to drink some wine. "He's my whole world."

"We're not so different after all," he said, almost to himself.

Chase sipped from the plastic spout, staring quizzically at Ricky from the corner of his eye, wondering what he meant by that.

"Do you have a secret child that I don't know about?"

"Me, sweetheart? I haven't gotten close enough to a vagina to even try." He laughed, looking up at the stars. "We've both been on our own for a long time."

Ricky had been alone by choice, but Chase had been alone because of his circumstances. Chase was open to love, but Ricky seemed closed off, and yet here he was on the date.

"It's no way to live life," said Chase.

"Oh, I don't know. I've done alright on my own."

"I don't doubt it, but don't you get lonely?"

"Do you?" Ricky twisted and stared deep into Chase's eyes. "Do you get lonely?"

Chase thought about it for a moment. He was so busy working and trying to raise his son that he barely had a moment alone to notice. He was about to tell Ricky he wasn't lonely, until he remembered those quiet hours when Dylan was in bed and he was on his own watching TV. Despite the constant noise in his life, he hated the quiet. Was that his loneliness?

"Maybe I am," he said, narrowing his eyes up at his flat. "It would be nice to have somebody to come home to. Don't you think?"

Ricky joined him in looking up at the flat, but he didn't

respond. Chase wondered if Ricky wanted to be on his own, or if he just thought he should be. He wanted so desperately to ask what had happened, but he was sure Ricky wouldn't tell him.

"I'm used to my own company, sweetheart."

"That's not the same thing."

"Isn't it?" Ricky laughed softly. "I have my friends, and I have my jobs. It's not so bleak."

"So you have three-quarters of the pie?" He handed the box to Ricky and watched as he gulped down more than was probably sensible. "What about the other slice?"

"What flavour is the pie?"

"Does it matter?"

"Depends." Ricky paused to wipe the red stain from his lips. "I don't like every flavour."

Chase understood why Tom had ranted on the phone to him. Trying to scratch below the surface was so frustrating, especially when he could feel there was so much more to learn.

"*Love* flavoured," he said.

"Sounds bitter."

"Have you ever been in love, Ricky?"

Ricky's response was to drink even more of the wine. He drank so much, it turned Chase's stomach, and he had to pull the box away from his mouth. He disguised it by drinking some himself, but he wasn't in the mood to drink.

"Have you?" asked Ricky, flipping the question.

"No," he said, not even having to think about it. "Not yet, anyway."

Ricky smiled, but it was filled with pain. It made Chase's stomach knot, and he wondered if that was the feeling he had always wondered about.

"Keep it that way," Ricky said bluntly.

"So you have been in love?"

"Did I say that?"

"I was always sceptical about romantic love," said Chase, looking up to his flat. "I love my son to death, but I never saw how I could feel that for another person who didn't have my blood in their veins. Looking into your eyes, I know you can, because I can see that you've felt it."

"It's getting cold out here," Ricky wrapped his suit jacket around his body and stuffed his hands into his armpits. "What time is it?"

"Stop changing the subject."

"I'm not!"

"Have you been in love, Ricky?"

Ricky pursed his lips and gritted his jaw. Chase wondered how often Ricky was put on the spot. He seemed to have created a bubble for himself that he wasn't comfortable leaving. Chase knew just sitting on the bench, having this conversation, Ricky was already way out of his bubble.

"Do I need to answer that?" said Ricky with a heavy sigh.

"I'm not putting a gun to your head."

"I should hope not, sweetheart! I'm not into that."

"*Ricky.*"

"What?"

"Answer the question."

Ricky's body relaxed and he stared back up at the night sky. He seemed to be tracing the constellations with his eyes as his mind ticked over.

"Yes," Ricky snapped. "I've been in love and it was wonderful, and it burned bright, until it didn't anymore."

"What happened?"

"I'm not answering anymore of your questions."

"Why?"

"Because it hurts, Chase," said Ricky bluntly.

Ricky stood up and took a step forward. He dragged his hands through his dark hair as he stared out into the night. A group of teenagers walked by, barely paying them any attention. Chase was waiting for Ricky to run away. He knew he had pushed him too far and he felt embarrassed for it.

"I'm sorry."

"Jesus, sweetheart, don't apologise. You haven't done anything."

"I shouldn't have pushed you." Chase stood up and hovered behind Ricky, resisting the urge to pull him into his body. "I didn't mean to upset you."

A bottle smashed in the distance, followed by teenage laughter. Chase pulled back.

"You haven't upset me. That was already there," said Ricky.

"Do you want to talk about it?"

"No, sweetheart." He turned around, his expression soft and his eyes firm. "I mean that. I don't want to talk about it because you don't need to know. What you do need to know is that I don't do this and the fact that I am standing here with you is a big thing for me. I haven't broken my rules in ten years. I've jumped in at the deep end, and my head is barely bobbing above the surface."

"If you want to go, I'll understand."

"I'd be gone if I wanted to go," he sighed. "I'm just not used to talking about how I feel, how I really feel. You're right, there are two Ricky's. In fact, there's a whole room full of Ricky's, all screaming and shouting at each other. Most people only see one version, but you keep dragging this one out."

"Is he the real one?"

"I don't know anymore. It's been so long, and I don't know what's real and what's not."

In a strange way, Chase knew exactly what he was saying. Between the secrets he was keeping from his family and the fake girlfriend he had invented, he didn't know what version of his own story he was living. He just knew that when he was with Ricky, he felt like he was living the only one that mattered.

"Right now is real," said Chase.

"I know, sweetheart."

"You're right, it's getting cold. Do you want to join me in my flat for a nightcap?"

Ricky looked up at the building, clearly wary of the invitation. Chase got the impression that Ricky hadn't been planning on staying out the whole night. He wondered if they had gotten a table at the restaurant, would Ricky have vanished before the dessert menu arrived?

"One drink," he said as he bent down and picked up the box of wine. "I'm bringing this, just in case you don't have anything decent."

They headed up to Chase's tiny flat. He poured them both a glass of Jameson Whiskey, which Barbara had given him for Christmas. Before they got a chance to drink it, they fell onto Chase's bed.

As they tore each other's clothes off in the dark, Chase began to wonder if he really had never been in love after all.

CHAPTER

SEVENTEEN

*B*ret banged on the ice, his white blonde hair dripping wet and his frosty skin the palest of blues. He screamed out, but no sound left his lips. Ricky banged his fists against the ice, but it didn't break. Bret stared desperately at him through the ice, begging Ricky to save him with his silent screams. Dragging his nails against the thick ice, Ricky opened his mouth to tell Bret everything was going to be okay. His lungs filled with arctic water, and he realised he was the one trapped under the frozen surface.

Ricky jolted out of his dream, naked and face down on a bed that wasn't his own. He jerked his head up and squinted at the tiny, open window. An icy cold draft fluttered the curtains and licked against his skin. Wiping the dribble from the side of his mouth, he remembered where he was.

He looked down at Chase's naked body tangled up in the sheets. The amount of times they had fucked last night flashed through his mind. He yawned, wondering how much sleep he had actually gotten.

There was a knock on the door and a rattle of the letterbox, and he recalled what had woken him up in the first place. This time, Chase jerked up and squinted up at Ricky, his eyes barely open.

"What time is it?" he groaned.

"There's someone at the door."

Chase's eyes fluttered for a moment until Ricky's words sank in. He jumped out of bed and pulled on his underwear. Seeming to think that his tattoos were enough coverage, he ran across the bedroom, opened the door and headed straight for the front door.

Ricky peered through the open door and realised that he could be seen from the front window. He wrapped the sheet around his body and hopped across the bedroom and hid out of sight.

As he fully woke up, he strained his ears to hear who was at the door. When he heard the unmistakable sound of a child, his heart dropped.

He hooked his toe in the belt of his trousers and slowly dragged them across the room. His underwear was still wrapped up inside, so he pulled them out and shimmied them up under the sheet.

"I heard you coming home last night. I'm meeting a friend in town. I would have taken Dylan with me, but I thought you might want him back," a soft, woman's voice drifted through to the bedroom.

Clutching the sheet under his armpits, he jumped into his trousers and attempted to pull them up. Instead of pushing his foot into the leg hole, it jammed in the pocket, and before he could rectify it, he felt his body starting to wobble. He reached out and grabbed hold of the wardrobe door. It flung open, sending him completely off balance. He tripped over the trousers and fell full force onto the floor and in the view of the door.

"What was that?" asked the woman. "Have you got somebody back here? Oh. Oh. I see. Erm. I better be going, love."

On his side, Ricky awkwardly smiled at the elderly woman, but she couldn't quite make eye contact. The little boy, who Ricky presumed was Dylan, tilted his head and frowned as he stared at Ricky.

"Daddy, who's that man?"

"He's just a friend," Chase said quickly.

"Why doesn't he have clothes on?"

"Because he's just woken up." Chase stumbled over his words as he stared at Ricky, horror loud and clear in his eyes. "Why don't you go and brush your teeth?"

Dylan nodded and walked through the flat, keeping his suspicious eyes trained on Ricky as he scrambled to his feet, trying to keep the sheet covering his body.

"Annie, it's not what it looks like," said Chase in a low voice. "It's —"

"No need to explain!" she cut him off and pushed up her roller set curls as she peered around his shoulder. "What you get up to behind closed doors is none of my business. I better be off."

She scurried away as quickly as she had appeared and Ricky caught her staring through the living room window at him as she went by. Feeling completely mortified, Ricky pulled on his shirt, but half of the buttons had been ripped off in their hurry to get undressed the night before.

"I should go," he said as he fiddled with his belt. "I'll call a cab and wait downstairs."

"Ricky, you don't have to rush off."

"I have somewhere I need to be," he lied.

"At least stay for some breakfast."

Ricky pulled on his suit jacket and buttoned it up in the middle to hide the fact his shirt was open. He pulled his phone from his pocket and punched in the taxi number before Chase could say anything.

"I really should go," he whispered as he waited for the operator. "Hello? Hebden Bridge please. Where am I? Oh. Chase. Where am I?"

Ten minutes and three cigarettes later, Ricky jumped into a taxi. The driver peered at him through the rear-view mirror the whole way home, as though he could smell the sex on Ricky.

"Why don't you take a picture?" he quipped as they pulled up outside of his cottage.

"That'll be forty quid."

"Forty bloody quid?" Ricky mumbled as he pulled the cash out of his wallet. "Daylight robbery."

He slammed the taxi door and hurried into his cottage. When he locked the door behind him, he exhaled and hit his head against the wood. The sudden jolt of pain brought him back to reality.

In his mind, he could still see Dylan staring at him, looking like a mini tattoo-less Chase. As he walked across his cottage to make some much needed coffee, he tried to understand the complicated mess he had got himself into.

He picked up the letter from the doormat. It was from the court. He ripped it open and skim read its contents. They had set a date for his trial. Not wanting to think about that yet, he folded the letter and stuffed it in a drawer.

As the day wore on and the sun started to fade from the sky, he sat down at his vanity. He wanted to feel ready for his big return to London Bridge, but he was distracted.

As he over lined his lips, a knock at the front door

provided further distraction. He peered through the peephole and saw a mass of dark curls.

"I said I'd drive you to the club," said Tom as he followed Ricky through to his bedroom. "Remember?"

"I don't need babysitting, sweetheart."

"For my own peace of mind, don't argue! So, how was it?"

Ricky sat back in front of his mirror and applied the liquid lipstick. He patted it as it dried down, knowing it wasn't going to move all night. He glanced at Tom in the mirror, who was waiting for him to answer the question.

"How was what, sweetheart?" he asked causally. "Make yourself useful and get me my short, red curly wig out of the wardrobe. I'm feeling colour tonight."

Tom walked across the room and slid open the wardrobe doors. He reached up onto the top shelf and picked out the right wig, clearly knowing Ricky's drag collection just as well as he did. He placed it on the pink, plastic head on the dressing table and sat back on the bed and leaned into the mirror.

"The date!"

"It was okay."

"Just okay?"

Ricky reached down and pulled open his lash drawer. He flicked through the fresh packets and picked out two packets of over the top dramatic lashes. He coated his lashes with mascara and applied black weave bond glue along the first strip. As he shook it waiting for it to get tacky, he pursed his lips at Tom in the mirror, who was still waiting for him to tell him everything.

"It was good."

"You need to give me something here, Ricky." Tom edged forward and leaned against the back of Ricky's chair. "Did something happen? Something bad?"

"I don't know," he leaned close to the mirror and applied the first lash. "I stayed over."

"At his flat?" Tom grinned from ear to ear. "And? Was it good? Did he bring you breakfast in bed?"

Ricky arched his higher than normal brow as he applied glue to the second lash. Marriage had turned his once just as cynical best friend into a hopeless romantic. Once upon a time, it had been Ricky who had been pushing for Tom to get a man. Perhaps if he had stayed out of his friend's business, he wouldn't feel like he needed to return the favour so heavily.

"His kid turned up," Ricky said carefully as he applied the second lash.

"And you ran, didn't you?"

"Naturally."

Tom sighed and slumped back onto the bed. He looked like an exhausted teacher who was frustrated that his student wasn't learning as fast as the other kids.

"Hold the back of this wig while I glue it down," he said as he slid the hair over his scalp cap.

Tom hooked his fingers into the back of the wig and pulled it down as Ricky positioned it. He glued down the lace and leaned back in the mirror, observing his artistry. Despite the shirtless torso of a man, Miss Kitty Litter was back.

"Does this mean you're not seeing him again?" asked Tom as he smoothed out some of the curls in the back of the wig.

Ricky looked at his friend's face in the soft glow of the vanity lights. He didn't respond. He peeked at his phone, which had been on silent mode all day. He had three missed calls from Chase.

He didn't know what was going to happen next, he just knew that he did have feelings for Chase, and he couldn't ignore them any longer because they were screaming at the top of their poor lungs after a decade of silence.

***

The gym was unusually quiet for a Friday night. Chase jumped off the treadmill and wiped the sweat from his face. He checked his phone, but Ricky hadn't returned his calls.

"You've been looking at that thing all day," Danny called across the gym. "Is Rachel giving you the cold shoulder?"

"Something like that."

"Women are complicated, bro." Danny tossed a protein bar to Chase. "You need to apologise, even when you haven't done something wrong. That's how they all work."

"But I haven't done anything wrong," he sighed as he unwrapped the bar.

"Exactly! Nice bit of jewellery and some flowers and you'll be back in the sheets in no time."

Chase crammed the bar into his mouth and chewed. The texture was stodgy and unpleasant, and he wasn't sure why he ate so many of them. He tossed the wrapper in the bin and wiped his face down with the towel again, wondering if his brother had a point.

He looked at his phone and considered trying to call Ricky. He doubted he would even pick up.

"The thing is, Rachel met Dylan by accident," he said, leaning on the counter and tapping his phone on the glass surface. "I wanted to wait a little longer until we were both sure, but I think it freaked her out."

"She sounds like the classic commitment-phobe."

"It's complicated."

"All women are," he laughed, snatching the phone out of Chase's hand. "I'll call her. I'll tell her to pull her finger out and get over here so you can talk."

"Not such a good idea," he took the phone back and pocketed it so his brother couldn't do anything stupid. "I think I just need to give him some space."

"Him?" Danny frowned and folded his arms.

"D-Dylan, I mean," he lied. "Space from Rachel. The poor kid was so confused this morning."

Chase hated lying, especially to his family, but it seemed to work. Danny's expression relaxed, and he dropped his arms back to his side. The truth was, Dylan hadn't asked any more questions after he came out of the bathroom and Ricky wasn't there. He wondered if it was because he believed that he was just a friend of Daddy's, or if his silence said something else.

"If she isn't answering the phone and you don't want her to come here, maybe you should go to her. Where does she live?"

"In the village."

"This village?" Danny rubbed his hands together, excitement alive in his eyes. "That's perfect, bro. Go now, I can pack up."

"I don't think that's a good idea."

"Why not? Scared you might find her with another man?"

Chase shook his head. That hadn't crossed his mind until his brother had said it. Was the reason Ricky wasn't answering his phone because he was busy getting the thought of Chase and Dylan out of his mind by letting another man into his bed? Pulling out his phone, he walked across the gym and listened to Ricky's answering message for the fourth time that day.

'Hello… Gotcha, sweetheart! I can't come to the phone right now because I'm very busy being fabulous and not answering your call. Don't be too devastated, because when

I've stopped talking, you can leave me a little message after the beep and I promise I might possibly think about getting back to you, if I like the sound of your voice. Do your thing, sweetheart.'

The voicemail beeped and Chase glanced over his shoulder, noticing that his brother's eyes were trained on him. He wondered how good his hearing was.

"It's me," he said quietly into the handset. "Just give me a call if you get this message, yeah? I'm worried about you."

He hung up and clutched the phone to his chest, wondering if that was the right thing to do. He knew he was probably making something out of nothing, but he needed to see Ricky's face to know that for sure. He ran out of the flat so fast, Chase hadn't had a chance to put things right. By the time he had reached the door to stop him, Ricky had already vanished down the stairwell.

When the time came to close the gym, they wiped down the machines, flicked off the lights and locked the doors. Chase immediately placed a cigarette between his lips before offering his brother one.

"Don't tell Natalie," said Danny as he accepted the lighter. "She's on my case about quitting again now that she's pregnant. She thinks it's a bad influence. I told her I wasn't an influence for another seven months, but she reckons babies can pick up on those things."

"Sounds like Natalie's usual bullshit," Chase mumbled under his breath. "She might have a point, though. I've been thinking about quitting for a while."

"You?" Danny laughed. "You've been smoking since you were a kid. You were the one who got me started!"

"It was those lads at the kickboxing club. They were all older than me. I wanted to fit in. There's nothing cool about dying in your sixties because you smoked yourself to death. I do everything I can for Dylan, and yet I still smoke."

"Sounds like you've been reading Natalie's books finally." Danny nudged him and winked. "She'll be well chuffed when I tell her. Maybe we can quit together?"

"Maybe."

Chase puffed hard on the cigarette and glanced down the road. He could see the tip of Ricky's garden gate and the soft glow of the living room lights.

"I'm going to take your advice and face this head on."

"Rather you than me, little brother." Danny slapped Chase encouragingly on the shoulders and pulled out his car keys. "Good luck!"

Chase waved his brother off and waited for Danny to disappear around the corner before he set off towards Ricky's flat. The last thing he wanted was Danny finding out that Rachel was really Ricky.

As he walked towards Ricky's cottage, he called him again, deciding to give him the benefit of the doubt. By the time he reached the gate, the voicemail kicked in. He pocketed his phone and unlatched the gate.

Before he walked up the garden path, he stared at the closed curtains, expecting to see figures moving inside. He didn't see anything. He knew it was likely Ricky wasn't in, but he also knew he had to try. If Ricky got to know Dylan, Chase knew he wouldn't be such an obstacle.

Inhaling deeply, he knocked heavily on the door. He waited to hear footprints across the wooden floors, but the cottage sounded painfully silent. He called Ricky again, and he heard his phone deep inside the cottage.

"Ricky, it's me." Chase banged on the door. "I know you're in there, open up!"

The door opened, but it wasn't Ricky. Chase stared down at the smiling man with dark curly hair. He wondered if this was who Ricky had been spending the day with.

"Chase, I believe?" The guy extended a hand. "We spoke on the phone."

"Tom?" Chase let out a sigh of relief, and he accepted the handshake. "Good to finally meet you. Is Ricky here?"

Glancing over his shoulder, Tom filled up the doorway, blocking Chase's view. He knew whatever he was going to say next was a lie.

"He's not here at the moment," he said, his smile shaking. "Can I take a message?"

With his phone still in his hand, he called Ricky again. With the front door open, he heard the phone ringing loud and clear.

"He left his phone," Tom said awkwardly. "Maybe you should come back later?"

"I've been calling him all day. I just want to make sure he's okay."

"He's fine."

"I know he's back there, Tom. He doesn't have to hide from me."

"It's not a good time," said Tom, scratching at his dark curls. "Come back tomorrow."

Chase heard a door open and close inside of the cottage, but he couldn't see past Tom. His imagination was running away, wondering what Tom was trying to hide.

"It's alright, sweetheart," he heard Ricky's voice from within the cottage. "Let him in."

Tom didn't move immediately. He stared ahead at Chase, fear in his eyes. Chase pushed his phone into his pocket, and he noticed that his hands were shaking.

Tom stepped back and opened the door. Chase put one foot in the cottage but he stopped in his tracks when he saw who was standing in the doorway of Ricky's bedroom. It wasn't Ricky, not as Chase knew him. Ricky was dressed like a woman.

Chase opened his mouth to speak, but no words came out. His eyes wandered up from the high, stiletto heels, to the tight fitting electric blue dress, up to the short, red, curly hair, and then to the make-up caked face. If it weren't for the eyes hidden behind the thick lashes and dark eyeliner, he wouldn't have even recognised it was Ricky.

"I don't understand," said Chase, his voice low and fragile. "What's going on?"

"I'm a drag queen, sweetheart," Ricky's voice came from the woman's body. "Tom, will you give us a minute?"

Tom looked from Chase to Ricky before walking quickly out of the cottage. He closed the door softly, leaving them alone. Ricky took a step forward, his heels clicking on the exposed wood floor. Chase took in the sight before him once more.

"Say something," Ricky laughed, his voice shaking. "You're scaring me."

Chase didn't know what to say. He had come to the cottage because he wanted to see Ricky's face after a day of being ignored, but as he stared at the altered bone structure, he struggled to see the man he had spent the previous night with.

"I think I need a drink," he said, unable to look Ricky in the eye.

"Take a seat, I'll fetch the vodka."

Chase perched on the edge of the yellow sofa and watched the woman pretending to be Ricky walk into the kitchen. She didn't walk like Ricky. Running his hands over his face, he tried to make sense of it all, but he couldn't.

Ricky sat next to Chase and handed him the bottle of vodka. Ricky's usual spicy aftershave, which Chase loved so much, had been replaced with a sweet, floral perfume. He unscrewed the vodka bottle and crammed the neck into his mouth.

"Is this why you didn't answer your phone?" he asked as he wiped the vodka from his lips with the back of his hand. "Because you were cross dressing?"

"It's not cross dressing." Ricky pulled the vodka from Chase's hands. He noticed the long red nails glued to the ends of Ricky's fingers. "It's drag. It's art. Nothing more, nothing less."

"Why didn't you tell me?"

Ricky pushed the vodka bottle into his mouth. He took a long drink before putting it on the low coffee table. He left behind a red lipstick print.

"This is the first time I've been in drag since the attack. The night I was attacked, I was working in the bar and after my shift I got out of drag and walked home. Those guys in the alley, they took my bag and they found my wig. They looked at me like you're looking at me now."

"So you remember now?"

"Bits and pieces."

Chase looked guiltily down to the floor. He hated to think he shared anything in common with the arseholes that had left Ricky for dead in the rain.

"I thought you were a DJ in the bar?"

"A drag queen DJ, and I'm bloody good at my job."

"So this is just a job?"

"It's more of a hobby. It's an outlet for me. I become somebody else for the night and I get to express a side of me that isn't so acceptable unless I'm in a wig and a dress. We all have an outlet."

Chase understood that. Whenever the world was getting too much for him, he worked out.

"So you don't want to be a woman?"

"God no, sweetheart! I couldn't deal with the hormones. No, I'm more than happy being a man. I'd miss the perks too much."

Chase laughed and reached out for the vodka bottle. He looked down at the lipstick before pushing it into his mouth. The vodka burned his throat, but he needed it to take the chatter off his brain.

"You've got a little –" Ricky reached out and wiped the lipstick from Chase's mouth. Their eyes met, and Chase's stomach knotted, just as it did whenever Ricky usually looked at him. "It's still me sweetheart. This washes off."

Chase nodded. The more he looked through the mask, the more he saw Ricky. In some ways, he even understood it.

"This isn't what I was expecting to find," he said. "I thought you'd have a guy here."

"Is this worse?"

"It's cool," he said. "It doesn't change anything. You're still you. It was just a shock to the system."

"Miss Kitty Litter is a shock to everybody's systems."

"Is that your drag name? Kitty Litter?"

"Miss Kitty Litter to you, sweetheart," he said with a wink. "And yes. Every weekend at London Bridge. Tonight's my big return."

"Is that why you ran out on me this morning?"

"Ah, that," he said, dropping his head low. "I'm a terrible human being. I panicked, again."

"It's fine. Tomorrow is a new day."

"So this hasn't scared you off?" Ricky pushed up the curls of his red wig and pursed his lips.

"It will take more than a frock and lipstick to scare me off, sweetheart."

"Don't go stealing my catchphrase now," he said, extending a long red nail, "or you'll be hearing from my lawyers. I need to set off soon, or I'll be late."

"Is there room in that car for one more?"

"Are you serious?"

"I'll have to make a call, but why not? I haven't been to the village since we met and I want to see if you're as good a DJ as you say."

Underneath the wildly overdrawn lips, Ricky smiled and nodded softly. He looked shocked; more shocked than Chase had been to see him dressed like a woman. It hurt Chase to realise that Ricky had kept it a secret because he thought Chase would reject him.

Chase was surprised by his own reaction. He felt like he had unlocked another piece of Ricky's puzzle and it made sense. He knew there were more pieces to discover, and he didn't doubt they would shock him just as much as this one had, but when he did, he knew it was one step closer to getting to know the real Ricky.

They climbed into Tom's Range Rover and set off into the city. Under the blanket of darkness, Chase reached across the backseat and looped his fingers gently through Ricky's.

CHAPTER

EIGHTEEN

On Saturday afternoon, the sun shone brightly over Barton Farm for their annual village fete. Ricky inhaled the country air, remembering how much he had enjoyed his time recuperating at the farm.

He looked over to Chase, who was deep in conversation with Cole. His inked skin glowed under the hot sun as he waved his arms around, telling a story to Cole.

Tom appeared by his side and handed him a cardboard cup of coffee. Ricky gladly accepted it and sipped from the tiny plastic hole.

"They're getting on," said Tom, nodding over to Dylan and Eva as Cole's Auntie Belinda led them around the riding school on two horses. "Looks like Eva's found herself a play date."

"He's a good kid," said Ricky as he sipped the coffee. "I

don't know what I was so scared of."

"Well, I have been saying that for years." Tom nudged him and winked in Cole and Chase's direction. "Looks like they're getting on too. I don't have to keep my eye on Chase, do I?"

"If me doing drag didn't scare him away, I doubt he's going to start hitting on your husband."

They sipped their coffee and leaned against the fence. Dylan waved to Chase and he waved right back. He had seen a different side of Chase all morning. He had always thought he was sweet and caring, but seeing the way he looked at Dylan added a whole new dimension to his personality. It warmed Ricky's old, cynical heart.

He finished the coffee, and the last remnants of the morning's hangover vanished from his system. It was a wonder they had woken up at all. After Ricky finished his shift at the bar, Tom went home, but Ricky and Chase carried on to the rest of the open bars after Ricky de-dragged. He vaguely remembered crawling into a taxi around the same time the sun appeared in the sky.

Dylan and Eva jumped down from their horses and ran across the riding school to their fathers. The next set of children headed towards Belinda, who received them with a warm, maternal smile.

"Did you enjoy that?" asked Chase as he ruffled Dylan's blonde hair.

"Can we get a horse?" asked Dylan, a wide smile on his small face.

"You're welcome here anytime," said Cole. "You can come and ride with Eva on the weekends, if you'd like that?"

Dylan nodded, and he and Eva ran off to the stables. Chase appeared by Ricky's side and he pulled out two cigarettes for them both.

"I'd love to raise Dylan somewhere like this," said Chase and he lit Ricky's cigarette for him. "That flat is no good for him."

"Like I said, you're welcome here anytime," said Cole again.

"Both of you," added Tom.

Chase glanced to Ricky and smiled as he blew smoke up into the air. Tom had been referring to them as a couple all morning, but that was still a foreign concept for Ricky. Inhaling the cigarette deeply, he forced himself not to go into his usual meltdown.

Tom and Cole got back to making sure the fete was ticking over, leaving Ricky and Chase to watch the kids. They leaned against the stables and watched as Dylan and Eva chased around a chicken.

"I still haven't found someone to look after him over the summer," said Chase. "They finish school next week."

"Shouldn't you have that sorted by now?"

"I did have, but my sister-in-law bailed on me. I'll think of something."

"Have you thought about asking Tom and Cole?" suggested Ricky. "They're here every day anyway."

Chase looked over to Tom and Cole as they wandered between the stalls, talking to people as they passed. Ricky could tell he was wondering if he should trust them, but Ricky hadn't met a more trust-worthy couple in his life.

"Do you think they would say yes? I was going to ask my neighbour, but I don't want to put that on her every single day."

"Are you kidding me? Mother Theresa has nothing on those two. Between them and Belinda, they'd have an eye on Dylan at all times. They wouldn't accept a penny either. This place has made them a small fortune."

Chase looked at Dylan again, as he chewed the inside of

his cheek. It was so obvious he cared more about his son than anything in the world. Ricky had cared about somebody that much once as well.

Bret would have loved the farm. He always used to drag Ricky out on long country walks on the weekends, much to his displeasure. Bret always used to say fresh air was the best medicine and that Ricky should trust him because he was a doctor. Fresh air hadn't been enough to save him from cancer.

Snapping his mind back to the present, he looked at Chase, as he stared at Tom and Cole.

"I might go and ask them now," he said, pushing away from the stables. "Can you watch Dylan for a minute?"

"Don't you want me to come with you?"

"I don't want them saying yes because they feel like they need to. It's better if I just ask them on my own. I'll only be a minute."

Ricky nodded. Before Chase headed into the fields to find Tom and Cole, he dove in and quickly kissed Ricky on the cheek. It was such a simple action, but it made Ricky's chest flutter. Smiling, he watched as Chase walked away, his narrow hips and broad shoulders swaying under his tight t-shirt.

He pulled his phone out of his pocket and checked through his notifications. He had dozens of messages from his hook-up app from the night before. He deleted them all and flicked through his apps. He hovered over the app for a second, remembering how many men it had brought to his bed. Aside from the blip arranging to meet BiBoiXO, the urge hadn't taken him since before he met Chase. Pressing down hard on the app, he sent it towards the trashcan. When it vanished, he didn't feel like he had lost anything.

"Ricky!" Rox, his former manager at London Bridge and heavily pregnant friend waddled towards him, her hands clutching her lower back. "Aren't you a sight for sore eyes?"

"How's the pregnancy, sweetheart?" Ricky asked as he kissed her on the cheek. "Treating you well?"

"I have the bladder of an eighty-year-old woman, and I haven't slept properly in weeks. She won't stop kicking. Here, feel."

She grabbed Ricky's hand and pressed it up against her stomach. Something squirmed under his palm, and he quickly ripped it away. He had only just come to terms with children being part of his life, but a baby was too much to think about.

"You look ready to drop, sweetheart."

"Any day now," she rubbed her firm tummy. "Little Ambrose can't come fast enough."

"Ambrose? Isn't that custard, sweetheart?"

"Shut up," she slapped his arm. "It's the only name me and JoJo could agree on."

"I'd hate to see the names you didn't agree on then. Apple? Sunflower? Cloud?"

She laughed and slapped him on the arm. He shouldn't have expected anything less from the woman who used to turn up to work with different coloured hair every shift. She may have been rocking demure, natural hair for her pregnancy, but he didn't doubt she would start dying it and chopping parts off the second her labour was over.

Ricky pulled out a cigarette and lit it. He blew the smoke away from Rox, but she breathed in and inhaled in deeply.

"Ugh, I've missed that smell."

"I'm quitting soon."

"Yeah, right," she laughed. "And pigs will fly. I heard a rumour that you've got yourself a boyfriend?"

"Who's spreading these vicious rumours? Is it Toxic Tonya again? I'll eat that bitch for dinner."

"A little birdy told me he also had a kid," she looked deep into his eyes and planted her hands on her hips. "Have I heard this right?"

"Fine, it's all true. I'm looking after the kid now, actually."

He looked over Rox's shoulder, but he couldn't see Dylan or Eva. The chicken was still there, pecking at something on the ground, but the children had vanished.

"Shit, sweetheart." He tossed the cigarette on the ground and quickly huffed the smoke out of his lungs. "They were there a second ago."

He ran to the place they had been, but he couldn't see them. Spinning around on the spot, the farm blurred and something similar to his morning hangover consumed his mind.

"Ricky?" Chase's voice pierced through the blurriness. "Are you alright?"

Firm hands grabbed his shoulder. He tried to speak, but his eyes were frantically searching the farm. Tom and Cole appeared with Eva by their side, and his heart stopped. Dylan wasn't with her.

"Where's Dylan?" he asked, his voice shaking. "He was here a second ago, I swear!"

"Eva just came running up to us," Tom pulled her into his side. "Dylan wasn't with her."

"We were playing hide and seek," Eva said, staring at the ground. "But I can't find him."

"Oh, God. What have I done?"

"Ricky, just calm down for a second," said Chase, pulling him to face him. "We'll all split up, and we'll find him in no time."

Ricky nodded. A memory of him getting lost at a car boot sale with his mother and auntie sprung to mind. He had spent almost an hour wandering around the fields looking for them, on the verge of tears. When he finally found them, they were so relieved to see him, they didn't even shout at him for leaving their side.

Rox volunteered to stay by the stables with Eva in case he came back, and the four of them split up to look over different parts of the farm.

The farm was overwhelmingly big. Between the farmhouse, the barns, the stables, the café, the riding school and the fields filled with hundreds of stalls and thousands of people, there were so many places Dylan could be.

After an hour of looking, he passed near Chase, but he couldn't look him in the eye. It was obvious he was starting to worry.

"Dylan!" Ricky cried out into the chicken barn. "The game's over now. Come out."

The chickens flapped their wings and hurried away from Ricky, but no child appeared. He doubled back and headed back to the stables, where Rox was sitting on an upturned bucket with Eva on her knee.

"Any luck?" she asked.

"Nothing. What have I done?"

"Kids wander off, Ricky. It's not your fault."

"No, it is. Chase asked me to watch him, and I wasn't watching. If I had been, I would have seen him walking away."

"He'll turn up," Rox said with a smile as she reached out to squeeze his hand. "Try not to worry."

It was impossible not to worry. Ricky looked out to the fields where Chase was stopping people and frantically asking them if they had seen his son. When they shook their head, he quickly moved onto the next person.

Ricky headed into the farmhouse for the second time. He checked under all of the beds again and under the tables. He opened the door to the kitchen and the sheepdogs jumped up at him. Mulder, the cat, lifted his head up on top of the fridge, but he didn't move.

"Dylan?" he said quietly. "Are you in here?"

He listened carefully, but there wasn't a response. Chase's voice echoed around the farm, crying out for his son. Ricky collapsed into a chair at the kitchen table and he pushed his face into his hands. After everything that had happened, he doubted Chase would talk to him after this. He was barely capable of looking after himself, let alone a child. How did he ever think any of this could work?

Something sneezed from behind him and he spun around in his chair. He thought it might have been Mulder, but he was still curled up and fast asleep. He looked down at the dogs as they looked up at him waiting for a treat, but they were all too big to make such a delicate sound.

Standing up carefully, he strained his ears to listen. He tried to tune out Chase's cries from the fields. He heard the sneeze again and the sound of rustling. It was coming from under the sink.

Ricky ripped open the cabinet doors and collapsed to his knees and closed his eyes when he saw Dylan curled up next to the mop bucket.

"Did I win?" Dylan asked sheepishly.

"You won." Ricky nodded his head and let out the longest sigh of relief of his life. "You can come out now."

Dylan crawled out of the tiny space and dusted himself down. Ricky pulled him into his chest and hugged him tightly. He didn't know much about the child, but he hadn't been able to think about anyone else for the past hour.

"Am I in trouble?" he asked softly as he wrapped his arms around Ricky's neck.

"No, you're not in trouble," Ricky said carefully as he pulled Dylan away. "You just scared us a little bit, that's all."

"Will my Daddy be mad?"

"Of course not." Ricky smiled softly. "Let's go and find him, okay, sweetheart?"

Dylan rubbed his dry eyes with his clenched fists and nodded solemnly. Ricky stood up, his knees creaking as he did. When he was on his feet, Dylan's tiny hand wrapped around Ricky's. It felt so fragile and delicate in his palm.

Hand in hand, they walked out of the back door and over to where Rox and Eva were sitting. Eva jumped up and ran over to them and hugged Dylan. He caught Chase's eye as he walked towards them and he let out the built up tension with one long huff. He reached up and clutched his hair and exposed his inked stomach.

"Dylan won, didn't he, Daddy?" said Ricky as Chase ran towards them. "He was hiding under the sink."

"Ugh, you had me worried to death," Chase dropped down to Dylan's level and clutched him tightly, but Dylan didn't let go of Ricky's hand. "Thank God you're alright."

"Did I do a naughty thing?" Dylan asked sheepishly.

Chase pulled away and clutched his tiny cheeks in his palm and said, "Of course not!"

When the farm started to calm down, they all headed into Belinda's living room, where they stayed long past sunset. Dylan fell asleep curled up in the corner of the sofa with Mulder crammed in between him and a pillow.

"I'm going to go to bed," said Belinda with a long yawn as she stood up. "It's been a long day."

"I'll get a taxi," said Rox with a long yawn. "JoJo is going to be freaking out that I've stayed out this late. Thanks for the tea, B."

"Anytime, love." She smiled as she kissed Rox on the cheek. "You boys are welcome to stay if you want. I'll make a bed up."

"I'll head home," said Ricky. "Thanks for the offer, though."

Tom and Cole both got up from the couch where they had been cuddling, and they started to clear away the leftovers of their Chinese takeaway. When they were alone, Chase leaned his head gently against Ricky's shoulder.

"I should get going too."

"You could always come to mine," Ricky suggested. "Both of you."

Chase smiled up at Ricky and nodded. Ricky almost couldn't believe he had said it, but the words had left his lips before he had a chance to overthink them. He had never been one to bite his tongue, but when it came to the matters of the heart, he would bite his tongue off before saying something he might potentially regret. Tonight, he didn't feel like he needed to.

Chase scooped Dylan up, and he wrapped his arms tightly around his father's neck as he slept on his shoulder. They set off into the night, down the long and winding road to the village. In the dark, Ricky looped his fingers around Chase's. They looked at each other, and Ricky could almost feel his heart stop.

"Did Tom and Cole say yes to looking after Dylan?" Ricky asked when they neared the bottom of the lane and the streetlights came into view.

"They can do Wednesdays, and I think Annie will be able to have him the rest of the days."

They transitioned from the dark muddy road to the firm concrete and the orange glow of the lights. They walked through the village, passing the gym as they headed to Ricky's flat. When they were at Ricky's gate, he pulled his keys out of his pocket and a strange thought came into his mind. Once again he didn't try to stop it.

"I could watch Dylan on Wednesdays. It's my day off

from the shop." He slotted the key into the old lock and fiddled with it until the door loosened.

"Are you sure? Don't feel like you need to offer."

"I want to. That's if, you want me to. I did lose Dylan after all, sweetheart."

"The main thing is you found him again," said Chase as they stepped into the dark cottage. "If you really want to, he's yours on Wednesdays."

Ricky flicked on a couple of the lamps and opened the door to the spare bedroom. He picked up his new dresses off the bed and tossed them over an armchair. He pulled back the sheets and Chase carefully placed him on the bed. Ricky pulled the sheets over his shoulders, and Chase leaned in and kissed him on the forehead.

They went through to the living room, and Ricky grabbed two beers out of the kitchen while Chase flicked through the channels on the TV.

Ricky handed Chase the beer and they settled next to each other on the sofa. Chase opened his arm and pulled Ricky into his side. Leaning his head against Chase's chest, he heard the thumping of his heart against his shirt.

As he sipped his beer and watched the TV, he couldn't remember the last time he had felt so normal.

CHAPTER

NINETEEN

Standing on the pavement outside of Ricky's shop, Chase looked up at the '*Books and Bondage*' sign. He had passed it a couple of times, but it was usually at night when it was closed. Checking his watch, he pushed on the door, knowing he had an hour before he needed to be at the gym for his shift.

"Just a second," Ricky's voice called from behind a beaded curtain. "I'll be right there, sweetheart."

Chase looked around the shop, unsure of where to look first. Most of the shop was taken up with rows of books and most of them looked pretty adult themed. He walked around the counter into the second half of the shop, where the walls were lined with gay porn DVDs. He picked out a case and turned it over in his hands.

"*Anal Avalanche 3*," said Ricky with a smirk as he

walked through the curtains. "Good choice, sweetheart."

"I can't believe they've made three of these."

"Avalanches can provide a lot of material, sweetheart. Snow can be sexy. I once knew a guy who got trapped in a cabin for Christmas with a hot lumberjack."

"That didn't actually happen, did it?" Chase placed the DVD back on the shelf and stuffed his hands in his pocket.

"It might have done. He swears it did," Ricky said with a wink as he leaned against the counter in the middle of the shop. "What brings you here this early in the morning? I thought you were working at the gym today?"

"I start at ten on Wednesdays. I've just dropped Dylan off at school, and I just thought I'd drop by and see how you were feeling."

Ricky suspiciously arched a brow as he refilled a tray of complimentary condoms on the counter.

"You mean you wanted to see if I was still okay to watch him after school?" he said, folding his arms and sitting on a stool. "I've told you already, sweetheart. I finish at two and I'll pick him up from school. I've already sorted the schedule so when he's off school for the summer holidays, I can have him all day on Wednesdays."

Chase nodded his appreciation. He was still so surprised, but grateful for Ricky's offer. After the way he had reacted to meeting Dylan, it felt like such a big turnaround in such a short space of time. Just thinking about the future made his heart flutter. They still hadn't officially defined their relationship, but it already felt like things were much more serious since their short-lived weekend at Coltrane House.

"What's through there?" Chase nodded to the red light seeping through the beaded curtain.

"Wonderland, sweetheart. C'mon, I'll show you."

Ricky hopped over the counter and locked the front door. He grabbed Chase by the shoulders and guided him towards the red light. The beads ran across his face, and it took his eyes a second to adjust to the dark hue.

Ricky let go of him and walked around him. He stood in the middle of the large room, smiling proudly.

"What is all of this?" asked Chase.

"*Sex*, sweetheart."

The walls were lined with shelves filled with more boxes of sex toys than Chase thought existed. He walked over to the nearest shelf and scanned the dildos. He never knew they came in so many shapes, colours, and sizes.

"And people buy this stuff?" Chase asked, picking up a large, heavy grey slab of rubber that looked far too big to fit inside anyone. "For real?"

"The War Hammer is one of our biggest sellers, sweetheart. Don't mock it till you've tried it."

"I'll pass."

"A lot of people like to see things before they buy them online. Pictures can be deceiving, and they know I'm not going to judge them. We all have our kinks, sweetheart."

Chase tried to think about his own. He loved it when guys looked up into his eyes when they gave him a blowjob, but he wasn't sure that was considered a kink. Perhaps it was the power he liked, rather than the action itself.

He crossed the room and peered in a large, glass display filled with leather restraints. He didn't know what most of them were used for, but he didn't doubt Ricky would know if he asked.

"I was doing the stock check when you came in," said Ricky, as he ran a black feather along the exposed flesh on Chase's neck.

"Do you like using this stuff?"

"Some of it," he smirked. "Not all of it. Jesus, sweetheart, you look absolutely terrified."

Chase laughed and tried to relax his face. It was a world

completely new to him, but one Ricky seemed more than at home in.

"You're just full of surprises, Ricky."

"I like to keep you on your toes."

Ricky grabbed his hands and yanked them behind his back. Before he had time to pull away, Ricky fastened something around his wrists, restricting them to the base of his spine. They felt like handcuffs, but thicker, almost leather like.

Chase turned around to face Ricky. They were inches away from each other. Without even needing to kiss Ricky, his cock was already hardening in his gym shorts. It sprung up, and Ricky looked down with a devilish smirk.

"How long did you say until your shift?" Ricky said slowly, his tongue running along his lips.

"I can be late."

Ricky smirked but instead of leaning in and kissing Chase, he took a step back and walked into a side room. Chase tried to pull his hands out of the restraints, but they were fastened tightly.

Ricky returned with an old wooden chair, and he put it in the middle of the room, directly under the red bulb. It shone like a crackling fire, making the wood look scorched. He pushed Chase down into the chair; neither of them said a word.

Chase heard the sound of the glass display behind him opening. Ricky appeared behind him again, and he attached something to the restraints around his wrists. He couldn't see what they were, but when he tried to move them, his hands were fastened to the chair.

He gulped hard, the aching in his shorts growing with each passing silent second. He wanted to reach down and touch it, but he was being denied that simple pleasure.

Something cold brushed against his neck as Ricky slowly

walked around the chair. Chase had no idea what he was holding, but he had a good idea of what Ricky was going to do with it.

Ricky hooked his fingers around the waistband of Chase's underwear and shorts, and he pulled them delicately over his solid cock and smooth thighs. He tore them down to his feet and pulled them over his trainers.

Looking up into Chase's eyes, Ricky grabbed his ankles and pushed them against the rough wood. The cold leather wrapped around his inked skin, fastening him in place. He tried to wriggle his feet, but he knew if he tried too hard, he would rock back and crash on the floor.

Maintaining the eye contact, Ricky dragged Chase's t-shirt up his body, and he hooked it over his head. Ricky's crotch was level with Chase's, and he could see Ricky was as hard as he was. He tried to reach out to touch him, but his wrists didn't move.

Ricky's lips tenderly pressed against the side of Chase's mouth, not quite touching his lips. Chase craved the kiss, but Ricky had other ideas. Clutching Chase's thighs with a grip of steel, he let his lips drag roughly down Chase's neck and chest. His heart pounded in his chest with every new inch of skin Ricky touched.

Clutching his fists, he watched as Ricky's tongue ran along his inner thigh. His cock twitched out of control, which only seemed to make Ricky go even slower. He seemed to be enjoying the power it was giving him.

Just when Chase didn't think he could take the teasing anymore, Ricky's lips brushed against the tip of his cock. The hairs on Chase's arms stood to attention, and so did his nipples. He inhaled deeply, ignoring the urge he had to grab the back of Ricky's head.

He took the tip of his shaft into his mouth, his eyes fixed on Chase's. He squirmed in his seat and bit deep into his bottom lip.

Ricky's hot breath trembled against his skin before he started to travel up and down Chase's cock. His expert lips and tongue knew exactly what they were doing and Chase wasn't sure how long he was going to be able to hold on for.

Clenching his eyes shut, he gritted his teeth and breathed slowly. He wanted so badly to run his fingers through Ricky's hair. He looked down at Ricky as he used his mouth and hand to give Chase a form of pleasure he never knew he could reach.

A ringing phone startled him, making him jump, causing the chair to lift off the ground for a second. The phone was in Ricky's pocket, but he ignored it.

The longer the phone rang, the faster he worked. Inhaling deeply, Chase tossed his head back as he let out a low moan. He wanted so badly to slow things down, but Ricky was the one holding the reins.

"I'm close," he mumbled.

Ricky didn't slow down. He sped up. Clutching the base of his shaft with one hand and Chase's thigh with the other, he looked up into his eyes as he bobbed up and down.

It was all that Chase needed to release. He tried to force his eyes to stay open, but it was too intense. His body thrashed against the restraints as his cock pulsed against Ricky's waiting tongue.

When it passed, he opened his eyes as the sweat ran down his inked skin. Ricky smiled up at him as he unfastened Chase's ankle restraints. After his feet were free, he unbuckled the ones keeping his wrists in place and he was a free man again. Leaning on his knees, his cock still solid, he rubbed his wrists as he smirked up at Ricky.

"That was new," he said, unsure how to feel post-orgasm.

"Like I said, sweetheart," said Ricky as pulled his phone

out of his pocket. "I'm full of surprises. They left a voicemail."

Ricky turned and headed through the beaded curtains, and he pushed his phone to his ear, leaving Chase to redress. He almost forgot he had a full shift at the gym to do. Sighing, he wished he could stay with Ricky all day. The more time they spent together, the harder it was becoming to leave. He had barely been home to his flat since the fete.

"I should get going," Chase called into the other room as he climbed into his underwear and shorts. "Danny is so stuffy about being late. You would forget we were equal partners the way he goes on."

As he pulled his t-shirt over his head, he waited for Ricky to respond but he didn't. He picked up the chair and took it through to the room Ricky had grabbed it from. It was a small office. It was dark and windowless, and the walls were lined with filing cabinets. A small desk cluttered with papers sat in the middle of the room. Chase set the chair down in front of the table, and something colourful jumped out at him on the desk. It was a travel brochure for the Canary Islands. He tried to remember if Ricky had mentioned going on holiday.

Dismissing it, he straightened out his t-shirt and walked back into the shop. The daylight stung his eyes after the low red haze he had been subjected to. He had no idea how long they had been in there, but he knew he was cutting it close getting to work on time.

Ricky leaned against the counter, his phone clutched to his chest, and his eyes glazed over. A deep sadness had washed over him, and he looked deep in thought.

"Is everything okay?" asked Chase.

"They've let him go," he said, his eyes staring dead ahead, but looking eerily through Chase to the wall behind him. "Terrance Hoole, the guy who attacked me, they've dropped the charges against him. The case has fallen through."

Chase had almost forgotten the case was still going on in the background. Whenever he made progress with Ricky, there always seemed to be something to take them back two steps.

***

"Do you want something to eat? Or a drink?"

Dylan shook his head as he perched awkwardly on the edge of Ricky's yellow sofa, still in his school coat and shoes. He peered around the flat, his eyes stopping on the pink sheet covering the large canvas print of two naked men above the fireplace. He frowned and sighed heavily.

Ricky hovered in the kitchen, his phone clutched in his hand. He considered calling Tom to ask for advice on how to deal with Dylan, but he didn't want to come across as weak. He had surprised everyone by offering to watch Dylan, even if it was only one day a week. He wanted to surprise everyone by showing he could do it without messing it up like he had at the fete.

The problem was, the chatty and fun Dylan he had spent the weekend with was gone, and he had been left with an almost mute, sad little boy. Ricky put it down to Chase not being there.

"Why don't you take your coat and shoes off and get comfy? I'll find you something to watch on TV."

Dylan nodded and slumped off the sofa. He walked over to the front door and kicked off his shoes. He shrugged his coat off and reached up to put it on the hooks. He couldn't reach, so he climbed up onto the small table where Ricky usually tossed his keys. He kneeled on the edge and put his coat on the hook. When he was done, he walked back over to the sofa and perched on the edge again.

Ricky flicked on the TV, asking if Dylan wanted to watch anything specific, but he just shrugged and huffed out his chest as he stared down at the carpet. Ricky opted for the first kid's TV channel he found among the hundreds of channels, and he tossed the remote control on last month's issue of Vogue magazine on the coffee table.

He walked back into the kitchen and opened the fridge. The bottle of vodka caught his eye. He reached out, knowing it would take the edge off, but he grabbed the bottle of milk instead.

After filling the kettle, he made a cup of coffee and leaned against the fridge. Sipping the hot, milky coffee, he watched Dylan watch the TV, but he didn't seem interested in the bright colours.

Ricky knew how he felt. Since listening to the voicemail that morning, he hadn't been able to concentrate on anything else. He had been trying not to think about the case, because the court date he had been given was so far away. The voicemail had asked him to call the station, but he hadn't been able to bring himself to make that call. He couldn't even begin to understand what could have led to the man who left him for dead, being let off his bail.

"How about a board game?" Ricky put the coffee cup on the edge of the counter and slapped his hands together. "Or I help you with your homework?"

Dylan shrugged and looked over at his tiny book bag he had brought with him. Ricky took that as an invitation. He picked it up from the floor and sat next to Dylan.

Dylan finally settled into the couch, resting his tiny hands in his lap. He concentrated on his fiddling fingers as Ricky unzipped the bag. He pulled out the small stack of books, along with pieces of creased paper and a couple of pencil crayons.

He flicked through the books and he found the one labelled '*homework*'. He skimmed to the most recent page, where a printed out assignment had been stapled to the top of the page.

"'*Draw your family tree*'," Ricky read it aloud. "'*You may need to ask a parent for help*'."

"It's for history," Dylan finally spoke. "Miss Wilkinson said we were learning about the Tudors and she wanted us to find out about our families."

Something within Ricky hurt when he heard the sadness and pain in Dylan's small voice. Ricky knew that pain.

"Is this why you look sad, Dylan? Because you don't want to do this homework?"

Dylan nodded. Ricky tossed the book on the table and leaned back on the sofa, putting his arm across the back.

"Tell me why," he said quietly. "I'm a good listener, sweetheart."

Dylan glanced up to Ricky, but he looked unsure. If it wasn't for what had happened at the fete, he doubted Dylan would have even talked to him in the first place.

"Everybody has a mummy, but I don't. Sarah Braxton has two. Billy Kay said I was an alien experiment and that's why I don't have a mummy."

"Billy Kay sounds like an idiot."

"He is," he laughed softly. "Daddy said my mummy is an angel in the sky, but I don't know what that means. Everybody else has one at school."

"Do people pick on you for being different?"

Dylan nodded heavily and sighed. Ricky knew that feeling. Even when he was six, he knew he was different. People started calling him gay before he even knew what the word meant. Ricky knew first-hand how cruel children could be.

"Have you told your daddy?"

Dylan shook his head. He sniffed hard and wiped his nose with the back of his hand. Ricky thought he was about to cry, but he just sighed again. It looked like Dylan had the weight of the world on his shoulders at such a young age.

"Why don't I have a mummy?" he asked, looking up into Ricky's eyes. "Do you have one?"

"I do, but I don't have a daddy. Sometimes, people have to leave, and they go up to the sky."

"You mean they die?"

"Yes, they die."

"I know my mummy is dead," he said in a matter-of-factly voice. "I don't know why. My daddy won't talk about it."

"People say mean things, but it doesn't mean you have to believe them. You have a daddy who loves you very much, and that's all that matters. Don't let anybody dim your shine, Dylan."

Dylan nodded, then crawled into Ricky's side and rested his head against his chest. It took Ricky by surprise, and his body tightened, unsure of what to do. When he finally relaxed, he brought his hand from the back of the sofa and rested it gently on Dylan's shoulder. Dylan wrapped his tiny arm around Ricky's waist, and he buried his face in Ricky's t-shirt.

Soft, silent sobs escaped his tiny eyes and it took all of Ricky's energy not to cry with him. He looked up at the ceiling as his mind wandered towards Bret. The usual guilt flooded his system again, followed by fear.

A knock at the door disturbed them, and Dylan sat up straight and wiped his red eyes. He leaned forward and picked up his homework workbook along with a blue pencil crayon. There was another knock at the door, forcing Ricky to get up off the sofa.

When he opened the door and saw Chief Inspector Patrick Brody, he almost closed the door again.

"What do you want?" Ricky asked harshly.

"Can I come in, Mr. Thompson?" he asked, taking his hat off and walking in without waiting for Ricky's response. "There have been some developments in your case, and I was in the area so I thought I would tell you in person."

"Granddad!" Dylan jumped up from the couch and ran over to Patrick.

"Granddad?" Ricky mumbled.

"What are you doing here, Dylan?" he asked, through gritted teeth. "Why is my grandson in your house, Mr. Thompson?"

"Grandson?" Ricky looked from Dylan to Patrick, trying to piece together what was in front of him. "I don't understand."

"I'm Chase's father," he said bluntly. "I'll ask you *again*, why is Dylan here?"

Ricky gulped hard, but his throat was as dry as the desert. He opened his mouth to speak, but no words came out. He noticed something of Chase in Patrick's cold, grey eyes and it made his stomach knot.

Trying to keep his cool, he coughed and ran his hands through his hair as he thought of what to say to the police officer.

"Chase was having trouble finding somebody to watch Dylan for the summer, so I offered," he said, shrugging casually. "We're friends."

"*Friends?*" Patrick repeated coldly. "Since when?"

"Couple of months."

"*Right.*" Patrick's brow twitched, but his expression barely changed.

Dylan left Patrick's side and he went and sat back on the couch. It was clear to Ricky how uncomfortable Patrick was with his grandson being in Ricky's cottage. Patrick's eyes darted over to the hidden portrait above the fireplace, just as they had done the last time he was in his cottage.

"I'll get straight to the point, Mr. Thompson," Patrick said, his voice flat and lifeless. "We've had to drop the charges against Terrance Hoole."

"I got a voicemail. I know."

"In preparation for his court appearance, his lawyer uncovered your original statement, and because you claimed not to remember anything until the identity parade, he managed to have you called an unreliable witness. Mr. Hoole had a good alibi from his wife and kids saying he was at home all night, so the only thing sticking was your identification."

"*Unreliable?*" Ricky muttered. "Are you being *serious*, sweetheart? *You* saw the bruises. *You* saw my broken nose. What about the CCTV?"

"It was grainy. We were unable to positively identify Terrance Hoole as the man in the tape," Patrick spoke as though he was reading from a pre-written script. "All charges against Mr. Hoole have been dropped, and due to insufficient evidence, we have decided not to pursue this case any further. You, of course, have the right to request a review of the case, but I have to tell you, Mr. Thompson, it rarely makes any difference."

"What are you saying?"

"Move on and get on with your life," Patrick said as he put his hat back on. "There's nothing more to be done about it."

He nodded his head to Ricky as he glanced in Dylan's direction before heading for the door. Anger bubbled up within Ricky, and he didn't know how it was going to explode. He turned around and watched Patrick walk through the door.

"You'd love that, wouldn't you?" Ricky said through gritted teeth in a low voice. "For the queer to shut up and stop making a fuss. You've thought so since the first moment we met."

"I beg your pardon! That is a *very* brazen claim, Mr. Thompson."

"Drop the act," Ricky snapped. "I know your sort, sweetheart. You're no different than the men who did this to me in the first place."

Before the Inspector could reply, Ricky slammed the heavy door in his face. He leaned against the hard wood and listened as his garden gate landed forcefully in its lock.

He hadn't been looking forward to giving evidence in court, but he would have done it. Now, he didn't even have his chance to face the man who left him for dead.

"How do you spell Barbara," Dylan peered over the couch, clutching his homework workbook.

Pushing his angry thoughts to the back of his mind, Ricky pushed forward and smiled as he sat back on the couch. He had always known life was unfair, he just hadn't expected it to bite him on the arse in this way. He tried to focus on the voice in his mind, which sounded a lot like Tom's, telling him to focus on the new positives in his life, but it was hard when the dark grey cloud was never far from circling above him.

CHAPTER

TWENTY

After his long shift at the gym, Chase walked to Ricky's cottage, excited to see them both together. He hadn't expected Ricky to drag him straight into the kitchen with thunder in his eyes.

"I can't believe you knew and you never told me!" cried Ricky as he paced back and forth in the kitchen after a whole minute of ranting. "Did you just expect that I wouldn't find out?"

"Ricky, please, calm down."

"*Calm down*? Didn't you think it was important for you to tell me your father was the guy dealing with my case?"

"I was embarrassed."

"Of me?"

"Of *him*," sighed Chase as he grabbed Ricky's arms. "Just listen to me. I didn't find out until you gave him my name, I swear. I almost told you, but I didn't want you to think I was like him. He's not a very nice man."

"I guessed that much." Ricky pulled away and carried on pacing. "From the start he didn't take me seriously, and now I find out he's your dad! Where does that leave us?"

"It doesn't change anything. We're not close."

"Dylan knew who he was. That's pretty close," he cried, looking over to where Dylan was sitting on the couch doing his homework. "How do you think he will react when you tell him the truth about me?"

Chase looked down at the floor, remembering all of the things his father had said about Ricky. He wanted to tell him all of the times he had defended him, but he knew his words would fall on deaf ears.

"I'll tell him right now. I'll call him and tell him the truth." Chase pulled out his phone and held it in front of his face. "I swear to you, I don't care what he says or thinks. I should never have kept this from you."

Ricky stopped pacing and he stared at the phone. Shaking his head, he pushed Chase's arm down. He pressed his body into the fridge and ran his hands messily through his hair.

"No, don't do that," he said. "Not yet."

"I thought that's what you wanted?"

"I just want you to be honest with me," he said, his voice low. "That's all I wanted."

"I'm not the only one with secrets, Ricky."

Ricky's jaw clenched, forcing the corners of his lip into a snarl. He pushed himself away from the fridge and pointed a long finger in Chase's face.

"That was a low blow," he sneered.

Feeling like he was digging his own grave, Chase took a step back and turned around. He watched Dylan as he scribbled in his homework workbook, totally oblivious to what was going on just a few feet away.

"I'm sorry," said Chase.

He turned back to face Ricky, but his expression had softened, and the anger had been replaced with exhaustion.

"I'm sorry too," Ricky exhaled. "I'm taking out these charges being dropped on you. I'm sorry."

Chase took a step forward, and he cupped Ricky's face in his palm. Ricky leaned into it and slowly closed his eyes, his dark lashes casting shadows down his stubble covered cheeks.

"I should have told you," said Chase. "It was wrong."

"Don't, sweetheart," Ricky pulled away and leaned against the counter, his head low. "Don't be nice to me. I don't deserve it right now."

Chase's heart tightened. How long was Ricky going to walk through life thinking he didn't deserve happiness? He had hoped that was behind them.

"I promise I'll be honest with you from now on, I swear." Chase rested his hands on Ricky's shoulders and squeezed gently. "About everything. I just have one condition."

"What's that, sweetheart?" he laughed deliberately.

"You do the same for me."

Chase's words made Ricky tense up under his touch. He shrugged Chase off, and he turned back, his head nodding.

"I will, but not tonight. Right now, I just want to be on my own."

"Are you sure?"

"I'm sure, sweetheart," he said through a forced smile. "I need to process."

Chase stepped back and stuffed his hands in his pockets, trying to understand. He tried not to be disappointed in Ricky, but he couldn't help it. He knew leaving Ricky alone was the worst thing he could do, but he knew he couldn't fight it. Ricky was too headstrong to have his mind changed in an instant.

When Dylan had his shoes and coat on, Ricky walked them both to the door. It dawned on Chase that it would be the first time he had slept at his flat since the fete.

"Call me if you need anything. Night or day."

"I will, sweetheart."

Dylan was staring at his shoes as he rubbed them into the exposed wood floor, so Chase quickly kissed Ricky on the lips. Ricky returned the kiss, but it felt forced.

Chase reluctantly left Ricky, and he walked with Dylan down to his car outside of the gym. Hovering at his door, he looked into the distance to Ricky's cottage, just at the moment he closed the curtains.

Chase didn't know how Ricky was going to spend his evening, but he knew he was making a mistake leaving him to spend it alone.

***

Walking towards G-A-Y, Ricky caught his reflection in the window. Considering he had got into full drag in under an hour, he was surprised by how good he looked. His short, red leather dress and cropped at the waist black leather jacket made his rushed makeup and messy wig look intentional.

"Kitty Litter." The bouncer, who he knew was called Rhys, smiled as he opened the door. "I haven't seen you around here in a while."

"That's *Miss* Kitty Litter to you, Rhys. And I've been away in Switzerland helping Toxic Tonya end it all, but I'm back now."

Ricky walked into the club. The familiarity of the over-played pop songs felt like a comforting blanket. It struck him that he hadn't been out in drag for the fun of it in a long time, even before the attack. He approached the bar, wondering why he wasn't there every night of the week.

"Kitty!" The bartender smiled. "Good to see you back on your feet."

Ricky couldn't remember the twenty-something's name, even if he had slept with him before.

"It's good to be back, sweetheart. Make me something fruity and make it strong."

The drink was on the house and he knew it wouldn't be the first free beverage of the night. Even if the drinks weren't coming from behind the bar, there was never a shortage of young, gay boys who wanted to buy the token drag queen a drink.

He sipped his free cocktail as he walked towards the dance floor. Even for early on a Wednesday night, it was quiet. Aside from a couple of people chatting on the couches, the bar was empty.

Pulling his cigarettes from his bra, he headed up the metal staircase to the smoking terrace.

He pushed open the door, and a cloud of smoke hit him. The handful of smokers looked in his direction. He recognised some of them, but none by name.

With his lit cigarette, Ricky sat on a wooden bench pushed up against the wall so he could observe the terrace. Puffing on his cigarette, he was beginning to remember why he hadn't been to the bars in drag for a while.

He wondered when it had become so mainstream and normal. He missed the days when he would walk into a room, and everybody would turn and stare. The attention pleased his narcissistic side, which was amplified the second he climbed into his heels. These days, drag queens were no longer the shocking ones on the scene. Every young gay boy in the village thought they were a drag queen and it only made Ricky feel like the old man hanging around the party. He finished his cigarette, realising why he never left the safety of his own bar.

He tossed the cigarette onto the ground and stamped it out with his heel. Looking up at the dark, starry sky, he sipped his drink. The attack played through his mind. He remembered not everybody was so tolerant of drag. He had stayed awake many nights since, wondering if any of it would have happened if it hadn't been for Miss Kitty Litter. That monster was back on the streets with his friends, but he doubted they would be stupid enough to return to the scene of the crime after getting away with it.

A man sat next to Ricky, breaking his thought. He looked like he was in his late twenties and he was classically beautiful, with soft skin, strong features and a thick head of dark hair. He pulled a cigarette from his packet and patted down his pocket.

"You got a light, love?" he asked Ricky.

Ricky produced the lighter from his bra and lit the man's cigarette. He winked his appreciation as he took his first puff of nicotine.

"Dead tonight, ain't it?" he said, glancing in Ricky's direction. "Makes me wish I'd stayed at home."

"I remember when Canal Street was busy every night, regardless of the day of the week." Ricky lit another cigarette and put his cocktail on the bench next to him. "It only seems to get busy when the gay tourists come down our way."

"Gay tourists?" asked the man with a smirk of intrigue.

"People who aren't part of the club who want to come ogle at the freaks. I can't remember the last time I played to a full club of gay people. Can't complain too much, somebody has to buy the drinks."

"I blame the apps," said the man. "You don't need to

leave your bed to get a shag. You just order whatever you want and it arrives within the hour."

Ricky laughed and nodded his agreement. He had been guilty of that himself. When he was first on the scene, he would be lucky if anybody replied to his online gay profiles when he checked them at the local library. He'd had no choice but to go to the bars if he wanted to get fucked.

"I'm Mark, by the way," he held out his hand.

"Miss Kitty Litter," he said. "Or Ricky."

"You exist? I thought Kitty Litter was a myth."

"*Miss* Kitty Litter," Ricky corrected him. "And a myth, sweetheart?"

Mark smirked as he came to the end of his cigarette. When he was finished, he blew the smoke into the air and tossed his cigarette into the overflowing ashtray. He smiled at Ricky, as though he should know exactly what he was talking about.

"All of my friends say they've fucked you," he laughed, shaking his head in disbelief. "I thought it was some kind of joke, or something, but here you are. You've been a private joke with my best friend since we were in college."

Ricky shifted uncomfortably in his seat, not doubting what Mark was saying was true. On more than one occasion, a group of friends had walked into London Bridge, and Ricky had fucked his way through the full set. He used to wear it proudly as a badge of honour, but it didn't make him feel proud tonight; it made him feel dirty.

"A private joke?" he asked.

"Whenever something sounds so ridiculous it can't be true, we call it a Kitty Litter," he said, his tone apologetic. "It's dumb really."

Ricky tried to laugh, but it was forced. The smoking area had emptied, leaving only a couple of people. Ricky had never cared about being the only person in a club before. He had always been the last one to leave at the end of the night, in or out of drag. He knew it wasn't even ten yet and it already felt so late.

"Let me buy you a drink," said Mark. "I'll call my mates, get them to come down. They'll never believe you're here."

He considered the offer for a moment. It wasn't too long ago that he would have accepted, just for the promise of a free drink and a shag at the end of it.

"No thanks, sweetheart," he said calmly as he stood up and brushed the creases out of his leather dress. "It's past my bedtime."

Ricky looked down at Mark's phone, noticing the date. August 3rd. His stomach dropped, and he almost threw up the cocktail he hadn't even finished.

Ricky headed down the steps two at a time. The nightclub had filled up, but he didn't care. He headed straight for the door. Rhys said something, but he wasn't listening. He just knew he needed to get out of there as quickly as possible.

Fumbling for his cigarettes, he headed to the top of the street, where Canal Street joined the main road. He turned left and walked over the bridge. Leaning over, he stared down into the dark canal as he tried to light his cigarette. His shaking hands dropped the lighter and it dropped down onto the path and ,bounced into the canal.

"Shit!" Ricky cried out, tossing his cigarettes in with them.

Turning, he slid down the wall and dropped to the street. People and cars passed by but nobody paid him attention. He was practically invisible to the world. He pulled his phone out and scrolled to the most recent contact.

"Hi, it's me. Can you come and get me?"

Staring ahead at the road, he couldn't believe he hadn't

noticed it was August 3rd. He had been so distracted by everything that had been happening, he had missed the anniversary of Bret's death.

CHAPTER

TWENTY
ONE

I n the hours since Dylan went to bed, Chase had been watching the clock. Time ticked by as he drummed his fingers on his phone screen, resisting the powerful urge to call Ricky. The only thing stopping him was his obvious cry for space. Chase knew he had to respect that.

He scooped up his cigarettes and walked out to the walkway out of his flat. Leaning over the concrete balcony, he watched the stars of the city twinkle in the blackness. He lit his cigarette and inhaled deeply, even if it didn't help the way it used to. It had become a bad habit and nothing more. He had always doubted his addiction to nicotine was strong enough to compel him to keep smoking.

A black and white cat walked dangerously along the concrete balcony edge. It sat in front of Chase and looked expectantly up at him. It purred softly as Chase tickled under its chin.

"What would you do?" he asked the cat.

The cat stood up and head butted Chase's shoulder. It wasn't wearing a collar and it looked like it hadn't eaten in a while. He stubbed his cigarette out on the ledge and doubled back to his flat. He grabbed a half-eaten pack of sliced ham from the fridge and emptied it onto a plate.

He put it on the floor, and the cat looked up at him suspiciously. Chase nodded his approval. He knew the cat wouldn't understand, but it grabbed a slice from the plate all the same.

Annie shuffled out of her flat wearing a pair of black slippers, pulling her pink robe tight around her frail body. Her grey hair was cluttered with rollers held in place by small metal clips.

"I thought I heard you come out," she said quietly as she closed her front door. "Can't sleep too?"

"I haven't tried." He bent down and tickled the cat's scalp as it ate the last of the ham at breakneck speed. "Met this little guy, though."

"That's Susan. Haven't seen her up here in a while. Tried to take her in a few times myself, but she can't be held down."

"Sounds like somebody I know," he said.

When the ham was finished, Susan scuttled off into the dark, licking her lips after her satisfying meal. Annie and Chase leaned against the balcony and looked out into the night together. It was a warm night, but the slight chill on the wind added some relief.

Chase wondered if there was some awkwardness between them. They had spoken plenty of times since she had seen Ricky on his bedroom floor, but never without Dylan as the buffer. Now they were alone in the night, it was all he could think about.

"You don't have to explain yourself," she said before he had a chance to speak. "I'm not one to judge, love. One of my sons is gay."

"I'm not gay."

"Oh?"

"Not technically." He lit up another cigarette and offered one to Annie, and to his surprise, she accepted it. "Here, let me light that for you."

She inhaled deeply and blew the smoke out of her nose like a dragon. A content smile relaxed her lips.

"Haven't had one of these since eighty-seven." She sent the ash tumbling over the edge with a delicate flick. "Quitting gave me another twenty years, make no mistakes, but I have missed the feeling."

Chase couldn't imagine Annie as a young woman. In his mind, she had always been in her eighties, and she would outlive them all. From the bulging of her joints and the translucency of her skin, he knew she didn't have many good years ahead of her.

"So if you're not gay, what are you, love?"

"Somewhere in between. I never thought I'd end up with a guy. I always thought Dylan needed a mother."

"Nonsense," she snapped, rolling her wide eyes. "My Rodger was a great father to our boys, but what's that boiled down to? A phone call once a month, and that's when they remember. The truth is, no matter how you raise your kids, they get to a certain age, and none of it matters anymore. All you can do is teach them good values and hope for the best. The rest is down to chance."

Chase inhaled the smoke and considered what she was saying. He had always been so worried about messing up Dylan's life with the dysfunctional nature of how he lived, but if it made no difference in the end, was he worrying about nothing?

"Maybe you're right."

"I've got fifty years on you, love. Of course I'm right." She decided she was finished with the cigarette half way down, so she dragged it along the concrete and pinched the end before tucking it in her robe pocket. "Your man friend is handsome. Not spending the night together?"

Chase wished they were. He finished his cigarette and flicked it over the edge.

"He needs some space."

"Space? You've only been together five minutes."

"It's complicated."

"Complicated?" she smirked coyly. "You kids have it so easy these days. You make your own problems with those phone things of yours, tapping away and ignoring the world."

"More complicated than that," he laughed. "I keep messing up."

Chase explained everything to Annie. He started with the night they met, right up to Ricky finding out who Chase's father was. She listened silently, nodding at the right parts and absorbing every nuance and detail. When he finished, he was surprised by how much they had fit into the short space of time they had known each other.

"He sounds like a piece of work," she said when he was finished. "Do you think he's worth it?"

"If I didn't, I wouldn't be risking everything to try. I haven't had a real relationship for years. I've been so focussed on Dylan, but I can't ignore the way I feel."

"Do you love him?"

Chase flicked opened his cigarette packet, but there were none left. He screwed up the box and tossed it into the night. The question made him feel more than a little uncomfortable.

"Your silence speaks a thousand words, love. Don't sleep on it. If you want to sort things out, don't wait around. Take it from an old bird like me, life is too short for regrets."

They said their goodbyes and they went back to their flats. Chase checked in on Dylan, who was fast asleep on his bed with his covers on the floor. Chase picked up the dinosaur duvet and placed it over his son. He stroked his pale blonde hair and kissed his forehead.

When he was sitting back in the living room watching the clock, he picked up his phone and hovered over Ricky's number. He stared at it for what felt like a lifetime before finally hitting the dial button.

Ricky didn't answer; Chase didn't leave a message.

***

Ricky looked down. He was wearing a wedding dress. He didn't need a mirror to know his face was free of makeup. Tightening his fingers around the bouquet of black roses, he felt the thorns pierce his flesh.

All eyes in the church were on him, but they looked sad. Why were they so sad? He reached the end of the aisle where a man in a suit was waiting for him. When he turned around and Ricky noticed it was Chase, he felt relieved. Chase reached out a hand for him. Ricky dropped the flowers and accepted Chase's hand, which was cold to the touch.

They turned to face the altar, but a deafening crash of thunder made them both turn around. The church doors burst open and the aisle turned into a calm, black river. A wooden coffin draped in the most vibrant flowers Ricky had ever seen floated along the river without making a ripple on the calm surface. He knew Bret was inside the coffin. He turned to Chase for reassurance, but he had disappeared. He tried to make eye contact with one of their guests, but they had also disappeared. The walls of the church burst into flames and crumbled to ash, leaving him alone with the coffin in a black void. Reaching out his hand, he tried to touch the wood, but it was impossibly out of reach. The flowers faded and crinkled, dying before his eyes. He took a careful step forward, but the floor evaporated and he fell into the darkness.

Ricky landed with a crash on Tom's sofa, the rising sun piercing through the curtains of the farmhouse living room and burning his eyes. He sat up and rubbed the crick out of his neck. Tom's cat, Mulder, was curled up at the bottom of his feet.

Ricky ruffled his short hair as he scratched Mulder's head. He jumped down from the couch and trotted away, leaving Ricky alone. He sat on the edge of the sofa for a moment, trying to think about the dream he had just had. It had already slipped away.

The remnants of his drag were folded neatly on the armchair, no doubt thanks to Belinda. After his shower last night, he crawled into some of Cole's spare clothes and crashed out on the sofa before Tom could start his interrogation.

Ricky listened out for other sounds of life on the farm, but it seemed he was the only one awake. Scratching under his arm, he yawned as he walked into the kitchen. The gang of sheepdogs jumped up excitedly, pawing gently at his grey sweatpants.

Having spent two weeks recovering on the farm after his attack, he had picked up the workings of the place. He filled Mulder's dish and put it on the dining table in the living room. According to Tom, it was the only place he would eat his food since moving from his tiny flat to the farmhouse. After feeding the dogs, he made a cup of coffee and headed out of the back door.

Inhaling the fresh country air, Ricky walked toward the stables, thinking over the events that had brought him to the farm again. Anxiety like he had never known knotted inside his stomach. With an odd twinge of embarrassment, he regretted going out. It had seemed like the logical thing to do in the circumstances; the cold light of day proved otherwise.

Stroking one of the horse's noses his thoughts wandered to Chase. He should have called him, but he had called Tom instead. He didn't want Chase to keep saving him.

He checked his phone, reassured that it was August 4th. He still couldn't believe he had forgotten Bret's anniversary. He usually spent it at home alone with a bottle of vodka and a bolt on the door.

Before he could dwell on it any longer, Tom appeared at the back door, already in his work clothes. A pair of well worn boots travelled halfway up his calf, making way to faded jeans and a grey knitted jumper, which smacked of Belinda's handy work.

"You're up early," said Tom. "Belinda's about to make some breakfast. Shall I tell her to make you up a plate?"

Ricky considered it for a moment, but he wanted nothing more than to go to his cottage. Breakfast would lead to lunch and lunch to dinner and before he would know it, Tom and Cole would be pouring their advice on him, attempting to force him to do things he didn't want to do.

"No thanks, sweetheart. I better head home."

Tom seemed uneasy about being denied an explanation for what had happened last night, but Ricky would have to give it another day. He was unsure himself. He just knew he had never felt more out of place somewhere he used to call his true home.

In his borrowed clothes and with his drag in a plastic

bag, he set off down the winding country lane toward the village. The sun scorched in the periwinkle sky, promising more hot summer before autumn claimed the weather. He let the rays lick his skin, wondering if jumping on a plane and jetting off to somewhere the sun never stopped shining would solve his problems. He thought about the brochure sitting on his desk at the shop, and for a fleeting moment, it seemed like the perfect idea.

The dirt road led him onto Hebden Bridge's high street. He considered walking the long way to avoid passing the gym, but he decided against it. He wasn't sure why he was avoiding Chase, but he felt like he needed to.

Clutching the handles of the plastic bag, he passed the window and he noticed Chase spotting for somebody in the weights area. Ricky wasn't sure if it was his imagination, but he looked distracted.

He pushed on the door, surprised by his own unpredictability. It was easy to pretend like he didn't want to see Chase, until he saw the clear cut lines of his profile and his muscles jutting out of the shorts and vest. Even through Ricky's sour mood, Chase didn't fail to cast a warm glow over him.

Tossing his plastic bag over his shoulder, he blended into the crowd of fitness fanatics. In Cole's sweatpants, tight white t-shirt, and running shoes he didn't look too out of place.

He hovered by the edge of the weights area and waited for Chase to catch his eye in the mirror. It only took a matter of seconds.

"You're doing great Chris," said Chase as he heaved the bar out of the overweight man's hands on the bench. "Why don't we have a five-minute break so you can catch your breath?"

Red faced and sweating, Chris nodded his appreciation

and sucked on the cap of his water bottle.

Chase didn't speak, he just walked in the direction of the changing rooms. Ricky followed him without question. It reminded him of being summoned to the Head Teacher's office, which had happened more than once in his five years at high school. Dying his hair bright pink and refusing to change it for two weeks was one of his personal favourite memories.

The changing room was empty, but it was clear the gym was full. Kit bags and towels draped the benches in the middle, and the sound of running water signalled the shower was in use. It reminded Ricky of their first, real encounter. A sense of urgency to repeat the act swept over him for a brief moment, so he swallowed it down and joined Chase in sitting on the benches.

"How are you feeling?" he asked, without a hint of annoyance or anger.

Ricky sucked the air between his teeth and tried to pin down one emotion. In Chase's presence, it was hard to think coherently. It was almost as if nothing else mattered, even if it would the moment he was alone.

"I went out in drag last night," Ricky said self-consciously, feeling the anxiety gnawing away at his once unapologetic choices. "I needed to blow off steam, but it all felt wrong."

"Did something happen? Did somebody do something to you?"

Ricky thought about the guy in the smoking area. He had already forgotten his name, but not what he had said. How could something he once wore as a badge of honour make him feel so sordid and wrong?

"I don't fit in there anymore," Ricky said. "I'm old and tired."

"You're not old." Chase squeezed Ricky's knee

affectionately. "Are you sure something didn't happen?"

Bret jumped to mind, but he pushed him away. He wasn't ready to process that guilt until he was alone.

"I'm sure, I just realised something, that's all," he inhaled deeply, wishing he had stopped off to buy a packet of cigarettes after throwing his away last night. "Doing drag in the gay village used to be my sanctuary. It was my safe place to feel good about myself, but it doesn't work anymore. It's turned into more of an asylum. It's springing leaks, and I can feel myself going down with the ship, sweetheart."

"The village has changed a lot recently."

"It's not the village that has changed," he said, the thought tearing at his insides. "It's me that's changed, but I don't know if I wanted to change. I liked my life before."

"Is this because of the attack?" he asked, squeezing his knee again.

"Maybe. Maybe not. *I don't know.* All I know is, I feel like a whole new person. I don't recognise myself in the mirror. To tell you the truth, sweetheart, it's freaking me out."

Chase's lips trembled with the need to smile, maybe even laugh. For a moment, Ricky felt defensive, but he realised his fears sounded so ridiculous out loud. Why were they eating away at him so viciously then?

"People change. It's part of life Ricky. You can't fight it."

"Can't I?" he laughed sarcastically. "I've been holding back evolution for years. Those religious nuts who don't believe Charles Darwin would be so proud."

Chase leaned on his knees, his tattoo smothered biceps tensing as he rested his fists under his chin. Out of the corner of his eye, he gave him such an adoring look, Ricky would swear he was looking at a newborn kitten.

"When we were at Coltrane House, you said you would take a leap of faith," he spoke with softness in his voice. "You leapt, but nothing bad happened. All of this, it's in your mind, Ricky."

Ricky appreciated the gesture, but his fears wouldn't vanish just because they weren't visible. The harsh voice in his mind was always the loudest in the room, even when Miss Kitty Litter was present.

Even staring at Chase's almost perfectly symmetrical face made Ricky ache with desire so strong it scared Ricky. He had once owned that feeling because he knew it was fleeting and ended the moment he kicked them out of bed, but the feeling for Chase never vanished.

Chase leaned in, his eyes attached to Ricky's. His lips were more persuasive than he wanted to admit. Their lips brushed together gently in a tender kiss, but it quickly turned explosive and exploratory. Chase's thick fingers travelled up Ricky's inner thigh, promising to do a whole manner of things, all of which weren't suitable for the changing room.

Ricky didn't stop him. The ache within him needed it. Chase's attention was a drug he couldn't kick. His cock hardened just by the movement of Chase's fingers clasping around it through the fabric. The noise from the machines and the chatter in the gym only turned him on more.

Chase's hand moved swiftly, tugging harder and faster as their kiss intensified. An audience could be watching them, and they wouldn't even know through their clenched eyes.

He wrapped his fingers firmly around the back of Chase's head, pulling him in even closer. Panting through the kissing, his chest heaved and his stomach retracted as Chase's fingers drove him closer to that sweet spot. It was so urgent and forbidden. Time wasn't on their side, so he wasn't going to hold back.

Digging his nails into Chase's neck, he moaned through the fumbling movement of their lips. Chase's fingers gripped his shaft even harder, pumping until Ricky was dangling on the edge of the rushed orgasm.

He unleashed, giving into the quick burst of unexpected pleasure. A wet patch formed in his borrowed underwear and sweatpants as his shaft thrust against Chase's grip and the material. Eyes still closed, he could feel Chase smiling through their motionless lips.

The sound of the running water stopped, and they tore their faces away from each other. A tall, classically handsome man with muscles to rival Chase's walked into the changing room with a towel around his waist. His eyes immediately went to the dark wet patch in Ricky's pants. They widened, and a knowing smirk threatened to consume his lips. Arching his brows, he grabbed his bag from his locker and walked slowly into a cubicle. When the door was locked, Ricky jumped up, but Chase didn't seem as concerned.

"I should get back to work," he said quietly, the pleasurable smile still spread across his face. "Don't worry too much. Things have a way of sorting themselves out."

Chase stood up and gripped Ricky's t-shirt. Despite almost being caught jerking him off, Chase pulled him in for one last prolonged kiss. When their lips parted, he didn't immediately pull away. His hazel eyes danced over Ricky's face, as though he was observing the most beautiful man in the world. Ricky couldn't understand it.

Chase opened his mouth to speak, but no words came out. Closing his lips, he sighed through his nose, his eyes half closing.

"Ricky, I love you," he said quietly and urgently.

The words hit Ricky like a piano falling from a ten-storey building. The changing room started to close in around him, and the damp patch in his underwear turned ice cold. His stomach coiled up into a tight knot, as did his thoughts, depriving him of speech.

Chase didn't seem to notice. He bit hard into his lip as he backed away. He winked at Ricky before heading to the changing room door. Before he went back to work, he turned to face Ricky one more time.

"I mean it."

Ricky could do nothing more than nod like a newborn baby without neck support. He couldn't think or speak, he just knew he needed to get out of there. Chase walked through the door, leaving Ricky alone.

The cubicle door opened, and the man walked out in his clothes, the same knowing smirk still on his lips. He knew what had happened, even if he had missed the main event. Ricky wouldn't be surprised if he had been sitting in the cubicle with his ear to the door.

"What are you looking at?" Ricky snapped venomously.

The man chuckled dryly before following Chase out of the changing room.

Clutching the plastic bag over his crotch, Ricky pushed hard on the door and hurried for the exit, avoiding everybody's gaze. The only gaze he caught was that of Chase's brother who was walking into the gym with a coffee in his hand at the same time Ricky was leaving. He looked confused and angry to see Ricky, but he wasn't going to stick around to ask why.

He hurried back to his cottage and locked the door, more scared than he had ever been. He immediately grabbed his old phonebook and flicked through the pages until he found the number he wanted. He hadn't tried calling it in years, but he knew it would still work.

"Brian?" he forced a smile into his voice, hiding the rumbling anxiety. "It's Ricky, sweetheart. About that job you keep telling me about?"

CHAPTER

TWENTY
TWO

The gym was always busy on Fridays and this week was no exception. Chase had taught back-to-back personal training sessions all morning, so when his lunch break rolled around, he was more than ready. He didn't get to have his full hour, but he managed to gobble down the tuna and cucumber sandwich he picked up from the pharmacist across the road.

It had been two days since Chase saw Ricky, and the same amount of days since Chase had declared his love. He had doubted the decision since, but he was trying not to overthink it. He had said it because he meant it. Ricky's sudden flu explained why he had dodged all of his calls and had only been replying via text message.

Chase opened the white paper bag and glanced at the

medication. He wasn't sure what difference it would make, but it gave him a valid excuse for dropping by Ricky's cottage after work. He had been given strict instructions to stay away, but Chase hadn't missed a flu shot since he was in high school. He screwed up the bag and headed back to work. The promise of seeing Ricky at the end of his shift lifted his mood and made the prospect of another seven hours seem like an easy feat.

"We need to hire someone else," said Danny as Chase approached the counter. "We're completely fully booked up. I've been turning away training sessions all week, and Beth's yoga class is brimming to bursting. I was thinking of asking if she wanted to add another class during the week? What do you think?"

"Won't that just eat up more of our profits?" Chase knew money wasn't as important to Danny as it was to Chase. "We've just gotten this place in the green."

"If we don't keep up with the rate of growth, we'll implode bro," he mumbled as he typed away on the laptop. "I was looking at the pet shop next door. They're looking to sell up, or so I've heard. Would make a good extension."

"I thought we agreed all decisions would be split?"

"You've been a little preoccupied, don't you think, bro?" Danny's eyes darted up and held Chase's gaze.

Chase frowned, uncertain of what his brother meant. Danny had been acting strange all week, and it hadn't gone unnoticed, even if Chase hadn't put his finger on why. He had been putting it down to Natalie's hormones getting on his nerves.

Deciding against confronting him in front of a full gym, Chase grabbed a bottle of water from the fridge and headed over to tidy some stray weights. In the mirror, he caught Danny watching him as he worked but he decided not to agonise over it. If his brother was in a bad mood, he didn't want it inflicted on him too.

When the weights were tidied away, he headed to the stock room to check the levels for Monday's order. Even though Danny's eyes were trained on the laptop under the desk, Chase could feel him glaring at him out of the corner of his eyes as he walked by.

Standing on a wooden crate, he shimmied open the tiny window and pulled his secret packet of cigarettes from the empty plant pot on the window ledge. He hated checking the stock levels, so a crafty cigarette break away from the hustle of the gym made it worth it. He lit his cigarette and blew the first puff of smoke out of the tiny gap in the window, his eye trained on the smoke alarm directly behind him.

His mind turned to Ricky. He hated the thought of him being home alone and sick in bed. It was likely Tom and Cole would have stopped by to check on him, if they hadn't been commanded to stay away too. Through the gap in the window, he could just about see a tiny portion of the high street. He caught a glimpse of two guys walking down the street, hand in hand. His heart fluttered, and he wondered if that would be Ricky and him one day. He had never been big on public displays of affection, but there was something about holding Ricky's hand that made him want to do it.

The stock room door burst open and Danny appeared in the doorway. Chase wasn't even halfway through his cigarette.

"Are you smoking in here?" he cried, wafting his hand. "Jane just said she could smell smoke. Bro, are you trying to get us shut down?"

Chase scratched his cigarette along the ledge until it was no longer lit and he slotted it back in the packet along with the green plastic lighter. He blew the last of the smoke out, wafted the air and clamped the tiny window shut. Turning around, he noticed a slight grey fog under the fluorescent lighting.

"I was just doing the stock check," he said as he stepped down from the wooden crate. "It's my gym too, Danny. Jesus, you're acting like my boss today."

"Somebody needs to be the responsible one."

"And that's suddenly you?" laughed Chase sarcastically. "Older doesn't mean wiser."

Danny stepped into the stock room and closed the door behind him, leaving the gym unattended. His bulky frame blocked the only exit, making Chase wish the window behind him was bigger. Whatever was on his brother's mind, he was sure he was about to hear about it.

"What's gotten into you recently?" his tone was chilly and blunt. "You've been treating this place like a drop-in centre. Coming and going when you please, leaving shifts early, giving away free out of hours training sessions to *that* guy."

Chase folded his arms across his chest and solidified his stance. He was confused by the unexpected mention of Ricky. Narrowing his eyes, he stared silently at his brother. Danny didn't elaborate on his point, so they stood in silence until one of them spoke.

"Why do you have such a problem with Ricky?" asked Chase, hoping his question wasn't too revealing.

"I just don't like him. Is that a crime?"

"You don't even know him."

"And you do?" he snapped pointedly. "I thought you were just his trainer?"

It was Danny's turn to fold his arms tightly across his chest. His stare darkened and his brows lowered. He looked as though he was waiting for Chase to say something, but he had no idea what to say. For a split second, he thought Danny had uncovered the truth about his relationship with

273

Ricky. He immediately dismissed that thought as being unfounded. It would take more than one huge jump to come to that conclusion without having all of the pieces of the jigsaw laid out in front of him.

"You don't think I talk to my clients?" said Chase as casually as he could, attempting to disguise the dryness in his throat. "It's good for business to be friendly with them, or would you rather I trained them in silence?"

"But it's not just that, is it?"

"What's that supposed to mean?" he snapped, glad that his shaking hands were tucked away.

"Dad told me about him babysitting Dylan. It's *not* right."

"Oh, don't you start that too! I'm still waiting for the outraged phone call from *Father Of The Year*: Patrick Brody. The only reason I had to ask other people to watch Dylan is because *your* wife went back on her promise."

"Did you want her to turn down an American book tour? This is huge for her. This could really put her on the map over there. Are you that selfish?"

"I'm selfish?" laughed Chase. "I do everything in my life for my son. He's the only one I care about."

"Really?" he ground the word between his teeth. "What about this so called girlfriend of yours? What was her name again?"

"Rachel," he answered quickly. "Of course I care about her. You've missed the point."

"When are we going to meet this Rachel? How long have you been dating again?"

Danny's questioning was edged with steel, and it drilled Chase into the ground. He felt a balloon rise up in his chest, forcing his lungs and air out of the way. It threatened to explode, and he didn't know what he would do when it did. It was clear Danny knew Rachel was a lie.

Chase considered coming clean to his brother. He was going to have to tell him the truth about Ricky eventually and now was a good a time as any. The words were on the tip of his tongue, but he couldn't commit to them. Fear knotted inside of him, and a shiver of panic slithered down his spine.

"You'll meet her when I'm ready for you to meet her," he said as calmly as he could. "Until then, get off my case, okay?"

Danny laughed and shook his head. He backed down and turned to the door. Before opening it, he muttered, "You're so full of shit, bro."

Chase knew his attempt to reinforce the lie hadn't worked. It might have even damaged his cause more than helped it. Following Danny back out to the gym, he wondered to what extent his brother knew the truth. Before he could find out, Danny grabbed his jacket and car keys and stormed out of the gym, leaving Chase to deal with the long line of irritated customers waiting at the counter with their membership cards in hand.

As Chase worked through the backlog, apologising blankly to each of them, numerous questions stabbed at his chest. If he didn't dampen the fires soon, the volcano that was his life was threatening to explode and burn everybody close.

Ever since meeting Ricky, he had been able to control how he continued to present himself to the world, especially his family, but he could feel that mask about to dissolve. He wasn't sure if he would ever be ready to deal with that fallout.

***

"Isn't all of this a little sudden?" asked Tom as he helped

Ricky pack his suitcase. "You didn't mention you had a gig in Gran Canaria."

"An old friend called me last night," he lied. "There's a tiny drag bar in the Yumbo Centre in Maspalomas and their host has come down with the flu. They need someone to fill in for a couple of weeks. I'm the first person he thought of. The bar's called *Ricky's Show Bar*, so it's destiny, sweetheart."

"And Chase is okay with you jetting off so suddenly?" said Tom with cooling disapproval. "What about your DJ gig in London Bridge?"

"Toxic Tonya's covering until I get back. I've already sorted it with Jackson. I'll be back in time for Pride. You won't even notice I'm gone."

Tom frowned as he continued to fold and pack Ricky's underwear. As he sorted through the makeup he would be taking, Ricky wondered how many lies he had told over the past two days.

The lies had started when he had called his old friend, Brian, who went by the drag name Miss Anita Dick. They had worked together way back when Ricky first got into drag, but Brian had traded in Manchester for the year-round sun of the Canary Islands. He had asked Ricky to go with him and he had got as far as the airport before deciding to stay. It had only been six months since Bret's funeral, and he hadn't been ready to say goodbye to all of the places they had been together.

Ten years later, he still wasn't sure if he was making the right decision. Brian had been Bret's oldest friend from childhood and even if he wouldn't admit it, Ricky was sure Brian had moved abroad to run away from facing what had happened. Staying behind, Ricky had chosen to imprison himself in a cycle of punishment and deprival. It was only in the last couple of weeks the cycle had started to lose its grip on his life.

Hearing Chase say the three words Ricky had dreaded for the last ten years had only strengthened the cycle. Looking back, he knew he should have gotten on that plane with Brian all those years ago.

As Ricky watched Tom through the mirror, he wondered how his best friend was going to react if he didn't come home after the two weeks. He had lied about Brian being the one to call him, but he hadn't lied about the hosting job in the bar. The host wasn't trapped in her apartment with the flu, she had spectacularly walked out in the middle of a Sister Act medley when one of the new girls stepped on her dress and made her trip off the stage and break her nose. Brian had told him she was threatening to sue and her return was looking more unlikely by the day, which was why he offered Ricky a two-week trial to see if Ricky liked the place. The trial wasn't to see if Brian liked Ricky as the host, because Brian knew how talented Ricky was.

Gathering up his foundation sticks, he thought of the other lies he had told. The host with the broken nose wasn't the only queen to have come down with a mysterious case of the sudden flu. His thoughts clouded with uneasiness at the thought of Chase thinking he was sick. He felt even worse knowing that he was running away without telling him.

Ricky knew it was the only way he could get clarity. He needed to get as far away from his life so he could finally move on. As long as the ghost of Bret hovered over his shoulder, reminding him of how much he had already lost, he was never going to move on. He had been kidding himself that he could do that with Chase.

"You're taking a lot of drag for two weeks, don't you think?" heaved Tom as he tried to zip up the first suitcase.

"Won't you be over the weight limit?"

"Are you calling me fat, sweetheart?" he quipped in the mirror. "A queen needs to have choices, so I bought extra baggage space on the plane. I want the Brits on their jollies to see that some of us queens do have a sense of style. Some of those queens abroad are rough."

"I didn't think you'd want to do drag for a while after what happened on Wednesday."

"A minor blip, sweetheart. I go where the money is. They're offering me a good rate for going at such short notice. Matthew and Brendon are fine with working full time at the shop, since they're off from uni for the summer. It's all worked out perfectly."

Tom grumbled deep in his throat, his brows heavy over his eyes. Ricky had become an expert at hiding how he really felt, but he knew Tom was one of the few people who could see right through it. Chase was another.

Ignoring the impending feeling of loss, he pulled out his fake eyelashes drawer and dumped the dozen or so boxes into his hand luggage. Glancing at the second suitcase, he started to think about his shoes.

Drag had always been his safety blanket, and he had worried that had gone away, leaving him exposed to the world, but drag had stepped in to save him once again, offering him an escape from reality.

After picking out nearly twenty different pairs of shoes, he dropped them messily into the case and tossed a handful of different wigs onto the mess. Checking his watch, he knew he had another six hours before he needed to be at the airport, but he wanted to set off sooner rather than later. He wasn't good at explanations and goodbyes.

"And you're sure you'll be back in time for Pride?" asked Tom. "You were looking forward to performing."

"Two days before, sweetheart. It's all sorted. Stop

questioning me!"

Before Tom could ask another question, there was a loud and firm knock at the door. Ricky knew it could only be one of a handful of people and he wasn't in the mood for seeing any of them right now. Intending to ignore the door, he opened his underwear drawer and stuffed a handful of fresh briefs into the side pocket of his bag.

The knock repeated on the door. Tom stared at Ricky as he tried to distract himself. He pretended not to have noticed, but the third knock was even louder and insistent than the first two.

"If you're not going to answer it," said Tom as he crawled across the clothes filled bed, "I will."

"Just stay here," he said, tossing his socks onto the bed and giving in to the fact he should answer his own front door. "Keep packing. I'll get rid of whoever it is."

Ricky slipped out of his bedroom and closed the door behind him. If it was who he thought it was, he didn't want Tom to see or hear a thing. Learning the real reason of Ricky's sudden trip would only make him determined to make him stay.

He tiptoed carefully across the living room, wondering if he could get away with pretending that nobody was home. The house was silent, but the curtains were closed. Through the frosted glass in his front door, he saw a large shadow.

The fourth knock shuddered through Ricky. There was anger in those knuckles. Holding his breath and moving methodically, he leaned in to glance through the peephole. He had been expecting to see Chase, not his brother.

Ricky wrapped his fingers slowly around the brass doorknob, unsure of what to do. Chase's brother had no reason to visit his cottage. He wasn't sure how he even knew where to find him. He considered if Chase had told him the truth about what they had been up to. If he had, he had the world's worst timing.

Sucking up his fear, he pulled open the door and stood strong in his doorframe. Chase's brother, whose nametag reminded him was called Danny, looked just like an older version of Chase. His features were strong and defined and even though his skin was a little more lined, he still looked youthful. If Ricky had to guess, he wouldn't have thought he was much older than himself.

Danny stared at Ricky, but he didn't immediately speak. He glanced over Ricky's shoulder, as though he was going to see something shocking. Just from looking into his eyes, he knew why Danny was there.

"Can I help you?" asked Ricky as casually as he could muster, deciding to play it dumb. "I'm a little busy right now."

"I need to speak to you," his tone was abrupt and demanding. "Now."

"What about, sweetheart?"

"I think you already know."

Danny pushed past Ricky and walked into his cottage without invitation. Ricky knew he could try his best to drag Danny out of his home or he could hear what he had to say. He decided he wanted to hear it.

"Please, sit," he said. "Can I get you a drink? A snack? How about the clothes off my back? From the way you barged in here, sweetheart, I'd say you were used to getting what you wanted."

"You'd know all about that," he laughed dryly. "I know what you've been doing with my brother."

Ricky pulled his packet of cigarettes out of his pocket and walked slowly around the sofa. He brushed the travel brochures off the sofa and collapsed into the yellow leather. He never smoked in his cottage, but he thought this was a good time to break that rule. He knew it was his rule breaking that had gotten him into this situation, so he didn't see the point in stopping now. He lit the cigarette and blew the smoke into the air. Danny didn't move from behind the sofa.

"Speak, sweetheart," he mumbled through the cigarette. "You came in here all Billy Big Bollocks. There's no point turning shy on me now."

Danny walked around the sofa so Ricky could see him but he didn't sit down. As he stared down on Ricky, he looked perplexed and lost for words. The more he looked at Danny's face, he realised he didn't look as much like Chase as he had first thought. He was nowhere near as good looking.

"Jake Kay told me what he saw in the changing room," he said dryly, his voice low as though he was talking about something sordid. "He told me how close you were sitting and what it looked like you were doing. I didn't want to believe it at first, but it's so fucking obvious, isn't it? Chase has always defended you far too much, I should have put the pieces together."

Guilt writhed in Ricky's chest but he ignored it. Puffing on the cigarette, he cast the thoughts of what he was about to do to the back of his mind. He didn't want to think about it until he was on the plane and he couldn't turn back.

"And what did Mr. Kay say he thought he saw?" he asked. "I'm *dying* to know."

"Are you taking the piss?" he cried.

"Don't take that tone of voice with me in my own house." Ricky's voice rose to match Danny, and he stood up and pointed his cigarette in his face. "I don't care who you think you are, you clearly don't know who I am, sweetheart. I'm not some little pushover. Tell me what he thought he saw."

Danny clearly hadn't been expecting a challenge, but he didn't back down. There was a tremor in the tightness in his jaw but his bleak expression didn't falter.

"You were kissing."

"Or so he says."

"So you weren't?"

"I didn't say that," Ricky said blankly as he stubbed the cigarette out against the wood of his coffee table. "What has Chase said?"

This time, Danny's expression did falter. He glanced at the door, as though looking through the wood and to the gym at the bottom of the winding high street. Ricky laughed softly and sat back down on the couch.

"He doesn't know you know," he said with a roll of his eyes. "What was your plan? Scare me away to keep your little brother safe? I'm afraid to tell you you're too late, sweetheart. I've already done that myself."

"My brother *isn't* gay," Danny said sternly. "He's got a kid."

"He's not straight either. I would know."

The vein in the side of Danny's forehead throbbed. He looked like he was trying to hold back anger while thinking of what to say next. He didn't strike Ricky as a man of high intelligence.

"Are you after his money? Is that why you seduced him?"

"Seduced him?" Ricky laughed heartily. "You've clearly got your wires crossed, sweetheart. I think you need to speak to your brother. He's a grown man. He knew what he was getting himself into, and he doesn't need your approval to do it."

"You're sick," Danny muttered under his breath. "Do you get a kick out of turning straight guys? I'm sick of *your* lot pushing your bloody rainbow flags on the rest of us. It's not right."

Ricky's fists clenched against his knees. Calming down quickly, he marked a strike next to Danny's name, but he wouldn't be giving him another one. Before his attack, Ricky would have found such ignorance amusing, but he knew first hand how dangerous that dismissal could be.

"Do you think this is one big conspiracy, sweetheart?" Ricky sighed. "Sexuality isn't black and white. Your brother might not be gay, but he's not straight either. Why should that matter?"

"Because he's a father!" Danny turned around and smashed his fist against the kitchen counter. "It's not right!"

"Who are you to say that?"

"God created Adam and Eve, not –"

"Adam and Steve?" Ricky jumped in. "You might want to be more original if you're going to try, sweetheart. I bet you're not even religious. Guys like you usually aren't, unless it's convenient for your cause. I was telling the truth when I said I was busy, so if you don't mind, you can show yourself out."

Ricky stood up. He almost walked the long way around to his bedroom, but he decided he was going to make a point. He pushed past Danny, just as he had done to gain entry to the cottage, and he made sure to stare him deep in the eye. When Danny's fingers tightened around the neck of Ricky's shirt, he knew it was just another of his mistakes.

Choking on his collar, Ricky stumbled back toward Danny. He thought he was going to fall, but the gym instructor's grip was firm. Their faces were within kissing distance. Danny's lips were snarled as he stared down into Ricky's face, despite them being similar heights.

"You think you're so smart?" Danny snarled, shaking Ricky with his clenched fist. "They should have finished you off in that alley so you could have left my brother and nephew out of your perverted life."

Ricky had already let one strike slide, but he couldn't let another. Adrenaline surged through his body and for a moment, he was back in that alley in the rain. Instinct took over as he stamped on Danny's foot and kneed him firmly in the crotch. He let go and keeled over as he let out a low and deep growl, but Ricky wasn't finished with him. Grabbing his hand, he twisted it up his back and with his other free hand, pushed his face down into the kitchen counter.

Standing over Danny, he stared down into his mushed face, tears fresh in his eyes. Ricky wasn't sure if it was the surprise or the perfect execution of the gooseneck hold Chase had shown him, but Danny wasn't trying to wriggle free.

"Not so brave now, huh?" Ricky whispered, leaning into Danny's face. "I'm not scared of you."

The face of Danny faded away and his attacker, Terrance Hoole's face blurred before him, as clear as if he was there in the room. For once, he felt like he was truly pulling that image from his own memory and not from the picture or the police line-up.

"I'm not scared of you," he repeated, pushing Danny's face into the marble. "Do you hear me, sweetheart? I'm not scared of you."

The bedroom door opened, and Tom's head popped around. When he saw what was happening, he rushed forward and pulled Ricky off of Danny. He was reluctant to let go, but Tom's strength surprised him. Clearly trying to keep his cool, Danny slowly raised himself, licking a fresh cut in the corner of his bottom lip.

"Stay away," he said, pointing a noncommittal finger at Ricky as he backed away to the door. "Or else."

"Like I said, sweetheart, I've already solved this problem

for you. My bags are already packed."

Danny turned on his heels and tore open the cottage door. He left it open and kicked through Ricky's gate, busting the lock. When he was out of sight, Ricky allowed his fear to peak for a moment before he pushed it down.

Pulling free of Tom's grip, he walked across the room and slammed the front door. Avoiding his friend's gaze, he picked up the pad and pen next to the phone and walked towards the bedroom.

"Aren't you going to tell me what just happened?" cried Tom hysterically.

"No."

Slamming his bedroom door just like he had the front door, he twisted the lock and walked over to the bed. Perched on the edge, he opened the pad and ripped out the scribbled down name of the apartments Brian lived in. He folded the paper and tucked it away in his pocket. He ripped the pen lid off with his teeth, ready to write his final note to Chase.

CHAPTER

TWENTY THREE

Three hours after his disappearance, Danny returned to the gym. His lip was cut and he stunk of beer. Chase didn't ask. He guessed his brother had been sulking in the pub and he didn't want to know.

Danny grabbed his keys from behind the counter, stumbling and blinking heavily as he did. For a moment, Chase watched him wander messily towards the door as he looked through his keys. Even if Chase didn't want to talk to him, he couldn't let him drive home in that state.

Thankfully, his brother didn't put up much of a fight, and he let Chase call him a taxi. When Danny's car keys were firmly in Chase's pocket, and Danny was in the back of a taxi, he announced that the gym was closing early.

There were a few grumbles, especially from the people

who had just shown up. The day had been long, and Chase was ready to get as far away from his workplace as he could. Chase hid behind the counter as the gym emptied, his face deep in the laptop as he stared at the rest of the schedule for the week. The long Saturday shift with just him and his brother jumped out at him. The thought of spending a full day with his brother felt like the opposite of what he wanted to do.

He deleted himself from the rota for the rest of the weekend. It would cause problems, but he would deal with them next week. Danny might have calmed down by then, but Chase knew he would probably be much worse. Danny was like their father in that respect; stubborn as an ox and too pig headed to notice.

All of the clients had left the gym, apart from one. Clare, who was a retired primary school teacher, worked out most evenings, and Chase could tell from the frosty expression on her face that she wasn't happy about being asked to leave. She looked like she might have been pretty in her youth, but years of excessive exercising and frowning had left her hollow and joyless. When she finally made her way to the door after carefully tightening the laces on her running shoes, he followed and locked the door.

He turned to look at the messy gym. He would never usually dream of leaving it in such a state, but he was going to. Danny could deal with it in the morning. Chase knew it was petty behaviour, but if that's how his brother wanted to act, Chase was going to match that. Danny might have been the older brother, but Chase had always known he was the wiser of the two, even if he hadn't said it aloud. Having a kid did that to a man. Flicking off the lights, he wondered if the baby in Natalie's stomach was going to change anything in the almost forty-year-old man.

The sun was still high in the sky, but the row of shops

across the road blocked off most of its light. An orange glow pushed through the windows, casting long shadows of the equipment along the length of the gym. Chase hurried through the dark to the changing room to grab his things. He checked the white paper bag again and the thought that he was about to see Ricky brightened his mood.

His phone rang as he headed for the front door. He pulled it out, expecting it to either be his brother or Ricky. It was neither.

"Annie?" he said after answering quickly. "Is everything okay?"

"Chase? Can you hear me?" she cried loudly down the handset. "It's Annie. I wasn't sure if I should call you at work, but I thought I'd better let you know. Dylan has had a little bit of a fall and he's scraped his knee. We were walking back from the shop, and he tripped over his shoelace. It's nothing to worry about, but he's asking for you, and I just thought him hearing you on the phone would calm him down a little."

"I'm finishing early," he said. "I'll be right there."

From the second he had seen Annie's name on his phone display, he had known something would be wrong. She had never called him before, despite having had his phone number since first moving in next door. She had made sure to take it down, in case of emergencies.

He unlocked the front door and stepped out onto the still busy high street. He looked down at the medicine bag and then to Ricky's cottage far in the distance. He considered quickly dropping it in before heading back to Manchester, but he decided against it when he noticed Tom's Land Rover sitting outside. It was a relief to know Ricky wasn't alone in his state. He had hoped his medicine drop would be more than a flying visit.

Venturing as far from the speed limit as he dared on the

motorway, he shaved ten minutes from his journey and pulled up in the car park under the towering concrete block of flats half an hour later.

Taking the steps two at a time, he sprinted up the piss-drenched, graffiti-riddled stairway to the fifth floor. When he reached Annie's flat, he didn't bother knocking.

"Blimey, that was quick, love," she pushed herself out of her armchair and greeted him with a quick kiss on the cheek. "Not to worry at all. You're fine, aren't you Dylan?"

Dylan nodded, barely looking up from the cartoons on the small TV screen as he dug his spoon exclusively into the chocolate portion of a tub of Neapolitan ice cream. Chase laughed softly to himself. He had never noticed his own habit had imprinted on his son.

"Let's have a look at you," he said as he heaved Dylan out of the chair and sat him on the kitchen counter next to the ceramic bulldog. "What have I told you about tying your laces? Were you a brave boy?"

"I cried," he said as he shook his head. "Granddad said big boys don't cry."

Chase's anger peaked momentarily. Just as his trick of eating each individual flavour in a Neapolitan ice cream had rubbed off on his son, he was beginning to wonder what other habits were being imprinted on his son's impressionable mind.

Annie had already cleaned and dressed the cut with a square, beige plaster. Chase put Dylan on the ground and when he ran back to his ice cream on the couch without a limp, he knew his son was fine.

"I shouldn't have called," Annie said to him, waving her hands dismissively as she sat at her small kitchen table. "Rodger always said I was an overprotective mother. I would call the doctor over the smallest thing. Mind you, that was back when the doctor knew your family, and they called round out of hours. Nice chap he was. Not like this NHS rubbish these days. You ring up, and they put you on hold for so long, you're dead by the time you make your appointment. Did you hear about Mary two floors below? She went in for a chest infection, and they kept telling her it was all in her mind. *Cancer!* Died before she reached seventy. Oh, here's me prattling on and I haven't even offered you a cup of tea. Sit down, and I'll make up a pot, love."

"Actually, I was thinking of heading over to see Ricky, if you don't mind having Dylan for a few more hours?"

"How many times do I need to tell you, love?" she said as she shuffled past him with the kettle to the sink. "You don't even have to ask. At my age, what else do I have to be doing with my time? They throw you on the scrapheap, and they act like you've got nothing else to say. That boy might be six-years-old, but he's been giving me the best conversations I've had in years. You've raised a good 'un there, love."

Chase was flattered by her praise. Coming from somebody who had raised five of her own sons, it meant a lot coming from her lips. He felt guilty for not paying his next-door neighbour much attention before she started being his on-call babysitter. It hadn't even occurred to him that the smiling woman next door was concealing her loneliness. The cups of tea she always brought him when he was having his late night cigarettes suddenly made much more sense.

"How's it going with your man?" she asked. "Are you still courting?"

She heaved the kettle over to the hob and dumped it on the gas ring. She twisted the dial and gas poured out without lighting. Sighing, she shuffled back across the kitchen, the smell of gas following her. She grabbed a lighter from the top of the fridge and shuffled back. Sticking her fingers under the kettle, she flicked the lighter and fire erupted in a bright ring.

"I took your advice, and I told him how I felt," he said. "I'm not sure how he took it. I didn't realise until later that he didn't say it back."

"Some men don't realise they don't need to," she said as she dumped two teabags into a white china teapot. "My Rodger only said it at Christmas and Birthdays. God bless him. I knew he did though, that's what counts."

Chase knew the words weren't as important as people pretended but he had said them because he truly meant them. Even if he hadn't realised it at the time, he had said them to hear them back. Wondering if Annie was right, he tried not to read too much into it

"He's sick in bed with the flu so I'm going to take him some medicine."

"You're a good lad," she said with a smile as the kettle started to whistle. "Feed a cold, starve a fever. That's what my mother always used to say. Lots of rest and plenty of fluids and he'll be back on his feet before you know it."

The kettle rattled on the hob as its high-pitched steam pierced through the air. She clicked off the hob and picked up the kettle to carefully pour it into the teapot. Chase held his breath, but she didn't falter. This was the kind of stubbornness he admired. Annie refused to give up, just because society told her she should. Chase was going to take that into his own life. Everybody around him might tell him to forget about Ricky, but Chase wasn't going to do that.

"If you want to stay out, I'll make a bed up for Dylan," she offered kindly as she set the teapot in the middle of the table. "It's no bother."

"I think I'll be home tonight. I'm all jabbed up but I

don't want to risk it, just in case. I don't want Dylan getting sick."

"Good idea." She nodded her agreement. "Any person is lucky to have you, Chase. You're such a thoughtful boy. Like father, like son. If I were twenty years younger, I'd still be too old, but I might try my luck."

Annie winked playfully as she poured her tea into a small china cup. Chase chuckled and pulled his car keys from his pocket. He kissed Dylan on the top of the head and promised he would be back in a couple of hours. Dylan nodded as he started on the strawberry slice of the ice cream, leaving the vanilla in the middle for last.

Chase walked back down the stairs and past a group of hooded teenagers loitering around the opening of the stairs. He noticed a couple of swiping hands out of the corner of his eye, drugs, no doubt. It only reinforced his want to move away from the estate he had raised Dylan on. Dylan deserved better, even if it meant leaving Annie on her own. He would make a conscious effort to visit her as often as he could.

Driving back to Hebden Bridge, he thought more about his future. Glancing to the white bag on the passenger seat, he allowed himself to imagine a scenario involving Ricky and Dylan. It was still summer but his mind jumped forward to Christmas. He could vividly see all three of them sitting around a Christmas tree in Ricky's cottage on Christmas morning. It felt like a fantasy, but he knew it could become a reality.

The sun finally started to slide out of the sky as he drove past the gym. It still would have been open, and he wondered how many people had tried pushing on the door, only to be disappointed. He glided past the gym and towards Ricky's cottage at the top of the high street. Tom's Land Rover was still parked up outside, taking up his usual parking space. He passed the cottage and noticed that the door was open. The lights hadn't been turned on yet, but he was sure he spotted a silhouette of Tom's curls. Turning the corner, he slid his car into an alley between a florist and a cake shop. It wasn't technically a parking space, but he knew the clampers had already clocked off for the evening. He killed the engine, grabbed the white bag and he slid out into the alley.

As he walked back to Ricky's cottage, he spotted Tom again. He was lifting a heavy looking pink and white suitcase into the boot of his car. Chase hurried over and took the bag from Tom.

"Let me," he said as he slid the case in between another pink and white case and a large black bag. "Looks heavy."

"Chase!" Tom cried, his eyes wide. "What are you doing here?"

"Thought I'd bring Ricky some stuff to help kick his flu," he said, lifting the bag up. "How's he holding up?"

Tom's lips trembled, but he didn't speak. He looked sharply over to the cottage and Chase's eyes followed him. He saw Ricky, wearing a black, leather jacket and carrying a large backpack over his shoulder. He didn't look sick.

Their eyes met, and he immediately sensed something wasn't right. He saw the dread in Ricky's eyes for the brief second that he managed to hold his gaze.

"What's going on?" Chase asked, hoping for a response from either of them.

Ricky walked out of the cottage, avoiding both of their gazes entirely. He fumbled with his keys and locked the door. Keeping his head low, he hurried down the garden path and towards the boot of Tom's car. Chase stepped back and watched as he added the bag to the collection. It struck him that only Ricky would have bright pink and white suitcases.

"Ricky?" he asked loudly. "What's going on?"

Instead of answering, Ricky hurried around the side of the car and called to Tom to get in.

Tom didn't immediately follow. He looked apologetically at Chase and said in a low voice, "Your brother was here."

"My brother?"

Tom didn't say another word and he jumped into the driver's seat of his Land Rover. The engine roared into life as Ricky joined him in the passenger seat.

Chase rushed around the car and stood at Ricky's window. Ricky glanced at him, then he looked down.

"Just drive," he said to Tom.

"Ricky?" Chase banged his hands on the window, the white paper bag still in his hand. "What are you doing?"

Tom was hesitating, but Chase knew the seconds were dripping away, even if time was trickling by slowly, as though he was in a dream. Tom reversed slightly, so Chase followed the car. He called out again, but he was ignored.

Ricky's eyes finally met his properly, and they were filled with tears.

"I'm sorry," Ricky said, his voice muffled by the glass.

Tom pulled out of the space, and Chase watched in stunned silence as the car drove away. It turned the corner and vanished from sight. Chase looked back to the cottage, trying to piece together what had just happened.

He spotted a piece of paper on the door. Wondering if it was an eviction notice, he walked quickly up the garden path and ripped it off the door. It was addressed to him.

With fumbling hands, he read over the short note, his lips tracing the words. Clenching the note in fist, his chest cracked. He sent the white paper bag crashing down to the stone path with a cry. It split, scattering the useless flu medication among the neat flowerbeds.

CHAPTER

TWENTY
FOUR

They drove silently down the high street. Ricky hoped that's how it would stay until they reached the airport. When Tom pulled into the opening of the country lane heading up to his farm, Ricky knew he wasn't going to be that lucky.

"You lied to me!" he cried as he pushed down on his handbrake. "You better explain everything to me right this second, Ricky Thompson, or I'm driving you up to my farm. You'll miss your flight."

They both knew it was an empty threat, but it was the kind of grand assumption he was used to hearing from Tom and his black and white view of the world. Ricky reached for the door handle, but Tom locked them.

"Is that how we're playing this?" Ricky laughed bitterly.

"I'm a grown adult, sweetheart. You can't stop me from leaving."

"You're not acting like an adult!"

"I knew I should have gotten a bloody taxi."

"You didn't tell Chase you were leaving! You said everything was fine between you," he banged his head on the steering wheel and sighed heavily. "Why are you always running away?"

"Because I can," he said as he pulled on the door handle. "Let me out, or I'll kick my way through the window. So God help me, sweetheart, I'm not fucking around right now."

Tom unlocked the doors, but Ricky didn't immediately jump out. The gesture was enough for him. Tom leaned back in his chair and let out an exhausted sigh.

"I can't keep up," said Tom quietly. "I thought things were fine between you."

"This was inevitable."

"Was it?" Tom turned to look at him, his brows pinched in the middle. "I've not seen you this happy since –"

"Don't."

"It's been ten years."

"I don't care."

"Bret wouldn't have wanted this," he said quietly.

"I forgot his anniversary. I've been too distracted."

Ricky's hand reached for the door, and he jumped down to the dirty path. With fury in each step, he marched to the boot of the car, but it didn't open for him. He heard Tom jump out of the car and he joined him at the back of the car, the keys in his fist.

"I'll let you go when you explain this to me, Ricky," Tom said firmly. "I need to understand."

"What does it have to do with you, sweetheart?"

"Because I love you!" he cried. "I'm sick of seeing you

hurt yourself like this."

Those three little words stung, but in a completely different way than they had when Chase had said them. He wondered why Chase couldn't have just kept them to himself. If he had, Ricky could have deluded himself a little longer.

"This is what I do, sweetheart."

"It doesn't have to be this way."

"This is the only way I know." Ricky reached for his cigarette packet; it was empty. "Ricky runs away before people can run away from him."

"Chase told you he loved you, didn't he?" said Tom as they both leaned against the back of the Land Rover. "That's why you're in such a hurry to get away, isn't it?"

Ricky didn't say anything as he screwed up the cigarette packet in his fist. It was scary how Tom had always been able to pin Ricky down so well. Even without fully understanding how his mind worked, he was the man who had gotten closest. Ricky was glad they had never had sex. Even if he didn't like people being able to figure him out, Tom was his one exception.

"I didn't want a fuss. I just wanted to slip away to the airport and get away. I need space to think, sweetheart. My mind needs clearing. I thought some distance would make it easier."

"You mean it's easier leaving Chase behind without explaining anything to him?"

"I left him a note."

He thought about Chase reading that note on the other side of the village and the guilty knife wedged deeper into his chest. He wished he had a cigarette to silence that unwanted emotion.

"Are you really only going for two weeks?" he asked.

Ricky looked at his best friend and he considered telling

him the truth about his real plans. He would be back in the country for his performance in two weeks' time, but he doubted he would be sticking around for long. Once he sorted out the shop and his cottage, he could slip away once again and forget all about the life he was leaving behind. A baggage free life under the sun seemed like the perfect escape.

"It's just two weeks," he lied. "We can talk about this when I get back. I don't want to miss my flight."

He tossed the cigarette packet into the dirt and walked back to the passenger seat. Tom followed him, and they were side by side once again. Before he drove away, he glanced to the church at the bottom of the lane. Ricky knew what he was thinking.

"When did you last see Bret?" he asked as he pulled out of the lane and back onto the road.

"Last week," he said, the lie dripping off his tongue too easily. "Let's get out of here."

Tom didn't question him as they drove silently through the village and towards the motorway. The entire journey to the airport, Ricky tried to remember the last time he had visited the graveyard. There had been snow on the ground, and he was trying to figure out how many winters it had been since it properly snowed in the village; he couldn't.

They pulled into the covered departures area at Manchester's Terminal One. He still had four hours until his flight, but that would fly by in the bar. He knew he needed to board the plane visibly sober, but he was an expert at hiding it. That first drink was already calling him.

Ricky unloaded the cases from the boot of the car as Tom ran to the sliding doors to grab a trolley. When all of the cases were loaded on the metal rack, it finally hit Ricky what he was doing. Chase's face was at the forefront of his mind, but he knew it would fade with time.

"Are you sure you're doing the right thing?" Tom whispered in his ear as he hugged him tightly. "It's not too late."

"I'm sure," Ricky said before he had a chance to think about it.

When Tom finally let go, Ricky wrapped his fingers around the cold handle of the trolley and headed towards the group of people smoking by the entrance of the terminal. He unzipped his bag and pulled out a fresh packet of cigarettes as he watched as Tom jumped back into his car. He wound down his window and waved to Ricky one last time. Even from his distance, he could see the tears streaming down his best friend's face.

As he lit the cigarette, he wiped away his own tear. He told himself the tear was for Tom, but he knew it wasn't.

"You can't smoke here," said a young guy in a high-visibility jacket branded with the airport's logo.

"Piss off, sweetheart," Ricky snapped back. "I'll do what I want."

"People like you usually do," the worker said with a sigh, shaking his head as he retreated back into the airport.

CHAPTER

TWENTY
FIVE

TWO WEEKS LATER

S itting in the driving seat of his car, Chase looked up at his brother's house. The front door was lined with blue balloons, all emblazed with the number seven. He wanted the afternoon over with as soon as possible.

"Nice house," whispered Annie from the passenger seat. "Your brother must have some money."

"His wife does," said Chase as he unbuckled his seatbelt. "We better go in before she sends out a search party."

He got out of his car and hurried over to Annie's side. She used his arm and the door to steady herself as she got out of the car. She was wearing a pretty pink floral dress, and her hair was tightly curled in neat rows. She evoked images of a nineteen-forties pinup, which was a nice change from her usual 'house clothes'.

Dylan unbuckled himself from his child's safety seat and tugged on the door handle, but the safety lock didn't budge. Chase pulled on the door, and he burst out in a bundle of energy. He looked up at the balloons, a wide grin on his face.

Chase tried to reflect that grin for his son's sake. He hadn't even thought about planning anything for his birthday, so when Natalie called him to say they were throwing a party for him, he could hardly refuse, even if he wanted to. He knew he could never throw a party to rival anything Natalie would do.

Dylan clutched his hand and dragged his dad to the front door. The sound of children's laughter and party music floated out of the house. A small specially printed banner saying 'Dylan's Birthday Bash' had been stuck to the front door. Deciding against walking in, he struck the knocker.

Barbara answered the door, and Dylan ran straight to the group of similarly aged boys and girls on the patio through the double French doors in the kitchen. Chase recognised some of them from Dylan's school and wondered how Natalie had gotten hold of their details.

"Chase," said Barbara as she pulled him in to kiss him on each cheek. "I feel like I haven't seen you in a lifetime."

Chase smiled awkwardly. He rarely saw Barbara and she had never remarked on not seeing him before. It became obvious Danny had made a big deal about the fact Chase hadn't been in to work for a whole two weeks.

"And this must be Annie," she said, pecking Annie quickly on the cheek. "Such a pretty dress. *Come in*! Come in. The ladies are in the garden and the men are in the living room."

Barbara whisked Annie through to the garden, leaving

Chase to linger near the open front door alone. Turning back to his car, he wondered if he could sneak out before being spotted by anyone else.

Before that could happen, Natalie glided down the stairs, a barely visible bump poking through her floating white Grecian dress, which looked like it had been chosen specifically to show off her pregnancy. Her usually ghostly skin had a glow, and he put it down to her weeks travelling America.

"Chase, so glad to finally see you," she said, her voice light and airy. "We were beginning to think you weren't going to show up."

"Traffic was murder," he said casually. "Thanks for going to all of this effort."

"No problem at all. Don't worry about trying to pay me back either."

He tried to keep his expression neutral. He hadn't offered her a penny, but he wasn't surprised she was once again trying to push her wealth on him. He had always wondered if she did that with everyone she knew. She had only been to his flat once, and she had acted as if she was stepping into a dirty crack den. Her hand sanitizer had made an appearance more than once.

"The men are in the living room," she said, nodding to the closed double doors. "The match is on."

As though to illustrate her point, there was a roar of cheers when one of the teams scored.

"I'll go out to the garden, if it's all the same to you?"

She pursed her lips tightly but she didn't argue. Natalie was a control freak and Chase was daring to go against her plan. He knew his brother was on the other side of that door and he wasn't about to willingly walk into that. He wouldn't be surprised if the whole party had been a reason to get them in the same room together.

She walked gracefully towards her white kitchen, her white dress floating elegantly behind her. Pregnancy seemed to suit her, in an odd way. On his way to the French doors, he grabbed a cold beer from the fridge and popped off the cap on the bottle opener attached to the side of the counter.

Sipping his beer, he walked out to the garden. The sun burned high in the sky after two weeks of straight rain. The weather had matched Chase's mood, and the sun felt wrong on his skin.

Dylan was sitting in the middle of a pile of wrapped gifts. Looking more excited than he had in a long time, he tore off the paper excitedly and examined each toy in turn. The children around him in an eager circle excitedly passed the new toys between them as the mothers were hovering right behind, making sure the rest of the mothers knew who had bought what and most likely who had spent the most money.

Taking a seat on the edge of the action, he looked up at the sky. He wondered if Ricky was under that same sky. Cursing himself for letting his mind wander there, he gulped down the beer.

Natalie's high-pitched, fake laugh pierced through the air, and he looked in her direction. She was sipping from a tall glass of orange juice as the women around her sipped chilled white wine. The woman who was sitting next to Annie jumped out at him, and it took him a moment to realise it was Beth, the yoga instructor from the gym. As though she could feel his eyes, she looked up over her wine glass and sent a smile his way. He smiled back; he didn't feel it.

The reason he didn't recognise her was because she was wearing a long, summer dress instead of a tracksuit, and her auburn hair was curled down her shoulders instead of scraped back in a ponytail. There was no denying Beth was a pretty girl, but she didn't do anything for him. He had never heard her mention having children, so he wasn't quite sure why she had been invited.

As he drained the last of his beer, his father appeared carrying a bag of coal. Patrick spotted Chase and nodded in his direction, but he didn't speak. He walked over to the BBQ and got to work setting it up. Half an hour later, freshly cooked beef burgers and sausages wafted through the garden. A line quickly formed and Patrick dished out the food. Chase noticed his brother wasn't one of the people in the line.

Deciding he wasn't hungry, he slipped back into the kitchen to grab another beer. When his foot hit the marble tiles, he spotted his brother at the fridge, grabbing his own beer. He turned on his heels, but he wasn't quick enough.

"Bro, wait up," Danny called to him.

Chase was wondering if he was imagining the apology in his voice. They hadn't spoken since Chase had bundled him into a taxi weeks ago. Chase had since lost interest in trying to find out how much his brother knew about his relationship with Ricky.

He took a cautious step into the kitchen and stood on the opposite side of the marble island. Danny grabbed a second beer from the fridge and slid it across the counter. It felt like a peace offering Chase wasn't ready for. Reluctantly, he accepted the beer and crammed the cold glass top in between his lips.

"How're you doing?" Danny asked him, his tone annoyingly casual. "I was wondering when you'd be back at the gym."

"I don't know."

"Which question are you answering?" he asked with an awkward laugh.

"Both."

They both drank their beers in silence, the tension loud and clear between them. There was more than a marble island between them. Chase had never felt further away from his brother in his life. He couldn't believe it was the same man he had willingly gone into business with less than a year ago.

"Fancy catching the end of the game?" he asked. "I'm not really hungry."

"You know I don't like football."

Danny sighed and rolled his eyes. He leaned against the counter and crammed the beer bottle in his mouth, sulking as he stared across the island at Chase.

"I'm trying here!"

"You don't need to," Chase said coolly.

"Bro, don't be like that."

"Like what?"

Chase heard the childishness in his voice. He sighed and sipped his beer. All of his emotions were still raw and near the surface, and his brother was a part of that.

"I know you went to see Ricky," said Chase, trying to stay as calm as possible. "Before he left."

His mind had replayed the night over and over. It had taken him a while to realise why Tom had told him, but it struck after a few days of constantly analysing the situation.

"Let's go and sit down, yeah?"

"I don't want to sit down."

"C'mon, bro," Danny laughed dryly. "This whole thing is over now, let's just forget it. Did you notice Beth out there? Go and talk to her."

Chase slammed his beer down on the counter, and he leaned his hands heavily against it. He shook his head, feeling like he was still trapped in the nightmare he had been in for over a fortnight.

"What did you say to him to make him leave?" Chase

asked calmly. "What did you do? I've been trying to work that out for weeks, and I can't understand what you said to scare him so much. Did you threaten him?"

Danny sipped his beer silently. His empty expression brought the anger prickling to the surface of Chase's skin. He ran around the island and pinned Danny into the fridge. He dropped the bottle of beer and it smashed with a crack against the marble tiles. Clutching the front of his shirt, Chase stared deep into his brother's eyes, searching for the answer. All he saw was fear.

"What did you do?" Chase cried, shaking him like a ragdoll. "What did you do to him?"

"I didn't do anything!" Danny pushed Chase away and straightened out his shirt. "What's the matter with you? I just went to see him, to tell him to back off but I didn't need to. His bags were already packed when I got there."

"You're lying."

"I swear on my unborn baby's life," Danny said, holding his hands up. "I swear on mum's life."

Chase's fists clenched. He was moments away from striking his brother's face but he refrained. He knew there was no way he would swear on such things if he were lying.

"What's going on in here?" Natalie's voice came from behind him. "I can hear the screaming outside. Are you always trying to embarrass us, Chase?"

Chase glanced over his shoulder at Natalie. Annie and his father were behind her and so was Dylan, poking out from behind Annie. Feeling the lump rising up in his throat, he took off out of the kitchen and into the downstairs bathroom. He locked the door and sat on the closed toilet.

Opening his wallet, he pulled out the crumpled up note and unfolded it carefully, his hands shaking like a leaf. He had read the words so many times he knew them by heart:

I can't do this. I'm sorry. It's for the best. I was always going to hurt you eventually. It's easier this way, sweetheart.

R.

He leaned his head back heavily on the tiles. He had spent weeks hoping his brother had done something to make Ricky leave, but deep down in his heart, he had known the real reason all along. He stood up and lifted up the toilet seat and dropped the note into the water. The ink bled until the words were nothing more than black scribbles. Flushing the toilet, he watched the note vanish, just like Ricky had vanished.

He wished he could make his feelings vanish so easily.

CHAPTER

TWENTY SIX

The Land Rover pulled up outside of Tom and Cole's farmhouse. From behind his sunglasses, Ricky looked up at the crystal clear sky.

"Looks like I've brought the good weather back with me, sweetheart," he exclaimed as Cole killed the engine.

Ricky had been expecting Tom to be the one who picked him up from the airport but he had been glad when he had seen Cole. He didn't doubt Tom had told Cole every detail, but Cole was less likely to ask any invasive questions. Aside from general murmurings about the weather and the bar Ricky had been working in, the drive had been pretty interrogation free. He was far too exhausted to answer any of Tom's questions, so he hoped he would be held up at the farmer's market for the rest of the day.

Ricky jumped out of the car and back onto Yorkshire soil. His dark glasses hid the dark circles around his eyes. He wanted nothing more than to crash out for a couple of hours but there was no time. He had expected the work in Gran Canaria to be hard, but he hadn't anticipated just how hard.

When he had arrived, Brian had picked him up from the airport and after an evening of adjustment and catching up, Ricky was put to work the next day. The bar was small, in the middle of the Yumbo Centre, which was an open-air mall, but filled with dozens of different gay bars.

The actual work itself was pretty straightforward. He was the host, which meant standing on a stage in drag to introduce the acts, banter with the audience and most importantly, keep them ordering drinks. Ricky could do it in his sleep.

Unlike Manchester, the days were long and hot, and so were the nights. The flow of customers never dried up and every day was identical to the last. Despite that, he already had his return flight booked for the same day of his Pride performance in two days.

Cole helped him unload his bags, and they dumped them in the hallway. Tom hadn't questioned him when he had asked to stay at the farmhouse for a couple of days. He seemed too happy to have Ricky in his sights that he didn't wonder why he was avoiding his own cottage.

"Ricky, love!" beamed Belinda with open arms as she walked in from the kitchen. "Look at the colour of you! You're glowing. Are you hungry? Course you are. Let me make you some breakfast."

Despite it being in the middle of the afternoon, Ricky didn't turn it down. Aside from a rushed sandwich on the four-hour plane journey, he hadn't eaten since the drunken

Burger King the night before. After his shift at the bar, Brian had insisted they spend the night enjoying the nightlife and Ricky had stupidly agreed. The alcohol only finally wore off when the plane's wheels touched down in Manchester.

Ricky wolfed down Belinda's breakfast and washed it down with a strong coffee. At the moment he put his knife and fork on the empty plate, the back door opened and Tom walked in.

"You're here!" Ricky grinned as he yanked him up into a tight hug. "Sorry, I couldn't pick you up. It's been hectic around here recently."

"Don't worry about it, sweetheart."

They sat at the kitchen table and Tom asked vague questions about his trip but he skated around the obvious elephant in the room. Ricky knew they would come when they were alone.

"Did you get what I asked from the cottage?" asked Ricky when Belinda and Cole went to muck out the horses.

Tom jumped up and walked into the hallway. He opened the airing cupboard outside of the bathroom and pulled out the birdcage. It felt like a lifetime ago he had even searched for the thing. It was uglier than he remembered.

"I got the spray paint too," he said, holding up a plastic bag. "We've got a couple of days yet."

"I want to get this sorted now, sweetheart," he stood up and grabbed the birdcage. "Miss Kitty Litter is performing at Manchester Gay Pride in two days, and it needs to be perfect."

Tom sighed, but he didn't argue. He passed the bag of spray paint to Ricky, and he gladly accepted it. With his supplies in hand, he walked out of the back door and dumped them on the gravelly ground. The sun burned down hard on him, making him feel like he hadn't left Gran Canaria. If it wasn't for the strong smell of manure on the wind, he could have pretended he wasn't back in the village he had run away from.

Tom laid out old newspapers on the ground, and Ricky started shaking up the cans. He stood back and looked at the metal birdcage, wondering what colour to paint it. When he couldn't decide, he picked the cans at random and started spraying it every shade of the rainbow. He was originally going to spray it a pale yellow so it would match his most expensive and favourite wig, but the last time he had seen it, it had been on a grainy video, and it had disappeared into the night in Terrance Hoole's fist.

"Grab my wig case will you?" Ricky said. "It's the pink one with the white stripes. I have just the wig for it."

Tom nodded and disappeared into the farmhouse. Ricky stood back and stared at the rainbow birdcage. It didn't look half bad considering he hadn't put much thought into its design. His original plan had been to create a dress made entirely of pure white feathers, but with everything that had been happening, he hadn't had the time. If he hadn't already been paid upfront for the performance, he wouldn't have bothered coming back. The only thing spurring him on was that it was a farewell performance of sorts, even if people didn't realise it.

Ever since becoming a drag queen, it had been a goal to perform on the main stage at Manchester Gay Pride. When they had offered him the gig, he had been surprised it was for his talent and not because he had slept with the right people. He tried to tap into that dream, to excite him, but it did nothing. It was a pit stop to recharge before heading back to the sun and nothing more.

When Tom didn't return with the case of wigs, Ricky followed him into the farmhouse. He was crouched over the cases, with a stack of papers in his hands.

"What are you doing?" asked Ricky as he hurried over. "That's private."

"Property listings?" cried Tom. "In Gran Canaria? Please tell me you're just looking at a holiday home, Ricky."

Ricky snatched the papers out of his hands and looked over the listing of small apartments. He had hoped he could slip out of the country and explain everything to Tom over the phone when he was on the other side. He thought about trying to lie his way out of the situation, but Tom would sniff him out.

"They've offered me a full time job," he said. "It's good money."

"Good money?" Tom attempted to get the papers back from Ricky but he didn't let go. "You can't just leave!"

Ricky folded the papers and stuffed them back in his bag. He grabbed the suitcase full of wigs and dragged it through to the kitchen. He heaved it up onto the table and yanked on the zip. His wigs were all matted together after two weeks of constant use. Feeling Tom's eyes on him, he dug through the hair.

"Ricky, talk to me."

"My mind is made up," he said. "I have nothing to stay here for. I should have realised that a long time ago. The one thing keeping me here is dead, so it's time I got out there to see more of the world."

Ricky was almost convincing himself, but he knew it wouldn't work on Tom. To his surprise, Tom didn't stick around to argue. He stormed out of the back door, slamming the door dramatically as he went.

Leaning against the table, Ricky inhaled deeply. Closing his eyes, he tried to focus his brain. It had been easier to do it halfway around the world with a cocktail in his hand and the sun beating down on him.

There wasn't another way. The alternative was staying in the same haunted village, bumping into the same people he had fucked, with Chase working down the street from him every day. Seeing him would be a reminder of what Ricky thought he could have had, if only for a fleeting moment. It brought to mind their weekend at Coltrane House. Chase had convinced him to take a leap of faith and he had. He wished he could go back to that moment to let Chase down gently. It would have been easier before 'love' was introduced to the already complicated mix.

The contents of his letter sprung to mind once more, and he felt justified in his decision. The heartbreak had been inevitable from the start, but to save his own heart, he had broken somebody else's. It didn't feel right, but it was a sacrifice he knew he had to make. It was like pulling out a splinter, and if he left it any longer, it would have only gotten worse.

"You would only hurt him in the end," he whispered as he pulled out the rainbow wig from the mix. "It's better this way."

Without truly understanding why, he began to sob.

***

Chase felt awful leaving his son's birthday party, but he couldn't bear the thought of sticking around. When Annie offered to bring Dylan home in a taxi when the party was over, he gratefully pushed a twenty pound note into her hand and got out of there. Nobody tried to stop him from leaving.

The electronic gates started to open as he crawled down the driveway. He edged his car forward, but they ground to a halt halfway leaving a gap too small to fit his car through. He reluctantly got out of his car, leaving the door open and engine running. With more force than he had intended, he dragged open one of the gates. It fought against him the whole way, the motor spluttering and coughing its protest. He jumped back into his car and sped away from the house.

He hadn't had a destination in mind, but he found himself driving into the gay village. He slowly passed Ricky's shop, *Books & Bondage*. It looked open, but he doubted Ricky was inside. That had been one of the first places he had looked. He drove further up the street and lingered outside of London Bridge. It was open, but aside from the staff, it looked empty. He thought about going in for a drink, but he decided against it. A taxi honked its horn behind him, forcing him further down the road.

He pulled into the alley next to London Bridge and waited for the car to pass. When the road was clear, he reversed and headed back the way he came. He noticed the banners draped above him advertising Manchester's Gay Pride weekend. The thought of any kind of celebration made his skin itch.

Barely paying attention to the road, he pushed aimlessly around a roundabout. One road would take him back to his flat, and another to Hebden Bridge. He hadn't worked out in two weeks, and his muscles were already starting to soften. He knew hitting the weights would release his frustration, but he decided against that too. He wasn't sure he wanted to get rid of that feeling. It was bubbling just under the surface of his skin, keeping him angry. He was angry with Ricky, and he was angry with his brother, but he was angrier with himself. Pulling on the wheel, he decided he should go home.

In the car park under his block of flats, he killed the engine and laid his head back on the rest. He stared ahead into the darkness with no desire to move.

After sitting in silence for nearly half an hour, his phone

rang, dragging him back to reality. It was an unknown number, and he almost let it ring out, but he was sure he recognised the last three digits.

"Hello?" he mumbled into the phone, pinching in between his brows. "Who is this?"

"Chase?" said a familiar voice. "Thank god you answered. It's Tom."

He almost hung up straight away, but he stopped himself. Tom was sweet, and he had been nothing but nice to Chase. Sighing into the silence, he sat up straight and leaned against the steering wheel.

"How's it going?" he asked, his tone flat, despite trying to inject a slither of interest into it.

"Can we meet?" Tom said. "Now?"

Chase checked the watch on his wrist. It would be hours until Annie returned home with Dylan and spending the afternoon alone in his flat was all he really wanted to do.

"What's it about? It's not really a good time."

"*Please*," Tom said desperately. "It's *urgent*."

Ricky's face burned bright in his mind, as though he was standing in front of him. Had something terrible happened to him? Chase's stomach knotted at the thought.

"Where are you?" Chase asked Tom reluctantly.

They agreed to meet in Churchill's, a small gay bar on Canal Street. Chase usually avoided it, but he picked it because he knew it would be busy regardless of the time of day. He wanted plenty of distractions just in case he didn't want to hear what Tom had to say.

He pulled up in the car park behind the pub and headed for its side entrance. It was Winston Churchill themed, but it was also filled with rainbow flags. Chase had always thought it was a bizarre choice for a pub in the middle of the gay village.

Avoiding the main part of the pub, he ordered a pint

and sat in a booth in the corner. It was a hot summer's day, so just as predicted, the bar was busy. The DJ played cheesy pop music for a group of women, all wearing bunny ears and pink sashes announcing '*Sarah's Hen Party*'.

Twenty minutes later, Tom walked in through the main entrance and pushed past the group of women, looking for Chase. When he caught his eye, he seemed relieved to see him.

Chase drained the last of his pint and walked over to the bar.

"What do you want?" he asked Tom.

Tom glanced behind the bar at what was on offer, settling for an orange juice. Chase almost ordered himself a second pint, but he remembered his car. He carried the two orange juices back to the booth and Tom followed him.

"Thanks for coming," said Tom with a nervous smile. "I've been trying to find you all afternoon. I forgot I still had your number on my phone after you called me from the hospital."

Chase thought back to that day. It had seemed like a lifetime ago. If he hadn't given his business card to Ricky, he probably wouldn't be sitting talking to Tom in Churchill's on a Thursday afternoon. An alternate reality where he hadn't followed Bailey into that alley on that dark night flashed through his mind. For a moment, he wished they had walked a different way, but that was followed by immense guilt. He sipped the orange juice, but it didn't have the same effect as the beer.

"Has something happened?" Chase asked Tom, who didn't look like he wanted to speak now that he was there.

Tom ruffled his curls and exhaled heavily. He pushed himself back into the chair, clearly exhausted. Chase knew only one person could have caused that.

"Ricky's back," said Tom quietly. "Cole picked him up

from the airport this morning."

Chase's stomach twisted as he sipped his orange juice. It settled strangely on his stomach, and he suddenly wished he hadn't been so quick to turn down the BBQ food at the party. He hadn't known Ricky had left the country but it had crossed his mind.

"Where has he been?"

"The Canary Islands," Tom said with a roll of his eyes. "Gran Canaria to be more specific. He said some old friend called him and offered him a job for two weeks. I didn't believe it, but he said he'd told you and you were fine with it."

Chase wondered if Ricky was used to lying so often. He had convinced himself that he had known Ricky, but he was now realising he knew nothing about the man he had professed his love for. He wanted to laugh, because just knowing that made him feel like a fool. The feeling still burned like fire in his chest and he hadn't been able to dampen it.

"I didn't know," said Chase. "He wrote me a note but it didn't explain anything."

"Sounds like Ricky."

"I wouldn't know," he said. "I don't know him, not really."

Tom smiled sympathetically. It became obvious to Chase that Tom felt the same way. If his friend of many years didn't really know him, Chase never stood a chance.

"You got closer than anybody else," Tom said with a soft smile. "I thought you were the real deal."

"Me too," the words jammed in his throat. "Why did you want to meet me, Tom? If it's just to talk about Ricky, I'm really not in the mood."

Tom sipped his orange juice silently, but Chase could hear the cogs turning in his mind. Something had happened, and Tom was trying to find the best way to put it. After drinking a generous amount, he put the half empty glass on the table, and he looked up at the ceiling as he chewed the inside of his lip.

"He wants to move to Gran Canaria," he said sternly. "*Permanently.*"

Chase let the words sink in like a knife into his back. Gritting his jaw, he tried not to let the flurry of emotions show on his face. He didn't know how he felt, but his anger was still the strongest of the bunch. It had been festering for two weeks and only growing stronger by the day.

"Good for him," Chase said, shrugging. "Best of luck to him."

"You don't mean that. This is serious! I found property listings for rented apartments out there. He's really leaving for good. He came back for his performance and then he's jumping straight back on a plane."

Chase screwed up his face and pinched between his brows. He wasn't sure how much he wanted to know, or why Tom was telling him any of this.

"He must really want to leave."

"I don't think he does," Tom whispered, leaning in closer. "Not really. This is what he does when he's scared. He almost left once before after Bret, but he didn't go through with it."

Chase had never heard Ricky mention Bret before. He wondered if he was another man he had strung along and dropped when things had gotten too serious. Whoever Bret was, he wished he had met him so he could have known what was coming.

"What does this have to do with me?" Chase asked.

Tom frowned and jerked his head back. He was looking at Chase as though he had missed something obvious. It was a shock that Ricky was going to the extreme of leaving the country, but it didn't change anything. Ricky had still left him standing on the side of the road, clutching a hastily written note. All of his questions hadn't been answered, and there had been two weeks to come to terms with that part of it.

"We can stop him!" said Tom urgently. "We *need* to stop him!"

"Why?" Chase asked bluntly. "Ricky is stubborn. If he wants to go, he'll go. If you stop him, he'll only go later when something, or someone else pops up."

The confusion on Tom's face deepened. He sipped his orange juice without taking his eyes away from Chase.

"There is no one else," he said. "There never has been."

"You just said he's done this before with another guy."

"I did?"

"Bret," he said. "You *just* said it."

Tom looked puzzled by what Chase had just said. His eyes widened and he stared darkly at him, his lips trembling but not forming words. He slammed himself back into the chair, his fists colliding with the table, making the glasses and Chase jump.

"This is just fucking *typical* Ricky!" Tom cried, a sarcastic laugh loud in his voice. "I *can't* believe he didn't tell you."

Hearing Tom swear shocked Chase. Ricky had always painted a Disney-esque view of Tom and his life. He wondered if Ricky had exaggerated to make Tom's life sound less appealing.

"Tell me what?" Chase asked, suddenly wanting to know. "Is Bret his big secret?"

Tom's eyes shifted from Chase to the bar. He looked uncomfortable being asked the question. Chase admired his strength to keep his best friend's secrets, even if Ricky didn't return the gratitude.

"I shouldn't," Tom mumbled. "It's not my place."

Chase drained his orange juice and stood up. He knew he should have turned Tom down on the phone. The only thing that had made him show up was the thought of getting an ounce of closure, but he only felt worse.

"I'm tired of these games," Chase said. "Sorry for dragging you to Manchester. See you around."

He headed for the door, not expecting Tom to follow him, and he didn't. He pulled his cigarette packet from his pocket as his foot hit the step down to the street.

"Wait!" Tom called after him. "Chase, *wait*!"

Sighing, he pushed the cigarette packet back into his pocket and turned back to the table. He stared at Tom, wondering if he should stick around to hear what he had to stay. The burning curiosity for answers made him sit back down.

"Ricky would kill me if he knew I was telling you this," Tom said. "In fact, he'd kill me if he knew I was here at all."

Chase wondered if Tom was expecting him to say he would keep their meeting a secret. He didn't owe either of them anything, but he nodded encouragingly.

"Bret was Ricky's fiancé," Tom said in a low voice. "Ten years ago."

It hadn't been what Chase was expecting to hear. Ricky had never hinted that he had ever been engaged and Chase had never suspected it. He had been expecting something much worse. He suddenly remembered Ricky's reaction when Chase had asked him if he had ever been in love.

"Don't tell me, he ditched this Bret at the altar?" Chase scoffed. "Wouldn't surprise me."

"They didn't get to the alter."

"Did Ricky leave behind another pathetic note?" Chase could hear the venom in his own voice but he couldn't control it. "I don't want to hear this."

He went to stand up but Tom's hand closed firmly around his wrist. Chase was about to pull away, but something in Tom's eyes made him sit back down.

"Bret died," Tom choked out, tears collecting in the corners of his eyes. "Cancer got him before the wedding."

Frowning, Chase pulled his arm away from Tom. He felt incalculably guilty for his words moments ago. So much about Ricky suddenly made sense, even if he still had unanswered questions.

"I don't understand why he wouldn't tell me."

"It changed Ricky," Tom said, wiping away a fallen tear from his cheek. "A lot. Ricky loved Bret more than anything in the world. They met in their early twenties at a party. Ricky was a different person back then. He wasn't jaded or distant. I met him when they were already together, so that's all I knew. They were perfect for each other in every way. On paper, it should never have worked, but it did. Bret was training to become a doctor, but he was diagnosed just after his graduation. They had only been engaged for a couple of months by that point. It was a hard time.

"When Bret died, Ricky locked himself away from the world. He went off the rails. He started partying most days of the week and he had a different guy in his bed every five minutes. He closed off his heart to the idea of love. I thought the Ricky I used to know would come back, but he didn't. He's still there under the surface, but Ricky locks him away to protect himself from that pain again. I finally saw the Ricky I used to know when he was with you."

Chase let the words absorb slowly but it was too much to listen to in one go. He stared ahead at the table, his eyes following the patterns in the wood grain.

"I told him I loved him and that's why he left," said

Chase. "He never said it back."

"He loves you, I know he does, he's just scared to admit it. Ricky thinks love and heartbreak are the same thing. He doesn't realise it's the journey that's important, not the destination. With you, he was changing, softening."

"But I wasn't enough."

"It's not you," he jumped in. "It's him. He just needs time."

"Well, he can have all of the time he wants when he leaves."

"*What*?" Tom cried. "How can you say that?"

Chase knew his words were cold and harsh. He thought back to how he had felt when Tracey died, and how difficult it had been. He hadn't even been in love with her, so he couldn't imagine how Ricky felt.

"How do you know anything I say will make Ricky change his mind?" he asked, calming his voice.

"I don't," Tom replied honestly. "But isn't it worth a shot?"

With a heavy sigh, Chase looked around the pub. He could easily slip out the door, head back to his car and go home, ignoring everything Tom had said. Logically, he knew talking to Ricky was a huge mistake, but his heart wasn't listening to logic. If it had, he wouldn't have had two weeks locked in his flat, trying to piece everything together and getting nowhere.

"Ricky has always thought loving somebody else would taint what he had with Bret," Tom said, resting his hand upon Chase's. "We just need to show him that isn't true."

Sighing heavily, Chase glanced to the door. He imagined Ricky still living with the pain of his fiancé's death for the past ten years. His heart ached for him. Looking back at Tom, he nodded, knowing that he had to at least try.

"What did you have in mind?"

CHAPTER

TWENTY
SEVEN

fter a restless night of strange dreams about being booed off stage, Ricky woke early on the morning of his performance. He quickly ate Belinda's breakfast, grabbed his things and headed to the station to head to London Bridge, declining Tom's offer of a lift.

He hated getting into drag at the bar. He usually got ready in the cellar with a mirror propped up against a barrel of beer under the single exposed light bulb. It always left him making questionable colour choices, but he would take mismatched contour and highlight over Tom's constant stream of noise.

Ricky had questioned his decision to stay at the farmhouse more than once over the last two days. Tom's questions were turning more pointed and emotionally charged by the day, making Ricky grateful for his flight in the early hours of the morning.

Brian had called him to make sure everything was still going ahead, and Ricky hadn't hesitated to tell him he would be back. He had travelled back to England with the smallest thought that something was going to change his mind but it had only reaffirmed his need to get away. Brian had explained the gruelling work schedule to him over the phone and it didn't sound like he was getting much time off until Christmas. With the summer season lasting right up until Winter Pride in November, Ricky was wondering when he would have time to sleep. It was a work schedule he wasn't used to.

Stepping off the train, he dragged his performance suitcase through Manchester Piccadilly station. As he walked through the city, he could feel a buzz in the air. The parade would start in a matter of hours, and the gay village would be flooded soon after. Manchester had always been his favourite city in the world. He still hadn't figured out how he would feel not having it around the corner.

He turned onto Canal Street and it was already decently busy considering it wasn't even ten in the morning. Bar staff and promoters were running around, putting the finishing touches to their decorations, ready for a weekend of over-priced, under-poured drinks.

"Hello, sweetheart," he called to Jackson as he struggled through the door with the case. "Give a hand with this, will you?"

Jackson left the bar and ran across the bar. Instead of grabbing the case, he grabbed Ricky around the neck.

"You're home!" he said. "God, I never thought I'd miss your face, but I have. Toxic Tonya doesn't have a patch on you. People haven't stopped asking about you."

"Naturally," he said as he handed his case over to

Jackson. "Put this in the cellar. I'm getting ready here."

Ricky was surprised people had been asking about him. Since the attack, Miss Kitty Litter's appearances in Manchester had been more than a little sporadic. He was touched people cared, but he couldn't dwell on that. It was no different than visiting your grandma's house and noticing the glass cabinet that had been there since the nineteen-sixties had suddenly vanished.

The bar was already busy, and Jackson had hired nearly a dozen extra pairs of hands. Most of them were behind the cramped bar, fighting over each other for space, while the rest were getting trays of shots ready to sell on the streets.

He followed Jackson into the cold and dark cellar, and he was glad it was quiet. He dragged up a chair and pulled his mirror out of his case.

"Your performance is at two, but I was wondering if you didn't mind being on the door before then. Y'know, get people in?"

"Why do you think I'm here at the crack of dawn, sweetheart?"

"You're a star," he slapped Ricky on the shoulders. "I better get back. The agency has sent a useless bunch."

"Actually, sweetheart, I wanted to talk to you quickly."

Jackson looked taken aback by the seriousness in Ricky's voice. He pulled up a barrel and sat next to him as Ricky laid out his makeup on a small fold out table.

"There's no easy way to say this," Ricky said as he stared in the mirror and pushed his hair out of his face with a headband. "I quit."

"Very funny," Jackson said with a laugh. "I've missed you."

"I'm being serious, sweetheart," he said solemnly, smiling at Jackson in the mirror. "I quit. I've been offered a great job abroad, and I've accepted."

"Oh."

Jackson frowned and stared at the floor as he scrambled for the right words. Ricky hoped he wasn't going to join Tom in trying to make him stay.

"But you can't go," he said. "London Bridge *is* your home. Miss Kitty Litter belongs here."

"I'm flattered, sweetheart, but I need to spread my wings and fly away."

"Is this about the money? I can call Benny and ask him if you can have a pay rise. I don't think it will be much, but there's no harm in asking."

Ricky wished it were as simple as that. He was flattered by the obvious sadness in Jackson's expression. He hadn't been the manager for long, but Ricky knew he was the best of a bad bunch and he hadn't minded working under him.

"It's not about the money, sweetheart."

"So what's it about? Is it because I hired Toxic Tonya when you were on the sick? Because if it is, she's dead to me. *Gone!* Just say the word."

Ricky laughed as he ran the cleansing pads along his cheeks.

"I need a change. That's all."

"So we'll redecorate," he sighed, resting his hand on Ricky's shoulder. "When do you leave?"

"Tonight," he said. "Well, tomorrow. Two in the morning."

"But there's no time to give you a farewell party! People will miss you!"

"Which will make it all the sweeter when I return for my farewell concert when I'm in my seventies. Works every time for Cher, doesn't it?" he said as he ran the pads along his jaw. "I'll just have to make this performance the best this village has ever seen."

Jackson stood up carefully, his eyes slightly glazed over.

He met Ricky's stare in the mirror, and he tried to smile. Ricky knew Miss Kitty Litter dragged money into the bar and Jackson was already panicking about how he was going to find another cashcow. When it came to being a drag DJ, Ricky didn't care about having an ego. He knew he was the best at his job and he wouldn't be surprised if the bar's profits had dropped in recent weeks.

Jackson patted Ricky on the shoulder before turning back to the stairs, leaving Ricky alone. Staring silently in the mirror, it struck him it was probably going to be the last time he got into drag in London Bridge, maybe even in the country. Trying not to think about it too much, he applied his moisturiser and got to work.

Creating Miss Kitty Litter had always been a joy for Ricky and today felt a little more special than usual. At some point during the process he escaped into the character, and they became one. He had always tried to pin down the point in the process when that happened, because for most of it, his makeup normally looked terrifying until the final touches.

When his face was done, he wriggled into his costume, which he had originally commissioned for the bars last New Year's Eve party. It was a gold, skin tight dress that hit the floor. A revealing slit from his hip down to his toes exposed one of his muscular, long legs. To hide the dark hairs, he pulled on five pairs of tan tights and one pair with a pearlescent sheen. He stepped away from the mirror and slipped into the matching gold heels. He looked like a giant Oscar award and in the low light, his exposed leg looking sleek and elegant.

He pulled on the tall wig, which he had spent the majority of two days constructing on the kitchen table in the farmhouse. The rainbow spray-painted cage sat in the middle of the construction, with the rainbow hair tangled around it, like vines creeping up a tree. He hadn't quite figured out how to find, catch and store a live bird, but Belinda had found a stuffed parrot in one of her drawers, which did the job.

After securing the construction to his head with half a packet of bobby pins, he glued down the edges to his forehead and clipped on the sleek, rainbow fringe that swooped over his right eye. The weight of the cage on his head was surprisingly lighter than he expected, which he was glad for. He hadn't had much time to plan his actual own stage performance, and he had only sent in his tracks to the organisers the night before.

Stepping back under the exposed bulb, he stared in the mirror. A small smile tickled his pink, overdrawn lips. It had been a while since he had seen himself so done up. The drag he had been doing in Gran Canaria had been comfortable and simple, with shake and go wigs and simple, sweat proof makeup.

He rolled deodorant onto his smooth pits, dowsed himself in Miss Kitty Litter's fruity signature scent and headed up the stairs. There was a flutter of nerves in his stomach that he hadn't had since his early days in drag. The more he tried to ignore them, the harder they burned.

The bar had started to get busy in his absence, and the first of the early drinkers were starting to fill the empty streets of the village. Ricky walked over to the bar where Jackson was waiting for him, an elaborate cocktail in front of him. He pulled a lighter out of his pocket and lit a sparkler in the drink. It fizzed like a firework as he pushed it across the bar to Ricky.

"I couldn't quite manage a party at such short notice," said Jackson. "This will have to do."

"It's Pride, sweetheart. We're at *the* party."

He gratefully accepted the drink, and he waited for the

sparkler to fizzle out before taking a sip. It was strong, fruity and sweet, just how Ricky liked it.

"You look stunning by the way," added Jackson. "Why didn't you put this much effort in for your weekend gigs?"

"Because it's not Pride every day, sweetheart."

Taking his drink, he walked to the front door and out onto the street. Gary, the security guard, had turned up. He nodded his recognition to Ricky, not commenting on his drag or sudden reappearance. He knew more security would appear during the course of the day.

"*Roll up, roll up*, gays, girls and everything in between," Ricky called out to the crowds walking slowly up and down the street. "Don't delay, we have the best priced and tastiest drinks in town."

A couple of people in the crowd headed into the bar, smiling at Ricky as they went. It hadn't been so easy in Gran Canaria. Most people like to stand outside of the bars, watching the drag show for free without having to pay for the drinks. His stomach flipped, so he drank more of the cocktail.

He couldn't dwell on the thought of what he had signed up for because he spotted somebody in the crowd. He probably wouldn't have noticed him, if the man hadn't been staring at him. He only lingered for a moment before slipping away unseen, but it had been long enough for Ricky to realise he knew that face and earring.

"Did you see that?" he asked Gary.

"See what?" Gary grunted.

Ricky thrust his drink into Gary's hand and he hurried off the pavement and onto the road. He crossed the street, pushing through the crowd. He peered down the empty alleyway, wondering if it had been a trick of his mind.

He hadn't given much thought to his attacker being released, because that was how Ricky dealt with things. He lingered by the mouth of the alley, wondering if he should venture further. Remembering that's how he had gotten into trouble in the first place, he walked carefully back to the front of the club and took his drink back from a stoic Gary.

"Trouble, boss?" he asked.

Ricky shook his head, careful not to shake too hard as to disrupt the art stacked up on his head.

"Trick of the light," he mumbled quietly, before turning his attention back to the street. "What's there to think about, you lot? Don't go in there, it stinks of piss. Come in here, it's much better! Free shots for everyone I want to fuck, so that's *all* of you, sweetheart."

Ricky slipped into Miss Kitty Litter like a comfortable pair of old jeans. Even if he knew those jeans were faded and no longer in fashion, he couldn't seem to throw them away. He had never needed anyone else in his life other than Miss Kitty Litter. She had been there for him when he had felt desperately alone, and she would be there with him on his next big adventure.

That was his only steadying thought as he heavily sucked on the straw, draining the vodka out of the bottom of the cocktail. Forcing on a smile, he pushed any doubts to the back of his mind and ignored them, just as he had always done.

CHAPTER

TWENTY
EIGHT

C hase watched Dylan eat his ham sandwich as he picked at his own. He couldn't bring himself to eat. Glancing at the clock, he knew he should have set off ten minutes ago if he was going to meet Tom on time.

He looked at the dozen red roses sitting in the vase on the counter. Tom had insisted that Chase needed to make a grand gesture and that roses were the ultimate romantic gift. Looking at the clock again, he wondered if he was going to get a chance to hand them over, not that he thought they were going to work.

A knock at the door dragged him from his thoughts. Looking through the peephole, he had expected to see Tom, not his brother. He hovered over the door handle, wondering if he should pretend he wasn't in, even if the cartoons on the TV made it obvious he was.

"Bro?" he knocked hard on the wood again. "Are you in there?"

Chase hadn't spoken to him since their argument at the party. Pinning him against the fridge flashed through his mind, and he felt embarrassed by his actions. He reluctantly opened the door.

Danny had already started to walk away, but he turned back, and he looked surprised to see him. Chase stepped to the side and held the door open. He walked in, his eyes immediately going to the flowers.

"I just wanted to see when you'd be back at work," he said, skipping the greetings as he ruffled Dylan's hair. "People are starting to wonder why their training sessions have been cancelled."

Guilt surged through Chase. He hadn't stepped foot in the gym since Ricky's disappearance. The thought of having to pretend everything was okay kept him away.

"I don't know," he said. "Dylan, go and get dressed and brush your teeth."

Dylan nodded and slid off the chair. He ran into his bedroom and closed the door behind him, leaving them alone. He hated mentioning anything to Dylan, but he knew he was picking up on things. He had asked more than once when he was staying at Ricky's cottage again.

"Who are the flowers from?" asked Danny cautiously. "Got a new admirer already?"

"If you've come to make wise cracks, don't bother," he snapped. "They're not for me, they're for somebody else."

Danny nodded and sat at the kitchen table. Still hovering by the door, Chase glanced at the clock again. He knew Tom would already be in the gay village waiting for him.

"I actually came to apologise," Danny said, a hint of

reluctance in his voice. "I've been out of order. I should never have tried to get involved in your life."

The apology surprised Chase. Danny had never been a guy to admit when he was wrong. He was like their father in that way. Leaving the safety of the door, he closed it and sat across the table from him. He started to pick at the edges of his uneaten sandwich.

"You're right," said Chase. "You shouldn't have gotten involved."

"I was worried about you."

"Worried I'd turned gay?"

Danny chewed the inside of his cheek and looked back to the roses, his eyes dancing over the scarlet petals.

"Something like that," Danny said quietly out of the corner of his mouth. "I'm not going to pretend to understand, because I don't, but I hate that you don't feel like you could have told me any of this. Makes me wonder what kind of brother I am to you."

Underneath Chase's anger, he felt a little touched that Danny was trying his best to open up. Chase had known he was going to have to tell him the truth one day, he had just never expected him to figure things out on his own.

"I fell in love with a man, Danny," he said sternly, surprised the words left his mouth so easily. "It's not the end of the world."

Danny looked taken aback by Chase's admission. Even after everything he had figured out on his own, he even looked surprised.

"*Love?*" Danny asked, the word almost jamming in his throat. "Are you *sure?*"

"More sure than anything," Chase said. "It doesn't matter. I told Ricky how I felt and that's why he left. You had nothing to do with it, I just needed somebody to take my anger out on."

"Why didn't you just tell me, bro?"

"Because you're turning into dad."

"What's that supposed to mean?" Danny looked genuinely perplexed, making Chase wonder if he even realised his own ignorance.

"The way he talks about gay people, it's not right," Chase said. "You're just as bad as he is sometimes."

"I didn't realise you were gay."

"I'm not," he said. "I'm just not straight either, whatever that means these days. But it shouldn't matter. Regardless of what I am, saying stuff like that about people who have done nothing to you is wrong. How am I supposed to feel, hearing you say that two men can't raise a child? Do you know how crazy that sounds?"

Danny shrugged slightly, looking at the roses again.

"So are those for him?"

"Ricky? You can say his name."

"This is just a lot to deal with at once."

"How do you think I feel? I confessed my love for a man, and he ran away. I never thought I'd be in a relationship with a man. I always thought I would meet another woman, for Dylan's sake. That's what you all told me, and I listened for a long time. When I met someone I genuinely cared about, I stopped listening."

"Bro, all I know is when you were dating, Rachel, who ended up being Ricky, you were happier than I've seen you in a long time," he leaned across the table, his voice low. "And you've been miserable ever since he left. Have you missed him?"

Chase nodded. He couldn't say the words out loud. The more he had tried to convince himself he could live a life without Ricky, the harder it became. He thought if he gave himself enough time and went back to work, things would go back to normal, but he wasn't sure if he wanted normal.

Life around Ricky was unpredictable and exciting, and he missed that fire. The thought of slipping back into his old routine scared him more than anything.

"It's probably too late," he said, gulping those feelings down. "He's moving abroad."

"But the roses?"

"His friend Tom came to see me. Convinced me I should do a grand last-ditch attempt to stop him from going. It's not going to work."

"Are you sure?"

He wasn't, but it felt like the truth. He couldn't imagine making a difference to Ricky's decision. If seeing him face to face didn't stop him from leaving in the first place, he wasn't sure what a dozen roses were going to do.

"I was all for the plan until about an hour ago," he said, glancing over to the roses. "It just feels like too little too late."

"Why do you even want to try if he's going to leave you so easily?"

Chase reached into his pocket and pulled out the piece of paper he had printed off at the library. Danny stared down at the obituary, clearly confused.

"Bret was Ricky's fiancé," he said, taking the paper back and reading over the words again. "He never told me that. I had to find out from Tom a couple of days ago. I went to the library to look at the old newspaper records and I found that. I just needed to see it with my own eyes, but I don't know if it changes anything."

Danny's fingers drummed on the table, as though he was holding back from saying something. Chase folded the paper and put it back in his pocket, nodding at his brother to talk.

"I can't believe I'm about to say this," he said quietly, laughing nervously under his breath, "but if you really love him, just fight for him, bro."

"What if it doesn't make a difference?"

Danny stood up and he walked over to the roses. He picked out the card, but aside from Ricky's name, it was blank. Chase hadn't been able to sum up his feelings into a snappy, short sentence. There was no way he could put his love, anger and disappointment into a Hallmark friendly catchphrase.

"Since when have you been afraid of failure?" Danny asked him. "You got up at five o'clock in the morning every day as a kid to go down to that kickboxing club. You didn't go to win, you went to fight."

"This is different."

"Why?" he pushed the card back into its stand in the flowers. "I just want my brother back, and if that means you being with a guy, I'll support you."

"It's not just about being with a guy. It's Ricky. It's been Ricky since the moment I met him."

"So fight for him," he repeated, picking up the roses and handing them out to Chase, "even if you don't think you'll win."

Chase stood up and accepted the flowers. He looked down at them. A couple of them were already starting to wilt at the corners, but most of them were still bright and thriving.

"Dad is going to freak out when he finds out," said Danny. "But I know mum wouldn't have cared one little bit."

Chase knew he was right. Their mother had been the most loving person he had known, and even though he had lived most of his life without her, her smile was still vivid in his memory. She would tell him to try.

Dylan emerged from his bedroom fully dressed, and he walked into the bathroom. The tap started to run, and the sound of his toothbrush hitting his teeth floated through. Chase knew he couldn't carry on being as miserable as he had been, if not for his sake, then for Dylan's.

"I'll even drive you if you want," said Danny, pulling his car keys from his pocket. "I owe you."

"What about the gym?"

"Some things are more important," he said with a small smile. "Like my brother being happy, regardless."

When Dylan had finished brushing his teeth, Chase took him next door to Annie, who remarked on how beautiful the flowers were. She asked who they were for, so he handed them over to her, plucking the card out as she admired their beauty.

"I thought they were for Ricky?" asked Danny as they headed down the stairwell to his car.

"They won't make a difference," said Chase. "But you're right, I might."

As he jumped into his brother's car, he knew he was taking a huge risk. The outcome most likely to happen was going to leave him feeling even worse, but somewhere in the darkness, there was a small glimmer of light. For the first time in two dark weeks, that light gave him hope.

***

Ricky peeked his head around the side of the stage and saw the thousands of people watching as the singer murdered a Britney classic. Ricky had never heard of her, but she was a '*YouTube Star*' according to the poster, not that Ricky knew what that meant.

"Ouch, sweetheart!" he cried as the production assistant nipped his back as they fitted the microphone pack under his dress. "Watch the skin!"

"Sorry, love," he mumbled as he zipped up the back of

Ricky's gold dress. "All done. You ready to go on?"

"Ready as I'll ever be."

Before he could let the nerves take over, Tom and Cole appeared, wearing their VIP Friends and Family wristbands. Ricky had forgotten all about organising them months ago.

"No Belinda?" he asked, looking over their shoulders.

"She's not feeling great," said Tom quickly. "How are you feeling? Nervous?"

"I wasn't until you asked me," he inhaled deeply. "How do I look?"

"Really good," said Cole.

"Just good, sweetheart? I don't want to look good, I want to look *great*. A piece of dry toast looks good, sweetheart."

"You look amazing," said Tom. "When do you go on?"

"In about eight minutes," Ricky replied, checking the clock on the wall. "When this wannabe has finished singing, it's Miss Kitty Litter's turn."

"Who is she?" asked Cole, peering over Ricky's shoulder to the stage. "The crowd looks like they're falling asleep."

"No fucking idea sweetheart, but the worse she does, the better I look."

Tom pulled his phone out of his pocket and started tapping on the screen. Before Ricky could see what he was doing, he pushed it back into his pocket and smiled up at him.

"Suppliers," he said before Ricky asked. "This is more important."

Ricky put his hand on his corseted stomach. Jackson had given him more cocktails than he should have and he was paying for it. It had been a long time since he had been nervous to go on a stage, but it was taking all of his power to stay on his feet.

The minutes ticked down and the girl on stage

announced she was about to sing her last song, which caused her first real cheer from the crowd. Ricky grabbed hold of a metal bar to steady himself as his head started to spin.

"Are you alright?" he heard Cole ask as he stared at the floor.

"Ricky, you've gone a funny colour."

"Kitty Litter, you're on in three," he heard the stage hand call over.

"*Miss* Kitty Litter," Ricky corrected him, straightening up and inhaling through his nose. "I'm *fine*, stop fussing."

Tom pulled his phone out again and furiously tapped on the screen. He pushed his phone into his ear and walked off into the shadows.

"What's he up to?" Ricky asked Cole.

"I don't know," Cole said with a shrug. "He's been acting weird all morning."

"You mean weirder than normal? I'm glad I'm leaving tonight. It's like living with my mother."

"He cares about you," said Cole with an air of sadness in his voice. "We all do."

"Two minutes, Miss Kitty Litter," the stagehand cried again.

"I can tell the time, sweetheart," he snapped, as he made sure the lace of his wig was pressed down. "Where's my bag? I need to powder my nose."

Somebody passed him his tiny clutch, and he pulled out the powder compact. He didn't realise how much his hands were shaking until he could barely see himself in the mirror. He picked up the pad, caked it in powder and pressed it in the centre of his forehead and on the sides of his nose.

"I'm sweating like a glass blower's arsehole," he laughed nervously as he crammed his clutch in Cole's hand. "I can't wait till this is all over."

"The performance?"

"Something like that."

When the stagehand announced the final minute until he had to go on stage, Tom reappeared, his hands crossed tightly across his chest and his teeth gnawing at the corner of his bottom lip.

"Can you go and stand in that corner?" Ricky snapped. "You're freaking me out. What's wrong with you?"

"Nothing." Tom glanced shiftily to Cole out of the corner of his eye. "When are you on?"

"In about forty seconds."

"Oh," said Tom, glancing over his shoulder. "Right. Okay."

"Have you taken up cocaine, sweetheart, because if you've chosen today of all days, your timing is terrible, as always."

"I'm fine," Tom said defensively. "Just focus on your performance."

The girl finished her song and ran off the opposite side of the stage. Ricky noticed the smile fade instantly from her face when she started screaming at somebody who looked like her manager. Without even realising it, somebody crammed a microphone into Ricky's hands as he listened to his name being announced to the crowd. There was a wave of cheers, which eased him a little.

"*Ricky?*"

He turned around, and the source of his nerves was standing behind Tom and Cole, with two security guards attempting to drag him away.

"C-Chase?" he mumbled, glancing from his sweat drenched face to Tom. "This was *you*, wasn't it?"

Tom stepped to the side, his eyes fixed on the floor. Chase pulled free of the security guards and headed straight for him, just as the backing track for '*I Will Survive*' started playing. Like a deer in headlights, Ricky stumbled out onto the stage, the sunlight piercing his eyes.

Staring out into the crowd, he heard his cue drift by him. He stared at the expectant faces as they looked among themselves, mumbling and laughing at the mute drag queen.

Clutching the microphone in front of his face, Ricky turned back to the wing, where Chase was standing, his hands on his head and desperation in his eyes.

"I can't do this."

Ricky dropped the microphone and ran towards the other side of the stage. The bottom of his heel caught on a wire, and he hit the ground with a thud, landing on his hands and knees. The force of the fall made his wig topple forward and slide completely off. The music cut off just in time for Ricky to hear the gasps of shock and awkward laughter from the crowd.

Clutching his wig, he dragged himself up to his feet. Tom and the time announcing stagehand rushed over, but before they reached him, he bolted off the stage, glancing back one last time to see two police officers dragging Chase away.

Ripping off his lashes as tears of embarrassment streaked down his face, he pushed through the confused crowd towards the nearest pub. He ran into Churchill's, ignoring the staring eyes. Pushing people out of the way, he made his way up the stairs to the toilets. He saw the one empty cubicle, and before the waiting line could fill it up, he pushed his way in and locked the door.

"*Oi!* I've been waiting for fifteen *fucking* minutes."

Ricky didn't respond. Under the strain of his corset, he panted for breath as he looked down at the birdcage in his lap. He pinched his arm, hoping it was all a bad dream, but his press-on nails nipped his skin before they snapped off.

Leaning his head against the dirty tiles, he closed his eyes and thought about his flight out of the country. It was a good job he was leaving, because he would never work in the town again.

He started to sob heavily into his hands. He felt the mascara and eyeliner run down his cheeks, blending in with his overdrawn lips. At first, he thought he was crying for his swift exit off the stage, but he knew it was deeper than that. He was crying for the complicated mess his life had become. He thought again about his flight later that night, but it didn't soothe him.

"You alright in there, love?" he heard a woman's voice cry from the other cubicle. "You can't be crying at Pride."

"I just got my period," he cried back through the tears. "I'll be fine. I always am. I'm Miss Kitty *Fucking* Litter."

"Who?"

"Doesn't matter."

Wrapping a length of toilet roll around his hand, he wiped away the tears, along with most of his makeup. He stood up, lifted the toilet seat and tossed the black and red stained tissue into the water. Flushing away his tears, he inhaled deeply and held his head high, despite the mess he was presenting to the world.

He opened the door and immediately caught his reflection in the mirror. It was worse than he thought. Ignoring the stares of the people in the bathroom, he ditched his wig on the floor and filled his hands with soap and water. Scrubbing his face, he melted away the clown. He splashed his face with cold water and patted it down with the hand tissues. Aside from the hint of eyeliner, Ricky stared back at him.

How he had ended up thirty-eight years old, standing in a gay bar bathroom, half in drag, he didn't know. It was not how he had seen his life turning out, but it felt somewhat inevitable. He knew he was only going to get deeper into that rabbit hole in Gran Canaria. He tried to imagine himself in ten years, still working under the sun as a chain-smoking drag queen. The thought didn't seem as appealing as it had done ten years previously.

He pushed through the line towards the door. The elderly woman in a headscarf sitting on a stool offered him a lollipop and a squirt of perfume, but he politely declined. It was going to take more than a nice scent to fix him.

Walking carefully down the stairs, having left his wig behind, he reached into his dress and pulled out his silicone breasts, dropping them on the floor. He yanked off his impossibly large earrings and also dropped them on the floor, shedding layers of drag like a snake would its skin. He decided he was going to go back to the London Bridge, change and decide his next move from there.

He pushed heavily on the door back into the packed pub. People stared in his direction and mumbled as they tried to suppress their laughter.

"Never seen a man in a dress?" he bit harshly at one woman when he heard her refer to him as '*rough*'.

He left the pub and joined the chaos of the street, where more eyes and whispering followed him down the strip. Deciding it was better to get off the main street, he turned the corner and joined the less busy alley system.

He reached into his empty bra and pulled out his packet of cigarettes. He pressed one in between his bare lips and reached into the other side of his bra for his lighter, but it wasn't there. Cursing under his breath, he pulled the cigarette out of his mouth and carried on walking. The smell of cigarette smoke drifted his way from behind a giant, yellow skip, so he followed his nose, wanting nothing more than a cigarette.

Steadying his heels on the cobbles and using the skip as

a railing, he made his way around, where he could see the cigarette smoke drifting up into the air.

"Can I borrow a lighter, sweetheart, I –,"

Ricky's voice trailed off when he saw the overweight, middle aged man with his pants around his ankles having his cock sucked by a much younger and much better looking guy with a septum nose piercing. Ricky immediately recognised the young guy as somebody who worked in one of the bars, but it took him longer to recognise the other guy. If it weren't for the silver earring, he would have written him off as any other man.

"*You*," Ricky mumbled.

"*Shit!*" The young bartender scrambled to his feet. "That's awkward."

"Not you," said Ricky. "*Him*. You're the guy who attacked me."

Terrance Hoole stared at Ricky, and for a moment, it was almost as if he didn't recognise Ricky at all. Had being arrested and almost charged not been enough for him? He quickly yanked up his pants and tucked away his below-average sized erection. Cigarette still hanging from his lips, he fumbled with the belt under his beer belly.

The young bartender slipped away unseen, leaving them alone. Ricky stared at the man as he struggled to fasten his belt. When he was done, he pushed past Ricky and swiftly walked away.

"*You!*" Ricky cried after him. "It was *you*, you piece of shit."

"I don't know what you're talking about," he called over his shoulder as he hurried down the alley.

Ricky started following him, trying his best not to fall over on his heels. Terrance glanced over his shoulder and sped up, until he was running away. Ricky didn't know what compelled him, but he bent down and yanked off his heels so that he was barefoot. He chased after Terrance, surprised at how quickly the fat little man could run.

After seeing him in the police line up looking angry and mean, Ricky had built him up to be something he wasn't in his mind. His memory had failed him. He was fatter and shorter than he had imagined. He looked somewhat pathetic.

Terrance ran out of the alley and onto Canal Street, disappearing into the crowd. Ricky jumped up on a metal chair, and everybody turned to look up at him, apart from one man scurrying towards the bottom of the street. Ricky jumped down and pushed through the crowd.

"*Move!*" he cried, his bare feet squelching against spilt drinks and cigarette butts. "Get out of the way!"

Ricky followed the man, all the way back up the long street. When he was back at Churchill's, Terrance turned left, away from the canal and down the quieter, backstreets.

Bursting out of the crowd, Ricky reached out, and his fingers closed in around the collar of Terrance's pink polo shirt. He yanked the man back, and he stumbled as he spun around, a Stanley knife clutched in his hand.

"Do you want me to finish you off?" Terrance cried, his eyes wide and his teeth gritted. "Do you have some kind of death wish, *faggot?*"

Ricky stepped back, but he didn't run away. Staring down at the blade, he suddenly remembered a useless piece of information Chase's father had told him. Terrance Hoole had a wife and children, who had been his alibi. The short blade of the knife glittered in the sun as he wondered if they had really believed he hadn't been anywhere near Manchester's gay village. Ricky couldn't imagine anyone's wife not knowing what their husband was up to on the weekends.

"You and me aren't so different after all," said Ricky,

surprised by his own confidence. "We've all got dirty little secrets."

Terrance swung the knife and Ricky jumped back. The edge of the blade struck his arm, and hot searing pain burned deep. He looked down at the bloody cut and clutched it with his other hand. Looking up at Terrance, he realised that he wasn't scared of the man, despite the knife.

"Do it, kill me," Ricky laughed. "You'll be doing me a favour."

Terrance frowned, his eyes widening even further. Ricky didn't doubt Terrance would do it. Clutching his bloody arm, he stared deep into Terrance's eyes, and he saw his own fear reflected. It suddenly occurred to him that they shared more than a love of having their cock sucked by other men in dark alleys.

Ricky hadn't been attacked because he was gay, he had been attacked because Terrance was scared of his own feelings. That's why he had been in the gay village in the first place. Ricky could have easily taken him back to his bed and fucked him if things had turned out differently.

Terrance had attacked what he was scared of, just like Ricky had. He was so scared of love and he had pushed Chase away because he loved him. He couldn't believe it had taken being faced with a knife to admit that to himself.

Suddenly, he wasn't as ready to give in. He took a step back, but Terrance copied, swinging the knife again. It snagged Ricky's dress and scraped along the corset.

"*Oh my God!* That man's got a *knife!*" a high-pitched voiced screamed from the crowd.

Terrance looked over to where the cry had come from, distracted just long enough for Ricky to send his foot crashing into his crotch. He yelped, and the knife tumbled to the ground as he keeled over. Ricky kicked the knife away, grabbed Terrance's arm and twisted it up in between his shoulders. He collapsed face first onto the road, with Ricky on top of him. He straddled him, ripping the inside seam of his bespoke dress.

"Get *off* me, you faggot!" he cried, wriggling under Ricky's weight.

"Don't fuck with me fella," he whispered into Terrance's ear as he pushed his face into the concrete. "This isn't my first time at the rodeo."

Two police officers appeared from the crowd, and they pulled Ricky off of the man. He returned to clutching his arm and truly acknowledged the pain and how much blood he was losing.

"Can we get a medic to the corner of Chorlton Street," said the female officer into her radio. "We have an injured civilian."

The male police officer dragged Terrance up to his feet as he read him his rights. He struggled, but the officer was built like a bodybuilder, and he wasn't going anywhere. Minutes later, a police car and a paramedic appeared. The paramedic tried to pull Ricky towards the back of an ambulance, but he wanted to make sure Terrance was in the car before he went anywhere.

"Can I take your name and a contact number?" asked the female police officer with a pad in her hand. "We'll need you to come into the station to make a statement when you're cleaned up."

"Don't worry, sweetheart. I was already on my way there."

CHAPTER

TWENTY NINE

There wasn't a window in Chase's cell, but he knew it was night time when they opened the door to tell him he was being let off with a caution.

"It's been a busy day," the officer explained as she led him out of his cell and down the brightly lit corridor. "Pride always is."

She took him to the counter where he had been informed he had been arrested for breach of the peace and trespassing hours earlier. The man behind the counter explained what a caution was, and how it might show up on certain searches before handing him back his phone, cigarettes, and wallet.

"You're free to leave," the officer said, already looking around Chase as a drunk man was dragged toward him.

Pocketing his things, he turned and headed for the exit, but he stopped in his tracks when he saw his father out of uniform sitting in the waiting area, flicking through a magazine of *Manchester Monthly*. Chase almost walked away without saying a word, but he decided against it, not knowing how long he had been there.

"What are you doing here?" he asked.

Patrick jumped and slapped the magazine shut.

"I could ask you the same bloody thing!" he cried angrily, standing up. "One of the boys called me to tell me you'd been *arrested*. Charging on to the stage at that freak show? What on earth were you doing there?"

"I'm too tired for this," Chase said, already turning around. "You didn't have to come."

He started to walk towards the exit, but his father grabbed his shoulder and pulled him back around.

"I think you have some explaining to do," Patrick said in a low, angry voice. "First you're hanging around with that freak, and then you're being arrested at that parade? What's gotten into you, son? It's like I don't know who you are these days."

Chase pulled away from his father and took a step back. He laughed, not only exhausted with being in the station all day, but also with his father's denial. He had all of the pieces in front of him, and he was still refusing to accept the obvious.

"Why do you think I was there, dad?" Chase asked, crossing his arms across his chest.

"I don't know," Patrick's brows lowered over his dark eyes. "That's why I asked you."

"I went there to tell somebody I loved them. Fat lot of good it did me. I need to go home. Annie will be worried sick."

Chase started to walk away again, but Patrick's fingers

closed tightly around his arm, dragging him back around as though he was a child.

"What do you think you're playing at?" he seethed through gritted teeth. "Don't walk away from me."

"Why?" Chase dragged his father's hand away. "I learned that from you. You should be proud."

"Proud?" Patrick laughed, shaking his head. "Proud that you're one of *them*? Is that what you're trying to tell me?"

"What if I am?"

"I don't accept it."

"I never asked for your acceptance," Chase laughed. "I don't know what I am, but maybe I am one of them. I don't really care. I just know I love a man who has now left the country because I've been stuck in this fucking station all night, twiddling my thumbs."

"Love a man?" Patrick scoffed bitterly. "You're sick."

"No, dad, I'm not," he said, walking away for real this time. "You are."

Chase pushed on the door and the cool night air hit him in an instant. He pulled his newly reclaimed packet of cigarettes from his pocket and crammed one in between his lips, lighting it instantly. He dragged hard, letting the nicotine flow through his blood after hours of deprival.

He hoped his father would stay inside, but he hurried straight out, looking around until he spotted Chase leaning against the wall.

"Is this my fault?" he asked loudly. "Is this because I left and you spent too much time with that mother of yours? She always was a bad influence."

"At least she was an influence. You only showed up when she died out of guilt. You needn't have bothered. I was doing fine without you, and I still am. The only reason I keep you around is for Dylan's sake."

"You don't mean that."

"I do," Chase said defiantly. "I really do. You've not been a father to me. You're so full of hate, you'd cut your own nose off to spite your face. I don't fit into your narrow view of what's right and normal in this world. I'm sorry I'm such a disappointment to you."

Patrick opened and closed his mouth, but no words came out. He lingered for a moment, but he shook his head heavily and headed to his car. After slamming the door, he sat staring at Chase through the dark for a moment before turning over the engine and quickly driving out of the car park.

Looking up at the ink black sky, the stars popped out at him. He didn't know what time it was. He wondered if Ricky was on the plane yet, or still waiting by his gate at the airport.

Puffing hard on his cigarette, he thought about the roses he had given to Annie. Had Tom been onto something about making a grand gesture? He hadn't had time to say two words to Ricky before being dragged away and handcuffed. He felt like he had been robbed. Ricky's outright rejection would have been easier to take, rather than his silence.

He thought about Ricky falling over. He had wanted so badly to run over and help him up. Why hadn't he just set off earlier like he should have? He finished his cigarette, tossed it to the ground and decided he was going to walk home. He hoped the air would help clear his head, but he doubted it would make a difference.

He set off walking, spotting a familiar black Land Rover parked in front of him. If it had been there the whole time, he hadn't noticed it. He squinted into the dark, and he saw Tom behind the wheel and somebody else in the passenger seat.

The door opened, and a man jumped out, wearing a pair

of black jeans, a black t-shirt and a dark grey hoody with rolled up sleeves.

"Ricky?" Chase squinted into the dark.

"Got any more of those cigarettes, sweetheart?" Ricky asked, a small, nervous smile on his lips. "I ran out."

Chase pulled out the packet of cigarettes in disbelief and slid open the lid. Ricky cautiously walked forward and pulled one out. Chase lit it for him. Chase noticed Ricky's left forearm was bandaged up.

"Guess who I bumped into," he said when he noticed Chase's eyes. "Terrance Hoole. He might have been in the cell next to you, sweetheart."

Chase looked back at the station, before looking back at Ricky. He blinked hard, lost for words and wondered if he had fallen asleep in his cell and this was all a dream. Ricky's distinctive aftershave floated on the night breeze with his cigarette smoke, letting Chase know he was more than awake.

"He cut me open good and proper, the little shit," Ricky said with an anxious laugh. "They got enough witness reports to charge him straight away. The bastard might get locked up after all. When the police tell his wife what I caught him doing in the back alley, I'm sure her alibi will suddenly crumble away."

Chase watched him smoke, trying to think of what to say first. All of the things he had planned to say to Ricky at Pride were jumbling in with the dozen new questions he had, and they were tripping over each other.

"Say something, sweetheart."

"Your flight?"

Ricky puffed hard on the cigarette, squinting his eyes up to the sky as a plane passed overhead.

"I might make it," he said. "It'll be close. Depends on the traffic."

"Right."

"Unless you want me to stay?" Ricky mumbled through the cigarette. "I wouldn't blame you if you didn't. I wouldn't want me to stay."

"What?"

"I tried to make a joke, sweetheart, because truth be told, I'm more nervous than a prostitute on her first anal booking."

Chase laughed softly as he stared at Ricky. If he had thought he was imaging it, he now knew for certain he wasn't. His own imagination would never have been able to conjure up such an obviously Ricky thing to say.

"You mean to tell me you'll stay if I say so?" asked Chase cautiously.

"That's the gist of it, sweetheart."

"What made you change your mind?"

Ricky tossed his cigarette down to the ground and stared at his bandaged up arm. Chase wondered how deep the cut went and if he had needed stitches. The dressing looked pretty thick.

"When we were at Coltrane house, you told me there was a hundred ways this could end and ninety-nine of them were probably bad. You were probably right, and there's still time for the other ninety-eight of those things to happen."

"What's your point?"

"If I have a one in ninety-eight chance of being happy with you," he said carefully, staring deeply into Chase's eyes. "They're the best odds I've had in a long time, sweetheart. I don't want to waste one of those ninety-eight chances running away again."

Chase couldn't help but smile. Even now, he still wanted to be angry with Ricky, but he couldn't bring himself to muster those emotions. His heart was throbbing in his chest and his brain was screaming at him to say something.

"I don't want to be your second choice," said Chase. "If you think there's any chance you're going to want to leave, you should go now."

Ricky bit into his lip, and he stuffed his hands in his pockets. He glanced back to look at Tom, who was leaning against his steering wheel with the window open, listening to every word.

"I never wanted to leave," Ricky said, almost reluctantly. "I knew I was running away. Truth is, sweetheart, I belong here."

"That's still not a reason for us to try."

"I'm confused," said Ricky, frowning heavily. "Did you, or did you not charge into Pride without paying, just to talk to me, only to get arrested?"

"I did," Chase said. "I just want to make sure that you really want this."

"You want the truth, sweetheart?" Ricky took a step forward. "I don't know what I want, I just know that I want to be happy and you made me happy. I freaked out and I can never apologise enough for that, but it was a blip."

"You don't have to apologise to me."

"Yes, I do. I've been a shit to you, and you didn't deserve it. You've never been anything other than amazing to me, sweetheart."

"Ricky." Chase stepped forward, gently grabbing Ricky's hands. "Of course I want you to stay. Just stop talking and kiss me."

"Okay," Ricky said, nodding his head and closing his eyes.

When their lips met, all of Chase's worries and fears melted away. Tom pushed hard on the horn, and they both laughed through the kiss. Nothing had ever felt more natural or right for Chase.

"I'm so glad you said that," whispered Ricky, his forehead pressed against Chase's. "Because that could have been very embarrassing."

"It's a good job I love you, isn't it?"

Chase waited for the freak out to come, but it didn't. Ricky looked nervous, but his shaky smile widened.

"I never told you about my fourth rule, did I?"

"You and those bloody rules."

"I promised myself I would never fall in love with someone," he said, squeezing Chase's hands hard. "I made that rule because I never thought I would meet someone who would make me even consider it."

"Is this the part where you tell me you've met someone else?"

"Shut up, sweetheart," Ricky laughed softly. "I love you, alright. Happy now?"

"I will be if you say it like you mean it."

"How about I show you?"

Ricky let go of Chase's hands and grabbed the back of his head. He pulled Chase into the most passionate kiss he had ever experienced. Chase grasped Ricky's face and opened his mouth to him, and their tongues danced against each other's. If this wasn't what love felt like, Chase was sure he would never find anything to top it.

"I guess that will do," said Chase when the kiss finally ended. "What now?"

"We go home."

"Dylan is still with the neighbour."

"I guess we'll drive to your flat, pick him up, and then go home."

"I'm pretty hungry."

"I guess we'll drive to your flat, pick up Dylan, go to the drive through and then go home," Ricky said as they walked back to the car, hand in hand. "Anything else, sweetheart?"

"No," he squeezed Ricky's hand hard. "That sounds pretty perfect to me."

They both jumped in the back seat of Tom's car, sitting side by side. Ricky told Tom to drive to Chase's flat, and he nodded without saying anything. Chase caught his eyes in the mirror, and Tom winked with a wide grin. Chase smiled back. He spread his arm out across the back of the chair, and Ricky snuggled up into his side.

Glancing over Ricky's head into the huge boot, he noticed a lack of Ricky's suitcases. Smiling, he kissed the top of Ricky's head, promising that he was never going to let Ricky feel like he needed to run away ever again.

CHAPTER

THIRTY

T he sun pierced through the open curtains, waking Ricky early. He climbed out of bed and looked down at Chase's tattooed naked body. He smiled as he leaned in and kissed him on the forehead. Chase groaned and rolled over, pulling the covers over his body.

Ricky checked his phone, and it wasn't even six, but he knew he wouldn't be able to get back to sleep. He dressed quickly and went into the kitchen to make his morning coffee. When it was ready, he took it out to the doorstep, where he usually sat and smoked his first cigarette of the day. He had missed the routine, but he opened the cigarette packet, and it was empty. Standing up, he walked back into his cottage and tossed it in the kitchen bin, deciding he wasn't going to buy another packet.

When he finished his coffee, he grabbed his keys and

softly closed the front door. He walked quickly down the high street and past the closed shops, inhaling the cool morning air. The bright sun pierced through a fog of clouds, hitting his grateful skin. He had expected to wake up under Gran Canaria's scorching sun, but he was happy to be in the village he had once fallen in love with.

He walked toward Hebden Bridge Parish Church, saying good morning to the vicar, who was collecting a flower delivery. He nodded his appreciation and wished Ricky a good day as he walked towards the graveyard.

In his two weeks away, Ricky had agonised over the date of the last time he had been to the graveyard to visit Bret. He had managed to figure out it had been on his birthday, nearly four years ago. Despite this, his feet took him to the exact plot without needing to think about it.

He hovered over the marble headstone and smiled. Bending down, he plucked out a sprouting yellow dandelion.

"Hello, sweetheart," he said, pressing his hand against the cold stone. "Sorry it's been a while."

Ricky sat cross-legged on the grass and he talked to Bret like he used to in the months after his funeral. He told him all about Chase and everything that happened. He laughed, he cried and when he finally stood up, he thanked Bret and kissed the stone.

Wiping away his tears, he made a promise to not leave it so long before his next visit. Feeling lighter, he headed back through the village, rerouting himself up to Tom and Cole's farm, where everything was already in full swing.

"Uncle Ricky!" Eva exclaimed, running over to him from the stables in her pink pyjamas. "Did you bring me a present from your holiday?"

"I did," he pulled out his wallet and stuffed a ten pound note into her hands. "Don't tell your dads and don't spend it all on sweets."

"Money!" she exclaimed. "Even *better* than presents!"

With her loot in her hands, she ran into the farmhouse, no doubt to stash her prize. Tom wandered out of the kitchen, a cup of coffee in his hands and sleep in his head.

"I thought I heard your voice," he said through a yawn. "Bit early for you, or have you not gone to sleep yet?"

"Those days are behind me," he laughed softly. "Just came up to see if Belinda could whip up her famous breakfast to go."

"Just one?" Tom asked cautiously.

"Two, you idiot," Ricky said. "Well, three actually. I guess kids eat food too."

"You worry me sometimes," Tom said through squinted eyes.

"I worry myself," he replied, pulling Tom into a tight hug. "I still need to thank you."

"What for?" Tom tried his best to hug him with the cup of coffee clutched in his fist.

"For being right," he said, pulling away. "For not letting me be me."

"Any time?" Tom said, confusion evident on his tired face.

"So, these breakfasts? I don't want Chase waking up and thinking I've done a runner."

"Café," Tom said, turning back to the farmhouse. "She's been up since the sunrise sorting through the fridges."

Ricky walked around the farm to the old converted barn. Belinda was behind the counter, scrubbing the cake display wearing a pair of pink rubber gloves with white fur around the edge.

"I need to borrow those gloves."

"Ricky!" Belinda jumped up, ditching her spray bleach and sponge. "Oh, I'm glad to see you. You didn't go!"

"You're stuck with me a little longer," he winked as she ran around the counter to hug him. "Isn't it a bit early to be cleaning?"

"Rox went into labour during her shift yesterday. She gave birth to a little baby girl. Eight pounds exactly. Let me see if I can get a picture."

Belinda snapped off her gloves and pulled her phone out of her pocket. After peering down her nose at the screen for what felt like a lifetime, she showed Ricky a picture of Rox and the baby.

"So that's little Ambrose."

"They went for Nicola in the end," she said. "Thank God."

Ricky stared down at the picture and smiled. He almost couldn't believe all of the old gang had found their happy endings, including himself.

"I couldn't trouble you for two full English breakfasts and one for a kid, could I?"

"Breakfast?" Belinda asked as she took back her phone. "Consider it done, love."

Fifteen minutes later, Ricky stepped into his cottage with three plates wrapped in foil in a plastic bag. Chase jumped up from the sofa wearing nothing more than his underwear and a look of relief.

"*Jesus*, Ricky. I've been worried sick!" he cried, pulling him into his third hug of the morning. "You didn't take your phone."

"But I did bring back breakfast, sweetheart," he said, holding the bag up as an apology. "I just had someone I needed to visit."

"Breakfast?"

"I went up to the farm. Nothing can beat Belinda's cooking."

"How's Tom?" Chase asked as he grabbed knives and

forks from the drawer.

"Didn't ask too many questions, surprisingly. I was expecting him to sit me down and shine a light in my face."

Chase dropped the cutlery on the table and wrapped his arms around Ricky's neck.

"No regrets?" he asked, glancing over to Ricky's suitcases, which were still by the door.

"No regrets," Ricky said softly. "I realised I don't need Miss Kitty Litter anymore. She got me through a tough time, but she's done her job. She deserves a holiday of her own."

"You're giving up drag?" Chase frowned. "Are you sure you want to do that?"

"Maybe for special occasions. You know how you said Dylan needed a mother and a father?"

"I'm happy with just Ricky," said Chase with a soft smile tickling his lips. "You're more than enough, for both of us."

"I'm happy with just Ricky, too."

Chase didn't ask any more questions. He woke Dylan, and all three of them sat in the living room, eating Belinda's breakfast on their knees with Sunday morning cartoons on the TV.

Ricky didn't feel any pressure or the need to run away. As he bit into a piece of toast, he watched Chase and Dylan eat their breakfast. They both spilled beans down their chests at the same time. He smiled to himself and turned his attention to the TV. For once, he had something normal to worry about, like how he was going to get out of the washing up.

EPILOGUE

CHRISTMAS EVE

The snow beat down at Barton Farm and Ricky snuggled in closer to the fire. He looked down at his lap and saw that Dylan had fallen asleep. He carefully reached over the back of the couch and pulled the blanket over him.

At the end of the sofa, Belinda had also fallen asleep, with a glass of sherry clutched in her hand. Ricky looked over at Tom and Cole as they cuddled on the other sofa with Eva crammed between them. *A Muppet's Christmas Carol* played on the TV above the fireplace, and the dogs and cats were all snuggled up on the hearthrug.

Ricky's eyes glanced to the front page clipping that Belinda had framed and hung on the wall. He read the headline '*Local Drag Queen's Pride Knife Attack!*' and he thought back to the interview he had given the reporters on the steps of the Crown Court after Terrance's sentencing. He was glad to have all of that behind him.

The front door opened, and heavy boots scratched against the doormat. Belinda shot up, as did the dogs. Nobody moved as Chase walked into the living room, a heavy scarf wrapped around his chin and one of Belinda's knitted hats low over his eyes.

"Had to park my car at the bottom and walk up," he said as he set down the bag full of Christmas presents. "How long's Dylan been out?"

"About ten minutes," said Ricky as he stroked Dylan's pale blonde hair. "He kept asking where you were."

"You know my brother. He insisted I have a drink with them."

Hearing the sound of his father's voice, Dylan's eyes fluttered open. He looked up at Ricky as he stretched, a soft smile on his face.

"Is it Christmas yet?" he whispered.

"Not quite yet," said Chase. "But Santa dropped off his presents."

"Can I open one?" he sat up and scratched his head.

"Can we?" Eva jumped up, suddenly wide-awake.

"Just one," said Tom.

Ricky reached under the tree and picked out the present he had bought for Dylan. He handed it to him, and he sat on the edge of the sofa and carefully started to unwrap its edges. Eva, on the other hand, ripped into hers with hurried excitement.

"It's a journal," explained Ricky, as Dylan turned the small, leather bound book over in his hands. "It's so you can write down your thoughts and feelings, and only you get to see it."

Dylan flicked open the book and looked through the

blank pages. For a moment, he looked confused, but he dropped the book and wrapped his arms around Ricky's neck.

"Thanks, Dad," he whispered. "I love it."

Ricky's heart swelled in his chest. It was the first time Dylan had called him dad. He looked over to Chase, who was smiling as he unwrapped his scarf from his neck. Dylan slid off the couch and joined Eva as she ripped open her new set of toy horses.

"Dad left a card for me at Danny's," Chase said as he sat next to Ricky. "It said '*To Chase and Ricky*'."

"Did he write it out?"

"It looked like Barbara's handwriting, but he signed it," Chase said as he cozied up. "Sounds like progress to me."

"Maybe it's a Christmas miracle."

Chase turned and kissed Ricky on the lips before resting his head on his shoulder.

"I had my Christmas miracle early this year, but I'll take another."

Ricky wrapped his hand around Chase's as he watched Dylan and Eva play together. It had not been the life he had expected, but it felt like the life he deserved.

WANT MORE ASHLEY JOHN?

Visit **ashleyjohn.co.uk** to discover his other books!

ABOUT THE AUTHOR

Ashley John lives in the North of England with his fiancé Reece, and his two cats, Jinx and Jeremy.

He's a sucker for a gripping love story. His characters are fighters, strong and complex, and they'll do anything to get the happy endings they deserve.

When Ashley isn't writing, he uses his creativity to paint and draw, and when he's not being creative, he's usually taking a nap.

Made in the USA
Lexington, KY
13 February 2017